Margaret Thornton was born in Blackpool and has lived there all her life. She is a qualified teacher but has retired in order to concentrate on her writing. She has two children and five grandchildren.

Her first novel, *It's a Lovely Day Tomorrow* ('a gentle novel whose lack of noise is a strength' *The Sunday Times*), was runner-up for the Netta Muskett Award, and is also available from Headline as are Margaret Thornton's other Blackpool sagas, *A Pair Of Sparkling Eyes*, *How Happy We Shall Be* and *There's A Silver Lining*.

Also by Margaret Thornton

It's A Lovely Day Tomorrow
A Pair Of Sparkling Eyes
How Happy We Shall Be
There's A Silver Lining
A Stick of Blackpool Rock

Forgive Our Foolish Ways

Margaret Thornton

HEADLINE

First published in 1996
by HEADLINE BOOK PUBLISHING

First published in paperback in 1996
by HEADLINE BOOK PUBLISHING

10 9 8 7 6 5 4 3

All characters in this publication are fictitious and any resemblance to real persons, living or dead, is purely coincidental.

ISBN 0 7472 5164 9

Typeset by Palimpsest Book Production Limited,
Polmont, Stirlingshire

Printed and bound in Great Britain by
Clays Ltd, St Ives plc

HEADLINE BOOK PUBLISHING
A division of Hodder Headline PLC
338 Euston Road
London NW1 3BH

This book is dedicated to the memory of the Blackpool Collegiate School for Girls, and to all the 'Old Girls' who were fortunate enough to attend this great school on Beech Avenue.

Chapter 1

Alice Rawlinson wondered however she would find the words to tell Josephine. She watched the child now, her dark head bent over her scrapbook, the tip of her tongue protruding with the effort of her concentration as she carefully cut round the shape of a red rose.

The child glanced up and looked thoughtfully at her aunt, frowning a little. The room was quiet apart from the ticking of the wooden clock on the mantelshelf and the silence seemed heavy and oppressive, weighted with sadness. Alice was so burdened with grief that surely the child, too, must sense that there was something amiss? No; her steadfast glance and the tiny frown that wrinkled her brow were obviously concerned with nothing more serious than the pile of coloured scraps in front of her, for Josephine suddenly smiled and her serious face was transformed.

'Look, Auntie Alice,' she said. 'I've cut out this big red rose. I'm going to put it right here in the middle, then I'm going to put these little blue flowers at the top and the bottom. I think they're called forget-me-nots. D'you like it, Auntie Alice? D'you think it'll look nice?'

The child's brown eyes, so like Samuel's, glowed with enthusiasm. Josephine was uncannily like her father; the same dark hair and dark brown eyes which burned almost black, like smouldering coals, when she was excited or angry. When she frowned, her eyebrows would almost meet, just as Samuel's did when he was in a bad mood. Alice did so hope that the child hadn't inherited her father's disposition as well as his looks. There had been a closeness between the aunt and her niece ever since Josephine was a tiny baby. It was just as well, under the circumstances . . .

Alice tried to smile at the child now, but her face felt so stiff that the muscles would hardly move. 'I'm sure it will be lovely, dear,' she replied. Dear God, she prayed silently. Please help me. Help me to find the right words to tell her. Please give me strength. She could feel her heart pounding against her ribs and a dryness in her mouth at the thought of the sad news she knew she must impart.

Josephine turned back to her task. She gave a little grunt of satisfaction as she painstakingly applied the flour and water paste to the back of each flower, then arranged them precisely on the piece of cardboard. She was always busy, with books and pencils and coloured crayons, and the book of brightly coloured scraps was her latest and most absorbing pastime.

Alice knew that the child had never cared much for dolls. Mary Jane, an elegant toy in a blue silk dress with matching bonnet – a present to Josephine from her parents on her last birthday, her sixth – sat on the top of the coal scuttle where her owner had abandoned her. She had a haughty look: she was not a doll to be cuddled or to give comfort. She had been brought along with Josephine's other belongings when the little girl had come to stay a few days ago.

'I'm sure Mummy will like this. D'you think so, Auntie Alice?' The child looked up again and smiled at her aunt. 'It's a bookmark. She can put it in her prayer-book when she goes to church. She hasn't been lately, with being poorly, but she'll be able to go again soon . . . when she's better. She will be better soon, won't she? I'll be able to go and see her . . .'

'Josephine . . . Josie, love, listen to me.' Alice crossed the room to where her niece was so happily occupied with her coloured cut-outs. A riot of flowers and fruit and brightly feathered birds lay scattered across the chenille tablecover and the protective layer of newspaper. She put her arm round the little girl and gently stroked the dark silken hair that hung, without the slightest semblance of a curl, to her thin shoulders. 'Josie, love . . . listen to me,' she said again. 'There's something I've got to tell you. Mummy . . . your mother . . . I'm afraid you won't be able to see her when you go home. She's not here any more, love. She's gone to heaven . . . to live with Jesus.'

Alice felt the child's body stiffen as she turned to look at her aunt. 'With Jesus? D'you mean . . . she's dead? Like all those people in the graveyard at the top of the hill? Is that what you mean, Auntie Alice?'

'Yes, my love. I'm sorry . . . That's just what I mean,' Alice sighed. 'And we'll all have to try to be very brave.'

'Why, Auntie Alice? Why did she want to go to live with Jesus? Didn't she want to stay with us, with me and our Bertie . . . and our dad?' Josephine's lower lip began to tremble and her deep brown eyes filled up with tears. Alice noticed however, that the child had failed to mention the youngest member of the family, the new baby, Frances, asleep at the moment in her makeshift cot at the far end of the room.

Alice shook her head in a gesture of bewilderment. How could she begin to explain? 'I'm sure she didn't want to leave you, lovey. But your mum was poorly, you know. She was very poorly when baby Frances came. And sometimes, when people are ill, they don't get better. But she will be safe now . . . now that she's with Jesus.'

Josephine was silent, and her aunt held her close while she wept. She dried her eyes and blew her nose on the handkerchief her aunt proffered, then she looked at Alice thoughtfully. 'I 'spect the King will be pleased,' she said quietly.

'The King?' Alice gave a start. Whatever was the child on about?

'Yes – the King. You told me the other day that the King had died, that he'd gone to heaven to live with Jesus. He'll be glad to see Mummy, won't he? She'll be able to keep him company.'

Yes, of course . . . The King. King George the Fifth. Alice had almost forgotten the national sadness and mourning in the face of her own much more personal bereavement. Last Monday night a poignant bulletin had been issued: 'The King's life is moving peacefully to its close.' Then, in the next morning's paper, had come the inevitable news that King George had died the previous night, January 20th, 1936, at the age of seventy.

How the Empire would fare under the new King remained to be seen. He – King Edward the Eighth – had arrived, bare-headed, in London, having actually flown there in an aeroplane from Sandringham. He was a dare-devil and no mistake! The Prince of Wales – no, Alice corrected herself, King Edward the Eighth as he now was, hard though it was to think of it – he wasn't one to be told what he must or must not do. He would be a different kettle of fish from his father, that was for sure.

Alice tried to answer her niece. 'Yes, my love. I daresay you're right. The King will be pleased . . .' After all, how did she know? The King might well be pleased to meet his subjects in heaven. They might all be equal there. How did any of us know? What was beyond the grave was a mystery. You could only go on trusting and believing and trying to hold on to the simple truths that you remembered from Sunday school so long ago.

Things had seemed so much more straightforward then. It had been easy to believe in a beautiful place *above the bright blue sky*; a place where, according to the old hymn writers, a glorious band of angels sang incessantly to the accompaniment of sweet harps, with golden crowns upon their heads. Perhaps Florence, her sister, was one of them now? And the King, too? But what remained of her sister, her earthly body, was at this moment lying in a coffin in Samuel Goodwin's tiny parlour a few doors away. Alice shuddered. Her beloved sister would soon lie in the churchyard, an elaborate stone set over her, no doubt, by her grieving husband. Samuel Goodwin would do the correct thing; he could always be relied on to behave in an exemplary manner and he wasn't afraid of parting with a bit of brass if it would impress folks. But how much he was really grieving, or for how long he would go on mourning his wife, Alice wasn't sure.

Florence was safe enough now, though, if the old hymns were to be believed. And the Bible, too. Hadn't Jesus himself promised, '*I go to prepare a place for you, that where I am, you may be also*'? That was what Florence had believed so implicitly and she, Alice, must try to believe it as well. She must believe it . . . but she was no longer sure that she did. She didn't know when the doubts had begun to creep in. She still went to church each Sunday, to St Luke's at the top of the hill, carrying her prayer-book and wearing her best hat and coat. And she still said her prayers. She had found herself praying just now when she had to break the news to Josephine; to pray had been an instinctive reaction . . . but she wasn't always sure that God was listening.

It wasn't so much that she didn't believe in God as that she had lost patience with some of the folks that went to church. Damned hypocrites a lot of them were, for all that they spent such a lot of time on their knees. Her brother-in-law, Samuel, for instance. He was a sidesman at St Luke's, full of his own importance as he strutted up and down the aisle, like the cock of the midden, showing folks to a vacant pew or passing round the collection plate.

He thought he was somebody, all right, did Samuel Goodwin, but Florence would never hear a wrong word said about him. She had gone on loving him, bearing his children . . . and it had been the death of her. The doctor had warned both of them, but Florence has insisted that they wanted another child. What a blessing it would be, she had said, whatever it was, but secretly she had wanted another girl. Well, it was a little lass all right, but whether baby Frances would turn out to be a blessing remained to be seen. She was Alice's responsibility for the moment and she seemed a placid enough baby to be sure. She had taken well to the bottle. It would be time for another feed soon; Alice could hear a faint mewling sound and could see tiny arms threshing the air.

She glanced across to the table where Josephine seemed to be busy again with her colourful creation. 'Come on, lovey. I think you'd best put that away now. Baby will be wanting her feed and your uncle Jack and the lads will be back soon for their tea. They'll be famished, I daresay.'

Josephine nodded. 'I've finished it now, Auntie . . . and I'm going to give it to you. The bookmark, I mean. I'm sure Mum won't mind.'

Alice felt the tears pricking her eyelids, but she answered as cheerfully as she could. 'Well, that will be grand, my love. Come on, there's a good girl. Side the table, then you can help me to get out the cups and saucers.'

They would be back before long, Jack and their Len, and little Bertie. It was dropping dark already, though it was only four o'clock. Jack had said that he would take the lads for a long walk across the moor, then they would have a look round the Saturday market.

'Don't fret yourself, lass,' he had assured her. 'I'll break the news to them. I don't suppose it'll upset our Len too much. It's only his aunt when all's said and done. I know he was fond of her, but it's not the same as losing his mam. And little Bertie's too young to know what it's all about. It's young Josie that I'm worried about. But you'll tell her, won't you, Alice?'

Well, she had told her now and it hadn't been as bad as she had anticipated. Some of the load had lifted from Alice's mind and she knew that she would do anything for that little girl. She loved her as much as she loved Jack and Len. She was fond of Bertie, too, and was glad that she could help out by looking after them while Samuel was busy, seeing the vicar and the undertaker, and coping with all the sad business that had to be attended to following a death. It was the least she could do for her dear sister, but what would happen after the funeral, the Lord only knew. She would just have to take a day at a time.

Alice glanced out of the window, across the stretch of moorland to the lights of Haliford shining in the valley and the mill chimneys thrusting upwards into the darkening sky. Haliford was one of the chief towns of the Yorkshire woollen industry, and it was in one of those mills, Hammond's, that Alice's husband, Jack Rawlinson, and her brother-in-law, Samuel Goodwin, were employed, though in widely differing capacities. Jack was a warehouseman, responsible only for humping bales of cloth and stacking heavy boxes; a job that didn't involve a great deal of skill or intelligence, but one that suited his easygoing nature. As long as there was enough money coming in on a Friday to keep himself and Alice and their Leonard, that was all Jack was bothered about. Enough for a pint or two a couple of nights a week at the Fox and Grapes, and a pouch of tobacco for his pipe.

Samuel, though, was ambitious; a go-getter if ever there was one. He didn't half throw his weight about now, Jack had reported to Alice, since he had been made head overseer. And that wasn't enough for him, Samuel Goodwin wouldn't rest till he was one of the bosses.

He was a hard worker, though, Alice had to give him his due. She was only surprised that the Goodwins still lived a few doors away in the terraced house that was identical to the one that Jack and Alice occupied. No; not quite identical because Samuel had had the boxroom over the front door converted into a tiny bathroom. There was hardly room to swing a cat round in it, but at least they now had running water upstairs and an indoor lavatory. The Rawlinsons still had to make do with a closet at the bottom of the back garden, like the rest of the inhabitants of Baldwin Terrace.

Her little family was coming up the lane now, the lads running ahead and Jack swinging his arms against the cold, his red woollen muffler wound several times round his neck and his flat cap pulled down low over his brow. A blast of cold air entered with them as Jack pushed open the door that led straight into the kitchen-cum-living-room.

'By heck, it's a cold 'un all right!' he remarked. 'Our

feet are like blocks of ice. We're frozen to the marrow, aren't we, lads?'

Len and little Bertie nodded automatically, but neither of them said a word. The light had gone from Leonard's eyes and Bertie, poor little soul, just looked bewildered.

'I've told 'em both,' Jack whispered to his wife.

But Alice could tell that he had by the look on their faces.

Josie tiptoed across the room to the cot. It wasn't really a cot at all; the real cot, the one that she and then their Bertie had slept in, and that she supposed the new baby would sleep in too, was at home, upstairs in the room where Mum had been poorly. This was just a big drawer that Auntie Alice had taken out of the sideboard and emptied of all its paraphernalia – old letters and bills, knitting needles and wool, sealing wax and rubber bands. She had made it comfy with sheets and blankets and then placed the baby inside it.

'There now, my little lamb,' she had cooed. 'You'll come to no harm, not while your auntie Alice is here to see to you. Poor little lamb – it's a shame, it is that.'

Baby Frances – that was what Dad had wanted her to be called, after his mother whom Josie didn't remember – was sleeping peacefully, satisfied with the warm milk that she had sucked hungrily from the feeding bottle that Auntie Alice held. Her little red mouth was making faint popping sounds and her tiny hands, like two miniature starfish, rested on either side of her head. Auntie Alice had told her that babies always slept like that when they were very little, with their hands above their heads.

Josie was puzzled now as she watched her new baby sister. She knew – she wasn't sure why or how, but all the same she knew – that it was because of baby Frances that her mother had gone to heaven to live with Jesus. It was all the baby's fault. Why did she have to come along, spoiling everything like this? In spite of herself, Josie reached out her finger, as she had seen her aunt do, and placed it in the baby's palm. Involuntarily, the tiny fingers curled and grasped hold of the finger. The little girl gave a start of surprise as the baby, for just a second or two, opened her eyes. For the face that looked up at her – though the blue eyes were unfocused and couldn't really see at all, only dim shapes, her aunt had told her – was Mummy's face. The palish blue eyes and finely drawn eyebrows and the straight nose were just like her mother's. So was the light blonde hair, wispy now, like the down on a day-old chick, but already showing the promise of a curl. Josie didn't want her to look like Mummy. She didn't want her . . . she didn't want her at all.

She pulled her finger away. 'I don't like you, baby,' she said, but in the softest whisper, putting her head near to the baby's. Auntie Alice mustn't hear. 'I don't like you one little bit. I shan't ever like you, so there!'

As soon as Josie had uttered the words she felt dreadful. She knew that if Auntie Alice heard her she would be very, very cross. She knew also that Jesus would not be pleased with her as well. Josie had learned at Sunday school that Jesus wanted you to love everyone, even your enemies. This new baby, she wasn't an enemy, but she was rather a nuisance and Josie didn't see how she could possibly love her, not yet anyway. But she knew that Jesus would want her to try. She leaned over the baby's makeshift cot again. 'I'm sorry, baby,' she whispered. 'I'm sorry I said I didn't like you.' Although she wasn't sure whether or not she meant it.

There was a clothes-maiden near the fire on which

were drying rows of nappies and miniature vests and nightdresses. The steam rose gently, permeating the air with a faint aroma of bleach and scented soap flakes. Josie crept inside the triangle formed by the clothes-maiden and sat down on the low stood near to the fire-guard. It was like a little house in here, a safe little house away from them all; Auntie Alice washing the pots in the kitchen, Uncle Jack reading the newspaper and gently puffing away on his pipe, and the boys, Len and Bertie, busy at their game with Leonard's toy soldiers.

Josie liked Len. He was much older than she was – nearly ten – but he was kind, like Auntie Alice, and quiet, like Uncle Jack. He didn't take much notice of Josie; boys of ten didn't care much for girls, she knew that, but perhaps he would when she was older. She wasn't bothered about him at the moment though; she wanted to be on her own, away from them all, and away from the baby. She would try not to think about the baby. She would just think about how much she liked everyone else, Len and Bertie, and Uncle Jack and Auntie Alice . . .

Josie loved her aunt Alice. She and Mum were sisters – not that anyone would ever think so, because they weren't very much alike – but Mum was a few years younger. Aunt Alice was small and round and rosy, like a ripe apple; she smelled of apples too, and cinnamon, because she was always baking, and of the lavender scent that she sprinkled on her handkerchief. Aunt Alice's eyes were dark brown, bright and shiny like a bird's, and everything in her house shone too. The brass fender and the brass candlesticks on the mantelpiece gleamed with constant burnishing and the windows and mirrors glistened. It wasn't a posh house; Josie had heard Dad complaining that it was shabby. The carpets and fireside chairs were threadbare and the rag rug had been made many years ago by Auntie Alice when she was a bride, so she had told Josie, from hundreds of tiny pieces of old cloth.

The house a few doors away, where Josie really lived, was much more splendid. They had recently had a new carpet square put down in the parlour, and on it stood a new three-piece suite in uncut moquette. But the best thing of all was the new bathroom. Aunt Alice's family had to make do with a closet at the end of the garden. It was a small, smelly place – Josie wrinkled her nose whenever she went inside – but Aunt Alice was forever scrubbing the wooden seat and whitewashing the walls. She provided real lavatory paper, too, in a square box, not pieces of newspaper threaded on a string, such as were used by most of the inhabitants of Baldwin Terrace.

Josie was glad that she didn't have to venture down the garden at night, though. Auntie Alice had told her to use the chamber-pot under her bed. It was a plain white one, but the one in her aunt and uncle's room was decorated with pink roses, to match the huge basin and jug that stood on the marble-topped washstand. Josie went in there to wash of a morning, in the icy-cold water that took her breath away. The tiny boxroom where she was sleeping at her aunt's was only big enough to hold a bed and a small chest of drawers. At home she shared the back bedroom with their Bertie, but Josie didn't know when she would be going home again. She was happy here for the moment, and now that Mum had . . . gone, perhaps Auntie Alice could be her mum and Bertie's mum as well? But what about baby Frances? Aunt Alice might not want to have all three of them. Josie did so hope that she wouldn't, then perhaps the baby could go . . . somewhere else.

* * *

On January 28th, 1936, King George the Fifth was laid to rest, with due pomp and ceremony, in St George's chapel, Windsor. Almost a million people filed past the coffin for four days as he lay in state at Westminster, while his four sons, in ceremonial dress, kept vigil. Vast crowds lined the route as the funeral procession made its way from King's Cross, the new king and his three brothers following the gun-carriage on foot. On top of the coffin was secured the Imperial Crown, but as the procession turned into New Palace Yard, the jewelled Maltese Cross on the top of the crown fell off into the gutter. 'A terrible omen,' was the report in one of the newspapers.

'It is that!' remarked Alice to her husband. 'A terrible omen . . . I can see trouble brewing with that Edward the Eighth, you mark my words.'

The next day, January 29th, Florence Goodwin, aged thirty-one, was laid to rest in St Luke's churchyard. There was no pomp, no ceremony other than a simple service, but she was mourned no less sincerely by her family and friends.

A biting north-east wind shook the bare branches of the elm trees and scattered the thin covering of powdery snow that lay on the ground. Alice's black coat was thin and worn, unsuitable for a funeral in the depths of winter, but she couldn't feel the cold. She couldn't feel anything but an overwhelming sadness and a foreboding for what the future might hold. She feared for the nation with the advent of the charismatic new monarch, but even more so for her immediate family, or rather her sister's family. What would become of them all, without Florence?

She watched it all as though in a dream. The lowering of her sister's body into the heavy clayish soil, the thud of the clods of earth as they fell on to the coffin, and the flowers, sprays of shaggy chrysanthemums like mop heads, some already wilting as they lay on the ground. She couldn't weep; she knew that once the tears started to flow they would never stop, and so she remained outwardly calm and detached. She had been too busy during the last few days, caring for the children and preparing the funeral feast, to give way to her emotions. Now they seemed frozen within her, as frozen as the icicles hanging from the church porch, and her heart felt as leaden as the wintry grey sky.

The funeral tea she had provided, with the money from Samuel's pocket, was a spread fit for a king. Samuel Goodwin wouldn't be able to say that she had stinted on anything. There were slices of ham and tongue, crusty bread, pickled onions and beetroot, apple pies, deep custard and curd tarts, and a huge fruit cake left over from Christmas with Wensleydale cheese to accompany it. And gallons of tea, hot and strong and sweet, now being avidly sipped from Florence's bone-china tea service, brought in from a few doors away, and from Alice's own white and blue earthenware cups. What a panacea for all ills was a pot of tea, the ideal way to bridge the gap caused by embarrassment or shyness . . . or by sadness and death.

Not that there seemed to be much sadness now, not from all quarters at any rate, thought Alice as she poured the dark brown liquid into the cups. She wondered if some of them had forgotten why they were here, judging from the gales of laughter issuing from one corner of the room. Or could it just be, she thought, that we sometimes laugh at the things we fear, and so we laugh at death? She had never really approved of the funeral tea, a gathering together of family and closest friends and neighbours, to reminisce about the one no longer in our midst. But she knew that it was a tradition, and quite necessary, too. Some of them had travelled a long way. Cousin Mabel had come from Skipton, and Aunt Bertha and Uncle Will from Huddersfield. You couldn't send them on their way without something warm inside them, not on such a cold day.

How Yorkshire folk loved a good funeral. She could hear the memories and anecdotes being exchanged now. Mrs Ollerenshaw, a neighbour from the other end of the terrace, never happy unless she was being miserable, was in full spate.

'Aye, I remember her when she first moved into t' terrace with young Samuel. A right bonny lass she were an' all, with that lovely long hair and her big blue eyes. And she were bonny right up to the end. When I saw her in her coffin, I said to our Bill as how she were still a bonny lass.'

'Aye, tha's right, Martha. But she were always weakly, like. A puff of wind 'ud have knocked her over. I allus thought she wouldn't be long for this world . . .'

Alice was glad that her mother couldn't hear it all. She glanced across the room to where the old lady sat, as motionless as a statue, in the big armchair near the fire.

'All right, Mother?' Alice mouthed, and her mother nodded, the black petersham bow, which had been added to rejuvenate her ancient velour hat, nodding to and fro.

Her mother's deafness was, at times, a blessing in disguise, cutting her off from the world and its problems. It was strange how Agnes Broadbent was often referred to as an old lady. She wasn't old – only in her early sixties – but her deafness made her seem so. She had aged prematurely many years ago, grief-stricken by the death of a son and two younger brothers in the carnage of the Great War, and of her husband who had died in the outbreak of Spanish flu that had scourged the country soon after. She had looked just the same for ten years or more, slight of build, still and wax-pale, frequently retreating into her own silent world. She seemed as insubstantial as a shadow, but her spirit was strong.

'Your ma's as tough as old boots,' Jack often remarked.

Indeed she was; frail though she looked, she had never ailed much and still lived alone in her small rented cottage at the far end of the lane.

'I'll ne'er budge from here till they carry me out feet first,' she had vowed.

It must be dreadful, Alice thought, to lose a child, a reversal of the natural order of things. You could expect to lose your parents eventually, and maybe your spouse, but to see a child that you have borne and nurtured snatched away by premature death – that didn't bear thinking about. And yet it had happened twice to Agnes Broadbent.

The buzz of conversation reverberating round the over-crowded little room progressed from memorable funerals, past and present, to the new King, and Stanley Baldwin, just re-elected as the Prime Minister of the National Government, and a fanatical little man called Hitler, who was beginning to make his presence felt in Germany. Alice's eyes searched the room, finally meeting the kindly glance of Jack, her husband. He looked ill at ease in his best navy suit and black tie and highly polished black boots; he was much more at home in a collarless shirt and cardigan, often referred to as a *ganzy* in their part of the world. His fingers were drumming nervously on the arm of the chair and Alice felt her heart warm with affection for him. She knew, with the wifely intuition that came with years of living in close proximity, that he was anxious to be off down the garden for a puff on his pipe. He wouldn't light up in here – it wouldn't be seemly, not at a funeral party. Nor could he leave the guests in his own house to follow their own devices. Jack was not a demonstrative husband, not openly affectionate, but Alice knew that he was as steadfast and dependable as the unchanging hills of his native Yorkshire and she grew more fond of him with every passing year.

She turned as she felt a hand on her arm. 'Samuel . . .' she nodded at her brother-in-law. 'I think it all went off all right, don't you? It was a lovely service. The vicar spoke real well of our Florence, and I think the folks have all had enough to eat.'

'Thanks to you, Alice, and don't think that I'm not appreciative of your efforts. For all you've done for the children these last few weeks, and for all this.' He waved his hand expansively at the banquet of food arrayed on the sideboard and table. 'You've done us proud.' He wasn't usually so ready with his compliments, Alice thought, not unless further favours were to be requested. They were. 'If you could see your way to looking after our Herbert and baby Frances for the next few weeks or so,' he went on, 'I'd be eternally grateful to you, Alice. Josephine will be at school, of course.'

He always gave his children their full names, Josephine and Herbert, whereas to most people they were usually Josie and Bertie; whilst he was known to everyone as Samuel, never Sam. And he's swallowed a dictionary an' all, thought Alice now. Him and his *eternally grateful*! But though he tried, when he remembered, to use fancy-sounding words, the flat vowel-sounds of the north of England betrayed him. In all fairness, though, he never sought to disguise that he was 'Yorkshire born and bred, and proud of it'.

'You know I'll look after the bairns,' Alice replied. 'Who else is there to do it, anyroad? Josie can come here when she finishes school until you get back from the mill, and I'll have young Bertie and the baby all day. Bertie's not a scrap of trouble, bless him, and as for little Frances, well, at the moment you wouldn't know she was there, she's that good.'

Samuel, to give him his due, did seem to be grateful. 'Thank you, Alice,' he said. 'I'll sce to it that you're not out of pocket, of course.' His dark eyes narrowed speculatively as he looked across the room. 'It may not be for very long. I may be able to come to . . . some other arrangement. But if you could carry on as you have been doing, just for now . . .' He nodded at her, but the brief smile didn't reach his eyes.

Alice watched as he crossed the room. In the far corner, by the back kitchen door, sat Iris Collier. She had long been a regular visitor to the Goodwin home, especially so of late, while Florence had been poorly. She was by far the most elegantly dressed person in the room although, admittedly, she didn't have much competition. A fox fur was draped elegantly over her smart black costume, the tail hanging down her back and the animal's head reclining on her shoulder, for all the world as though it was about to snap off her ear. Her hat was small – what the French people would call *chic* – perched atop of her dark but already greying hair. Iris was a buxom woman; all bust and bum was how Jack had once described her. Her chest stuck out like a pouter pigeon and her long skirt hid the bandiness of her legs.

Samuel pulled up a chair and sat next to Iris Collier. She lowered her head as he spoke to her, then smiled at him and nodded. Alice felt a spasm of premonition run through her as she watched them. She knew that not by the slightest word or glance would Samuel step out of line, not in public view, at any rate; he could always be relied upon to act circumspectly. All the same, Alice was uneasy. So that was the way the land was lying, was it? Iris Collier was a widow . . .

Chapter 2

'Well, he's not wasted much time about it and that's for sure! Our poor Florence only in her grave these last couple of months and he's talking about getting wed again. Mind you, I've seen it coming . . .' Alice put down her knitting and leaned forward. She nodded her head slowly as she looked at her husband, sitting in the opposite fireside chair. 'That Iris Collier's never been off the doorstep since the day of the funeral. Oh aye, I could see how things were shaping.'

'I don't suppose you can blame him, lass.' Jack looked over the top of his *Haliford Chronicle*, then, seeing the worried expression on his wife's face, he folded the newspaper and tucked it down the side of the chair. 'Don't take on so about it, Alice. It'll happen work out all right. Like I say, you can't blame him. It's hard for a chap working all day at the mill then coming home of an evening and starting again. Men aren't used to making meals and messing about in the kitchen like womenfolk do.'

'Samuel's not done so much messing about in the kitchen and well you know it, Jack Rawlinson, so don't go sticking up for him.' Alice's eyes flashed with annoyance. 'It's me that's been looking after those bairns these last few months . . . and I'd be only too happy to go on doing it an' all. They're no trouble to me, bless 'em. The little 'uns are as good as gold. Bertie's a grand little lad and as for the baby, you hardly know she's there. And Josie's getting to be a real good help to me in the kitchen, siding the table and drying the pots. She even helped me make an apple pie the other day.'

'It's not natural, though, for a fellow to live alone,' said Jack. 'I don't care what you say, Alice. A chap needs somebody to look after him, to see to his meals and creature comforts an' all that . . . as well as the other thing,' he added under his breath. 'And Samuel's a young man still. What will he be now? Not much more than thirty-two or three?'

'And she's old enough to be his mother!' Alice picked up her knitting again. Her needles clicked together furiously as she stared fixedly at the grey sock taking shape beneath her flying fingers. 'Cradle-snatching, that's what she's doing.'

'Aw, come on now, lass. I think you're laying it on a bit thick there. Old enough to be his mother, indeed! Nowt of the sort.'

'I'll bet she can give him ten years though.' Alice glared at her husband indignantly. 'Iris Collier must be well turned forty. She's been a widow these past five years or so and she was no chicken then. I don't know whatever he's thinking about. When I think of our poor Florence, such a bonny lass she was, and as dainty as a fairy. That Iris Collier couldn't hold a candle to her.'

'Aye, I'll grant you that. Iris wasn't on the front row when looks were given out, and that's for sure.' Jack grinned wickedly. 'And them legs of hers. She couldn't stop a pig in an entry!'

'Jack! What a thing to say!' Alice laughed in spite of herself. 'You can't blame the poor woman for that, now can you? That's what comes of standing long hours at a loom, and that's just what Iris did when she was a youngster. She used to work all hours God sent, from all accounts, when she was a lass. There was a big family of 'em, I believe, lived on the other side of town.'

'She did all right for herself though, when she got wed,' replied Jack. 'She didn't do much standing on the mill floor once she'd wed Alfred Collier. And she's still doing pretty well out of the business from what I've heard tell. She must be worth a bob or two.'

The red and black lorries with their eye-catching slogan, *Colliers for Coke and Coal*, were a familiar sight as they trundled up and down the steep cobbled streets around Haliford and district. The business had been started by Alfred, and was now carried on by his two younger brothers. Iris, however, it was said, was still a major shareholder and had a lot to do with the running of the business.

'Yes, I daresay she's pretty well heeled.' Alice sighed. 'And I wouldn't be surprised if that's the main reason Samuel's taken up with her. He's had his eye on the main chance these last few years. But he can suit himself. I'm not all that concerned about Samuel Goodwin. It's those youngsters I'm worried about.'

'He'll see to it that they're all right. Don't fret yourself, lass.' Jack leaned across and placed his hand comfortingly over his wife's. 'Whatever else you say about Samuel, he does look after his children. They're always nicely turned out and they don't want for anything. And he's as pleased as Punch when he takes them all out of a Sunday. Right proud of them, he is.'

'And why is he proud of them? Just tell me that. It's because he likes folks to say that they're a credit to him. Whatever Samuel Goodwin does, it's for Samuel Goodwin's benefit.' Alice scowled at her husband. 'What those youngsters want is a bit of love and affection, never mind new clothes and posh bathrooms an' all that. And what does that woman know about bringing up children? She's never had any of her own. She'll not know where to begin, you take it from me.'

'I daresay she'll learn,' said Jack, a trifle edgily. 'It comes natural to a woman, doesn't it, looking after children? And you've said yourself that they're not much bother. Don't get so het up about it, Alice, love.'

'I didn't expect you to take that attitude, Jack,' said Alice, feeling hurt and let down. At least she had expected Jack to agree with her if no one else did. 'You seem to be siding with him . . . and with her. I shall be lost without those bairns after all this time.'

Jack sighed. 'Whatever we do or say, it's not going to make a ha'p'orth of difference. So we'd best look on the bright side. That's all I'm trying to do. I'm just trying to cheer you up. Happen it'll all be for the best. And you'll have a bit more time to yourself, Alice. You've been rushed off your feet these last few months.'

Alice smiled and quickly wiped away a stray tear from the corner of her eye. 'Yes, I daresay you're right, Jack. And I ought to know by now that you'd try to see some good in the devil himself. Yes, it'll no doubt sort itself out . . . but it's them moving away from Baldwin Lane that's upsetting me. When will I get to see the children?'

'It's not as though they're going a hundred miles away. Gladstone Avenue's only twenty minutes' walk if it's that. And that house 'ud be a bit cramped with five of 'em in it, you must admit.'

'Plenty folks have to manage with less,' said Alice

pointedly. 'But of course a poky two-up two-down at the end of a terrace wouldn't be good enough for the likes of Iris Collier.' She stared thoughtfully into the fire, then looked up at her husband and gave a tight little smile. 'Like you say, Jack, we must look on the bright side. And I'll try to be charitable to the woman. I'll have to be for the sake of the little 'uns. It's no good us getting off on the wrong foot. It wouldn't be fair to the youngsters for us to be at loggerheads from the start.'

'Good lass. That's the spirit.' Jack patted her hand. 'And you'll be able to see the children, don't you worry. When all's said and done, they're your sister's children. Your own flesh and blood.'

Alice nodded slowly. 'Little Josie . . . she's just like my own child. She always has been, right from the start. And it's her that I'm worried about. Not the other two, they're young enough to adapt. Baby Frances has never known her real mother and young Bertie, bless him, I daresay he'll soon forget. But Josie . . . she's a spirited lass. I can see that there'll be sparks flying before she's much older.'

'Don't meet trouble before it comes,' said her husband patiently. He gave her a worried glance, but Alice was absorbed once more in her knitting, her brow furrowed with concentration as she turned the heel of the sock. Jack picked up the *Haliford Chronicle* again. All the worrying in the world wouldn't make a scrap of difference.

Iris Collier was not unaware of the strong feelings, in some quarters, regarding her forthcoming marriage. The gossip of the folk at church didn't worry her. She could do her share of scandal-mongering; what women didn't when they were on their own, away from their menfolk? Iris knew that while they were talking about her they were leaving someone else alone, and in any case, it would all be a nine day's wonder. But she was most mindful of the quiet antagonism of Alice Rawlinson . . . and of young Josephine.

Not that there was anything she could put her finger on, not with Alice at any rate. In fact the woman had gone out of her way to be friendly, inviting Iris round for a cup of tea and a chat after the Mothers' Union meeting. Iris had complimented Alice on her sponge cake – light as a feather, it was – and they had exchanged recipes. Iris had given Alice a recipe for parkin made with black treacle that had been one of Alfred's favourites, and they had parted on the best of terms.

Iris had had no ulterior motive when she first started visiting the Goodwins' home. At that time, of course, Florence had been alive, ailing though, and very big with her third child. The poor lass had hardly been able to walk about, the protuberance that had swollen her slender body to such grotesque proportions seeming not to be a part of her at all. Iris had felt sorry for her. She was a pleasant lass, though rather a milk-and-water sort of person, overshadowed by the dominant personality of her husband. Iris had befriended her, taking her under her wing at the Mothers' Union meetings. So it had been inevitable that Iris should start calling at the home with little offerings of nourishing chicken broth or appetizing cakes and custards. It had been a great shock when the poor girl had died. Iris had been sorely distressed at the news, not realizing that the situation was so serious, and had called to offer her condolences.

Samuel was grateful. She had begun to see him then, for the first time, from a purely feminine point of view. Formerly he had just been the husband of her friend. Now the shrewd glance of his deep brown eyes kindled a similar response in her own. They had looked at one another, and had gone on looking for several seconds more than it was necessary. Each of them recognized in the other's eyes an awareness, an acknowledgement, the very beginnings of desire. Neither of them said a word, though; sometimes words were not necessary.

Iris had lived alone since her husband, Alfred, had died, a state of affairs that didn't suit her at all. It was different for men; they could take a woman to their bed on the quiet – or quite openly, for that matter – and very little would be said. It was assumed that men were like that; it was just 'the nature of the beast'. But what could a woman do? Very little if she wanted to keep her self-esteem. Iris, at the time of her husband's death, had been anxious to hold on to the good opinion that others had of her, and to maintain her up-and-coming position in the hierarchy, such as it was, in the town of Haliford.

Marrying Alfred had been a step up the social ladder. She had married him mainly for the security and the ease that his wealth could bring her although she had been fond of him as well. His modest affluence had been riches untold after the poverty in which Iris had been brought up. She had been one of a family of ten children, raised in a back-to-back house in a grimy cul-de-sac, where the mill chimneys incessantly belched out their putrid smoke. Alfred's semi-detached house on Gladstone Avenue had seemed like a palace to the nineteen-year-old girl. He was twenty-five years her senior, but what did that matter? He could offer her a comfortable home and affection. She didn't know whether it could be termed love; she had nothing with which to compare their feelings for one another. Iris's life, up to that point, had consisted of standing for up to fourteen hours a day on the mill floor, then helping her downtrodden mother to care for the vast brood of children to which, every eighteen months or so, another was added. There had been little time to spare for walking out with lads. Alfred had been her first encounter with the opposite sex – except for her drunken bully of a father – and Alfred had been her salvation, her means of escape.

He had proved to be an adequate lover. What they had enjoyed together once a week in the commodious feather bed had been mutually satisfying. But Alfred was considerably older than his wife and, moreover, was becoming increasingly preoccupied with his business affairs. Sexual desire, on Alfred's part at least, had waned. With Iris it had been merely put on one side. But the spark was there, and at Samuel's knowing glance it was immediately rekindled.

When he asked her, about six weeks after Florence's death, if she would consider marrying him, she didn't hesitate, except to remind him of the difference in their ages.

'I've long turned forty, you know, Samuel. Folks will say I'm cradle-snatching.' Iris gave him an amused glance which he quickly countered.

'To hell with what folks say!' he replied. 'I shouldn't have thought it would worry you, Iris. I daresay folks had enough to say when you married Alfred, didn't they? Let them think what they like – it's our affair, and we've nobody to answer to but ourselves.'

Your children, Samuel, thought Iris. What about your children?

She was thoughtful for a moment. Yes, there had been talk all right when she married Alfred, not only that he was more than old enough to be her father, but that she was feathering her nest very nicely. The age difference was the other way round this time, but it didn't worry her. She felt more than adequate to cope with Samuel's youthfulness. The thought of it excited her . . . But she had the sense to know that it wouldn't all be plain sailing.

She replied to him now, 'Nobody to answer to, you say? There are your children, Samuel. Josephine and Bertie. Baby Frances is too young to have any memories, but the other two will go on remembering their mother. I wouldn't want them to make comparisons. Well, I suppose they're bound to, but I just hope I get on all right with them.'

Samuel shrugged. 'They'll forget,' he said casually.

Too casually, Iris thought. She wouldn't want the children to forget their mother, but she hoped that she would be able to compensate them, if only slightly, for the sadness of their loss. She knew only too well that Samuel, in asking her to marry him, was thinking of himself first and foremost. She had no illusions about him. Samuel, she knew, would always look after number one. She was well aware that her wealth was part of the attraction, and also the fact that there would be someone on hand all the time to look after his three children. But she didn't think those were the only reasons. She had read the desire in his eyes, a feeling that, on her part, was eagerly reciprocated.

'They'll soon forget,' he repeated. 'Josephine was very fond of her mother, I know that, but children don't worry very much, so long as there's someone there to see to them. They're all selfish little beasts at heart. They think of their own needs first, it stands to reason. Why do you think a baby cries? Because it wants attention, and once it's got what it wants, it stops crying. No, children don't care a damn for anybody else, only for themselves.'

And some of them don't change very much once they've grown up, thought Iris, but she kept her thoughts to herself.

What she said was, 'You're quite the philosopher, Samuel.' She smiled wryly. 'Yes, you're right . . . to a point. Very young children don't care who looks after them, so long as there's someone there to see that they're fed and watered. But Josephine's growing up. She's six now, isn't she? And sometimes she seems a lot older than that. At any rate, she's plenty old enough to start making up her own mind about things. And I don't think she's taken to me all that well.'

'Of course she has. You're imagining it.' Samuel's tone was indifferent. 'Never mind about the children. They'll soon get used to you, you'll see. It's us that's important, Iris my love, you and me.' He came to sit next to her on the settee and slipped an arm round her shoulders. His hand wandered down to her breast, quickly finding the opening in her blouse. She responded eagerly to his touch and returned his kiss with more than an equal ardour. Not that it would do to get too excited. Samuel, she knew, would go little further, not with the children upstairs in bed. Samuel always behaved correctly; he was well able to keep his emotions on a tight rein . . . for the moment. But she couldn't wait for the wedding day.

Josephine, though, was the bone of contention. Iris knew that she wasn't imagining it when she said that the child hadn't taken to her. She had seen the thoughtful look in Josephine's eyes – so like her father's – a look that was weighing up Iris, wondering what to make of her. The child couldn't possibly know, yet, that Iris was to be her new stepmother. They had decided it would be better to wait awhile before breaking the news to Josephine and Bertie. But the child knew that something was afoot; there was no need for her to be told. The knowledge was there, in her remoteness, in the way she refused to get too close to Iris.

Iris had tried with her. She decided she must try even harder. On her next visit to the Goodwins' home she picked up Josephine's elegant doll who seemed to have a permanent position on top of the sewing machine.

'I like your doll,' she began chattily. 'Do you know, Josephine, when I was a little girl I always wanted a doll just like this. But my mother could never afford to buy me one. There were a lot of us in our family you see, dear. We didn't have many toys . . .' Her voice petered out as the child stared at her fixedly. 'What is she . . . what do you call her?' she asked falteringly.

'Mary Jane. That's what she's called,' said Josie, not showing much interest.

Iris stroked the doll's silken dress and lifted the skirt to reveal lace-edged pantaloons of the type worn by Victorian children. 'She's very posh, your Mary Jane . . . but she's torn her dress. What do you suppose she's been doing? Fighting with the teddy bear while you're fast asleep?' She smiled at Josephine, but evoked very little response. The child just looked at her, frowning slightly.

Iris persisted. 'Would you like me to make her a new dress? I've got some pretty pink material at home that would just suit Mary Jane.'

'If you like,' Josephine replied. 'I don't mind. I don't play with her very much. I don't like dolls.'

'Oh dear – I thought all little girls liked dolls.' Iris was aware that her voice sounded fatuous. Damn the child! Such a little scrap of a thing she was, but she was making Iris feel so helpless, a feeling Iris wasn't used to at all. 'What do you like then, dear?' she asked.

'Story-books, cutting-out, drawing . . .' The child's voice

was still detached. She paused, then a slightly more responsive look crept over her face. She pulled open the sideboard drawer and took out a book of coloured scraps. 'Look – Mummy bought me these just before she . . . before she was poorly. I made her a bookmark to put in her prayer-book, but then she . . . I gave it to Auntie Alice. She says she uses it every Sunday.'

Iris felt a sigh of relief escape from her. This seemed like a breakthrough, albeit a minor one. 'That's lovely,' she said. 'May I have a look, dear?' She held out her hand and the child passed her the book of multi-coloured scraps. 'That's lovely,' said Iris again as she turned the pages. Flowers, fruit, trees, gaudily coloured parrots and birds of paradise. 'That's lovely,' she repeated, beginning to feel like a parrot herself. 'Do you think you could make me a bookmark, Josephine? I'd really love one.'

'Yes . . .' The child smiled and her face lit up immediately. Iris hadn't seen her smile very much; she was a serious little girl most of the time, but it was amazing what a difference the relaxing of her facial muscles made. She looked animated now, almost pretty, and her dark eyes shone with interest. She pointed to the scrap book. 'Would you like to choose the ones you want?'

Iris had noticed that Josephine didn't call her anything. Bertie had quickly fallen into the way of calling her Auntie Iris; most grown up persons, friends of the family, were given the courtesy title of Auntie or Uncle. But it was obvious, the way Josephine always left the sentence unfinished. Iris decided not to press the matter. She had already begun to make a little headway with the child; it would be better not to rush things. She smiled at the little girl and began to look through the book, exclaiming over-enthusiastically at the array of colourful characters. She stopped at a page full of dogs, impossible-looking poodles and Pekinese, and soulful spaniels with drooping ears.

'What a dear little dog,' she said, pointing to a Scottish terrier wearing a tartan bow. 'Do you think I could have him on my bookmark, dear? And perhaps some of those pretty blue flowers to match his bow. When I was a little girl there was a dog just like him that lived next door to my gran. I always wished that he belonged to me . . .' She stopped, aware that she was prattling foolishly, and looked at the child. 'Do you like dogs, dear?'

'Not much. I'd rather have cats,' Josephine replied.

Iris gave a sigh. She had thought she was doing so well with the child. Now she felt deflated and, for the moment, utterly at a loss.

She started as she felt a small hand touch her knee, and she smiled warmly at little Bertie. He had been engrossed with his toy cars on the hearthrug, so quiet that she had forgotten he was there. Now his big brown eyes looked up at her pleadingly. 'Will you read me a story, Auntie Iris?'

'Of course I will, love.' Iris lifted the child up on to her comfortable lap and he rested his head against her shoulder. 'Now, which one shall we have? What about *The Three Little Pigs*?'

Bertie nodded contentedly and Iris began to read . . .

He was a dear little lad, so well behaved and biddable. He resembled his father in looks, as Josephine did; like three peas in a pod they were, with their dark hair and dark eyes. But there, as far as Bertie was concerned, the resemblance ended. He had inherited none of his father's temperament. The child was very young of course, but so far there was no sign of Samuel's driving force nor, it must be admitted, of his self-centredness. Bertie was showing the promise of a much gentler nature – like his mother's – which was probably why Samuel took very little notice of his son. Not that he paid that much attention to any of his brood. He cared for their material needs – there was very little that they lacked – but if there was someone else there to look after them, then Samuel was only too happy to relinquish his responsibilities. He was completely ignoring them all now, enveloped in the depths of his Sunday newspaper.

It was becoming quite a Sunday afternoon ritual, as though they were a proper family already; a sedate walk in the municipal park, then back to Baldwin Terrace for tea. It would soon be time for Iris to don her pinny and prepare the meal. Samuel, of course, took it for granted that she would do so, and she couldn't blame him. It was what he had always been used to. What went on in the kitchen – cooking, baking, washing-up – that was women's work, in Samuel's opinion. You couldn't expect a man to start buttering the bread and peeling potatoes or to shove his hands in a bowl of soapy suds, not when he'd been working hard all day. Samuel hadn't been working today, of course, but Sunday, as everyone knew, was a day of rest. For the men . . . There was precious little rest for the women, but that was just the way things were. Iris wouldn't have expected it to be any other way. Not for the moment, at any rate. But Samuel would change once they got married. She had no intention of waiting on him hand and foot as his first wife had done, but it would be soon enough for him to find that out once they were wed. For the moment she would be the dutiful little woman, if that was what he wanted . . .

'And the big bad wolf fell into the pan of boiling water . . . and that was the end of him. And the three little pigs lived happily ever after.' Iris finished the story and closed the book. 'There now, did you like that? Come on now, love. You'd best go and play with your cars again and Auntie Iris will start to make the tea. And Frances will be wanting her bottle soon, won't she?'

Iris tiptoed across the room to where the baby was sleeping peacefully in her pram. They hadn't taken her out when they returned from their walk; it had seemed a shame to disturb her rest, but it was time she was waking up now. Iris gently joggled the pram. 'Come on, sleeping beauty. Let's be having you.' She leaned closer, breathing in the warm aroma of talcum powder and milk, the distinctive smell of a tiny baby. She felt her heart contract so that it almost hurt as the child opened her big blue eyes and looked straight at Iris.

'You're a little beauty, you are that. You're a lovely little girl,' she crooned softly as she placed her forefinger in the baby's palm and felt the thrill she always felt as the tiny fingers closed around her own.

Iris had never been a great one for cooing into prams or asking if she could hold newborn babies. She thought she had seen enough of babies to last her a lifetime. Her childhood home had been full of them; bare-bottomed toddlers with dummies in their mouths, and older children with nits in their hair, grubby threadbare jumpers and seats falling out of their trousers. Iris's mother had tried hard, at the beginning, to keep them all clean and well clothed, but she had been fighting a losing battle. Eventually she had been defeated by the grime and poverty and the sameness of life, the dull routine as one endless day followed another. Three of the children had died in infancy. She had wept, but it had, in a heart-rending way, been a relief. Three less mouths to feed, three less rapidly growing bodies to clothe.

This child was beautiful. Little Frances Goodwin was the image of Florence, her mother. But Florence was dead and in her grave these past few months, and baby Frances would soon have a new mother to care for her. Iris realized, as she bent close to the child in the pram, that this was one of her main reasons for marrying Samuel; not only her rapidly growing affection for him, but the desire to look after this little child.

The discovery came as a shock to Iris. She had been married to Alfred for almost eighteen years and no babies had come along. They hadn't sought for a reason, but had just accepted that this was the way it was to be. They had been content enough with each other and with the increasing responsibilities of the business without the added worries that a family would bring. Iris had experienced little joy in family life and had felt that it was bliss beyond compare to live in a house where she wasn't constantly falling over piles of washing, or working her way through mountains of dirty crockery; a house that smelt of lavender furniture polish and freshly baked bread, not of stale cabbage and urine . . . or worse.

Her brothers and sisters had been an unattractive brood, skinny and sallow-featured, and Iris had felt little affection for any of them. They mostly still lived in or near Haliford, but she saw very little of them. Save for Fred, the brother nearest to her in age, who, like Iris, had managed to scramble out of the mire. Fred had a white-collar job in the office at Hammond's mill. He had married a girl that his family considered 'a cut above him', and they lived in a nice little semi on the other side of Haliford. Yes, Fred, like his sister Iris, had bettered himself.

Iris knew only too well what was said about her, not so much now, maybe, but when she had first married Alfred.

A 'jumped-up nowt', they said, who was riding for a fall. Her own mother had warned her that no good could come of marrying out of her class.

'Fur coat and no drawers,' one of their old neighbours had whispered to a friend when Iris had turned up at her father's funeral in her new sable coat. It hadn't been intended that Iris should hear the remark, indeed she hadn't done so; she had just read the woman's lips and seen the sardonic smile on her face. Iris was skilled at lip-reading, as many mill workers were. It was an art they acquired over the years, enabling them to converse amid the clatter and clamour of the looms.

Iris was not immune to the cynical comments that were made about her; she found them hurtful, but she knew, too, that there were those who were envious because she had done so well for herself. Yes, she thought, looking back on the hard times, there had been occasions in her childhood when she had lacked certain articles of underclothing, as her sarcastic neighbour had suggested. But not now. Now she could afford a change for every day of the week.

Her mirror told her that her face and figure left a lot to be desired. Her cheeks were florid, a network of broken capillaries: her wiry brown hair was greying at the temples and she was – she had to admit it – fat. But where nature had failed, artifice could succeed, and Iris knew that when she attended St Luke's she was the best-dressed woman in the congregation.

She was forty-two now. Whether it had been her fault or Alfred's that no children had come along she would never know, but she was certain now that she would never give birth, nor did she wish to do so. She had seen her mother too often in the throes of childbirth to have any desire to experience it for herself.

But with this lovely child she was being given a chance. The thought thrilled her beyond words. What a joy it would be to dress her up in pretty clothes, to cuddle her and sing her to sleep, and, above all, to have a hand in her upbringing. Iris was well aware that she was taking on a big responsibility with the care of three children who were not her own flesh and blood, but she was more than willing to try. The two elder ones might not be easy, especially Josephine, but with this tiny baby it would be like writing on a clean page. Iris felt, for a moment, almost humble at the thought of it all, but not the least bit afraid. She had never been faint-hearted.

She straightened up, aware that Josephine was watching her. 'Your sister's awake now,' she said, more cheerfully than she was feeling. Josephine's quiet resentment disturbed her. 'Come along, dear, and help me make baby's bottle. Then you can set the table for me, there's a good girl.'

Josephine looked at Iris, then she turned and looked at her father. Iris sighed inwardly. It was no use either of them looking to Samuel for assistance. He was still engrossed in his newspaper.

'Josephine . . . I don't think you heard me.' Iris's voice was steady and controlled, but there was no mistaking that she meant to be obeyed. 'Come and help me to get the tea ready. Now!'

Josephine put down her book, but she still stayed where she was.

'At once, Josephine! I'm not going to say it again . . .'

This time Josephine moved.

Chapter 3

'I shall miss you, Auntie Alice,' said Josie, leaning against the wooden draining-board in the kitchen. She was sucking abstractedly at the end of one of her long dark plaits, something that she had started doing only recently. 'It'll be horrid, going to that house in Gladstone Avenue instead of coming here to you when I finish school. I shan't like it, you know. I shan't like it one little bit.'

'Nonsense! Of course you will.' Alice purposely made her voice sound sharp, though her instinct was to put her arms round the child and hug her tightly. But Josie had to be steered away from this propensity towards self-pity and made to come to terms with what was going to happen. What couldn't be cured had to be endured; it was no use telling the child that, but Alice knew that it was true and the message had to be got across somehow.

'Don't suck you hair like that, dear,' she said. 'You're making it all nasty. And just look, your ribbon's coming undone.' Alice deftly tied the red ribbon into a bow and tucked the plait behind Josie's shoulder. 'There – all shipshape again.' The child had not looked as spruce since Florence went, partly because, understandably, Samuel hadn't got the touch that a woman would have, nor the time to bother of a morning; but also because Josie had stopped caring so much about how she looked. She went off to school looking reasonably well turned out, but sometimes when she returned at four o'clock she looked as though she had been dragged through a hedge backwards.

'Of course you'll like it at Gladstone Avenue,' said Alice again. 'Aren't you going to have a bedroom to yourself, like a big girl, instead of sharing with Bertie?' Josie nodded. 'Well, there you are then. That'll be grand. Proper grown up you'll be. And it's not all that far away you know, lovey.' Alice couldn't help herself putting an arm round the child's thin shoulders. She hated to see her looking so dejected. 'You'll be able to come and see us quite often. Perhaps we could arrange with your dad to bring you here on a Saturday? Or if Auntie Iris would let you come one day a week after school, like you do now, then maybe your dad could come round for you later, when you've had your tea. Would you like that?'

Josie nodded again. 'But I come every day now, don't I?' she replied. 'You said once a week . . . That's not very much.'

Alice sighed. The child could be so difficult when she was 'wrong side out', very much like her father. 'Well, I'm afraid it will have to do, Josephine,' she replied more firmly than she would have wished. 'I've told you, your home will be in Gladstone Avenue in a few weeks' time . . . and it's all going to be grand. Now, come on, love. We'd best shape ourselves and get this table set. Our Len'll be in soon, ready to eat me out of house and home. He always does when he's been playing football. Now, I'll cut the bread and you can spread the butter on it. How's that?'

Alice was pleased to see that the little girl cheered up slightly as they prepared the tea. She answered in monosyllables at first. Yes, she was looking forward to school finishing in two weeks' time. And yes, she would be in the big school, the Juniors, when she went back in September, as opposed to the Infant school that she attended now. Then, 'We're going on our holidays,' she volunteered, somewhat hesitantly. 'All of us. Me and our Bertie and Dad . . . and Auntie Iris and the baby,' she added in an undertone. 'We're going to Blackpool.'

At this Alice threw up her hands in a gesture of surprise and delight, as if she hadn't already known that Samuel proposed taking not only his new bride but all the family with him on his honeymoon to the seaside. 'Blackpool! Well, I never did! Aren't you the lucky one? Fancy going to Blackpool.'

At her aunt's enthusiastic response a glimmer of interest began to stir in Josie's dark eyes. 'Is it nice at Blackpool, Auntie Alice? Have you been?'

'Nice? I'll say it's nice,' replied Alice. 'There's nowhere in this wide world like Blackpool. There's the sea, and miles and miles of sand, and the Pleasure Beach. And the dear little donkeys on the beach. You'll be able to have a donkey ride, Josie. Yes, I've been to Blackpool. Your uncle Jack and I went there when we got married. And we went back once when Leonard was a tiny lad. But we haven't been for ages. I wish I was coming with you, I do that. You are a lucky little girl, going to Blackpool.'

'Perhaps you could come with us, Auntie Alice.' Josie was looking at her intently, her dark eyes serious and her brows drawn together in a questioning frown. 'D'you think p'raps you could? I'd like it a lot better if you were there.'

'Oh no, that wouldn't do at all.' Alice hastily patted her shoulder. 'Don't you worry about me, love. I didn't really mean that I wanted to come. I know I can't. No . . . this is a holiday just for your family. But you'll have to send me a postcard, mind. One with the Tower on. And bring me back a stick of pink rock, then I won't mind so much being left behind.'

Alice was pleased to see that Josie looked much more cheerful now. 'That'll be in August,' the little girl said, as she placed the slices of bread and butter carefully on the bottom tier of the cake stand, the way she had seen her aunt do. 'The middle of August, Dad said. But before that there's going to be the wedding and a party at the Quarp Café.'

Alice smiled at the child's pronunciation. 'Co-op,' she said. 'The Co-operative Café. Say "Co-op", Josie. That's how you say it.'

'Co . . . op,' repeated Josie, frowning slightly. 'And she says . . . Auntie Iris says that she's going to take me to the big Co-op in town, so that I can choose a new frock and hat for the wedding. For meself, I mean. She's already got her new frock, Auntie Iris has, but she says it's a big secret. We can't see it until the day.'

'Well, I never did!' said Alice again. 'New clothes and holidays in Blackpool. Whatever next!' She had noticed the child's slight discomfiture when she spoke of Auntie Iris, but at least she was giving the woman a name now, instead of referring to her as 'she' as she had done in the beginning.

'Who's *she*? The cat's mother?' Alice had said to her repeatedly, though jokingly, at first, until Josie got into the way of calling Iris Collier 'Auntie'. She doubted if the child would ever be able to call the woman Mother or Mum as she supposed baby Frances would learn to do. Frances, of course, would never be able to remember her real mother and little Bertie, too, might soon forget.

Eh, dearie me, it's a sad business, Alice thought to herself as she placed four tomatoes – one each – in a glass dish and four slices of boiled ham on the plates. Poor little bairns, losing their mother at such a tender age and then being pitchforked into a new relationship before you had time to say Jack Robinson. She flicked away a tear that had formed in the corner of her eye. She thought she had done all her weeping for her beloved sister, but still, at odd moments, this feeling of desolation came over her. It was imperative, however, that she should keep cheerful for the children's sake.

'Put these plates on the table,' she called to Josie, 'then I'll just mash the tea and we'll make a start. I'm not waiting any longer for our Len. If I've told him once I've told him a hundred times that tea's at five o'clock sharp. I'll be having your uncle Jack in before I can turn round and the sparks'll fly if his dinner's not ready for him, I can tell you.' Alice knew that this was not strictly true. Mild-mannered Jack Rawlinson would not say a word if, for once, his evening meal was not ready and waiting for him when he returned home from work. But it always was, and his slippers warming by the hearth as well. They were what he called his creature comforts, and Alice knew that he appreciated them, though he didn't often tell her so. The little homely touches that Samuel, no doubt, was missing at the moment . . . but not for much longer.

'And give Bertie a shout, will you, there's a good girl. And make sure he washes his hands before he sits down . . .' Four-year-old Bertie was playing with his ball in the back garden. Such an obedient little lad he was, so quiet and baby Frances, too, seemed as though she would be very little trouble. She was lying happily in her pram now in the corner of the big kitchen-cum-living-room, kicking her legs and making the occasional gurgling sound of contentment as she did when she had just had her bottle. Yes, they were good, well-behaved children but, for all that, Alice was finding that looking after them, day in, day out, was exceedingly tiring. She wouldn't be sorry when, in a few weeks' time she handed over the reins to Iris Collier. Or Iris Goodwin, as she would be by then. So long as it worked out all right for Josie, that was Alice's only worry. She did so hope and pray that it would.

When Josie came in through the back door holding her little brother by the hand, Len came in as well. Or he would have done if his mother hadn't stopped him. 'Hold on a minute, lad.' She pushed him back over the step with the flat of her hand. 'You're not setting foot on my clean kitchen floor in them muddy boots. Take 'em off and leave 'em outside. And wash them mucky hands and your face an' all. You've mud up to your eyeballs . . . And you're late, as usual.'

Len grinned good-naturedly. He was so like his father, easygoing and even-tempered and with the same mild blue-grey eyes and tousled fairish hair. It was impossible to stay mad with him for more than a minute or two.

'All right, Mam,' he said, 'keep your hair on. I'm not all that late, anyroad. If I were late you'd be sitting round the table, wouldn't you? And you're not, so I can't be late. It's just summat you like to say, isn't it, Mam? Come on, Bertie, let's get us hands washed or we'll be in even more bother.'

He picked up his little cousin and carried him over to the stone sink, at the same time giving Josie a conspiratorial wink. Alice noticed how the little girl lowered her eyelids and blushed faintly as she smiled back at him. Alice knew that Josie adored her big cousin, although it wasn't very often that he had very much to do with her. Bertie seemed to like him, too, and Len was good at entertaining the little lad, that was when he wasn't out playing his blinking football. All too soon, though, Alice reminded herself, the Goodwins would be someone else's responsibility.

Josie had been pleased, in spite of her wariness of the woman who seemed to be taking over their lives, when Iris had said that she was going to take her to the Co-op to choose a new outfit. Josie had been brought up on shopping at the Co-op, or the 'Quarp' as Auntie Iris insisted on saying, much to Auntie Alice's amusement. She remembered, as a tiny little girl, going into the grocer's shop just down the road with her mother, and sniffing appreciatively at the fragrant aroma of cheese and coffee that assailed her nostrils as she went through the door, combined with the more pungent scent of white Windsor soap, paraffin and fire-lighters emanating from the hardware counter opposite. The shop sold bread, too, and oven-bottom muffins, fruit pies and deep egg custards (for those housewives too lazy or imcompetent to make their own), all done up in twists of white tissue-paper, but somehow the strong scents from the other quarters never seemed to taint these delicacies, or if they did then no one remarked on it.

Just before her mother died Josie had started being entrusted with messages to do on her own. 'Don't lose the divvy check,' her mother always reminded her, 'and mind you take care of the change. And you know the number, don't you? It's one, four, six, nine.'

Josie knew the number very well. It was impressed upon her mind because her mother reeled it off every time they bought anything at the shop. The little coloured check was proof of purchase, and these checks were painstakingly stuck into a book and then exchanged for 'divvy' a couple of times a year. Money which was often used to buy new clothes or to help pay for a holiday at the seaside. Dad always professed to be amused at her mum and her auntie Alice's shopping habits. 'Proper Co-opites,' he called them, and Josie got the impression that he really thought it was beneath the Goodwins to do their shopping there. But now it seemed that Auntie Iris was the biggest 'Co-opite' of all. Josie had heard Auntie Alice saying so to Mrs Jackson over the backyard fence.

There were six Co-ops in and around the town of Haliford, but it was the one near her home, on Baldwin Lane, that Josie knew best, that one and the big Emporium in town where they went to buy new clothes and articles of furniture. It was to this Emporium that Josie went with Iris, one Saturday afternoon towards the end of July, to buy her outfit for the wedding. The imposing building, four storeys high, stood in the centre of Haliford and Josie was already acquainted with it. Her mother had taken her there once a year to buy her a frock and a hat for Walking Day, the day in early June each year when processions from the various churches paraded round the town to the accompaniment of brass bands and waving banners. She had gone to the Emporium on other occasions, of course, but this annual trip to buy clothes was the important one. Josie guessed that the outing today would be pretty much the same, but she hoped that Auntie Iris would let her do some of the choosing herself. Mum had always let her do so, just guiding her gently in the right direction, which, Josie realized afterwards, was towards those garments that Mum had picked out in the first place.

Auntie Iris was such a bossy boots, though, and Josie knew, before she set foot in the shop, that she wouldn't be so ready to listen to her advice as she had been to Mum's. And she did so hope that Auntie Iris wouldn't insist on pink. Josie detested pink, and it was a colour of which Iris Collier seemed to be particularly fond.

Josie's misgivings disappeared momentarily when they entered the shop through the glass swing doors into the foyer, from which wide stairs led down to the basement and upward to the other three floors. This was such an exciting place, even more so than the local Co-op on Baldwin Lane and, like that establishment, it had its own distinctive aromas. The smell of face powder and scent was drifting into the foyer now from the counter nearest the door. A pretty girl in a pink overall who looked no more than fourteen was trying lipsticks on the back of her hand for an elegantly dressed customer.

Josie stopped for a moment. She liked this floor with its colourful array of scarves and gloves and handbags, and, at the far end – Josie could just catch a glimpse of it – what they called lingerie. Pink satin petticoats with matching wide-legged knickers, as different as you could possibly imagine from the serviceable navy-blue ones that Josie wore with her vest and liberty bodice. Pink corsets, too, funny-looking things with tapes and hooks and eyes with suspenders dangling from them. Auntie Iris would be in her element amongst this vast array of pink, and Josie found herself wondering, fleetingly, if her father's bride-to-be might be going in there to buy herself a new corset. It was obvious that she wore one – you could see the bones showing underneath her tight marocain dress – but, even so, her tummy bulged and her bottom waggled. Josie felt a smile pulling at the corners of her mouth.

'What d'you think you're grinning at? Come on – we're not going on that floor today; there's not time.' She smiled at Josie in a friendly way. 'Thinking about your new dress, are you? It's always exciting getting new clothes, isn't it? I know I love it.'

Josie nodded. 'I was just wondering if you might be going to buy a new . . . lipstick, Auntie Iris,' she said demurely. Iris quite openly used lipstick, and powder and rouge as well, though Josie knew that some ladies – like Auntie Alice – thought that it was 'fast'. Her mother had never used it.

'No, not today, dear,' Iris smiled very charmingly. 'But I do intend getting a new colour of lipstick to match my new outfit. I'll come down on my own some day when they're not so busy. The counter gets very crowded on a Saturday.' Obviously it must be a pink dress then, thought Josie, or red, if the lipstick was going to match it. You would hardly wear a blue lipstick, or green, or yellow . . . She almost laughed again at the thought of Auntie Iris painted up like a circus clown. 'And I might treat myself to some of my favourite perfume, Evening in Paris,' Iris was saying. 'After all, it's not every day that you get married, is it?' She took hold of Josie's arm in a companionable 'all girls together' way, and Josie wasn't sure whether she liked it or not. 'Come on, let's go and see about this dress. That's what we've come for, isn't it?'

The clothing department for both ladies and children was on the first floor. There were racks of coats, suits and frocks and several full-busted dummies – rather like Auntie Iris without a head – wearing a selection of the garments. But they marched straight through this array to the children's section at the end. Iris flicked through the rail of dresses, occasionally stopping at a garment, pursing her lips and putting her head on one side. Inevitably she drew out a pink one, all frills and flounces and lace, which made Josie immediately think 'Ugh!', and held it against her for size. Josie was relieved when Iris said, 'No, I don't think so.'

'No, neither do I,' said Josie. 'I don't really like pink, Auntie Iris,' she added, more hesitantly than was her normal manner. After all, Auntie Iris was being kind enough to buy her a dress. 'Not for myself, I mean. But I know you like it.'

'Perhaps you're right,' said Iris, sliding the dress back on to the rail. 'I don't think pink's your colour. Anyway, we can't have you outdoing the bride, can we?' she added coyly.

'Can I help you, modom?' A black-suited assistant appeared then, and, between them, the two women picked out three dresses for Josie to try on, a pale blue, a pale green and a lemon one, none of which was too fussy or fancy. The assistant seemed to be quite a discerning lady and she whispered to Josie, while Iris was at the other end of the rail, 'You don't want too many frills, do you, dear? It wouldn't be you.'

'No,' Josie whispered back, grinning at her, although by this time she was getting rather bored. Grown-ups always took such an age about everything, especially choosing clothes; but she decided that she quite liked this lady.

Eventually they decided on the lemon one. It was made of a soft rayon material patterned with tiny white daisies, with short puffed sleeves and a little white lace-edged collar. Josie knew that she looked nice in it, though it looked rather odd with her heavy brown Clarks sandals. Iris saw her looking at her feet and said, 'Black patent-leather shoes, I think, and white ankle socks, don't you?' She looked inquiringly at the assistant who nodded in agreement.

'It looks lovely with your dark hair, dear,' the lady said,

and Josie gave a little nod of approval. She was glad that, in spite of all her worst fears, she wasn't to be decked out like the fairy on a Christmas tree.

There was still the hat to choose, but Josie didn't mind so much about that, knowing that it was bound to be a straw one. Straw hats were standard wear for little girls in Sunday school processions and suchlike; straw bonnets that tied beneath the chin with wide ribbons when you were very little, progressing to more grown-up hats when you were seven or so, like Josie was now. The one they chose was white instead of the customary straw-yellow, with pale lemon ribbons, the same colour as the dress, hanging down the back and a little spray of white daisies at the side. The assistant had taken it out of a deep, deep drawer where the hats were kept, wrapped in masses of white tissue-paper. She held up a large wooden-framed mirror for Josie to see the back with the ribbon streamers.

'It's the back that people see most when you're in church,' Iris commented. 'It's for a wedding, you see,' she added, in tones of some importance to the assistant, who nodded interestedly.

'Very nice, modom. It looks very smart. Is the little girl going to be a bridesmaid?'

'No, we're not having any bridesmaids. But we want her to look nice, me and her father. It's my wedding, you see.' She moved closer to the assistant, mouthing the words, 'I'm marrying her father.'

'Oh, very nice. Congratulations, modom,' said the assistant, and Iris preened herself and smiled, even blushing a little. She patted at her dark hair as she looked at her reflection in one of the many mirrors, then she gently touched a stylish hat that was displayed, in solitary splendour, on a hat stand. 'That's lovely,' she said, her head on one side.

'It's right bonny, that is. And it would set my outfit off a treat. It's the only thing I haven't got, the hat.'

'Yes, very smart, isn't it, modom? It's lacquered straw, very fashionable at the moment. Would modom like to try it on . . . ?'

'No thanks, not just now. I'd better not . . . I'll come back when I've more time, perhaps on Monday.' Iris longingly, almost reverently, fingered the brim of the hat. 'It's bonny though, it is that.'

Josie thought the hat looked daft. That long feather sticking out from the shallow crown and the brim dipping over to one side reminded her of a picture of Robin Hood that she had seen in one of her story-books, except that his hat was bright green and not deep pink as this one was. Still, if Auntie Iris thought it was smart – and the assistant, too – then she supposed it must be. She had heard some of the ladies at church saying how smartly Iris Collier dressed. Sometimes adding, 'Of course, it's all right for some.' Or, 'We haven't all got brass to chuck about.' Remarks that Josie didn't altogether understand and probably wasn't meant to hear, but there wasn't much that the little girl missed.

She thought to herself as they made their way back down the stairs with their purchases, carefully wrapped in brown paper and tied up with string, that Auntie Iris had spent what her auntie Alice would term 'a bob or two', this afternoon. Josie wasn't quite sure who was footing the bill for all this finery, whether it was Iris or her dad; but, whoever it was, she felt quite happy, much happier than she had expected to be, spending a whole afternoon on her own with Auntie Iris.

'Thank you . . . Auntie Iris,' she said now, a little shyly. 'It's a lovely dress and hat.'

'Glad you like it, dear,' Iris beamed. 'I think your dad'll be pleased. Not that he takes much notice most of the time. Fellows don't . . . Now, we've just one more errand to do, then we'll go and have a nice cup of tea . . . or an ice-cream, perhaps. You'd like that better, wouldn't you, Josephine?'

Auntie Iris couldn't be all that bad if she was suggesting ice-cream, thought Josie, trying hard to contain her impatience as that lady wandered up and down the basement of the Emporium between the rolls of oilcloth and linoleum and the rows of carpet squares. Josie was bored now, and she didn't like the smell so much down here. It was a funny, musty odour and it was starting to make her feel dizzy. She gave an exaggerated sigh and flopped down on the end of a gigantic roll of carpet. To her credit, Iris decided that enough was enough.

'I'll come back on Monday,' she said, like she had done about the hat. 'I want a new carpet square for the parlour and some lino for the surrounds, but it'll have to keep.' She nodded understandingly at Josie. 'We've done enough for one day, don't you think so, Josephine? Now – next stop, tea and ice-cream. I'm fairly gasping for a cuppa.'

By the end of the afternoon Josie had decided that she liked her Auntie Iris after all.

'Well, I never did!' Alice had remarked to her husband when she first heard of the final wedding arrangements. A deckle-edged card had arrived that morning, encouraging her once again to give voice to her feelings on the matter.

'Samuel Goodwin and Iris May Collier request the pleasure of the company of Mr and Mrs John Rawlinson and their son, Leonard, at their marriage,' it stated,

'. . . at St Luke's Church at 2 p.m. and afterwards at the Co-operative Café, New Street, Haliford.'

'Fancy 'em having a service in church,' Alice remarked, as she had already done several times. 'I would have thought, under the circumstances, that it might be more seemly for them to go to the register office. Some of the folks at St Luke's have got quite a lot to say about it, I can tell you. Our poor Florence hardly cold in her grave . . .'

'Aye, I don't doubt they have,' said Jack drily, '. . . as usual,' he added under his breath. 'But you've got to give Samuel and Iris their due, they're asking God's blessing on it, and that's a darned sight better than a hole-and-corner affair in a register office. You know you've never thought much of the register office before, Alice, so I don't see why you should change your tune now just because it's Samuel and his fancy woman. Of course, whatever they did, it would be wrong in your eyes, wouldn't it?'

'I've tried, Jack. You've got to admit, I've tried,' said Alice, aggrieved at Jack's sardonic tone. She and Jack had had more words than they had ever had in the whole of their married life about Samuel Goodwin and his forthcoming nuptials. 'In fact, I've got quite friendly with Iris lately. She's not so bad when you get to know her. I have to admit that she's no side to her. She dresses posh an' all that, but she's not stuck-up. She calls a spade a spade, as they say round here. Anyroad, I'll be ready to forgive her anything, you know that, Jack, so long as she treats my little Josie all right.'

'Josie'll survive. She's a fighter,' remarked Jack. 'I wonder who's paying for all this lot,' he said, tapping at the gilt-edged wedding invitation with a nicotine-stained finger. 'The wording's a bit different, isn't it? When it's a young couple that's getting wed it's the parents that send the invitation. But this seems to be from t' pair of 'em, Samuel and Iris.'

'I don't know, Jack, I'm sure,' replied Alice. 'Samuel hasn't taken me into his confidence to that extent. I daresay they'll be splitting the cost between them.' Like any true Yorkshireman Jack Rawlinson was always concerned about the cost of things and who was paying for what. 'Just as I don't know who'll be giving Iris away. Her father died a while back – a drunken old so-and-so he was, from all accounts – and I don't think she's very close to the rest of her family. And I don't know who she's having for a bridesmaid either, except that it's not our Josie. Bridesmaid, I ask you, at her age!'

'Happen she won't have one at all,' said Jack, 'or she might have what they call a matron of honour. I'm sure she won't want an affair like a three-ring circus, not at her time of life. She seems a sensible sort of woman to me,' he added, casting a wary look at Alice. 'Anyroad, I'm glad Samuel didn't ask me to be best man.' He ran his finger round the neck of his collarless shirt; he had removed the collar as he always did when he came home from work. 'You know I'm not much of a one for dressing up – stiff collars and bowler hats and all that, although I'll have to get my best blue suit out of mothballs for t'wedding, I reckon. I mustn't let the side down.'

Alice smiled at him, knowing that he was 'having her on'. Certainly he was more at home in his slippers and cardigan than his Sunday suit, but her Jack could look as smart as any of them when he put his mind to it. 'You'll do fine, lad,' she said affectionately. 'And I've got to admit that this do has given me an excuse to get a new frock. The Lord knows it's time I had one. One of Samuel's brothers'll be best man,' she added. 'Happen the one from Leeds, although I know he doesn't see much of them. He'd hardly be likely to ask you when he's got brothers of his own. Anyroad, time'll tell. We'll know soon enough who he's going to have. It's only a few weeks off now.'

The wedding reception, by courtesy of the Co-op, the very best that the caterers could provide, was on the top floor of the Emporium, above the clothing and furniture departments. But this, of course, was after the service at St Luke's church at 2 p.m. on a sweltering hot Saturday afternoon in August. It was the beginning of the Haliford holiday week, known throughout the North of England as 'Wakes' week, and, as Samuel had confided to Alice, not an ideal day for the wedding, but they had no choice. Hammond's mill was closing down for the week. It was an enforced holiday for the employees – and one with pay, too, which wasn't to be sniffed at – and as Samuel was determined to have a honeymoon with his new bride he was, therefore, obliged to get married on this very busy Saturday. To take a week off at any other time would be unthinkable; it would very likely earn him his cards or, at the very least, put a spoke in the wheel of his promotion prospects.

It was Samuel's eldest brother, Harold, the one from Leeds, who stood next to him in church as his best man; and Iris's matron of honour was her next-door neighbour and friend from Gladstone Avenue, Mabel Whittaker, discreetly dressed in pale blue, so as not to overshadow the bride. Iris was given away by an elderly man whom Alice had heard tell was a favourite uncle on her mother's side, and as she walked down the aisle on his arm, smiling proudly, but – for Iris – unusually demurely, Alice had to admit to herself that she had never seen Iris Collier look so bonny.

Bonny was the right word, because the woman was undeniably plump, but it wasn't quite so obvious today, her ample proportions skilfully hidden under the elegant deep pink costume. It was of very lightweight wool, with a hip-length jacket, which covered her very rounded rear end, and a mid-calf-length skirt, the gentle flares of which hid the imperfections of her legs. The ruffles of the paler pink blouse which showed at the wrists and neck might – if they had been any larger – have made her look like dog Toby at a Punch and Judy show. But they didn't. Iris looked extremely elegant, Alice thought; and the little straw hat with the pink feather, which Josie had described to her aunt, added the finishing touch to the ensemble. She had been wise, too, in not carrying an over-large bouquet of flowers, just a discreet posy of pink rosebuds attached to a white prayer-book.

That outfit – apart from the hat – certainly hadn't come from the Emporium, thought Alice; more likely Marshall and Snelgrove's or Schofield's in Leeds. Alice felt dowdy in her marocain two-piece. She had chosen a serviceable colour, navy blue; nothing too pale because it was more than likely that baby Frances would dribble all over it, or worse, before the afternoon was out. Her little white straw hat, trimmed with a navy petersham ribbon, and the white silky rayon blouse, the collar of which showed at the neck of her jacket, had looked very smart in the shop. But now, in comparison with Iris, Alice felt like a dull grey pigeon next to a bird of paradise. Not that she wanted to be compared with Iris, she reminded herself – it was, when all was said and done, Iris's day – and the navy costume would stand her in good stead for 'best' for many years to come.

Alice was holding Frances, now seven months old, in her arms. She had offered to take care of the child during the service, and it would be up to her as well to see that she was settled down in her pram to have a sleep during the wedding breakfast. Two o'clock was usually the time that the baby had her afternoon nap, but at the moment she was wide awake, staring around as though afraid of missing anything. Her big blue eyes, with their faint air of puzzlement, looked today more than ever like her dear dead mother's, Alice thought with a pang of sadness. Baby Frances looked lovely, like a big doll, in her new pale pink dress, with the frills and flounces that Iris loved so much covering the bulk of her nappy. Alice was glad that Iris had had the sense not to deck Josie in a similarly fussy dress. The pale lemon shade was just right for the little girl, and Bertie, too, looked very well turned out in his new tweed jacket and trousers and highly polished brown shoes. Altogether, they were a very attractive trio who were receiving, this afternoon, a goodly share of fond and admiring glances from the assembled relatives and friends.

Alice shifted Frances to the other arm – the child was getting to be a ton weight – at the same time gently fingering the bracelet of smooth flesh around the chubby wrist. She would miss this lovely baby, there was no doubt about that. Samuel had, quite heedlessly, left everything to Alice throughout the weeks whilst he was at work, taking his family back in the evenings and at weekends in a most nonchalant manner. Iris Collier would never allow herself to be taken for granted in such a way, Alice thought now as she watched the pair of them standing together at the chancel steps. She felt, with a sudden premonition, that Samuel Goodwin might find that marriage to Iris wouldn't be entirely a bed of roses. But Alice didn't give two hoots for Samuel, not so long as the children were all right. Folks were saying already that Iris was real fond of the baby, and that little Bertie seemed to have taken to her very well. But Josie . . . she would be a much tougher nut to crack.

Alice listened as the vicar recited the reasons for which matrimony was ordained. '. . . For the procreation of children,' she heard, to her bemusement, although she had known, of course, that this was one of the reasons. It did say in a footnote, somewhere in the prayer-book, that these words could be omitted if the woman was past child-bearing age. But Iris wasn't past it. All the same, the idea of Iris having children was one that hadn't occurred to Alice. The thought that she might do so only served to heighten her apprehension.

She forced herself to listen to the rest of the service, the responses, the joining of hands and the moment in which Samuel and Iris became – for better or for worse – man and wife; the singing of the twenty-third psalm and the vicar's brief homily wishing the couple well. Then they all rose to sing the final hymn before the bridal couple and their attendants departed to the vestry to sign the register.

> Dear Lord and Father of mankind,
> Forgive our foolish ways . . .

Alice sang with the rest of the congregation, wondering as she did so whether this was an entirely wise choice of hymn for a wedding? Would they – Samuel or Iris or both of them – think before long that their precipitate marriage had, indeed, been foolish? Iris had probably not given these words a thought when she had chosen the hymn. It was, after all, one that was often chosen by brides, the incongruity of the words not always being apparent to them. The sentiments expressed were straightforward and sincere, those of committing one's life to the Lord 'in simple trust', just like the disciples had done so long ago by the Sea of Galilee. It was one of Alice's favourite hymns, not least because of the combination of a tuneful melody and poetic words. She automatically found herself praying as she sang that she might, as it said in the hymn, know the beauty of His peace.

> Breathe through the heats of our desire
> The coolness and thy balm.
> Let sense be dumb, let flesh retire . . .

The congregation sang the last verse lustily, and Alice reflected again as to the suitability of these words. The hymn-writer probably hadn't had carnal desire in mind; it was just the archaic way the early Victorians expressed themselves, she told herself. All the same, Alice couldn't help pondering about Samuel and Iris and the wedding night ahead of them, in the boarding-house in Blackpool.

Chapter 4

Samuel, too, was thinking of his wedding night as he sat with his new wife at the middle of the long table. His eyes scanned the assembled company of relatives and friends who had gathered here, at the Co-op Café, to join with them in their celebrations and to wish them well. At least, Samuel presumed that most of them wished them well, although he had noticed a few less than favourable glances in his direction, even today; and in the weeks leading up to the wedding he would have had to have been blind and deaf to miss the snide remarks and the innuendoes from certain quarters. Some of the less charitable remarks had been repeated to him, in true St Luke's fashion, usually with an added word of reassurance, such as, 'Of course, *we* don't think like that, but we thought you ought to know what some folks are saying . . .'

I'd like *them* to try and bring up a family single-handed, Samuel thought to himself, and a young baby into the bargain. Alice had been grand, he had to give her her due. Samuel didn't know what he would have done without her, but an aunt wasn't the same as a mother and that was what his three needed. A real mother, and he could see already that that was what Iris would be to his brood. She doted on baby Frances, and young Herbert. As for Josephine, she would just have to get used to the new regime, because it was what he, Samuel Goodwin, wanted, and what Samuel wanted he always made jolly sure he got.

Yes, Alice had been a godsend to him all these months. Samuel glanced at her now, further down the table, little Frances on her knee and Herbert and Josephine each side of her, with Leonard and Jack Rawlinson at the end. She was spooning a tiny morsel of her own trifle into the child's mouth, smiling indulgently as the baby licked at her lips and dribbled the gooey mess down her bib. Frances was still wide awake, the little tinker. She should have been asleep ages ago, but obviously the excitement of the day was proving too much for her. Perhaps, with a bit of luck, she would sleep all the way to Blackpool. Samuel knew that he should have expressed his gratitude to Alice much more than he had. He'd try to make it up to her, he thought, feeling suddenly benevolent. They'd bring her a nice present from Blackpool; he'd get Iris to choose something for her.

When he came to think of it the guests here today were, by and large, the same folk that had gathered at the graveside of Florence, only seven months ago. As Samuel looked from one to another of them, all now tucking into their pudding in true Yorkshire fashion – as though they didn't know where the next meal was coming from – he felt, just for a moment, somewhat chastened. But life had to go on, and Florence wouldn't have wanted him to be miserable. That was a truism often trotted out on such occasions and one in which Samuel took great comfort. He was only thirty-three; he had a whole life ahead of him. In the company of Iris, for better or for worse . . .

He turned to her now. 'Happy, love?' he asked, his hand resting fleetingly on her work-roughened one.

''Course I'm happy,' she answered, grinning broadly, in

answer to his question. 'It's all gone so well, hasn't it? The service was lovely, and it's a marvellous spread here. The Quarp have done us real proud.'

Samuel nodded his agreement that the Co-operative Society had put on a magnificent meal. There had been half a grapefruit each to start with, with a glacé cherry in the centre adding just that touch of refinement, followed by roast chicken, roast and boiled potatoes, vegetables and all the trimmings. And sherry trifle for dessert, which, judging from the scraping of spoons on dishes, everyone was now finishing.

Samuel was suddenly aware of how warm it was in the room. He could feel a film of perspiration on his forehead and, looking at Iris, he could see that she was likewise affected.

'Hot, isn't it?' she said, mopping at her face with her serviette. She had toned down her florid complexion earlier in the day with more face powder than usual, but the make-up had melted away now and her face was its normal reddish hue. Samuel found himself thinking, incongruously, that Florence had always been so pale. Pink-and-white-complexioned, flaxen-haired, like an angel . . . Samuel's thoughts were running off at a tangent and he tried to bring them back to the present, to the woman who was now his wife.

'D'you know what I'd like to do? I'd like to plunge straight into a cold bath,' Iris was saying, as she continued to wipe her face. 'Get out of all this clobber and splash cold water all over me. Phew! It's a scorcher today if ever there was one.'

'It is that,' agreed Samuel, musingly. A picture had flashed into his mind of Iris in a bath-tub of water – sensually warm though, not cold – and of himself joining her. He could feel a stirring in his loins at the thought of it. She might not be beautiful, but she was sensual and desirable. Florence had been a lady, but his new wife was a real woman.

'You'll be able to paddle in the sea at Blackpool,' he said now, smiling at her. 'That'll cool you down right enough. The sea's cold enough there to bite your toes off, even on a hot day.'

He looked at her appraisingly. No, she couldn't really be called beautiful. Her face was ruddy and her features unremarkable, and her dark hair, already showing streaks of grey here and there, was coarse and wiry.

'What d'you think you're staring at?' Iris asked, grinning impudently. 'I bet I know what you're thinking, Samuel Goodwin,' she added in an undertone, leaning closer to him.

Her deep grey eyes were luminous, glowing with desire, a desire that was coupled with affection and understanding, and in that instant Iris did look beautiful.

'I daresay you do, lass,' Samuel whispered to her, realizing that his new wife's dark shining eyes were undoubtedly her best feature. The ardour in his eyes as he smiled back at her matched her own. After a few seconds he looked away. 'Hey up . . . Our Harold's getting to his feet. I reckon it must be time for the speeches.'

Harold Goodwin was Samuel's elder brother, the one from Leeds. Samuel saw very little of his brothers and sister and their respective families, except on big occasions such as today. They got on well enough when they met and had never had any serious disagreements, but they had their own lives to lead just as he, Samuel, had his. He had moved to Haliford when he met and married Florence, lured by the prospect of faster promotion at Hammond's mill, a smaller business, but one with a much more personal touch than some of its rivals in the bigger wool towns.

Harold's speech was circumspect, proposing the toast to the matron of honour, then to the happy couple, wishing them well. There were no lewd jokes or ribald comments, either from Harold or from the guests, as they raised their glasses of dark brown sherry. Such bawdiness, often the norm at a gathering like this, would have been inappropriate at a wedding that had followed so hard on the heels of a funeral; besides, Harold, for all he was his brother, had never really known Samuel all that intimately. Samuel and Iris rose to cut the cake, hands locked together over the handle of the breadknife as they plunged it into the rock-hard icing. They made only a tiny indentation in the white smoothness of the bottom layer, but the icing shattered and fragments of it were scattered over the damask tablecloth. A waitress in a black dress and frilly apron and cap bore it away, to half-hearted applause, before they could do any more damage.

Samuel thanked the guests for attending, on behalf of his wife and himself, and there was the usual polite laughter and a few handclaps at the familiar wisecrack. But he was anxious by now to be on his way and he had a good idea that Iris felt the same. They had both decided that they wanted a proper 'do', not a hurried, furtive affair – after all, they had nothing to be ashamed of – but now it all seemed to have fallen rather flat. Samuel came, somewhat belatedly, to the conclusion that his marriage was 'nowt to do with any of these folk here', and he and Iris would make their exit just as soon as they could. Anyway, they had a train to catch soon after six o'clock.

Samuel hoped that, by then, the enormous queue at the station to board the holiday trains would have dwindled to a mere trickle. They had caught a glimpse of the queue when they had passed by the station approach in the taxi on the way to the Emporium; three and four abreast, snaking right up the cobbled incline and round into the High Street. And that was at nearly three o'clock in the afternoon. Goodness knows what it must have been like in the early morning. There were tales that had come to be part of Haliford lore – and which lost nothing in the telling – of queues of up to half a mile long at the start of Wakes week, comprised of surprisingly patient people, on the whole, who were all longing to leave behind the grime of the mill town for a blissful few days at the seaside.

The queue had, indeed, lessened considerably by the time Samuel, Iris and the children tagged on to the end of it at a quarter to six. They had been back to Gladstone Avenue – the place which would, a week from today, become home to Samuel and his offspring for the first time – to pick up their suitcases which had been packed the night before. They were all still wearing their wedding clothes, although Iris had exchanged her smart hat for a less showy one of white straw. But there was nothing to show that the pair of them were a newly-married couple; how could they be with three children in tow? There had been no confetti thrown as they left the Co-op Emporium, and no one had come with them now to speed them on their journey.

Samuel was relieved. He wanted to get away with the minimum of fuss. He had deplored the idea of going away on holiday – especially on honeymoon – with all the world and his wife, as was always the case during Wakes week, but he had had no choice in the matter. At least by waiting until late afternoon it meant that they didn't have to queue for so long. Samuel had bought the tickets a couple of days before but, even so, they would have to wait their turn.

Josie could hardly contain her impatience. She skipped up and down the cobbled street while the rest of the queue crept resignedly towards the station entrance.

'Be still now, there's a good girl.' Iris put a restraining hand on the child's arm as she danced past for the umpteenth time. 'We're nearly there. Keep with us, else they'll not let you through without a ticket. Walk nicely like Bertie. He's not jumping up and down.'

It had fallen to Samuel to push the big black pram to the station while the rest of the family had come in yet another taxi. Pushing a pram was a woman's job, although Samuel had had to do his share recently, with Florence being taken so soon after the child's birth; but he hoped that he wouldn't be doing so much of it from now on. He could see, though, that today there had been no alternative.

Josie poked her head into the pram now, right beneath the raised hood. 'What are you going to do with the pram on the train? We can't take it in the compartment with us, can we? There won't be room, and I shouldn't think it'll fit in the corridor either . . .'

Iris gave a sigh. 'For heaven's sake, child, stop your worriting. It'll go in the guard's van, won't it? I thought a big sensible girl like you would have realized that.' Iris added the last words more gently, as Samuel looked at her sharply. Tempers were, understandably, getting a little frayed, he thought. It had been a long day, but they would soon be on their way, thank goodness.

'And the baby as well? Is she going in the guard's van?' Josie persisted. 'She'll wonder where she is if she wakes up. She might start crying . . .'

'Of course not, you little goose.' Samuel smiled at her. 'She'll come with us in the compartment. Auntie Iris'll hold her. But she might sleep all the way to Blackpool with a bit of luck.'

'D'you think all these people are going to Blackpool, like us?' asked Josie. 'A girl in my class said she was going to Scarborough for Wakes week, and another 'un's going to Bridlington. But none of 'em said they were going to Blackpool . . . like me,' she added proudly.

'I should think the folk in this queue will be, yes,' replied Samuel. 'This is the last excursion train to Blackpool today. It goes straight there, so we don't have to change, luckily. There'll have been trains to all sorts of places today, though, like you say, Josephine. Bridlington, Filey, Scarborough, but there'll have been a fair number to Blackpool. Exciting, isn't it?' He smiled at her again and she nodded, stopping her continual jack-in-a-box antics as they passed through the barrier and on to the platform.

Samuel went to see the guard about the pram and then, with baby Frances still asleep in Iris's arms, they boarded the train. Everybody seemed to be in a holiday mood, giving one another a hand to hoist weighty suitcases on to the luggage racks and shuffling more closely together, like sardines in a tin, to ensure that as many folk as possible got a seat. It would be a long journey, and Samuel was relieved to see that it was a corridor train – many of them weren't – as it would be asking too much of Josephine and little Herbert to travel all that way without spending a penny. To say nothing of himself and Iris. He looked at his new bride now in the seat opposite, her head bent dotingly towards the baby bundled in her fluffy pink blanket. He leaned back and tried to relax, as much as he was able, in the few inches of space allotted to him, closing his eyes and listening to the rhythmic clatter – diddle-de-dum, diddle-de-dum – of the train wheels as they speeded him and his family ever nearer to their destination. Dusk fell in the following hour or two and the excited chatter of the children – his own and a couple more in the compartment – ceased. Bertie went to sleep leaning against Iris, and Josie next to her father.

It was completely dark when they arrived in Blackpool; it had been too dark, in fact, to play the usual game of visitors to the Fylde Coast of 'first to spot the Tower'. But it was there when they emerged from Central Station, the tracery of iron girders looming above them, black against the dark grey of the sky.

Samuel nudged his son and daughter, both still drowsy and yawning, tottering along the unfamiliar pavement like a couple of miniature drunkards. 'Look, there it is, see . . . Blackpool Tower.'

Josie was wide awake in an instant, rubbing the sleep from her eyes as she craned her neck to stare heavenward. 'Gosh! It's 'normous, isn't it, Dad? Are we going to go up it? Can we, please, Dad?'

'We'll have to see,' Samuel answered, the age-old reply to children's entreaties. 'What do you think about it, Herbert lad?' He scooped up his son in one arm, pointing upward with the other. 'Blackpool Tower, look. Isn't it grand?' But Bertie only nodded solemnly, laying his head against his father's shoulder and closing his eyes.

'Come on, Samuel,' said Iris, a trifle edgily. 'We can't stand here gawping on the pavement, not at this time of night. It's time these little 'uns were in bed. Bertie's dead on his feet. But you'll have to put him down, you've the cases to carry. Come on, let's find this 'ere boarding-house. Albert Road's just round this corner.' She picked up Bertie and plonked him on top of the pram. 'Now, sit tight, and mind you don't squash the baby's feet.' Then she strode ahead pushing the pram, with Josie clinging to the handle, bravely trying to keep up with her, and Samuel, bow-legged beneath the weight of two massive suitcases, tagging along behind.

'I thought you said it was a private hotel, not a boarding-house,' he called after her. Iris had insisted that it was to be no common or garden boarding-house where they were to spend their honeymoon.

'So it is,' she retorted, without turning round. 'Keep your eyes skinned for it. It's called "Elinorm".'

Very original, thought Samuel, grinning to himself. No prizes for guessing what the boarding-house keepers – no, he corrected himself, private hotel keepers – were called. Norman and Elinor, no doubt . . . or Elizabeth. Or it could be that he was Eli and she was Norma . . . What the hell did it matter! He was dog-tired and all he wanted at that moment was his bed.

'It's here.' Iris stopped the pram and Samuel, with a sigh of relief, put the cases on the pavement. He clenched and unclenched his hands which felt red-raw and wriggled his aching shoulders; he had feared his arms were going to be pulled out of their sockets. It hadn't seemed worth getting a taxi, not for what was only a few minutes' walk, although it had felt like hours.

'Come on then, what are we waiting for?' He kicked open the iron gate with his foot and led the way up the path. 'Oh, crikey, no!' he gasped, catching sight of the short flight of stone steps, carefully edged in white with a donkey stone, which led up to the front door. 'How the hell are we going to get the pram up that lot?'

'I think they look proper posh, them steps. We can manage them as easy as winking,' Iris replied. 'I'll push and you pull.' She plonked a dazed Bertie on to the path and deftly turned the pram round. 'Josie, go and ring the bell, there's a good girl, then they'll know we're here. Now Samuel, get behind that hood and lift up the back . . .'

The front door opened whilst they were in the middle of their manoeuvres. A buxom woman, roughly the same build as Iris, but blonde where Iris was brunette, greeted them. 'Mr and Mrs Goodwin? I'm glad you've got here at last. We were beginning to wonder what had happened to you, my hubby and me!' She turned round, yelling into the passage beyond the open door, 'Norman . . . Come and give us a hand, will you? There's a pram here as big as a bus, and some cases an' all.'

Norman appeared, a beanpole of a man with a prominent Adam's apple revealed by his open-necked shirt. He pushed up his sleeves baring sinewy arms, ready for action. 'Right y'are, then.' He picked up the suitcases as though they weighed no more than a few ounces. But then he hadn't carried them a few hundred yards, thought Samuel, perspiring freely from his exertions. He glanced uncertainly at the pram which seemed to fill the narrow hallway. It wasn't in Samuel's nature to be apologetic, but they did seem to be causing rather a commotion, he and his brood. A curious face had appeared round the door of what a notice proclaimed to be the lounge, and another looked down from the top of a flight of stairs. 'It seems to be in the way,' he said. 'We hadn't realized—'

'Not a bit of it,' replied the buxom landlady cheerfully. 'There's a nice big space at the back of the dining room. It can stand there when you're not using it, no problem at all. All part of the service. See to it, will you, Norman?'

The obedient Norman pushed open the door marked *Dining Room* and wheeled the pram into the darkened room. Samuel could see that the tables, each seating four or six, were already laid for the next morning's breakfast; white cloths, gleaming in the semi-darkness, white earthenware cups, each upturned in its saucer, and in the centre of each table, next to the cruet, the three bottles without which no northern meal would be complete – vinegar, tomato ketchup and HP sauce.

'Now, how about a nice pot of tea?' said the landlady, beaming at them. 'I'll bet you're gasping for one after that journey. All our other guests arrived hours ago, but it's a fair old journey from your neck of the woods, isn't it? We usually serve tea in the lounge at half past nine, for those that want it, but I think we could make an exception tonight and let you have it in your bedroom. It'll help to make up for the two meals you've missed. I believe in letting my guests have these nice little extras. I'll go and put the kettle on again and Norman'll carry your cases up. See to it, will you, Norman? I'm Eliza, by the way, Eliza Pendleton, and he's Norman, my hubby.' She nodded towards him, adding, 'We're a good pair, aren't we, Norm, you and me?'

Samuel noticed the smile of real comradeship that passed between them and he thought that maybe he had been mistaken in his first impression that poor old Norman was henpecked. Perhaps his wife couldn't help being a bossy-boots and maybe Norman was used to her. Maybe you did get used to it after a while . . . There had been music-hall jokes bandied about for years now about Blackpool landladies, buxom, beetroot-faced and broad-spoken, and their insignificant little husbands; skivvies who were reputed to spend the summer months in the depths of the cellar, peeling endless piles of potatoes and only emerging when the season ended. Samuel didn't think that Norman quite belonged to that category – if, indeed, any of them did – although he had jumped to it quickly enough at his wife's command. Perhaps it was easier to take the line of least resistance. She seemed nice though, Mrs Pendleton, friendly and obliging. Samuel was thoughtful as he climbed the stairs in the wake of Norman, Iris and the children.

Iris echoed his thoughts a little while later as they sat on the edge of the bed, on top of the billowing silky pink eiderdown. Josie and Bertie had been put to bed in the adjoining very small room, and baby Frances was now guzzling at the last drops of her bottle which Mrs Pendleton had been pleased to warm up for them. The baby was to occupy a cot at the foot of Samuel and Iris's double bed.

'Nice, isn't she, that Mrs Pendleton,' said Iris. 'Very friendly, like, and eager to help.' She took another gulp of the strong tea. 'By heck, that's a good cup of tea! I don't think I've ever tasted one as good, but then I was ready for it after that journey. Yes, she's right nice, I think, don't you, Samuel? I like the way she says she provides those 'little extras'. That's why I chose this place, of course, because I thought it would have that little bit extra. Wash-basins in the bedrooms . . .' She pointed to the white porcelain one in the corner, 'instead of the old jug and bowl. Some places still have them, you know. Of course you've got to go down the corridor to the . . . er . . . WC, but lots of folks still have to go down the yard, don't they, at home? Your sister-in-law does,' she added with a tight little smile.

'Never mind about her,' said Samuel gruffly. 'I'm glad you're satisfied with the place, anyroad.'

'Oh, I am, Samuel, I am. Very satisfied. They've got a lounge an' all. Somewhere to sit of an evening, 'cause we won't be able to go out so much, not with having the kiddies with us. But I wouldn't have wanted to leave our little Frances behind, bless her. In some places, you know, there's nowhere to sit except on the form outside the front window. And some landladies turn you out of the dining room as soon as the meal's finished, so they can get ready for the next. It's just the same if it's raining; that's why you see so many folk huddled in the shelters all along the prom. But I knew it wouldn't be like that here, not in a *private hotel.*' There was a distinct emphasis on the words as Iris uttered them. 'That's where you have to go if you want the little extras.'

Samuel chuckled. 'You want to beware of little extras. What they do is stick it on the bill at the end of the week. Have you never heard of charging for the cruet?'

'Oh, that was in the old days, when folk used to bring their own food,' protested Iris. 'In the lodging-houses. I don't think there's so many of them do that now.'

'And has anybody ever told you that you talk too much?' said Samuel, moving closer to her and taking the empty cup out of her hand. He placed it on the tin tray on the chair at the side of the bed. 'Never mind about those little extras. What about a little extra for me, eh?' He smiled at her, almost shyly, as he began to unfasten the pearl buttons on her frilly pink – and now rather creased – wedding blouse.

Minor irritations and misgivings had all been forgotten half an hour later, as Samuel lay in the depths of the feather mattress, his arm across the buxom figure of his wife. One thing was certain; marriage to Iris would certainly not be dull.

Chapter 5

Josie was awakened on her first morning in Blackpool by her father gently shaking her. 'Come on, lazybones, wake up. Let's be having you.'

She opened puzzled eyes, staring confusedly for a moment around the unfamiliar room. Then she remembered. She was in Blackpool. They were all in Blackpool on their holidays, her and Bertie, Dad . . . and Auntie Iris and the baby. And there was Bertie sitting up in the other bed just a few feet away from her, his striped pyjamas all rucked up round his fat tummy, tight fists rubbing the sleep out of his eyes.

Dad was smiling in a jovial way that Josie had never seen before – well, not often, anyway – and he looked different, all relaxed and casually dressed in a pale yellow open-necked shirt, grey flannel trousers and a tweed jacket. 'It's a grand day,' he said. 'Too nice to stay in bed. Up you get, the pair of you, and we'll go and have a walk on the sands before breakfast.'

'All of us?' asked Josie.

'No . . . Auntie Iris is still in bed,' Samuel told her. 'And when the baby wakes up she'll have to see to her, won't she? Baby Frances is an old sleepyhead as well this morning, but it was an exciting day yesterday, wasn't it? She didn't close her eyes very much. Now, hurry up and get dressed, Josie, and have a wash. There's some nice hot water in the tap – and see to our Bertie as well, will you? There's a good girl. Come and knock on our door when you're ready, then we'll be off.'

Josie didn't need any second bidding. She leapt out of bed, wide awake now, but still hardly recognizing this bright and breezy father. She and Bertie seemed to have acquired new names as well, Josie and Bertie instead of Josephine and Herbert, which was what their father usually called them. She decided that they must be holiday names.

'What about my hair, Dad?' she asked. 'My plaits. I can't do them myself.' Samuel usually plaited her hair, after a fashion, or Auntie Alice if she happened to be around.

'Oh, never mind about them,' said Samuel, in a casual way. 'Just leave it. It looks nice like that anyway, all loose. Auntie Iris'll do it when we get back. Be sharp now, or we won't have time.' He turned when he got to the door. 'Oh, the lav's just at the end of the landing – you know, where you went last night. Don't forget to pull the chain, Josie, after our Bertie's been. He can't reach.'

Josie was quite used to seeing to herself of a morning now, since Mum had not been there, and to looking after Bertie as well. In a few moments they were knocking at the door of the next room, then the three of them, like conspirators off to a clandestine meeting, crept down the stairs and along the passage to the front door. The rest of the house seemed still to be deep in slumber – it was only half past seven – but from the kitchen region at the rear of the ground floor they could hear a clattering and banging and the rattle of pots.

'That's what I like to hear,' said Samuel, beaming. 'Mrs Pendleton's on the job already, and the obedient Norman as well, no doubt. Our breakfast'll be ready when we get back.'

It had been dark when they had arrived the night before. Now Josie could see that Elinorm was just one of a long, long row of tall thin red-brick houses. Three-storeyed, some with tiny attic windows poking out on top of the roof, some with the proprietor's name on a glass-framed notice by the front door, others – like Elinorm – with the name emblazoned in large letters over the dining-room window: Astoria, Rosedale, Tower View . . . The Tower, indeed, was in view over the rooftops, looming ever larger as they made their way down the long street.

Albert Road was quiet at that time of the morning. Through the front windows Josie could see that all the tables were laid ready for breakfast, although no one was, as yet, partaking of the meal. They passed a few men, clad similarly to Samuel, with morning papers in their hands, one holding the newspaper in front of him, reading the headlines as he sauntered back up the road.

'No newspapers for me this week,' Samuel remarked. 'Not while we're on holiday. Time enough to think about the world and its problems when we return home.'

A woman halfway down the road was mopping her steps, a short flight of them, like there was at Elinorm, and on the forms in the tiny front gardens a few men were sitting, puffing away on pipes or just sprawling, eyes closed and faces uplifted, anxious to get the full benefit of the sunshine. It was a watery sun as yet, just appearing over the rooftops, but the sky was clear and cloudless, holding the promise of a glorious day.

'Nice to see a bit of blue sky,' Samuel remarked, reiterating what Josie was thinking but was unable to put into words. 'It isn't often we see a blue sky like that back home, is it, Josie? Or the sun. It's usually hidden by the smoke from the mill chimneys. It's only during Wakes week that you get a glimpse of the sun, when you live in a mill town like Haliford.'

'And we're here, aren't we, Dad, not there,' said Josie, grinning up at him.

'We are that,' answered Samuel, grabbing hold of their hands, Josie's and Bertie's, one on each side of him, and swinging them wildly. 'Come on; I can't wait to see the sea, can you?'

The three of them ran, laughing excitedly, across the road towards the canopied entrance to Central Station where they had arrived only a few hours before. Samuel stopped in his tracks, pointing across the promenade. 'Look, you two. There it is – the sea.'

It wasn't Josie's first glimpse of the sea. She had seen it at Bridlington, where they had been for the day, and at Filey, where they had once spent a week. But her memories, at seven years of age, were hazy. She was sure, though, that never before had she seen such a vast expanse of sand. Golden-brown and rippled, it stretched for miles, northward and southward, and west to the distant sea, silvery-grey and sparkling in the early morning light. They crossed the road near to the Palatine Hotel, then halted at the tram-track, looking carefully both ways.

'We'll have to mind out for the trams while we're here,' Samuel told them. 'It's a bit dangerous, that unfenced track, but we'll be all right so long as we watch what we're doing. Now, hold my hand while we cross.'

There was a tram coming now, cream and green and streamlined, humming along the track, then giving a warning 'toot-toot', though not too loud, at a couple who were crossing a few yards in front of it. Josie gazed in wonder as the tram passed them, then, alerted by the clip-clop of horses' hooves, she turned to watch a landau go by on the road behind her. But there was no time to stop and stare because ahead of them, down a flight of steep wooden steps, the sands beckoned.

The ridges in the sand, left by the outgoing tide, were unbroken, but soon their pristine freshness was shattered by three pairs of feet, one large and two small, as the little family walked seaward, sniffing the salt-laden air and listening to the harsh cry of the seagulls wheeling leisurely in the air just above their heads.

'There's no donkeys,' said Josie, gazing around. 'Auntie Alice said there'd be donkeys on the Blackpool sands, and Punch and Judy and ice-cream stalls as well.'

Samuel laughed. 'The donkeys'll be here all right, in another couple of hours. And the stalls, too . . . and hundreds of people. We're very early, you know. You don't often see a Blackpool beach deserted like this. I don't suppose we'll do this every day, either. I'll be wanting a lie-in some of the time . . . We'll just walk as far as the sea, then we'll have to turn round and go back. We mustn't miss breakfast, must we? That 'ud never do.'

Tiny foam-capped wavelets lapped gently at their feet as they stood at the water's edge, gazing out at the limitless grey-green ocean. 'The Isle of Man's over there,' Samuel remarked. 'Never seen it myself, I must admit, but they say you can see it on a clear day. And the hills of Barrow over yonder.' He waved his arm northward. 'You can see them clearly enough.'

Josie looked at the range of small black hills, just visible on the distant horizon; but it was only Blackpool that interested her at that moment; and the thought of all they would be doing there over the coming week.

'Is the tide coming in or going out, Dad?' she asked. 'If it's coming in, we won't be able to go on the sands this morning, will we?'

'Blessed if I know,' said Samuel. 'Seems to be standing still at the moment, doesn't it? I suppose there comes a point where it's on the turn before it comes back again. But don't worry – there's always sands at Blackpool, some time of the day at any rate, afternoon if not morning. There'll be plenty of time for building sandcastles and paddling.'

'And donkey rides?' asked Josie.

'Yes, donkey rides as well. Now, I don't know about you, but I'm feeling decidedly peckish. Let's go and see what our Mrs Pendleton's got for breakfast.'

They arrived back to the appetizing smell of frying bacon. Auntie Iris was sitting in the lounge wearing a navy-blue cotton dress with white polka dots as big as pennies. Josie thought it made her look fatter than ever. She was dandling baby Frances on her knee, who was being cooed over by a couple of middle-aged ladies. Iris looked pleased and proud.

'Ah, here's the rest of my family,' she said, beaming at them and putting an arm round Josie's waist in an affectionate manner. 'Had your first taste of the Blackpool breezes, have you? It's their first visit here,' she said, turning to the two baby-worshippers. 'Proper excited they were, I can tell you.' Her voice sounded different, a bit false and la-di-dah, not much like Auntie Iris at all. Josie felt herself stiffen and she wriggled away from Iris's restraining arm.

'When's breakfast, Dad?' she asked.

At that moment there was a loud sound from the brass gong that Josie had seen in the hallway.

'There you are,' said Samuel, 'right on cue.' He led the way to the dining room, leaving Iris to follow on behind and settle baby Frances in her pram, before starting on her own breakfast. They were ravenous after their early morning walk, and the bacon, sausage, eggs and black pudding – a delicacy Josie hadn't come across before – went down a treat.

As the day progressed, Josie and Bertie began to sample the many more delights that Blackpool had to offer. The tide had turned and was on its way in when they arrived back at the beach mid-morning. They had stopped on the way to buy gaily patterned tin buckets, and spades – a wooden one for Bertie and a more grown-up one with a red metal blade for Josie – paper flags for the tops of sand pies and castles, a fishing-net, two round sun-hats and two pairs of sand-shoes, blue with white piping round them.

'My goodness, Samuel,' Iris remarked. 'You're throwing your money about like a man with no arms. You'll have to go steady or it'll be bread and jam for a month after we get home.'

She was laughing, though, so Josie knew that it was only a joke, especially when her dad replied, 'You only come to Blackpool once a year, if that, so we may as well make the most of it. Time enough to pull on the reins when you've not got it.'

Josie guessed he was talking about money. On this holiday her father was certainly a very different man from the one she knew at home. Sometimes Dad didn't take much notice of her and Bertie, and she'd heard Auntie Alice say to Uncle Jack – when she wasn't supposed to be listening – that Samuel Goodwin was sometimes so tight-fisted that he'd cut a currant in half. Josie remembered, too, that sometimes her mum had been short of money. Auntie Iris had 'a bob or two', though. Josie had heard that as well, so she supposed her dad could afford to be generous now.

At all events, he was a different man – jolly and carefree and open-handed – and Josie was glad of it.

There was time that morning for her and Bertie to make a few sand pies, paddle in a rock pool, and to have their longed-for donkey ride before the tide defeated them. Josie's hair streamed backward in the stiff breeze – she hadn't, after all, had it made into plaits that morning – her cheeks were flushed and she laughed out loud for the sheer joy of it as the donkey, the bells on its harness jingling, trotted, then broke into a brisk canter across the broad expanse of sand. Bertie, more timidly, followed along in her tracks, his donkey led by the man in charge of them.

'That was ever so good, Auntie Iris,' Josie cried, flinging herself down on the churned-up sand near the deck-chairs. 'Why don't you have a go? Why don't you, Dad? You'd like it, really you would. There are some grown-ups on them, look.'

'No, not for me, dear.' Iris shook her head. 'I'm too . . . No, I never really fancied a donkey ride, even when I was a child . . . We couldn't afford it either, when I was little,' she added quietly, as if to herself. 'I'm glad you enjoyed it anyway, dear.'

Josie glanced back at the little group of donkeys. There were some adults mounting them, as she had said, but, come to think of it, they were all thin people. Of course Auntie Iris would be too fat. A picture came into Josie's mind of Iris's fat bottom, encased in the navy and white spotted dress, on top of the little donkey; she had to turn away because she could feel a giggle starting. But Iris hadn't noticed because she and Samuel were gathering up all their paraphernalia in order to retreat before the tide. Deck-chairs, buckets and spades, striped towel, brown canvas bag bulging with nappies and feeding bottles, not to forget the baby herself and the huge pram which they had wheeled down the cobbled slope that led on to the sands near Central Pier.

The picture of Iris on a donkey stayed in Josie's mind; and so, later that day, when they went into a shop to buy postcards, she spent some of her precious spending money that Auntie Alice had given her on a drawing-book and some coloured crayons. In the seclusion of her bedroom each night, after Bertie had gone to sleep and her dad and Auntie Iris were chatting in the lounge to the other visitors, Josie drew and coloured to her heart's content. She had always loved drawing, but now, inspired by the comic postcards she had seen on the stalls all over Blackpool, Josie's artistic bent took on a different dimension.

'Come away from those things,' Auntie Iris said, whenever she stopped to stare at the garishly coloured postcards, a vivid contrast to the black and white and sepia views of Blackpool – the Tower, North Pier, the three-tiered promenade, the Boating Pool – which Iris and Samuel were choosing to send home to their friends and relations. 'Rude, they are. Proper vulgar! Now, what about this nice picture of Stanley Park to send to your auntie Alice? We'll be going there one day this week, I daresay.'

But Josie sneaked a crafty look whenever she could at the 'rude' pictures of red-faced women with bulging breasts and big fat bottoms, of tiny men in striped pyjamas with their hair sticking up on end and a surprised look on their faces, of lace-edged knickers and shapely legs, red-nosed men lifting glasses of frothy-topped beer, saucy waitresses in frilly caps and aprons; and she reproduced some of them in her own little drawing-book with the pattern of teddy bears on the cover, adding quite a few ideas of her own.

The first thing she drew was Iris on the donkey. *Fat Iris on a donkey*, she captioned it, in a fit of pique, on the evening that Iris had sent her to bed sooner than she thought she ought to go. She drew Eliza Pendleton, their landlady – another corpulent figure, the likes of whom were a godsend to the comic postcard artists – with her blonde sausage curls and the flowered crossover pinny she always wore; and Norman at her side, tall as a lamp-post, scratching his head in the bemused way he often did. She drew lots of other things as well, not always portrayed in an amusing way, all the ingredients that made up her first exciting, unforgettable visit to Blackpool. The seagulls and the sand; paddling at the edge of the sea; Bertie fishing in the rock pools with his fishing-net as tall as himself; the big dipper at the Pleasure Beach (too daring, even, for the intrepid Josie); the flower-beds, now a riot of colour in the Italian Gardens in Stanley Park; and, appearing time and time again in Josie's sketchbook, Blackpool Tower, the symbol of the place that Josie was beginning to think must surely be the best place on earth.

It was, on the whole, a very happy week for the Goodwin family and their new mother. There were a few disagreements, to be sure, but nothing rankled for very long. Iris was delighted to find, early in the week, a stupendous new Co-op Emporium, even bigger and better and brighter than the one in Haliford, on Coronation Street, very near to their Albert Road hotel. Josie and Iris spent a happy morning mooching around the store, sniffing at the scent, fingering the bolts of cloth, examining pots and pans and cutlery (with no intention of buying). And, eventually, when Josie was becoming just a little bit bored, buying a new pair of court shoes for Iris and two lengths of wide satin hair ribbon, one tartan and one yellow-spotted, for Josie.

And then – undreamed-of bliss! – they found it. The place that was to become, above all others, Josie's very favourite place in the whole of Blackpool. Pablo's ice-cream parlour, tucked away down a little back alley near to the Co-op Emporium, so hidden away that you might even miss it. But obviously, judging from the queue that confronted them when they entered the back street, lots of other people knew the whereabouts of this enchanting place. The building was unprepossessing, a cream-painted, box-like structure, but the ice-cream was out of this world. The queue was quickly dealt with and that morning Josie and Iris both enjoyed their first taste of the unbelievably delicious confection; two scoops each of ice-cream, served in a shallow glass dish, with a dollop of fresh cream at the side. Iris's was covered in chocolate sauce and nuts, but Josie opted for the raspberry juice which she squeezed on herself out of a shaker that looked just like a vinegar bottle.

'Isn't this fun?' said Iris, in the conspiratorial way she sometimes did when she and Josie were alone together. Josie had not been altogether sure at first that she liked this, but she was getting more used to Iris now. It had certainly been good fun this morning and it was kind of Auntie Iris to buy her the hair ribbon and the ice-cream.

'Mmm . . .' said Josie, not wanting to waste time talking whilst a scrap of ice-cream remained in her dish. She scooped up the last remaining morsel, licked her lips and gave a sigh of contentment. 'We'll have to bring Dad and Bertie here, won't we, Auntie Iris? And Frances,' she added. She sometimes forgot about Frances. 'It wouldn't be fair, would it, to keep it to ourselves.' And Josie knew that she, too, would want to come back, again and again, if she was allowed.

'Of course we'll bring them,' said Iris, smiling at her. 'Nothing more sure than that.'

'This afternoon?' Josie asked eagerly.

'No, I don't think so,' replied Iris, laughing. 'Enough is as good as a feast, as they say. We mustn't go overdoing things. Perhaps tomorrow . . . We thought we might go to Stanley Park this afternoon if it's not too far to walk. It's a bit awkward with the pram, not being able to take it on buses and trams. Anyway, we'd best get back to the beach now and rescue your poor old dad. The baby'll want her nappy changing no doubt, and he's no great shakes at that, I can tell you, Josie.'

As Iris had remarked, it was difficult with the pram, but they managed very well, taking it in turns to look after baby Frances so that the other two children could get the full benefit of the holiday. When Samuel, Josie and Bertie rode on a tram to the Pleasure Beach Iris stayed on the sands, reading her *People's Friend* and writing postcards, with Frances sleeping in the pram at her side. Iris, in fact, spent quite a lot of time that week ensconced in a deck-chair whilst the others paddled or built sandcastles, walked on the pier or watched the antics of Punch and Judy. Samuel and Josie, dark-haired and swarthy-skinned, turned brown very quickly in the sun's powerful rays; but Bertie, although he, too, had brown hair and brown eyes, had inherited his mother's delicate colouring.

Iris, also, in spite of her dark hair and ruddy complexion, found that the heat was rather too much for her. Bertie's bare shoulders soon became red and sore and he was forced, in spite of his squeals of protest, to wear his shirt and his sun-hat all the time, whilst poor Iris spent a lot of the time with a newspaper over her head, fanning herself frantically with her magazine and turning as red as the nose of Doodles the clown whom they had seen at the circus.

But the sun didn't shine all the time. On Friday, their last day, it rained, so they decided to spend the day inside the Tower. The fact that, seemingly, thousands of their fellow holiday-makers had opted to do the same thing didn't detract from their enjoyment. They left the pram at the hotel this time, Samuel and Iris taking it in turns to carry the baby whilst the family sampled the myriad delights that the Tower had to offer. Strange exotic fish in the dimly lit, green-hued aquarium at the bottom of the building, a place of mysterious caverns and sinister rock formations; lions, apes and monkeys, somewhat mangy and bad-tempered, in the upstairs zoo; Lilliput Land in the roof gardens, where a community of midgets lived, performing dances and acrobatic feats for a fascinated and incredulous audience; a host of slot-machines offering peep-shows, spinning balls and metal hands outstretched to grab at alluring prizes.

And the famous Tower ballroom, open in the afternoon not for ballroom dancing but for the Children's Ballet. Josie and Bertie watched entranced whilst scores of local children from various dancing schools went through their routines. There were fairies – inevitably – butterflies and birds, elves, pixies and clowns; and a long line of little girls, pert and pretty, all dressed in identical short red skirts, crisp white blouses and red boleros, with shiny red tap-shoes flashing in and out like quicksilver to the accompaniment of the resonant tones of the Tower organ. Josie thought they were very clever, but she didn't envy them. She had never wanted to have dancing lessons, but she decided that she would draw them in her book when she got home.

'It's a pity we've not been able to come dancing this

week, Samuel,' Iris said wistfully, after the performance had finished. 'I think it would be real lovely to dance to the Tower organ, but we couldn't leave the kiddies at night, I realize that, and it 'ud be too late for them to stay up.'

'Hold on a minute – you might get your wish,' said Samuel. 'Look there . . .' The last of the scenery had been shifted away from the ballroom floor and now, as the organ broke into the lively strains of 'Let's Face the Music and Dance', a few couples were taking to the floor.

'Come on,' said Samuel, smiling at his new wife. 'Let's take a turn, shall we? Let's face the music and dance. It's a quickstep . . . I'm quite good at that. It's ages since I danced, and then it was only at a church hop. But this is something like . . . Josie love, you sit down there with Bertie and I'll put the baby on your lap.'

'Ooh, Samuel, d'you think we should?' Iris looked anxious. 'She's only a bairn herself. I wouldn't want her to drop her.'

''Course she won't drop her,' said Samuel. 'Frances is fast asleep, and it's about time Josie started learning, anyroad. Girls can't start too soon.'

So Josie and Bertie sat on the red plush seats at the edge of the ballroom while Iris and Samuel stepped on to the floor. Josie, keeping one eye on the baby, stared round fascinated at the glittering scene; the gilded balconies and columns, the painted ceilings and the gleaming crystal chandeliers, the magnificent floor of inlaid mahogany, oak and walnut and the white-coated figure seated high on the organ, the melodious tune bursting forth at the touch of his flying fingers. And she watched her father and Iris dancing together. They looked very happy, gazing from time to time into one another's eyes and moving round the floor without the slightest stumble or hesitation in their steps. Josie knew that it was the man who 'led' when a couple danced, but it seemed as though it was Iris who was taking the lead now. She looked remarkably light on her feet for someone who was so plump. Josie had thought she would dance like a baby elephant – like the ones they had seen performing at the circus – but there she was, as graceful as a fairy, and, in that instant, looking almost slim.

Josie was beginning to feel rather lost and alone. There were her dad and Auntie Iris smiling at each another, all lovey-dovey, and here she was left holding the baby and looking after Bertie.

At that moment the baby gave a mewling sound and Josie looked down. Frances opened her eyes, those pale blue eyes that looked so much like Mum's, and stared up at her sister. In spite of herself, Josie felt a surge of fondness for the child on her lap, the baby whom she had vowed, only a few months ago, that she would never like, the baby who had caused her mother to be taken from her. Frances recognized her and gave a gummy smile; then, realizing that this wasn't the person who was usually there when she awoke, her mouth puckered and she began to whimper, twisting her head round, looking for Iris and security.

'Oh, stop it,' said Josie, feeling uneasy. She had been beginning to think that baby Frances wasn't too bad after all, but now she was wriggling like an eel and going red in the face. Josie clung on tightly to the warm, slightly damp bundle. 'Stop it, can't you? They'll think I can't look after you. There, there,' she cooed, as she had heard Iris do. 'Please don't start crying, you silly baby.'

And then, to her immense relief, Iris and her dad were at her side, not appearing to notice her discomfiture. Auntie Iris actually beamed at her. 'Thank you, Josie, you're a good girl. That was a lovely end to the afternoon.'

They joined the crowds of holiday-makers swarming back up Albert Road and the other streets close to the Tower, all looking forward to their five o'clock tea. As well as the sea, which ebbed and flowed unfailingly twice a day, there was also the four-times-daily tide of visitors, thousands of them, moving between their boarding-houses and the promenade; seaward at nine-thirty in the morning after a hearty breakfast, back inland at twelve-thirty to partake of another gigantic meal, out again at two and back at five. And so it went on, day in and day out.

Through the dining-room window of Elinorm they could see the tables laid for tea; dishes of beetroot and pickled onions and a bottle of salad cream in the centre, and a three-tiered cake stand holding triangular slices of bread and butter (both brown and white), buttered scones and a selection of delectable iced fancies.

'Salad today,' Iris remarked. 'And what d'you bet it'll be red salmon for our last tea?' She was right.

Josie found it hard to get to sleep that night, a thousand and one memories of the happy week crowding into her mind. She was still awake, in fact, when Iris and her father came up to bed. She heard the bedroom door close and then the sound of muffled voices. They were shouting a bit; not exactly angrily, but Josie could tell there was a 'bit of a barney' going on. She knew that she shouldn't, but she knelt up in bed and put her ear close to the wall.

'Have you taken leave of your senses, woman?' Samuel was saying. 'I only hope you're joking . . . but I somehow don't think you are.'

'I don't mean *yet*, Samuel, of course I don't,' Iris replied. 'But I think it might be an idea for . . . sometime in the future.'

'Well, I don't,' said Samuel. 'Blackpool's fine for a holiday, but nobody in their right mind would want to live here. And a boarding-house! You must be barmy.'

'Hotel, Samuel,' Iris replied. 'A private hotel, like this one—'

'Oh, what the hell!' It wasn't often that Josie heard her father swear. 'It's the same difference. Hotel or boarding-house, they're all a lot of damned hard work, and you won't catch me with a pinny on, like old Norman there.'

'Don't get cross, Sammy love. Don't be cross with your little Iris.' Josie's eyes opened wide at the soppy sort of voice that she hadn't heard before. 'Come here to me . . . There, that's better . . . I told you, Sammy, I don't mean yet . . .'

'Not ever – not if I live to be a hundred. And don't call me Sammy. Stop it, Iris . . . Honestly . . .' Her father didn't sound as cross now; in fact, he was laughing, and after that Josie didn't hear any more words.

But if they were talking about what she thought they were, then it all sounded very exciting – unbelievable, in fact – and this time Josie agreed wholeheartedly with Auntie Iris. It would be wonderful to actually live in Blackpool . . . But Josie had the sense to know that she mustn't repeat what she had heard, not to anyone.

Chapter 6

Iris had little doubt that she would be able to talk Samuel round to her way of thinking, eventually; but common sense told her that it would be as well to drop the subject of Blackpool for the moment. Having had a few chats with Eliza Pendleton during the week and finding in her a kindred spirit – so much so that the two women had promised to keep in touch by letter – Iris saw herself as the proprietress of a private hotel, not as a common or garden seaside landlady. She had learned that Eliza was anxious to better herself, to move away from the Albert Road area to North Shore, to the promenade if possible.

That was the ultimate goal of all landladies – those that saw themselves as rather more than boarding-house keepers – to move into a hotel, however small, on or near the promenade. Eliza had already taken the first step, she explained, by classing her residence as a private hotel, but it was, when all was said and done, slap-bang in the centre of the boarding-house hinterland. Eliza desired something more salubrious, and she would get it; Iris had no doubt about that. Eliza was a very determined lady and it took one to know one.

For the moment, however, Iris knew that she must content herself with arranging things the way she wanted them in Haliford. Samuel hadn't needed much persuading to sell his own little terraced house on Baldwin Lane and move into the house that Iris owned – left to her by Alfred – on Gladstone Avenue. It meant that Samuel had a few hundred pounds in the bank, a nice little nest egg, as he called it; but to Iris the most important thing was that the house where the Goodwin family were now living was still in her name . . . and she intended to keep it that way. It had been a blessing that Samuel had owned his property. Many families on that terrace, including his sister-in-law and her husband, Alice and Jack, only rented theirs. Iris wasn't at all sure that she would have agreed to marry Samuel if he hadn't owned his own house . . . but, in all events, she had married him, and it seemed to be working out quite nicely.

She didn't intend staying there, though. Gladstone Avenue was all very well, a 'desirable semi-detached residence', the estate agents called such properties, but it was opposite a row of shops, with a fish and chip shop at the end of the block and a pub on the next corner. Hardly what you would call 'residential'. Not like the Victoria Park area on the outskirts of the town. That was where Iris had set her sights, but she knew she would have to wait a little while; a few months . . . get Christmas over, maybe, then they would see.

In the meantime she had her new family to organize. Frances was a delightful little girl, all that Iris had ever dreamed of in a daughter. She was gratified – humbled, in fact – to think that the child would grow up thinking of her as her mother. She was at the enchanting stage now, just beginning to sit up in her pram, gurgling and grinning at admiring strangers in the street, her blue eyes wide with wonder and her wispy blonde hair gradually thickening and curling round her pink and white china-doll face. Iris delighted in dressing her up in frilly pink frocks and hand-knitted matinée coats, bonnets edged with swansdown and bootees of the softest suede and calf leather. Some might say – Samuel had already hinted – that she was spoiling the child, but Iris didn't care. Little Frances brought out all the maternal instincts that had lain dormant for so long, almost annihilated, in fact, by her own unlovely brothers and sisters.

Bertie, too, was an affectionate little boy, well-behaved and biddable and ready to fall in with Iris's new ways. He never mentioned his real mother and was gradually, Iris thought, coming to look upon her as his mother. The name of Auntie Iris, readily accepted by Bertie when he first got to know her, had now been replaced, most of the time, by Mum or Mummy.

Iris could not help but be aware of Josie's questioning glance whenever she heard her brother use this appellation. For Josie still saw her father's new wife as Auntie Iris, and Iris feared that it might never be any different. Josie was very quick to tell her, 'Mum never used to do that,' when, for instance, she put down sheets of newspaper after scrubbing the kitchen floor, or – only once, and that was in an emergency – popped out to the shop wearing a scarf over her curling-pins. Or to say, with a slight pouting of her lips, 'Why can't I? Mum used to let me,' when Iris refused to let her go to church in her playing-out clothes, or to let her wear her hair all loose round her shoulders. Iris knew that that wasn't true anyway. Florence Goodwin had always insisted on correctness in dress, as in everything else. The folk at church always used to say that Samuel and Florence's children were the best turned-out pair you could ever wish to see, and Iris intended to keep it that way. She wasn't going to have it said that standards had declined in the Goodwin household since Samuel married her.

Josie seemed to be taking a delight, recently, in looking untidy. Iris suspected that the child, at times, was deliberately being difficult. But if Josie wanted to be awkward, then she would find that she had met her match. Iris had the advantage in that she was still living in her own home, not stepping into another woman's quarters. Nevertheless, Samuel had brought with him, as well as some furniture, various articles that had been treasured by his first wife; family photographs, vases and knick-knacks bought as presents or on holiday, brass candlesticks, decorative bells and horse-brasses, and Florence's silver-plated dressing-table set which now had pride of place, though it was somewhat tarnished, in Josie's bedroom.

It was this that aroused a defiant spark in Iris, one morning when Josie had been particularly difficult. The child had wanted to dash out immediately after breakfast to play with a new friend she had made down the road, instead of helping Iris to clear the table and wash the pots; and when she had been forced to do so she had done it with a very bad grace. When Josie returned at dinner-time it was to find that her dressing-table set had disappeared.

'Where's it gone?' she stormed, confronting Iris in the kitchen.

Iris met Josie's belligerent stare with a slight smile and raised eyebrows.

'Where's what gone, dear?' She drained the water from the potatoes and proceeded to mash them as though Josie's outburst concerned her not a bit.

'Me brush and comb and mirror, what belonged to me mum. What've you done with them?'

'Oh, those silver things.' Iris added a dash of milk and a knob of butter to the potatoes, then went on mashing. 'Until you can take care of them, Josephine, they'll have to go away. I'll look after them . . . until you're a big girl.' Iris knew that she wouldn't dare – indeed, it would be downright wicked – to go any further. She had no intention of getting rid of the lovely dressing-table set, a present to Florence from Samuel, which, understandably, Josie prized; but the child made her see red at times, made her behave in ways that she knew to be uncharitable and certainly unchristian, and for which, afterwards, she hated herself.

'What d'you mean?' Josie spluttered. 'I can take care of them. They're mine. Me dad gave them to me. You've no right—'

'I've every right,' Iris replied calmly, far more calmly than she was feeling. She was feeling, in fact, rather mean and horrid. 'I've every right so long as I'm doing the cleaning in this house. And that's what I meant, Josephine. Your dressing-table set is filthy. Black bright, it is, all tarnished and nasty, and I certainly haven't time to clean it with everything else I have to do. So until you're a big girl and can look after it yourself then it had better stay where it is, in the cupboard in my bedroom.'

'Right then, if that's all you want, I'll clean it.' Iris was astonished at the look of confidence on Josie's face. Although she was only just turned seven the child seemed to possess, at times, the maturity of a much older girl.

'*You* clean it?' replied Iris. 'That'll be the day. Look at the fuss you made this morning when I asked you to dry a few pots.' But the vehemence had gone out of her words. She was beginning to wish she'd never started this. 'Come on now, wash your hands, there's a good girl, and sit down at the table. It's your favourite today, sausage and mash. Bertie's all ready and waiting, aren't you, lovey?'

Iris tried to ignore Josie's murmurs of 'It's not fair!' as she washed her hands; and she was relieved to see, a few moments later, the child tucking with gusto into the fluffy potatoes and the crisply browned, succulent sausages. She didn't say thank you for a nice meal, though. Perhaps that would be asking too much at this stage. All the Goodwin brood, in fact, seemed to take Iris's housekeeping – her well-cooked meals and smoothly run home – for granted. At least she had managed to get Samuel out of the habit of getting up from the table and sitting down immediately with his newspaper or library book. Now he followed her into the kitchen, ready to dry the pots as she washed them. She hadn't yet seen him with his hands in a bowl of soap suds, but that day would come, or her name wasn't Iris Goodwin.

Iris's new family was coming to learn that she didn't intend being a skivvy for them all, pandering to their every whim in the way that she knew a lot of northern women fussed over their menfolk; in the way that Florence, before her, had so obviously done, but Iris was made of sterner stuff than her predecessor.

Silence reigned for a little while as Iris and the two children ate their dinner – Samuel would have his in the evening when he returned from the mill – and when Josie spoke it was in slightly less aggressive, though still quite determined, tones. 'I will clean them, Auntie Iris, honest I will. Give them back to me . . . please.'

'All right then,' Iris relented, finding that she was relieved to do so. 'I'll get the Silvo out and some clean cloths and you can have a go at them this afternoon . . . before you go and play out again. I'll show you how to do it, then you'll have to get on with it yourself.'

There was as much of the pungent, whitish-grey liquid on Josie's fingers and on the newspaper covering the kitchen table as there was on the dressing-table set; but the child persevered, her eyebrows meeting in a frown of concentration and her tongue peeping out from between her teeth as she rubbed and polished. And when the gleaming silver set was once more in its place on Josie's dressing table, Iris was not sure who had been the victor.

'Very nice, dear. You've done well,' said Iris. She must give credit when it was due. 'Leave all the mess downstairs and I'll clear it away. Remember though – you'll have to do them at least once a fortnight or they'll get all tarnished again.'

'All right,' said Josie airily, though sounding a little aggrieved. Perhaps she, too, was thinking that her triumph had been hardly won. 'Now can I go out to play?'

Iris decided to leave the brassware – the candlesticks, horse-brasses and bells – where it was for the moment, though possibly in a slightly less prominent position. She quite liked it really; it was bright and cheerful, though the very devil to keep clean. Perhaps she could suggest to Samuel that he should do that job, seeing that it had come from his former home. She contented herself with rearranging the framed photographs, moving the ones that Samuel had brought to the back of the sideboard and putting in pride of place on the mantelpiece the one they had had taken in Blackpool of herself, Samuel and the three children, in a photo booth on the Golden Mile.

And that hideous blue vase with the gilded flowers would have to go. She had seen it on the mantelpiece in the Goodwin home when Florence was alive, and now it had found its way here. For her own part she would never have given it houseroom, but it just showed that some women's taste was all in their mouths. She shoved it away in the sideboard, then, thinking better of it, took it out again and placed it on the window-ledge at the top of the stairs. It wouldn't be quite so conspicuous there.

Samuel was very well aware of Iris's strategic moves to eradicate all memories of his former marriage, to establish beyond all doubt that she was his wife now; and that it was her home, more than it was his, by right of possession. He tried to turn a blind eye to much of it. He was also aware – though he was sure Iris didn't realize it – that whilst he perused the *Daily Express* and the *Haliford Chronicle* for the national and local news, respectively, his wife couldn't wait to get her hands on the page of Houses for Sale. She wasn't much of a one for newspapers – women's magazines were more to her liking – but she read this page avidly. Samuel didn't doubt that they would be on the move before long, and when they did he would make sure that the next property would be in both their names. Never mind the fact that this house was Iris's and that the sale of it would almost, if not entirely, pay for the next one; he would have a little cash to contribute as well.

Besides, he was the male, and as such he should he regarded as the householder. The sole one, in Samuel's opinion, but the Married Woman's Property Act, towards the end of the last century, had deemed it otherwise. A retrograde step, in Samuel's view, giving married women the same rights as their husbands with regard to property. You couldn't argue with an Act of Parliament, but Samuel intended to make certain that his name featured on the next set of deeds. At least Iris seemed to have given up on that barmy idea of moving to Blackpool. It had never been mentioned since they returned home.

For the present, though, he was content. This was a far superior house to the one he had lived in on Baldwin Lane and Iris was making him very comfortable. He was even willing to wipe a few pots now and again if it kept her happy, a little thank-you, as it were, for the pleasure that she gave him in the marriage bed. Samuel was finding that Iris was as different as could be from Florence in that, as in most other ways. Her lovemaking was ardent and uninhibited and Samuel felt, for the first time in his life, that he was receiving, in the act of love, as much as he was giving . . . more, in fact, at times. Florence had always been a passive, almost reluctant, recipient of his lovemaking, but Iris brought to it a fervour and a passion that more than matched his own. Not that it was without tenderness; there was a very loving, caring side to his new wife's often brusque and abrasive personality.

He wished, though, that she and Josie were more compatible. Maybe it was just that they were seeing too much of one another at the moment. The school holidays were too long – he had always thought so, and Iris had said only last night that she would be glad when Josie went back to school next week. Young Bertie would be going with her, for the first time. It was fortunate that the school was an easy distance from Gladstone Avenue, just as it had been from Baldwin Lane, though in the opposite direction. Josie wouldn't have taken kindly, he knew, to a change of school as well as a change of home . . . and of mother.

Ah well, there was no point in worrying his head about the children. They were adaptable. You had to learn to change in this world or you'd go under. He reached for his *Daily Express*. He would spend a few moments perusing the world news before joining Iris upstairs; not that he was overly concerned with world affairs – he was more concerned with what went on in his own little world – but he liked to keep abreast of the times. It was largely doom and gloom as usual. The civil war which had started last month was still waging fiercely in Spain, and sixteen of Stalin's opponents in Russia had been executed after a mockery of a trial. They certainly didn't mess about there, just as they didn't in the present regime in Germany. Samuel could foresee trouble with that maniac, Hitler, before long . . . Roosevelt had been elected President for a second term in America, though. That was good news; he would be a valuable ally, if one was ever needed . . .

'What are we going to do for Christmas, Jack?' asked Alice Rawlinson, one evening towards the end of November. 'We'll have to be deciding.'

'Christmas? How the heck should I know?' Jack looked up reluctantly from his *Haliford Chronicle*. 'It's ages off yet, isn't it? Why d'you want to go worrying your head about Christmas?'

'Because things have to be decided, that's why,' said Alice. 'And it isn't ages off, it's only a matter of weeks. You know as well as I do that we've always had the Goodwins round at Christmas – our Florence and Samuel and the two children, and my mother, too, of course. Well, it's different this year, isn't it? Our Florence has gone, God rest her soul, and there's Iris there instead, and our poor Florence's bairn. And I don't rightly know what to do, Jack . . .'

Jack put down his newspaper then and looked at his wife with the kindly concern that she knew to expect when she was really troubled about something. 'What d'you want to do, lass?' he said gently. 'That's the most important thing – that's the way I see it. What d'you feel like doing?'

Alice sighed and gave a slight shake of her head. 'Carry on the way we've always done, I suppose. Although it can never really be the same . . . I love to see those kiddies at Christmas, you know I do, especially Josie. If I don't invite them I won't have the pleasure of seeing them open their presents, but I don't know how Iris will feel about it. She might have made other plans. She's very good at organizing them all, from what I hear.'

'Well, you won't know until you ask,' said Jack, prosaically as ever. 'Ask Iris and see how she feels about it. She can only say no.'

'And think how upset I'll be if she does refuse . . .'

'There you are then,' said Jack. 'You've got your answer, haven't you? You want 'em to come. You've just admitted it . . . And I should think Iris'll jump at the offer. She's probably only waiting to be asked.'

'Aye, happen you're right,' said Alice slowly. 'You know what we've always done. Christmas Day at our house and Boxing Day at theirs, turn and turn about. We went to our Florence's last time for Christmas Day, although she was so poorly with the baby coming, poor lass, that I ended up cooking the dinner for us all. It's awful to think that it's less than a year ago, and all this has happened. Samuel fussing around that woman as though she's eggshell china. It's as though our Florence never existed.'

'Don't start taking on again, Alice love,' said Jack kindly. 'You can't live in the past. And it seems to be working out all right, you've got to admit it. You still see quite a lot of young Josie, don't you? And that was what you were worried about, that you'd never see her. She's here, regular as clockwork, a couple of times a week for her tea, and sometimes Saturday as well.'

'She probably comes to get away from her,' said Alice thoughtfully. 'No . . . perhaps I'm being uncharitable. I know she likes to see us, and our Len, and she doesn't say too much about Iris. I daresay if she was really unhappy she'd tell me . . . Yes, I've decided, Jack – thank you for helping me, love – I'll ask them for Christmas Day. I think it'd be a Christian gesture, like. I'll see Iris after church on Sunday. And maybe she'll ask us to Gladstone Avenue for Boxing Day, d'you reckon? I'd like to see what sort of a show she puts on.'

Jack smiled and shook his head. 'You're a caution, Alice, you are really.'

'What d'you mean?' Alice looked at him sharply. 'Why? What've I said?'

'Nothing, nothing at all. Just go ahead and ask 'em. You've made the right decision, love.'

'That was a grand meal, Alice. You've done us proud,' said Iris, with obvious sincerity. 'And that pudding – I don't think I've ever tasted one as good. You made it yourself, didn't you?'

'Of course I did,' replied Alice, smiling at the compliment. 'None of your shop-bought stuff for me. Not that the Co-op don't do a very nice one – I bought one earlier this year when they were selling them off after last Christmas – but this one is home-made. Made 'em all at the beginning of November, I did, and my Christmas cake and mincemeat.'

'And very nice it is too,' said Iris. 'Rum sauce always helps it to go down a treat, doesn't it? Good job we're not

Methodists, eh?' She laughed, patting at her red lips with the damask serviette. Lipstick stains are the very devil to get off, thought Alice, watching her. But she mustn't be unchristian. It was Christmas and they were enjoying a happy day together, the Goodwins and the Rawlinsons and Alice's mother, Agnes Broadbent.

'Glad you liked it,' said Alice. She couldn't help preening herself a little as she beamed at the satisfyingly replete group of people around her dining table. The table was fully extended today, with the extra leaf in place, and it almost filled the dining end of the kitchen-cum-living-room. 'Now, go and sit yourselves down in the parlour and I'll stack these pots together and make us a nice cup of tea. I can wash 'em later when we've had a bit of a sit-down. We've got to let our dinner digest before I set to and make the tea.'

In spite of the gargantuan meal of turkey, roast potatoes, sprouts, carrots and peas, not to forget the apple sauce and sage and onion stuffing, followed by the pudding which had so impressed Iris, Alice knew that her guests would expect, in a few hours' time, to sit down again to an enormous tea. Turkey sandwiches – the carcass of the huge bird, now lying broken and dejected on the kitchen dresser, would be dissected until not a morsel remained – sherry trifle, mince pies and Alice's *pièce de résistance*, the iced and marzipanned Christmas cake. She wouldn't cut that, though; if they were all too full to enjoy it she would put it away and bring it out again at New Year.

'It's strange, isn't it?' Agnes Broadbent remarked. 'This time last year we were sitting here – well, we weren't here; we were at our Florence's – listening to the old King's broadcast, and now he's dead and gone, poor soul, and we've got another 'un in his place.' The five adults were sitting, nursing their cups of tea on their laps, around the roaring fire in the Rawlinsons' small parlour.

'And a very good King he is too, Mother,' said Alice, raising her voice and mouthing her words exaggeratedly as she always did when speaking to the deaf old lady, who sometimes, Alice couldn't help thinking, heard more than she let on. 'George the Sixth'll do very well for us, you mark my words, in spite of what some folks are saying.'

'Why, what are they saying, our Alice?' Agnes inclined her head, looking at her daughter inquiringly.

'Well, that he hasn't got the personality of his brother. He's not as flashy, I'll grant you that, but I think he'll be a good 'un.'

'It's a pity he couldn't have broadcast to us, though,' Iris remarked, 'like his father always did on Christmas Day. It's a tradition, like.'

'Only a recent tradition,' Alice put in quickly. 'It's only been the last three or four years, and some of us couldn't afford wireless sets. We've only had ours since last year, haven't we, Jack?' She didn't wait for her husband's reply; the remark, indeed, didn't warrant one. 'Anyroad, you can't expect the new King to make a broadcast, poor chap. I reckon he's still in a state of shock. It's only a fortnight since he was left holding the baby, with that other one absconding.'

'He's got a stammer, too,' said Iris. 'A speech impediment. Happen that's why he's not doing it. Happen he'll never be able to do it.'

'And happen he will,' replied Alice. 'He'll overcome it, you'll see. He's taking lessons from a speech fellow, a thera—whatsit. He'll make the grade, all right. And as for that Edward the eighth, the Duke of Windsor, as they're calling him now, I always said he wasn't cut out to be King. That one'll never be crowned, you mark my words, I said to Jack. Didn't I, Jack? Isn't that what I said?'

'Indeed you did, my dear,' replied Jack quietly, continuing to stare into the fire.

'And what beats me is how they kept us all in the dark for so long.' Alice was on her hobby-horse now. 'Downright disgusting, I call it. If something so important could be kept from us ordinary folks all that time, what else might they be hiding from us? All them politicians and bigwigs that are supposed to be in charge, that's what I'd like to know.'

'Aye, you're right, Alice. You're quite right,' added Jack, agreeing with her, as he so often did – or pretended to – for the sake of a quiet life, as Alice well knew.

'And a divorced woman at that!' she went on. 'Not only once, but twice. Whatever are things coming to, I ask you? Divorce has always been considered a disgrace, in my book.' Alice nodded, somewhat piously. 'And all right-thinking folk 'ud agree with me. If the Royal Family are going to accept divorce, then there isn't much hope for the rest of us, is there?'

'But they didn't accept it, did they?' Samuel pointed out. 'That's why he had to go.'

'Well, I think it's a shame,' said Iris. 'I always liked him. I don't see why he had to go. Why couldn't he marry the woman he loved, same as other folks do – and let her be Queen an' all – without all this silly fuss?'

'Because it wouldn't be right, that's why,' said Alice primly. 'We've got our standards in Great Britain.' Trust Iris to take the opposite point of view, she thought. She might have known she would. 'That Mrs Simpson – she's no better than she ought to be. She's no more than a common—'

'Hark the herald angels sing,
Mrs Simpson's pinched our King . . .'

chimed Leonard's voice from the back of the room where the three children were happily engaged in a game of snakes and ladders.

Everyone laughed, and the atmosphere, which had been threatening to become tense, was lightened. Alice laughed too, and her rebuke to her son was a light-hearted one. 'That's enough of your cheek, our Len. You're not supposed to be listening to us grown-ups. Honestly! The things he comes out with since he became a choirboy at St Luke's. You wouldn't credit it.' Alice was proud of him, though; and she wasn't the only one, she thought, looking at Josie's pink-tinged cheeks and her eyes shining with admiration as she smiled at her cousin. 'Right now I reckon I'd better tackle this washing-up. Any volunteers? You two fellows stay where you are. I can't be doing with men cluttering up my kitchen . . . Anyroad, I don't suppose you'd be offering, would you?'

Iris rose to her feet. 'Oh, he has to do his bit at home, don't you, Samuel? He's learning, I can tell you, but I'll let him off today. I'll help you, Alice. A bit of help's worth a lot of pity, that's what I say.'

To Alice's surprise, Josie got up as well. 'I'll help, Auntie Alice. We've finished our game . . . and I won!'

'Good girl,' said Alice. 'Come on then, and I'll find another pot towel.'

'My, my! Wonders'll never cease,' remarked Iris as they followed Alice into the kitchen. 'What's got into you, young lady? New Year's resolutions ahead of time, is that it? Honestly, Alice, you should see the face she pulls when I ask her to help. Stop a clock it would, sometimes.'

'It's Christmas,' said Josie brightly. 'There's a lot of work to do at Christmas, isn't there, Auntie Alice? Besides . . . I like helping Auntie Alice.' She looked pointedly at Iris.

Oh dear! thought Alice. Don't let's have any trouble at t' mill, not on Christmas Day. But Iris was not rising to the bait, most likely deciding to live and let live on this of all days. From what Alice could see, it did seem to be a case of six of one and half a dozen of the other as far as those two were concerned. They had both behaved quite well today, but there was an undercurrent between them that Alice, attuned to the situation as she was, couldn't help noticing.

Josie had, however, proudly displayed the Fair Isle jumper that Iris had knitted for her Christmas present, and very nice it was, too; and Iris had shown off the bright pink lipstick that Josie had given her, Woolie's best, if Alice was any judge – certainly not Yardley or Max Factor – but Iris had seemed well pleased. It did, after all, take a while to adjust to another person's ways, and it was only four months since Samuel and Iris had married. No doubt things would improve as time went on. The little girl was sure to think about her mother, though, and make comparisons. The two of them had been very close.

Iris squatted down by the cupboard in Josie's bedroom. She had been asking the girl for ages to tidy it and to sort out her old games and jigsaw puzzles before they moved to their new house. She had been asking her since March, in fact, when they first started house-hunting in earnest, and now it was the end of April. But all to no avail; Josie had taken not a scrap of notice. When Iris opened the cupboard door the whole lot fell out on to the carpet.

Broken-down boxes of ludo and tiddly-winks lay before

her, odd pieces of jigsaws, draughts and snap cards, a sorry-looking felt rabbit with only one ear, a baby doll in a dirty white dress – Josie wasn't much of a one for dolls – and a half-knitted scarf and a ball of wool with the needles pushed through it. Ouch! Iris jumped as she caught her hand on the knitting-needle. Drat the child! She'd be the death of her, she would really. And she had never got the hang of knitting, which Iris had tried so painstakingly to teach her. Oh well, it would serve the young madam right if some of the things she wanted got thrown away. Iris had decided that she would have to tidy the cupboard herself, and tonight, whilst Josie was staying the night at her aunt Alice's, was a good opportunity.

They were moving in a few weeks' time to Victoria Grove, the select little cul-de-sac on the fringe of Victoria Park where Iris had found the semi of her dreams. Samuel had been quite amenable about it, once he had managed to get her to agree that his name, as well as hers, must go on the deeds. She had aquiesced, knowing that if she didn't he might never move at all. And the children, Josie and Bertie, seemed quite happy about it all as they would still be able to go to the same school.

In half an hour Iris had finished, and if Josie decided she wanted some of the things that had been thrown away then it was just too bad. Iris pulled open the small drawer at the top of the cupboard. This, strangely enough, seemed to be tidy. Oh yes, she thought, as she saw Josie's pencils, crayons and paints, all neatly put away in their boxes. This was the one thing that really interested the child, so she would try to keep it in apple-pie order. Iris had to admit that she seemed good at it, too. Some of the paintings and drawings that Josie brought home from school showed real promise.

She pulled out a book from the back of the drawer, recognizing the pattern on the cover. This was the one that Josie had bought for herself in Blackpool, although Iris had never seen the drawings the child had done. She'd been very secretive about it all. Iris opened the book now. Blackpool Tower – very good, too, although it was leaning a tiny bit, like that leaning tower of Pisa; and that was a very lifelike seagull. Iris smiled to herself as she turned the pages . . .

Then her smile turned to a frown, then a gasp of horror. What on earth was this? The rear view of a very large person on a donkey . . . and the navy-blue spotted dress was unmistakable. *Fat Iris on a Donkey*, she read, unbelievingly. The cheeky young minx! Iris's florid cheeks flamed more brightly than ever and her eyes burned with humiliation as she marched down the stairs, the book in her hand, to show her husband.

Chapter 7

'Just look at this!' Iris thrust the book under her husband's nose. 'Put that blessed library book down and look at this. I've never seen anything like it in all my born days, the impudent young madam!'

Samuel gave a quiet sigh, almost under his breath, and put his library book down on the arm of the chair. He opened the drawing-book. 'Ah yes, Blackpool Tower,' he said, turning to the first page. 'Brings back some memories, doesn't it, love? These are Josie's, aren't they? Yes, I remember her scribbling away . . . Can't see anything to get worked up about, though . . .'

'Can't you? Well, look a bit further then.'

Samuel turned the pages while Iris stood at his side watching him. He stopped at the page with the large lady on the donkey and there was silence as he scrutinized it. Then, to Iris's astonishment, he threw back his head and laughed. 'Oh yes, Iris, she's captured you there all right. It's you to a tee, that is. I know it's only the back view and you never went on a donkey, of course, but—'

'What! How dare you!' Iris seized hold of the library book which was, fortunately, only a slim volume, and hit him over the head with it. 'You're just as bad as she is. How dare you side with her? The cheeky little—'

'Hold on, hold on . . .' Samuel put up his hands, warding

off the blows that were raining down on him. 'Calm down, woman. You're going to have apoplexy if you carry on like that.' But he was still smiling. 'You've got to admit it's rather funny.'

'Funny! I don't think it's funny.' Iris's breath was coming in short pants and she was feeling very near to tears. 'I think you're horrible, Samuel, laughing like that. I did think I might get a bit of support from you. But no . . . I suppose it's what I should have expected. You couldn't care less what that daughter of yours gets up to. So long as your meals are ready and your washing's done and I'm there at your beck and call, that's all you care about. She's getting out of control. A proper little madam she is, and you just don't care. It's always up to me to see to her—'

'And you look after her very well, my love. You look after us all very well. I don't know what we'd do without you,' said Samuel placatingly. He put his arm round his wife's waist. 'Oh, come on, Iris. Don't take on so. I'm sure the child didn't mean any harm. It was just a bit of fun. I know she can be a handful. She's a high-spirited girl and I know the sparks fly now and again between the pair of you. It's only natural. But you do very well—'

'Oh, thank you kindly, I'm sure.' Iris's tone was sarcastic. 'I could do with a bit of support now and again, Samuel.'

'Aye . . . I know.' Samuel nodded. He was trying hard, Iris could see, to look contrite, but she hadn't forgiven him yet. 'I know it's not easy for you, looking after three kiddies, but I'm not always here, am I?' Samuel rubbed the side of his nose thoughtfully. 'I'm at work all day, and they go to bed soon after I get home. It's you that sees them more than I do, that's why I leave 'em to you most of the time. Don't see what I can do, anyroad . . .'

'No, you never do, do you? You could be a bit firmer with them, that's what. Josephine deserves a damned good hiding for this, and I've a jolly good mind to—'

'Now, steady on, Iris. You know I've never approved of smacking them. I don't know that it does any good, and you know that you don't approve of it either. You've told me so.'

'Yes . . . I know I have.' Iris remembered only too well the beatings she had suffered as a child from her drunken bully of a father, and all for something and nothing, just because he couldn't control his temper. She had vowed from a very early age that she would never treat any child of hers in that way. And nor would she, even now. But there were other ways . . . 'But she can't get away with it. By heck, she can't! No wonder she was so secretive on holiday, rushing up to her room and not letting us see what she was up to, the little minx! And I'm very hurt, Samuel, that you did nothing but laugh. Very hurt indeed.'

'Sorry, love,' said Samuel. 'I'll have a word with her.' But Iris knew that he wouldn't. He slowly turned the pages and as Iris looked over his shoulder she had to admit, in spite of herself, that the little girl was very talented. 'Oh, I say, look at this.' Samuel held the book at arm's length. 'She's captured Eliza and Norman all right there, hasn't she?'

Iris gave a wan smile at the caricature of Eliza Pendleton in her flowered apron, holding a frying-pan, and Norman, pot towel in hand, with a long-suffering expression on his face. 'There's another one of me on the next page,' she said dispiritedly. 'At least I think it's supposed to be me.' Her rage had subsided a little now, to be replaced by a deep distress at Samuel's attitude. How dare he laugh? He was trying hard to be more supportive now, but the damage had been done.

'Oh yes . . .' said Samuel reflectively, looking at the next picture in the book, but not laughing this time. He'd better not if he knew what was good for him! 'It could be anybody, Iris,' he commented, a tiny smile pulling at the corners of his mouth. 'She hasn't said it's you . . .'

The picture, again, showed a fat lady in a deck-chair, her skirt hitched up, showing a voluminous amount of pink knickers, the sort that came down to your knees . . . 'I never wear things like that,' said Iris, prodding her finger at the offending underwear. She remembered how, on her honeymoon, she had worn her new French knickers of pale pink satin and how they had been much admired by her husband. Ever since she had been able to afford it, Iris's undergarments had been of the most exquisite kind.

'Indeed you don't, love,' said Samuel seriously. 'And you would certainly never show your knickers on Blackpool sands.'

She gave him a sharp look. 'Are you laughing at me again, Samuel?'

'No . . . of course not, dear.'

'And I certainly don't snore either,' said Iris indignantly, pointing to the balloon coming out of the woman's mouth, with a *Zzzz . . . Zzzz . . .* inside it, like something out of the *Dandy* comic. 'Of all the things!' But the navy spotted dress in the picture was unmistakable.

'Samuel . . .' said Iris now, glancing down at her generous waistline and the bulge of her tummy. 'I'm fat, aren't I?'

'Oh . . . I wouldn't go so far as to say that.' Samuel put his arm round her waist again and gave her a squeeze. 'Well proportioned, perhaps, but I like a woman to have a bit of meat on her. All the more to cuddle up to. You've never heard me complain, have you?'

'No . . .' Iris smiled uncertainly as she felt his hand move down, caressing her bottom. Things were always all right in that department, thank goodness. But she didn't feel like it just now. She pushed his hand away. 'Give over, Samuel. I'm not in the mood. I've never really worried too much before, about being on the large side, I mean. It runs in the family. My father was a big fellow, and my aunt Maud was like a house-side. But I've decided – I'm going to lose some weight. I'm not going to have folks poking fun at me, certainly not a little madam like Josephine. And that's what she is, whether you like it or not, and we're going to have to take a firm line with her.'

'Oh, come on, love. I don't think she's all that bad . . .'

'Not all that bad? She's dreadful, Samuel, and she's getting worse by the minute. Very well then, if you don't intend to do anything about it, then I certainly will.' Iris's rage was returning, inflamed by the nonchalant attitude of her husband. 'It's a good job she's not here tonight, that's all I can say. I'd wring her neck – I would that!'

'Steady on, love,' said Samuel again. He was looking a trifle anxious now. 'Sleep on it . . . You'll happen feel better in the morning, see things more in perspective, like. I still think that the child didn't mean any harm. Just try to calm down, then you can have a quiet word with her when she comes back from Alice's in the morning. Tell her that it's not very kind to make fun of people, if that's what you feel you must do . . .' He stopped, frowning slightly. 'Although, if it was up to me, I'd be inclined to ignore the matter altogether. You might only make things worse between the pair of you.'

'I can't ignore it, Samuel. That's just like you, isn't it?

Bury your head in the sand and it'll all go away. And it shows how much notice you take of what's going on. She isn't coming back here in the morning. She's going straight to school from Alice's. I won't see her till dinner-time.'

'Oh yes . . . I see.' Samuel nodded in a somewhat abashed manner. 'Who's taking our Herbert to school then?'

'Who d'you think? Muggins here.' Iris pointed a finger at herself. 'It's too far for him to walk there on his own, so it means I have to get the baby ready, and meself as well, and trail all the way to school and back. But Josie doesn't care, so long as she's getting what she wants . . . Going to her precious auntie Alice's.'

'I don't suppose she's given it a thought,' said Samuel calmly, 'about you having to take Herbert to school. She's only a child, Iris, when all's said and done.'

'That's right! You stick up for her.'

'Oh, come on, love, this is getting us nowhere.' Samuel rose from his chair, resignedly placing his library book on the sideboard. He put his arms round his wife, stroking her hair and nuzzling his chin into the soft skin of her neck. 'We mustn't fall out about the children. It's just not worth it. It's you and me that's important, isn't it?'

Iris nodded in spite of herself, feeling her temper gradually beginning to abate. Samuel's strong arms always had that effect on her. She responded to his kiss, though not so ardently as she sometimes did. She was unusually worked up tonight, and would take more than a little coaxing and calming down. So when he suggested an early night she told him, again, that she wasn't in the mood.

'But I must admit I'm tired,' she said, 'with all the tidying up I've been doing after your daughter. So I think I'll go to bed – but it'll be to sleep,' she added meaningfully.

'OK, then,' Samuel grinned ruefully. 'Tell you what. You go and nip into bed, and I'll make you a nice pot of tea. You never say no to a cup of tea, now, do you?'

And Iris found, after the cup of tea, that she was, after all, more than ready for Samuel's amorous advances. But he needn't think I've forgotten, she thought to herself afterwards, as she lay in the darkness listening to his rhythmic snores. I'll be ready for her when she comes home from school. I will that!

Iris thought of little else all morning as she went about her chores. Fortunately it was not one of the days when she had her cleaning lady, Mrs Murphy, in to 'do' for her. That lady loved a good old chin-wag, but Iris, preoccupied with her own concerns, was certainly not in a gossiping mood that morning. By the time twelve o'clock came round, with the lamb casserole gently simmering in the oven and the potatoes bubbling away on top of the stove, Iris found, to her surprise, that she had calmed down considerably. She was even coming round to Samuel's point of view, that the matter might be best left alone.

But no, the child couldn't be allowed to get away with it, Iris told herself. She had to be made to realize that she had been rude and cheeky and that, as Samuel had said, it was unkind to poke fun at people. Iris knew, though, that there would be nothing gained by losing her temper, as she had done last night with Samuel. She must take things calmly and quietly, talking rationally and appealing to the child's better nature.

So Iris reasoned; but it was the sight of Josie bursting in through the door looking, as Iris frequently told her she did, like 'the wreck of the Hesperus' that upset her again. One ribbon on the end of her plait was undone, the other plait had come completely unravelled and her hair was flowing untidily round her shoulders. Her black shoes were scuffed, her socks concertinaed round her ankles and the belt on her navy-blue gaberdine was trailing loose. Bertie, on the other hand, was looking just as neat and tidy as he had when Iris had said goodbye to him at the school gate that morning.

Iris bit her tongue, merely saying, 'Get your hands washed and sit at the table, the pair of you.' There was a nice dinner waiting and there was no sense in letting good food go cold while you ranted and raved. No, Iris reminded herself, there was to be no ranting and raving. But Josie, unfortunately, seemed to be wrong side out today, complaining of gristle on her meat, then spilling gravy down her gymslip. It was the last straw when Iris produced the apple pie and custard for afters to be told that she had had the same thing last night at her auntie Alice's.

'It's lovely, me auntie Alice's apple pie,' Josie declared, at the same time, Iris noticed, tucking wholeheartedly into the dish in front of her.

'I've no doubt it is,' said Iris darkly. 'If everything your auntie Alice does is so wonderful then happen you'd better go and live there.' This was something she had often felt like saying to the child but, so far, had resisted the temptation. Now, as soon as the words were out, she regretted them. Especially as Josie, head down, scraping the bowl clean, muttered, 'Wish I could.'

Iris felt her temper rising and she had to almost sit on her hands to prevent herself from lashing out at the child. Instead, 'Don't be silly, Josephine,' she said, through clenched teeth. 'And don't be so cheeky. You know very well you can't go and live there.'

'Why d'you say it, then?'

'Because I'm sick of you going on about her, that's why. It's Auntie Alice this, and Auntie Alice that, morning, noon and night. You'd soon get fed up if you were there all the time, I'll tell you, traipsing down the yard to the lav and boiling a kettle of water every time you wanted a good wash.'

'Wouldn't mind,' said Josie sullenly.

'Well, you're not going and that's that,' snapped Iris. 'And I want to talk to you when you've finished your dinner.'

'I've finished now. What d'you want to talk to me about? You're always on at me—'

'We'll have less of your cheek, Josephine. Get down from the table and go into the lounge.' Iris turned to Bertie. 'Look after baby Frances for a few minutes, will you, Bertie, there's a good boy.' She lifted the baby from her high chair, unable to resist, as she did so, planting a kiss on the soft pink and white cheek. She was aware of Josie hovering in the doorway, her eyebrows knit together in a frown and her eyes dark with resentment.

'Go on, Josephine, I said,' she shouted. 'Go into the other room. I'll be there in a minute.' She placed the baby in her play-pen with her teddy bear, fluffy pink rabbit, a collection of rattles and a couple of well-chewed rag books. 'There you are, darling,' she cooed, her voice taking on a very different tone now. 'Bertie'll look after you while I go and talk to that naughty sister of yours. Such a naughty little girl she is, I don't know what we're going to do with her, I really don't.'

Josie was standing by the fireplace, moodily kicking her toe against the chromium-plated fender when Iris entered the room.

'Give over, can't you?' snapped Iris. 'You'll make it all mucky, to say nothing of scuffing your shoes up even more. Proper little ragamuffin you look, and we'll have to get that hair tidied up an' all before you go back to school. Now, sit down. I've got something to say to you.'

Josie gave an exaggerated sigh. 'What now?' she said, flinging herself down on to the sofa so forcibly that the springs gave a metallic twang. 'What've I done now?'

Iris again resisted the urge to slap the child. Instead she picked up the drawing-book from where she had placed it on top of the display cabinet. 'This is what you've done,' she said, as calmly as she was able. 'These drawings. What've you got to say for yourself?'

Iris noticed that the child went pink and, for a moment, looked very discomfited. At least she did have some sense of guilt. Then her mouth set in a stubborn line and her eyebrows drew together again as she looked at the floor, not speaking.

'Come along, Josephine. What have you to say? I'm waiting.'

'Nothing,' the child mumbled, still not looking at Iris. 'What d'you want me to say? I never meant you to see them. They're mine . . . they're private. You've no business to go messing about with my things. They've got nothing to do with you.'

'Oh, haven't they, young lady? I'd say they had everything to do with me, especially as you've seen fit to poke fun at me, to make me a laughing-stock.' Iris found that all her good intentions, to behave calmly and rationally, were flying out of the window in the face of Josie's stubbornness. 'For a child of eight – no, seven, you were then – to think up such disgusting things, well, I just couldn't believe it when I first set eyes on them. There's a nasty streak in you, Josephine, real nasty, and where you get it from I can't imagine. Not from your father . . . and certainly not from your mother.'

'Don't you dare mention my mother!' Josie's eyes blazed with fury as she looked for the first time at Iris. 'I loved my mother. And she would never—'

Iris didn't wait to find out what it was that Josie's mother would never have done. Tell her off, maybe; show her who was boss? That was what the child was short of. 'I shall mention who I like,' Iris retorted. 'I'm not saying anything wrong about her. I'm just saying you're not much like her. You're rude and cheeky, and deceitful as well . . . keeping those dreadful drawings all this time, laughing about them, I don't doubt. Sniggering away behind my back . . .'

Her temper was really aroused now, and her next reaction was almost an involuntary one. 'I'll show you what I think about your drawings,' Iris raged, waving the book in front of Josie's face. 'This is what I think about them.' In one savage movement she tore the book in half, then at Josie's gasp of horror she tore it across again and flung the pieces into the grate. 'There . . . that's all they're fit for – burning. Nasty, disgusting things.'

There was no fire in the grate, just coals and folded paper and a piece of fire-lighter, ready for putting a match to in the evening. Some of the offending pictures fluttered to the hearth; the top half of Blackpool Tower, a seagull's wing and, most pertinently, a prominent rear end clad in a navy-blue spotted dress.

Iris hated herself the moment she had done it, but by then it was too late. She could see that Josie's face had blanched and her mouth was quivering. 'I can't stop you from drawing, but there are other things I can stop you from doing. There'll be no more visits to your aunt Alice, not until you've learned to behave yourself.'

'No!' Josie's brown eyes moistened as she stared unbelievingly at Iris. 'You can't stop me from seeing me auntie Alice. You've no right—'

'I've told you before, I've every right,' said Iris, more quietly now. 'You'll see Alice on a Sunday at church, but as for going to tea and your Saturday afternoon jaunts – no, not until I can see that you're trying to be a good girl. And not until you've said that you're sorry. That's what I've been waiting for, Josephine.'

If the apology had come then – and Iris had given the girl every chance – she might well have relented. But Josie didn't apologize. Her eyes were dark with animosity, with hurt and pain, too, as she stared at Iris. 'It's been awful ever since you came,' she said, 'and you don't need to think I'll ever call you Mummy, like our Bertie and Frances, 'cause I shan't!' Her voice grew louder. 'And our Frances is a spoiled little brat. That's what me auntie Alice says and—'

'Never mind what your aunt Alice says,' replied Iris, getting to her feet and finding that her legs were unsteady. 'I've told you, you've seen the last of Alice Rawlinson for the time being. Whether you like it or not, Josephine, I'm your mother now. Your father married me and he expects me to look after you, and I'm going to make you behave yourself if it's the last thing I do. Now, come here and let's get that hair fixed before you go back to school.'

Josie got up without a word and stood, motionless and silent, on the hearthrug as Iris combed and re-plaited her hair. Iris's instinct was to tug the comb through the long silky locks, but she found herself treating the girl with gentleness, and, as she tied the blue ribbon on the end of the plait, wondering, as she had done before, just who had been the victor in this fight.

'Whatever d'you suppose our Josie did to upset Iris so much?' Alice Rawlinson said to her husband one evening at the beginning of May. 'She can be a little monkey, I know, and I've seen trouble brewing between the pair of them for a while now. Ever since Samuel married her, in fact, as well you know, Jack – I've always had my doubts about it. But for her to stop the child coming to see us, it must be something real bad.'

''Dunno, I'm sure, love,' said Jack. He put his newspaper down; it was useless to try and read when Alice was determined to make him talk. Besides, he knew that he would miss young Josie's visits almost as much as his wife. The child was like a breath of fresh air sweeping through the place. 'What did Josie have to say for herself? Didn't she tell you what it was all about?'

'She couldn't very well, could she, with Iris there. No, she just stood there looking sullen and shuffling her feet around while Iris told me that she couldn't come to see us for a while. She'd been rude, she said, rude and cheeky and . . . disrespectful, that was the word. I suppose the child's been giving her cheek, answering her back.'

'Aye, she's a spirited lass,' said Jack. 'But you've got to admit that Iris is right to take a firm line with her. She can't let her get away with it – whatever it is. She's got to show her who's boss. The woman's in an awkward position, I've always thought so. Three youngsters to bring up and Samuel to cope with as well. It can't be easy for her.'

'No . . . I daresay you're right,' Alice answered, somewhat surprisingly. For once she was not accusing her husband of sticking up for Iris Goodwin, as she so often did. 'I must admit that Iris didn't rant and rave about it. Of course, she couldn't very well, not with all the folks milling around outside church. No, she just pointed out to me that Josie had to be punished for being cheeky . . . She seemed almost apologetic about it, come to think of it, as though she might be having second thoughts.'

'But not wanting to back down?'

'Yes, that's it exactly, Jack. I wish I knew what it was all about.'

'I know,' chimed in Len's voice from the back of the room. He looked up from his football scrapbook and the newspaper pictures spread all over the table. 'I know why Josie can't come to see us. She told me when I saw her in the playground.'

'You know?' Alice looked at him in astonishment. 'Then why on earth didn't you tell me?'

Len shrugged. 'Thought you knew, Mam.'

'Well, I didn't. Go on then, lad. Spill the beans. What has the lass done?'

Leonard grinned. 'Drawn some rude pictures.'

'Rude pictures? Whatever do you mean?' Alice asked guardedly, wondering if she ought not to pursue the matter too closely, but, at the same time, dying to find out.

'It was when they were away on holiday,' explained Len. 'When Uncle Samuel got married, but Iris – Auntie Iris – has only just found out. Josie drew a picture of her on a donkey – her back view, Mam – and wrote 'Fat Iris' underneath it. And there was another one of her in a deck-chair, showing her . . . underwear.'

Alice bit her lip to stop herself from laughing, but she could feel the tears of merriment springing to her eyes. 'And she told you all this? In the playground? I thought the boys and girls had separate yards.'

'Oh yes, we do, Mam. There's a only a little wall between, but we're supposed to play separately. Josie beckoned to me when the teacher wasn't watching and I went over to have a word with her. I knew it was something important or she wouldn't have interrupted our game.'

'Josie did that? She interrupted your football game?'

'We were only kicking around. Anyway, the lads are used to Josie watching us. They like her, Mam. She's a good sort . . . for a girl.'

Jack Rawlinson hadn't even tried to stem the mirth that his son's words had aroused. He was laughing now, unrestrainedly, shaking his head back and forth. 'Eeh, that's a good 'un. Wish I could see them pictures. Iris on the back of a donkey. Heaven help the poor donkey, eh, Len?'

'Stop it, the pair of you,' said Alice, but laughing herself now. She had wondered what Len meant by 'rude' drawings, but now she could see that it was probably nothing too lewd or suggestive. Just cheeky and disrespectful. Iris would have been made to feel a fool and it was little wonder that the woman had felt hurt when she found them. But that didn't alter the fact that Josie had been banned from coming to see them, and Alice did miss the child. 'That's all it is, then?' she said to Len. 'These drawings?'

'Seems like it. But Iris – Auntie Iris – expects Josie to say she's sorry, and Josie won't because she's torn up the pictures.'

'Iris has?'

Len nodded. 'That's all I know. We had to go in then because the teacher blew the whistle.'

Alice was thoughtful for a moment. Poor Josie. That was a wicked thing to do, to tear up the child's drawings. On the other hand, she supposed Iris had seen red and you could hardly blame her. 'I shall go and see her,' she said. 'Josie, I mean. I'll go and meet her when she comes out of school tomorrow. Iris doesn't come to meet them, does she?' Len shook his head. 'Very well then. I'll go and try to persuade her to say she's sorry. We can't all be punished like this because of a few silly drawings, and if that's all Iris is waiting for, for Josie to apologize . . .'

'Yes, I reckon that's a good idea,' said Jack. 'Josie'll listen to you, won't she? If she'll listen to anyone. Best to get it sorted out soon. Once they get to Victoria Grove it'll be even further for the child to come and see us. Victoria Grove . . .' repeated Jack dreamily. 'By heck! The Goodwins are going up in the world, aren't they? It was only politicians at first – Baldwin Lane and Gladstone Avenue – and now it's royalty. Victoria Grove, no less.'

'Oh yes, I hadn't realized that,' said Alice smiling. 'Very apt. Victoria Grove's posh all right. On the edge of the park, where the nobs live. Happen Iris'll be satisfied now. But the main thing is to make things right between her and Josie, if I can. I'll go and see her tomorrow.'

'Auntie Alice!' Josie let go of Bertie's hand and ran to the school gate. She flung her arms round the small plump figure, burying her head against the soft roundness. 'Oh, I'm so glad to see you. What are you doing here?'

Alice laid a gentle hand on the child's head. 'I've come to see you, love, about this spot of bother you're in.' She tried to speak reprovingly and to make her face look stern. 'From what I can gather your auntie Iris has had every reason to be annoyed . . . and I think you should tell her that you're sorry.'

'I suppose Len's told you what she did; but I'm not sorry. She's mean and horrible and she had no right to tear up my drawings and to stop me from seeing you. I hate her . . .'

Alice didn't want to comment as to the rights or wrongs of it all. She paused to smile at Bertie who had just joined them and slipped his hand into hers. 'Hello, Bertie love . . . Don't say you hate your aunt Iris, Josie,' she went on, speaking quietly. 'That isn't kind and I'm sure it isn't true. You're just feeling cross with her. Listen, love, why don't you get it over with, right now? Go home and tell her that you're sorry, that you know you've been rather . . . rude, then it can all be forgotten. The longer it goes on, the worse it'll be, and goodness knows when you'll be able to come and see us again if you don't try to do as I say. Won't you do it, love, just for me?'

Josie looked at her aunt, her brown eyes perplexed, but no longer quite as belligerent. 'Don't know . . .' she murmured.

'I'd get into awful bother with your aunt Iris if she knew I was here,' Alice went on. 'You do realize that, don't you, Josie? She'd say I was interfering.' Josie nodded. 'I've only come because I think such a lot about you, and I want you to come back to us.'

'I might then,' said Josie slowly. 'Just for you, though, Auntie Alice. It's only because you want me to.'

'All right then.' Alice sighed. 'That's a good girl . . . but don't let on to Iris that that's the reason, will you?'

'You don't think I'm that daft, do you?' said Josie, sounding much older than her eight years.

Alice smiled and motioned towards Bertie who was standing there quietly. 'I'm a bit worried about Bertie here,' she said in a whisper. 'I knew I was taking a chance, coming to see you. He won't say anything, will he?'

'Not if I tell him he mustn't,' said Josie confidently.

'Our Bertie always does as I say. He doesn't say very much anyway.'

Oh dear, thought Alice. So much deceitfulness, it really wasn't right; but if it meant that Josie could start her visits again then a little slyness could perhaps be excused. 'You'll say you're sorry then?' she asked.

Josie nodded, then gave a sigh. 'Yes, I'll say I'm sorry.'

The Goodwin family moved at the beginning of June, 1937, to their new address, number twenty-one Victoria Grove, Victoria Park, Haliford. Iris looked round, gratified, as the removal van drew away, at the large lounge where there would be more than enough room for her three-piece suite, her display cabinet, wind-up gramophone and tasselled standard lamp. They had been decidedly cramped in the small lounge at Gladstone Avenue. The room was overflowing with packing cases at the moment, but they would soon get that lot shifted. Iris had never been afraid of hard work and Samuel would give her a hand when he came home from the mill. He hadn't been able to get a day off for the removal, but it didn't matter. Iris was glad, on this first day, to be alone as the mistress of their new domain.

The other 'reception room' – the estate agent's wording – downstairs, was of the same large size, the kitchen was adequate, and, an added bonus, there was a brick-built wash-house a few feet away down the garden, so that the steam didn't enter the house.

Iris wandered upstairs, caressing the smooth oak balustrade. There were three good-sized bedrooms. Even the little one over the front door, where Bertie would sleep, was a good deal bigger than the average boxroom. And Josie should be thrilled to bits with her room at the back, overlooking the garden with the small lawn and rockery and the single apple tree at the bottom. This garden was a definite improvement; at Gladstone Avenue they had only had a paved yard and a flower border.

Josie was a very lucky girl, Iris mused, to have a room to herself. She remembered how, at the same age, she had been crowded into a double bed with several of her siblings – both boys and girls. Top to toe, they had been, and with nowhere to put their clothes either – such clothes as they had – except behind a curtain in the corner. Josie had her own dressing table, wardrobe and bookcase, though she might have to share the room with Frances when the baby grew too big for the cot in her parents' room.

Josephine's behaviour was much improved recently, Iris found herself thinking. Ever since the girl had, so surprisingly, apologized for her rudeness, there had been little further trouble. It had been a somewhat grudging apology, but Iris had been relieved that it had come at all. She had, therefore, been glad to accept it and to allow the child to resume her visits to her aunt. She had felt dreadful about that.

There's plenty of room in here for two single beds, thought Iris, looking at the one bed that was there now, piled high with pillows, sheets and pillowcases, spare blankets and bedspreads. Josie wouldn't want to share with her sister – Iris knew that – but the girl would have to like it or lump it. Unless . . . Iris was thoughtful. Perhaps by the time Frances was three – in another eighteen months or so – they might be able to move again to a four-bedroomed house. After all, number twenty-one Victoria Grove was only a semi . . .

[illegible]

[illegible]

Chapter 8

Samuel wondered sometimes where it would all end. He stared out of one of the back bedroom windows of number six Jubilee Gardens, at the wide expanse of lawn, the garage, garden shed and shrubbery, across to Victoria Park. He was enjoying a couple of hours' well-earned rest after mowing the lawn, a job to which he was gradually becoming accustomed; it was all part and parcel of his new lifestyle. Iris was in town with the two younger children, buying new shoes, and Josie was with her aunt Alice. Perhaps this time, he reflected, Iris would be satisfied. She had got her four-bedroomed detached house in an area of Haliford that couldn't be bettered. Maybe, now, they could all settle down. But somehow he doubted it. Iris was not the settling-down sort.

They had stayed in Victoria Grove for two years – too long for Iris's liking, Samuel suspected – and now, in the June of 1939, they had moved to what Iris avowed to be the house of her dreams. She had, however, said that last time . . .

Samuel had to admit, though, that he had gone up in the world since he married Iris, and not just as far as their property was concerned. He was now an under-manager at Hammond's mill and vicar's warden at St Luke's. He was justifiably proud of himself on ceremonial occasions –

the visit of the Bishop, for instance, or the carol service or harvest festival – when he preceded the clergy up the aisle carrying his staff of office. This didn't happen as often as Samuel might have wished because St Luke's was quite low church, not given to a great deal of pomp and ceremony. But Samuel felt that it was a well-deserved feather in his cap, brought about not only through his own efforts but also, in no small measure, by the persuasive powers of his wife. He had not been without a good deal of get up and go before he married her, but this trait in him had been heightened by Iris's ambition which was not only for herself but for her husband as well. It had been Iris who had put it into the minds of the vicar and the Parochial Church Council that Samuel was just the man they were looking for, when the previous warden had died suddenly of a heart attack.

Yes, Iris was getting to be a force to be reckoned with at church and at the Townswomen's Guild which she had recently joined, as well as at home. She had long been a force to be reckoned with in the family and Samuel knew that he had a lot to thank her for, not least her money. It was her income from her shares in the coal business, started by her first husband, that had paid largely for this present property; but so long as his name, too, was on the deeds – which it was – Samuel didn't much care who had paid for it. He was proud to be seen with her, especially since she had lost weight, following that unfortunate incident with Josephine and the drawings.

They had all been made to suffer because of that. No more puddings, pastries and cakes, Iris had declared, and that went for all of them – more fresh fruit and vegetables, and, for herself, no more sugar in her tea. It had resulted in a new, not exactly slimline, but more evenly proportioned Iris, who wore her new clothes – and there had been many of them, Samuel thought ruefully – with aplomb and self-confidence, a quality that she hadn't exactly been short of before.

And, to crown it all, they now owned a car. A brand-new Austin Ten sat in the garage, from where it was taken out each morning for Samuel to drive to the mill. It had been a necessity as the new house was on the far side of Victoria Park, a couple of miles from Hammond's mill, almost in the country. Samuel had mastered the gears and steering and all the mechanics of driving quite easily. Iris, too, had had a try, but hadn't quite got the hang of it yet. Samuel was glad that there was at least one area in which he was the master. He feared that life was, at times, a battle for supremacy between the pair of them, each of them convinced that they knew best and often resulting, to Samuel's chagrin, in his wife getting the upper hand.

Samuel sighed as he thought of the uneasy truce between his wife and elder daughter. Just as there had been an uneasy truce for the past year between Great Britain and Germany. But you couldn't trust Hitler. Samuel had never trusted him, and he had never had any confidence in Neville Chamberlain's 'peace in our time' nonsense either. Samuel had feared, when Chamberlain succeeded Baldwin a couple of years ago, that the fellow wasn't right for the job. Appeasement, indeed! Chamberlain's critics had been vindicated all right now, with Hitler walking into Czechoslovakia in that high-handed way. The Prime Minister had been forced to admit that Britain would go to war if Poland's independence, too, was threatened, which now seemed more than likely.

War . . . The thought of it filled Samuel with dread. He remembered only too well his father enlisting in 1914, when Samuel was eleven years old, having no idea at that time what he was letting himself in for. He had gone cheerfully and philosophically, but he had come back a changed man. He had been lucky, Samuel supposed, to come back at all; so many of his friends, lads that he had been to school with and worked with in the Bradford mill had not returned. And Harold Goodwin, Samuel's father, had not lasted long. The outbreak of Spanish flu that had swept through the country soon after the end of the war had proved too much for his weakened constitution.

Samuel's eyes wandered to a couple of souvenirs of that dreadful time which hung on their bedroom wall and which, surprisingly, Iris hadn't banished to the back of a cupboard. One was a photograph of a group of soldiers, Harold and his Bradford pals, all looking incredibly young and naive, as they had done when they had volunteered. They had all been killed, save for Harold and two other lads, and Samuel recalled how his father had returned with sunken cheeks and hollow eyes, a far cry from that picture of fresh-faced innocence. The other souvenir was a sepia photograph of Samuel's mother, Frances – after whom his youngest child had been named – superimposed on a china plate and surrounded by roses against a background picture of the town of Ypres. It had been his mother's most treasured possession, Samuel remembered, as he looked at it thoughtfully.

This next war which, alas, seemed to be imminent, would be a very different carry-on from the last lot, though. He had read somewhere that priority would be given to air defence, but already the military training of young men aged twenty had begun. Samuel was now thirty-six. He could no longer be classed as a young man; he wouldn't, therefore, be called up – would he?

Not at first . . . Eventually, though, it might come to that. Unless he volunteered, before he had a chance to be conscripted. His father had done so, and Samuel had always held the greatest admiration for his father. Besides, he thought, almost guiltily, it might be something of an escape. Sometimes – just sometimes – he felt that his life was not his own . . .

Josie had received the news that they were to move – again – to a detached house in Jubilee Gardens, with mixed feelings. In some ways she was glad because it meant that she could once more have a bedroom to herself, as she had done until Auntie Iris had moved Frances in with her about a year ago. Frances was a nuisance, waking up early and shouting and singing when Josie wanted to snatch a few more minutes under the covers; or preventing her from reading in bed because the light might wake her up. And she was forever messing about with Josie's things . . . and Auntie Iris didn't stop her either. There had been a big row when Josie had come home from school and found her best crayons scattered all over the floor and Frances scribbling away in one of her drawing-books. Fortunately, the child hadn't spoiled any existing drawings, just wasted pages and pages of brand-new paper.

'She's only a baby,' Auntie Iris had said, when Josie nearly hit the roof. 'She's not doing any harm. You should learn to share your things. Never mind, my pet . . .' This to a tearful Frances who was pouting, as she often did, when she was thwarted. 'Mummy will buy you a nice new drawing-book, all to yourself, when we go into town. Never mind what your sister says. She's a crosspatch, isn't she? That's what she is.'

'That's right, stick up for her as usual,' Josie had

muttered, but under her breath so that Iris couldn't hear, as she hid her precious drawing things away at the top of the wardrobe. Drawing was a sore point between her and Iris since that Blackpool incident, and Josie didn't want to add any more fuel to the fire. She was blazing mad, though. Frances got all her own way.

So it would be nice to be free of the child; and it would be good, too, to live nearer to the countryside, away from the grime of the woollen mills, belching black smoke into the air, and the noisy clang of the railway which had passed quite near to their house in Gladstone Avenue. Jubilee Gardens was admirably sited, part of a new estate which had Victoria Park on one side and moorland on the other. The Jubilee referred to in the name was not old Queen Victoria's – the revered personage after whom so many places in Haliford had been named – but that of George the Fifth who in 1935 had celebrated twenty-five years on the throne.

So the house was only four years old, with many up-to-the-minute features which had been very attractive to Iris. A modern Aga cooker in the kitchen; a fireplace in the lounge which burned coke instead of coal and had a gas burner incorporated in the grate; and, best of all, a garage for the new car which they had bought. Josie was pleased about the car because her main objection to the house was that it was so far away from everything: from Auntie Alice's, from St Luke's church, and, most importantly, from school.

'Goody,' Josie said, when she first saw the shiny black Austin Ten sitting at the kerbside in Victoria Grove. It was a Saturday tea-time and the car had just been delivered. Samuel had bought it a few weeks before they were due to move, in order to learn to drive in readiness for his longer journey to work. 'You'll be able to take us to school, won't you, Dad? Bertie and me? It'll be too far for us to walk from the new house.'

'The car's for my convenience, not yours, young lady,' Samuel replied. 'Take you to school, indeed! That I won't. What d'you think I am, a blooming chauffeur? Anyroad, I start work long before you go to school – you know full well I do, Josephine – so I couldn't take you even if I wanted to. No, your mother . . .' He hesitated as he saw the resentment in Josie's eyes, then reworded his sentence: '. . . Your aunt Iris and I have been talking, and we've decided you'll both have to go to a different school. Like you say, Queen Street school, where you go now, would be too far—'

'So you're going to Beechwood,' Iris joined in. 'It's a nice little school, only a few minutes' walk away from the new house—'

'Oh no! That's not fair,' Josie interrupted. 'Why didn't you tell me! You never said—'

'I'm telling you now, Josephine,' said Iris. 'I knew you'd make a fuss, that's why I didn't say anything before. What a silly girl you are, anyway, thinking you could go all that way to Queen Street, and expecting your father to take you. Of all the things! No, you'll go to Beechwood. Happen they'll teach you some manners there, young lady. From what I've heard it's a very good school and they don't stand for any nonsense.'

'It's not fair,' said Josie again. She had been trying so hard lately to behave, not wanting to be deprived of going to her auntie Alice's. 'I don't want to go to silly old Beechwood,' she went on. 'Stuck-up, toffee-nosed kids they are, what goes there. I've seen 'em in their green uniforms and daft hats. Think they're it, they do, 'cause they wear a different colour to everybody else. It's a potty school and I don't want to wear a daft green gymslip. I'm not going!'

Josie had never even considered that the move to Jubilee Gardens might involve a change of schools. She was very happy at Queen Street. She had been there since she was four and a half – that was more than five years – and all her friends were there. And she liked the teachers, too, as much as you could like teachers. Josie didn't, as a rule, find it hard to make friends, but the thought of that snooty lot at Beechwood, to say nothing of the stupid uniform . . .

'You're going, Josephine,' said Iris in an ominous tone. 'I've already been to see the headmaster. He's got room for you and for Bertie, so you'll be starting there the Monday after we move. And you needn't worry about the green gymslip, because I shan't be buying you one anyway. You've got a perfectly good navy-blue one, and the way you treat your clothes – like a scarecrow you are – you needn't think I'm going to throw good money away on a new uniform for you. No, I've explained to the headmaster and he says it's quite all right for you to wear your blue one. You've only another year to do anyway, then you'll be going to the grammar school . . . that is, if you work hard and pass your scholarship exam.'

Josie found that she was, temporarily, at a loss for words. There seemed to be no answer to what Auntie Iris had said and she knew there was no point in arguing any further. She wouldn't have to wear that daft uniform anyway, which was one blessing. She contented herself with mumbling, 'Don't care. Still don't want to go. Don't see why I've got to . . .' then she proceeded to eat the rest of her tea in silence.

Iris ignored her and addressed her next remarks to her husband. 'Like I say, Samuel, it's a very good school; not a private one, of course, but the next best thing. Mr Edwards – that's the headmaster – says that the pupils don't have to wear the green uniform, but most of them do. I shall buy new for Bertie, of course. He's just going into the Juniors now he's seven, so he'll be ready for some new jumpers and shirts and a gaberdine mac. And the green cap they wear, an' all.'

Samuel nodded and Josie thought from his expression that he was more concerned with the plate of baked beans on toast in front of him. He left matters such as schools and uniforms and new clothes to his wife, as, indeed, he left most things to her, and Josie had never known him to take a great deal of interest in her school work. She was surprised, therefore, when he cast her an unusually sympathetic glance before he turned back to his wife and said, 'I don't know about that, Iris. Doesn't seem fair, does it? I think we could run to a new gymslip for the lass, couldn't we? We don't want her to be the odd one out.'

'Huh! Since when has Josephine ever cared about that?' Iris retorted. 'She likes being different, doesn't she? Besides, she says she's not bothered. You heard her. "I don't want to wear a daft green gymslip," she said. And Mr Edwards says it doesn't matter, so she'll have to wear her navy one. It's practically brand new anyway. And I don't believe in—'

'No, you don't believe in throwing good money away,' Samuel finished for her in a slightly mocking tone. 'All right, all right, I've heard it all before . . . but I hope you know what you're doing,' he added darkly.

No, it doesn't seem fair . . . and it jolly well isn't fair, thought Josie, listening silently to this exchange. If Bertie was having a new uniform for this potty new school then so should she. She had forgotten for the moment that she had said she would never wear their daft uniform; now she was only concerned with Iris's meanness in giving preferential treatment to Bertie, and in her father's remark that she might be the odd one out. Don't care if I am, she tried to tell herself, but she knew that she did care. And she was determined now to take the opposite view from Iris. If Iris wanted her to wear her navy gymslip, then she, Josie, would stick out for a green one.

Josie wasn't aware of how much she did care until the Monday morning in the middle of June when she found herself almost the only child, in a mixed class of thirty boys and girls, without a green uniform. It was a chilly, cheerless day, such as one often gets in the approach to what was supposed to be summer. The girls, at this time of the year, sometimes wore summer dresses instead of gymslips; but the few that were doing so, Josie noticed, were all clad in varying shades of green. Candy-striped, spotted, or checked gingham dresses, some with hand-knitted or shop-bought green cardigans on top of them. Most of the girls, however, because of the inclement weather, were wearing their bottle-green gymslips with a white blouse, green and white striped tie and a green and white woven girdle at the waist.

The boys, of course, wore knee-length serge or grey flannel trousers, but they all had green pullovers; except for two boys – unusually untidy-looking boys for Beechwood – who sat together at one of the double desks. The ginger-haired one wore a shabby grey jumper with holes in the elbows and the dark boy next to him wore a red one, of all things, which looked as though it might have been handed down from an elder sister. There was a smattering of such unkempt-looking children in most Junior school classes. There had been more than a few at Queen Street, Josie's previous school, from homes where the father was out of work, or the mother was feckless, or where there were just too many children to cope with, but she was surprised to see any at Beechwood. The ginger-haired lad had grinned at her when she entered the classroom with Mr Edwards and she had warmed to him immediately.

The teacher, Miss Longbottom, seemed nice enough, small and mouselike, but well able to keep order. Josie suppressed a grin on hearing her name, wondering if it might provoke rude jokes, but probably not, from the well-behaved children of Beechwood. Even at Queen Street, where there had been a few unruly children, it would have been a brave soul who had dared to make fun of a teacher. You didn't have to like teachers – some of them you positively hated or dreaded ending up in their class – but you knew that you had to respect them.

Josie's neighbour in the double desk, a tall girl with long dark plaits like Josie's, didn't seem particularly friendly or inclined to talk. The class, as a whole, didn't chatter much, getting on with their work in an exemplary manner. Josie ignored her neighbour – two could play at that game – and, likewise, got on with the morning's work, which she found very easy. Pounds, shillings and pence sums of the kind Josie had learned ages ago, and an English exercise which she completed in five minutes while many of the children were still chewing their pencils, their brows furrowed in puzzlement. For goodness' sake, Josie thought, she'd known all about nouns, verbs and adjectives ever since she was seven. So much for Auntie Iris insisting that it was a 'good school'. Obedient and neat and tidy these pupils certainly were – most of them – but as far as cleverness was concerned, Josie was sure that the Queen

Street kids could knock spots off them. She knew that *she* could!

Well behaved in class they might have been, but once in the school yard at playtime it was a vastly different story. It was then that Josie found out, as her father had feared she might, what it was like to be the odd one out.

'Where've you come from?' This from the tall dark girl who sat next to her in class and who was now looking her up and down as though she were something out of Noah's ark. 'And why aren't you wearing green, same as the rest of us?'

'I'm from Queen Street,' said Josie, sticking out her chin defiantly and looking the girl right in the eyes. She was very slightly cross-eyed, Josie thought with a stab of malicious glee. 'And they wear blue uniforms there, not daft green ones like what you wear. Anything else you'd like to know?'

'Yes, plenty,' replied the girl. 'Wouldn't we, Vera?' She turned to another girl who had just joined them, a pale, freckled girl with the reddest hair Josie had ever seen. 'We want to know why you're pretending to be such a clever clogs, finishing your work dead quick and then staring round as though you owned the place.'

'Ye-eh, she was, wasn't she, Hilda?' agreed Vera with the red hair. 'I saw her looking round at us as though we were dirt and I thought, who the heck does she think she is?'

'I wasn't!' Josie replied hotly. 'I was looking round 'cause I'd finished my work. Dead easy it was, baby work. Huh! We did that in Standard Two at Queen Street.'

'Oh, we did that in Standard Two at rotten old Queen Street,' mimicked Hilda. 'Why d'you leave then, if it was so wonderful? Why d'you come here?'

Josie felt, to her horror, that her eyes were ever so slightly moist, something that hardly ever happened to her. She mustn't cry, she mustn't, not in front of these awful girls. She blinked rapidly, determined to give as good as she got. 'What's it got to do with you?' she retorted. 'If you must know, I've had to come to this rotten old school because we've moved to a new house. A big posh house,' she went on, staring at them defiantly. 'We've got four bedrooms, an' a right big garden, an' a garage . . . an' a new car an' all,' she added, although by now her voice was petering out unsteadily.

'Oh, hark at her! A new car an' all,' mimicked Vera, turning to grin at a small group of girls who had sidled up, showing interest in the fracas. 'My dad's got two cars, an' our house has got five bedrooms.'

'Ours has got six, and we've got a swimming pool,' joined in Hilda, putting her face right up to Josie's and practically spitting at her. 'So there, you swankpot . . .'

'You're a rotten liar, Hilda Ormerod!' The scruffy ginger-haired boy who had grinned at Josie earlier that morning had now wandered over with his mate. 'Swimming pool, my aunt Fanny!' he sneered. 'Don't take any notice of 'er, kid.' He winked at Josie and gave an impudent grin. 'She's a bloody liar, ain't she, Derek?'

The dark boy with the red jumper nodded. 'Aye. And d'you know what her dad does? He's a rag-and-bone man.' He turned to the small group of girls. 'I'n't he? A bloody rag-and-bone man!' He burst into raucous laughter, joined by his ginger-haired friend, but not, Josie noticed, by the group of girls.

'You shut up, Derek Watson! And you an' all, Jimmy Clegg. Mind your own rotten business,' retorted Hilda. 'And you won't half catch it if Miss Longbottom hears you swearing,' she added, somewhat self-righteously. 'I've a good mind to tell her . . .'

'You do and we'll bloody well get you at home-time!' Derek seized hold of one of Hilda's long plaits, pulling the green ribbon undone and making her lose her balance.

'Leave go!' Hilda shouted at him. She aimed a kick at his shin, which didn't make its mark, but Josie couldn't help feeling a grudging admiration for her.

'Come on, Derek. We'd best leave her,' said Jimmy, the ginger-haired lad, nudging his friend, 'or else we'll have Miss coming over here.' They both glanced in the direction of the teacher at the far end of the yard who was casting a curious look in their direction. She took a step towards them and Jimmy and Derek scuttled away. 'You tell us, kid, if that Hilda Ormerod gives you any bother,' said Jimmy in a low voice as he passed her. 'Me and Derek, we'll bloody well sort her out. We'll stick up for you.'

Josie grinned her thanks, thinking how this playground at Beechwood, for all its veneer of respectability, seemed to be a much more vicious place than the one at Queen Street. Probably because here, at Beechwood, the boys and girls, fewer in number that at Queen Street, played together in the same yard. They each, however, by an unwritten rule, kept to their own territory except when, as just now, there seemed to be something worthy of investigation taking place.

Josie couldn't help but feel that, in different circumstances, she and the dark-haired Hilda Ormerod might have been friends. The girl was only exercising her proprietary rights over her school, her friends, her part of the playground . . . but in a very high-handed manner. Josie had already gathered that the girl was something of a leader, looked up to by children of a less dominant personality. Most likely she and the red-haired Vera egged one another on in displays of spitefulness, which they might not do if they were on their own. The other girls, Josie had noticed, hadn't risen to the bait offered by the irrepressible Derek and Jimmy, that Hilda's father was a rag-and-bone man, keeping instead a loyal silence. Josie wondered if it could possibly be true. Surely not . . .

Hilda and Vera were not openly taunting her now, but were walking behind her, talking to one another in loud voices which she knew they fully intended her to hear.

''Spect she's wearing a funny old blue gymslip 'cause her mum and dad can't afford a green one.'

'Ye-eh, they'll have spent all their money on the new car . . .'

'And the big posh house with four bedrooms . . .' They both giggled.

'Queen Street's a right mucky old school. D'you know where it is? Right near to the gasworks and the Corporation tip. Wonder what her dad does? P'raps he's a dustbin man . . .'

This last remark was from Vera, and there was a significant silence while Hilda digested it before she replied. 'It wasn't right, you know, what that awful Derek Watson said about my dad. He's not a rag-and-bone man. He's got a shop – it's what they call an antique shop. Of course, he does go round buying stuff . . .'

The conversation came to an end as the teacher blew the whistle and all the classes lined up to walk sedately back into school. They were certainly well disciplined and it was no doubt this regimentation that gave outsiders the impression that Beechwood was a 'good school'. Josie couldn't have put her thoughts into coherent words, but she knew that something was lacking at this new school that they had had in abundance at Queen Street. There, there had been friendliness and comradeship and an absence of petty rivalries and jealousies. The affluent children – not all that many of them – the less well-to-do and the undeniably poor had all mingled together, taking little heed of their differences.

And newcomers were always made to feel welcome. Josie could recall several instances where she, or one of the other children who, like Josie, was not short of self-confidence, had been asked to take a new classmate under their wing and help them to find their feet. Josie wondered why Miss Longbottom hadn't done this. If she had done so then things might have been very different. As it was, Josie knew that she had got off on the wrong foot with Hilda Ormerod and that, instead of friendship, there might soon be out and out rivalry between the pair of them.

It wasn't long before Josie realized that Hilda was a clever and intelligent girl. Hilda was used to being top of the class, and her biggest bone of contention against the newcomer was that there was now someone in Standard Three who seemed to be streets ahead of all of them. Josie continued to find the work simple. In spelling or mental arithmetic tests she usually got nineteen or even twenty out of twenty, whilst the majority of the class struggled away in the low teens. Even the previous number one, Hilda, rarely managed more than eighteen.

It was the same with reading aloud. Josie, a fluent reader, was very soon put into the top reading-group where she provoked giggles and more than a few dirty looks from her classmates with her loud clear voice and the expression which she put into her delivery. Many of the other children tended to mumble, reading in expressionless voices and making little sense of the text. Reading had been a priority at Queen Street school and Josie loved it, almost as much as she loved drawing.

And that was another thing which had antagonized the class – some of them, at least – led on, of course, by the ubiquitous Hilda. The first Art lesson, to which Josie had been looking forward, took place on the Friday afternoon of the first week. The drawing which Josie did of a spray of wild roses – gathered from the hedgerow by Miss Longbottom and displayed in a jamjar on her desk – had been so much praised by that teacher that she had even sent her along to show it to the headmaster.

'Rotten old show-off!' mocked Hilda at playtime. 'Who cares, anyway, about going to see Mr Edwards? I bet he didn't take any notice. I bet he thought it was a daft old drawing.' Art was not a subject at which Hilda excelled, and her own effort had looked more like a lollipop on a stick.

This was what Josie told her, in no uncertain terms, leading, for the first time, to an actual physical brawl between the pair of them. Several of the children looked on apprehensively – it was almost unheard-of for girls to fight – as the two adversaries lashed out at one another, fists and feet flying as they tried to pull one another's hair, to scratch, to punch, to kick . . .

'Go on . . . Thump 'er, Josie. Let 'er 'ave it,' yelled Jimmy and Derek, whilst Hilda's champions, led by Vera, were too bewildered to open their mouths.

Fortunately the fight didn't last long enough for either of them to be seriously hurt as it was soon stopped by the teacher on playground duty. And so for the second time that afternoon Josie found herself confronting the headmaster.

'We're not used to this sort of behaviour at Beechwood,'

he told her severely. 'And as for you, Hilda Ormerod, I'm ashamed of you. I thought you would know better. This isn't Queen Street, you know,' he went on, looking back at Josie. 'Whatever they do at Queen Street you'd better forget it, because we don't behave like that here.'

Josie thought it was most unfair of him. What did he know about Queen Street school? They didn't fight there anyway – not much – because there wasn't anything to fight about.

'And after you'd done such a nice drawing,' Mr Edwards said, more kindly. 'I was really very impressed with it, Josephine, and now you've gone and spoiled yourself.' He gave a sigh. 'I'm going to let you off this time. I don't believe in caning girls, but you've both behaved very badly and the next time I won't be so lenient . . . but there had better not be a next time. I know it's difficult for you, Josephine, at a new school.' As he looked at her Josie was aware that his eyes were on her navy-blue gymslip. 'And you, Hilda, you should be trying to make friends instead of fighting like this. Now – off you go, and remember what I've said.'

In the corridor outside the headmaster's room the two girls looked sheepishly at one another.

'Shall we?' said Hilda, not smiling, but looking at Josie in a much more affable manner.

'Shall we what?'

'Shall we be friends, like he said?'

Josie wasn't going to be won over easily, but she wanted at least one friend at this awful place, and if she made friends with Hilda the rest of the girls would most likely follow suit. 'I might,' she said nonchalantly. 'I'll have to think about it.'

* * *

'Josie's not happy at that new school,' Samuel remarked to Iris on Saturday evening, after the three children had gone to bed. 'Bertie seems to have settled down all right, but not Josie. It's funny, that . . . I thought it might have been the other way round. Bertie's much more nervous than his sister. Of course, he's got the right uniform, and that helps.' He gave his wife a meaningful look which Iris quickly countered.

'Don't you start! She's been going on about that green uniform all week. Contrary Mary she is, and no mistake. She said she didn't care, and now, because I say she's to wear the blue one up she's decided she won't.'

'I think you should give in to her about this,' said Samuel thoughtfully. 'Just this once . . . It's not just the uniform, but she might feel better if she was the same as the other girls. From what she says she doesn't seem to get on with them.'

'I'm not surprised! She'd made up her mind before she went that she wouldn't like that school.'

'I think you're being too hard on her, Iris. She says the children don't like her because she's cleverer than they are.'

'Yes, I heard her. I don't wonder they don't like her if she's showing off like that. You don't believe her, do you? Beechwood's a good school. Everybody says so.'

'Yes, as a matter of fact, I do believe her,' replied Samuel. 'A school's only as good as its teachers, and I happen to believe that the ones at Queen Street took some beating. Josie was doing very well there. Anyroad, she's my daughter . . .' The look he gave his wife was unusually ominous, '. . . and I'm telling you I'd be a lot happier if she had some nice friends at this new place, like she had at Queen Street. And the first thing to sort out is this blasted uniform. You'd better get her a proper one, and jolly soon, too! Now, think on!'

Husband and wife stared at one another doggedly and there was silence for a few moments before Iris replied. 'All right then. I'll get her one before they go back in September. It's hardly worth it now; they'll be finishing for the summer holidays in a week or two.'

But by the time September came there were other much more important things to think about. Thoughts of school uniforms, as of many other matters, paled into insignificance at the news that Britain was now at war with Germany.

And, soon after the outbreak of war, Josie did make a new friend.

Chapter 9

'Seems as though it might work against you, us having four bedrooms,' Samuel remarked to his wife on the evening of Sunday the third of September. 'You and your big house! I daresay they'll be knocking on the door before long asking us if we'll take some evacuees.'

'And d'you think I'd mind?' Iris retorted. 'You don't know me very well, Samuel Goodwin, that's all I can say, if you think I'd mind giving a home to a couple of kiddies. We've loads of room . . . as you keep reminding me. God forbid that the day should ever come when I refuse to help those who are less fortunate than I am. We've got to show a bit of Christian charity, especially now. I'm very hurt, Samuel, that you should think I wouldn't want to help.'

'Don't take on so, Iris love,' Samuel said, leaning forward in his armchair and patting her knee. 'I wasn't getting at you, honestly I wasn't. I was only saying that it's more than likely they'll ask us to take a couple of those kiddies from Liverpool, and you may well think you've got enough to do looking after our own three.'

'I daresay I have. They're a full-time job and no mistake,' Iris sighed, 'but I've got to do my bit. We all have. You'll have to do some self-sacrificing an' all, Samuel. That lawn you're so proud of'll have to go.' Iris knew that she would hate to see the velvet-smooth lawn disappear just as much as Samuel would. It had been his pride and joy since they moved here, but sacrifices would have to be made all round. 'I see the chap next door has already started digging,' she added.

'Yes, I was thinking of getting ready for one of them Anderson shelters,' said Samuel, 'and I'll dig part of the lawn up and put some vegetables in. I don't really see why I have to bother, though, not yet. Perhaps it might be best to wait and see what happens. The Government might just be panicking about something and nothing.'

'Hardly something and nothing when war has been declared,' Iris replied. 'We've all been given gas masks, and they're sending the kiddies away, so they're obviously expecting a big air attack . . . and soon an' all.' She cast an apprehensive glance towards the window, but she couldn't see out. The green damask curtains had already been drawn against the September dusk on top of the new lining of blackout material. No longer would they be able to leave their curtains open to watch the twilight deepening over the stretch of moorland and to see the twinkling street lamps and lighted windows in the next village, something Iris had loved to do. There would be no street lamps lit or windows left uncovered for the foreseeable future. 'Happen we're reasonably safe here though,' she added, 'in Haliford. I suppose we must be, or they wouldn't have sent the evacuees here, would they?'

'Haliford's safe enough,' Samuel answered. 'A darned sight safer than Liverpool will be, or Leeds or Bradford, if the raids do start. We've not much industry here, only a few woollen mills, no shipyards or big engineering works like they've got in the big cities.'

'And we're safer than most here, aren't we? On the edge of the moor,' said Iris, somewhat fearfully.

The words of Neville Chamberlain that morning, although they hadn't been entirely unexpected, had filled her with horror and dread that kept coming over her in spasms. She remembered very well the Great War, as it was now called, although it hadn't affected her all that personally. At the start of it she had been twenty and already married to Alfred Collier. He hadn't served in the war, being forty-five years of age and having a job of vital importance as a coal and haulage contractor. Her father had gone to France, but, like a bad penny, he had turned up again at the end of it all, seemingly no worse for his experiences; unlike Samuel's father who, she knew, had suffered badly from his ordeal. Iris wouldn't have cared if her father hadn't returned at all and she was sure her mother had been of the same opinion, although she had never said so.

William, one of Iris's brothers, had been killed on the Somme. She remembered that her mother had grieved – along with countless other women in the neighbourhood who had also lost their sons – and then had got on with her drab, pitiful life. For her part, Iris had hardly known her brother William at all. He had been just one of a throng of children in the hovel that she had escaped from as soon as she was able, and now she couldn't even recall his features.

She was disturbed by feelings of guilt, though, from time to time, about the uncaring attitude of her earlier years and she was determined to make amends with her new family. She had showered Frances with love and affection, and she had tried hard, too, with Josie and Bertie – and now she would give a home to some poor little evacuee children.

'I shan't wait for them to come and knock on the door,' she told Samuel. 'I shall go down to that reception place – in the church hall, I think it is – and choose two of them myself. That's all I shall have, mind you, one of each. The girl can share with Josie and the boy with Bertie. Happen I could have a brother and sister.'

'You seem to have got it all worked out.' Samuel grinned at her. 'I heard there was a train-load arrived on Friday, even before war was declared, and I daresay there'll be another lot tomorrow. Happen it'll be somebody for our Josie to pal up with,' he added thoughtfully. 'She doesn't seem as unhappy though, does she? Since she went back to school last week. I expect having the right uniform has helped.' He nodded significantly at his wife. 'I'm glad you decided to give in to her, love, just this once,' he added. 'It couldn't have been very nice for her, being an odd one out.'

'I expect the children have other things on their minds now, besides uniforms,' said Iris, 'like the rest of us.'

As her father had said, having the new uniform did help, and when Josie had returned to Beechwood school just a couple of days before war broke out, she no longer felt excluded from Hilda and Vera's gang. This was to be her final year at the Junior school, what was always spoken of in portentous tones as 'scholarship year', for in February she and her classmates would be sitting the all-important examination which would decide their futures. Josie had never even considered that she might not pass. She was confident of her capabilities and was quite sure that a place at Haliford High School – an all girls' school – would be hers without too much effort on her behalf. Anyway, that was all in the future. There were other things to think about at the moment; chiefly, the war, which everyone was saying would soon break out between Britain and Germany . . . and a new girl to sit next to in class.

The teacher in 4A didn't know everyone's names on the first day. It usually took a few days to connect the names on the register with the sea of faces sitting in front of her (or him). It was a him this time, Mr Laycock, a tall dark man, slightly balding, whom Josie thought looked about the same age as her father. He did, however, seem to know Josie's name, and he asked her to look after the new girl, Pamela Coates.

Josie remembered only too well her own first day at the place, and she immediately felt sorry for the girl as she watched her shamble, head down, to her seat next to Josie. She was dressed in a dark grey gymslip which straight away branded her as an outsider; and Josie felt her hackles rise as she saw Hilda and Vera, seated together this term at a desk across the aisle, nudge one another and grin. They were no doubt planning how they could take a rise out of the new girl, just as they had done with her, but this time, if they started their antics Josie would be ready for them.

Pamela Coates had a head of the tightest curls Josie had ever seen, like that child star, Shirley Temple, but not of the same startling blonde colour. Pamela's hair was mid-brown and her eyes were pale blue and slightly protuberant. Her pugnacious jawline and the set of her small determined mouth indicated that she might be of a rebellious nature, but she seemed decidedly cowed at the moment. Josie thought that the girl must be unhappy and she wondered why, apart from the fact, of course, that she had just come into a classroom full of strangers. She smiled at her and the new girl, uncertainly, smiled back.

'Where've you come from? Why've you come to this school?' Josie asked in a whisper, as soon as Mr Laycock had finished calling the names from his new register. But Mr Laycock was obviously a teacher who was not going to allow talking in his class. Sometimes, in some classes, there was a minor riot whenever the teacher turned his (or her) back, but Mr Laycock wasn't one to put up with that.

He rapped on his desk with a ruler. 'Stop talking! You, Josephine Goodwin, stop talking at once. That is one thing I don't allow, so you'd better all learn it right away. You can find out all about Pamela later,' he added, a little more kindly.

It was playtime before Josie had a chance to find out about Pamela Coates. It was then she learned that the girl was a sort of evacuee – a word which they were beginning to hear quite a lot and which they would hear much more before very long – but not what you might call a proper one. The true evacuees arrived in train- or bus-loads and were billeted on complete strangers, whereas Pamela had been brought to Haliford by her parents and was staying with an aunt and uncle.

'We live in Manchester, y'see,' she explained – she pronounced it Manchister – 'and me mam and dad want me out of the road before Hitler starts dropping bombs. So I've come to live with me auntie Mary and uncle Bill.' She seemed to have cheered up quite a lot now and Josie sensed that this girl could turn out to be the real friend she had longed for.

'D'you think he will?' Josie asked now.

'D'you think who'll do what?' asked Derek who, with Jimmy at his side, had wandered over for a chat.

'D'you think that Hitler'll start dropping bombs? D'you think there's really going to be a war?'

''Course there is,' said Jimmy. 'I've heard me mam and dad talking about it. Me dad's going to join the Army. There'll be bombs dropping all over t' show when old Hitler gets going. That's what me dad says. That's why she's come 'ere.' He pointed a thumb in Pamela's direction. 'You 'eard 'er, that's what she said.' He turned to Pamela. 'You're one of them 'vacuees, ain't you?'

'Yes . . . I suppose so,' Pamela answered a little sulkily.

'There'll be loads more of 'em coming soon,' added Derek. 'I've heard me mam say so. We ain't having any at our 'ouse, though. We've go too many kids already.'

'So've we,' agreed Jimmy. 'You'll be 'aving some at your 'ouse, though, Josie, you with your four bedrooms.' He spoke in a mocking tone, but he was grinning, and when Josie replied it was, likewise, good-naturedly.

'Shurrup you,' she answered, pushing at him, and he pretended to fall to the ground in an exaggerated manner.

Derek and Jimmy departed, wheeling across the yard like bomber aircraft, making the appropriate swooping and diving movements and explosive noises. In other parts of the yard, boys were pointing imaginary guns at one another and there were yells of 'Stick 'em up,' and, reeling and clutching at their chests, 'Aw . . . he's got me. I'm a goner . . .'; scenes which owed more to the cowboy and gangster films they had seen than the imminent war with the Germans.

'They're all right, aren't they?' said Pamela, as Derek and Jimmy sped away.

'Ye-eh . . . not bad,' agreed Josie. She was thinking about what they had said about the war and evacuees and bombs. She knew something about it – who didn't? – but she guessed that in her family conversation wasn't always quite as uninhibited as it was in the Clegg and Watson households, and that her father and Auntie Iris only spoke of grown-up matters when the children were safely tucked away in bed. In any event, this war, which seemed to be looming large in everyone's mind, had brought her a new friend, and for that she was thankful.

The two evacuees that Iris brought home the following Monday didn't, however, stay very long in the Goodwin household. They were a sister and brother, Betty and Johnnie, from Liverpool, aged eight and six respectively. Betty was far too young for Josie to make a friend of, whilst Johnnie, continually missing his mum, spent a lot of the time snivelling and a few times he wet the bed. Josie was surprised to see that Auntie Iris was unusually patient with them – far more so than she was with Josie – but at the end of November their mother came and took them home again. The danger they had all been anticipating with such dread hadn't materialized. It wasn't exactly a false alarm – Britain was undeniably at war – but the bombs were not falling, children were missing their mums and vice versa, and by Christmas most of the evacuees had gone home.

A few more evacuees besides Pamela had arrived to swell the numbers in the classes at Beechwood school, but not all that many. In some schools, Josie had heard, there were so many evacuees that they had to resort to part-time schooling, the regular children being taught in the morning and the evacuees in the afternoon. Josie thought that that would have been a very good idea, as did the rest of her classmates, but no such luck. Beechwood school was modern, the classrooms were large and the classes reasonably small, and the extra children were easily assimilated. Besides, by Christmas they had nearly all gone. Pamela Coates, though, had stayed, and very soon she and Josie were bosom pals.

The chief indication that there was a war on was the blackout. Josie, ever since she was a tiny girl, had loved to watch the lamplighter going on his rounds, putting his ladder against the iron arms of the lamp-post and climbing up to light the gas jets. This is what had happened when they lived in Baldwin Lane – ages ago, it now seemed – but in Gladstone Avenue and Victoria Grove the gas lamps had been lit by a more modern clockwork mechanism. And in Jubilee Gardens they were very up to the minute with electric lighting. But now all the lights had been extinguished and everyone moved around in a world of darkness. On the rare occasions that Josie did go out in the evening, always with the rest of the family, of course – returning home from Auntie Alice's or from an occasional visit to the cinema – her dad carried a large silver torch to light the way. The kerbs had white lines painted on them, and the trees that edged some of the roads were likewise painted with white stripes, like a zebra; and it was a good job you knew your way home because all the street signs had been taken down.

Her father no longer used his car for pleasure, only for work, which was why they had to walk everywhere or to use the very infrequent buses. Josie thought it was fun to travel on a bus at night, with only a dim blue light illuminating the interior. It made everyone's face look dead white, like a ghost, with purple lips, and you had to travel very slowly so as not to collide with the other traffic on the roads, although there was never very much of it, not in Haliford anyway, just a few cars and buses, all with dimmed headlights.

'Don't know why I bothered to buy that blooming car,' Samuel grumbled to Iris. 'I've only had it a few months and now I can't damn well use it.' Petrol rationing had started in September and everyone was now using 'pool' petrol which had replaced the branded makes. Petrol for commercial vehicles was dyed red to prevent its illicit use by civilians. 'I've heard there's a lot of fiddling going on, though,' Josie heard her father telling her aunt Iris. 'I've heard of some of the chaps at work straining that red petrol through a gas-mask filter to get rid of the dye. It's one way, I suppose, to get round these damned restrictions, but I wouldn't like to try it.'

'I should think not, indeed!' Iris replied vehemently. 'It would be downright unpatriotic – to say nothing of being dishonest. You've got your five gallons a month that you're entitled to and that will have to be sufficient.'

'Yes, I suppose so,' Samuel replied, somewhat doubtfully. 'I tell you what, though, Iris. If I take part in this Government scheme for free lifts – "Help Your Neighbour", it's called – then I'd be entitled to a bit more. I could happen give some of the other chaps a lift to work.'

Iris sniffed. 'Suit yourself, Samuel. As far as the children and I are concerned, we'll walk or we'll go on the bus. It's more patriotic.'

Patriotic . . . That was a word that Josie was hearing a lot recently, both at home and at school. It had been *patriotic* for her dad to dig over his nice new lawn, ready to plant vegetable seeds in the spring and to make room for an air-raid shelter. He was now, in the autumn of 1939, in the process of erecting an Anderson shelter from the bits of corrugated iron that the council workmen had left. You had to build it yourself, three feet below the ground, and there was a lot of head-scratching and sweating and occasional swearing before the thing was eventually completed.

'Blessed if I know why I've bothered,' he remarked to Iris. 'There are still no bombs falling, and I'm just about knackered with this lot.' He laughed. 'You can leave me alone tonight, lass. I'll be too tired for that there, I can tell you.'

A remark that Josie didn't entirely understand, and one which she probably wasn't meant to overhear. She knew that her dad was fed up. He had never been a gardener, not until they moved here; now he seemed to be doing nothing but dig, dig, dig, like the seven dwarfs. 'Digging for Victory', it was called. And when he wasn't digging he was out practising his fire-fighting.

Not that there were any fires to fight as yet, but it was a *patriotic* thing to do, seeing that he hadn't yet been called up.

That was another thing Josie frequently heard being discussed at school, dads being called up. As yet, not many of them had been, as the fathers of her classmates were mostly of Samuel's age group, the middle to late thirties. A few of the younger ones had already gone, and a few others, including Derek's and Jimmy's fathers, had volunteered to join the Army. But most of them were still waiting. In theory every man between the ages of eighteen and forty-one was liable for conscription, but arms, uniforms and accommodation were all in short supply, so the call-up procedure was slow.

At school it was patriotic to wear red, white and blue ribbons in your hair, to carry your gas mask at all times – this was obligatory – and to make fun of the Germans.

> Whistle while you work,
> Hitler is a twerp,
> Goering's barmy, so's his army,
> Whistle while you work,

they sang cheerfully in the school yard, or,

We're gonna hang out the washing on the Siegfried line,
Have you any dirty washing, Mother dear?

without having any real idea where or what the Siegfried line was.

However, Mr Laycock, Josie's teacher, had pinned a large map of Europe on the wall so that they did have some idea where the various countries were, and how large they were in contrast to Great Britain. Such a tiny little island it looked on the map compared with France, Germany and the vast expanse of Russia. And at home there was the *Daily Express* war map hanging in Bertie's bedroom, decorated with little coloured flags representing the various armies and their progress – the British, French, German and Russian forces – but, for the moment, nothing much seemed to be happening.

They had gas-mask practice, though, quite regularly, at school. They all trooped into the air-raid shelter, one of the Anderson type, like the one Josie's dad was trying to build at home, but much bigger, all wearing their gas masks. It was good fun really, and a welcome diversion from regular lessons, sitting in the damp, gloomy shelter reciting their twelve times table; especially when Jimmy Clegg and Derek Watson got up to their tricks.

Gas masks were strange things and everybody had them, even horses. Young children had jolly red and blue ones that looked like Mickey Mouse faces – Frances had one of those – but Josie and her brother Bertie and the rest of the school had grey ones, like the grown-ups, with a silvery-green nozzle at the end with little holes that you breathed through. There was a large perspex window for the eyes to see out of, but the moment you put it on the window clouded up and you couldn't see properly. Getting it on and off was an art which had to be practised time and time again, tucking your chin deep into the mask, then pulling the straps back over your head. It made your face hot and sweaty, and you were as red as a beetroot when you took it off. When you breathed out it made a noise like somebody breaking wind, and if you breathed out really hard you could make a very rude noise indeed. And this, of course, was what Jimmy and Derek delighted in doing, sending the rest of the class into gales of laughter.

As yet, it was all a game, and Josie, along with countless others, wondered when and if the real war would ever start. She didn't worry about it unduly, however, because it was her friendship with Pamela Coates that was occupying much of her time and her thoughts, both in and out of school.

'I'm glad our Josephine has made a new friend at any rate,' Samuel remarked to his wife one evening in October. 'It's Pamela this, Pamela that, all the time, and she doesn't grumble about school now. There's a big change in her. She seems much happier, don't you think so, love?'

'Yes, I must admit you're right,' agreed Iris. 'She's easier to deal with at home and I'm very thankful for that. She's asked me once or twice, though, about going to the pictures on a Saturday afternoon – they have a special matinée for children, you know, at the Regal – and apparently Pamela goes, and some more children from their class. To hear Josie talk it sounds as though everybody goes but her, but I know jolly well that's not true. But I've got to say that she did ask quite nicely, not pestering all the while and saying "It's not fair," like she sometimes does. She asked me again this dinner-time.'

'And what did you say?'

'I told her I'd think about it . . . that I'd talk to you.' Iris grinned at him ruefully.

'Can't see that it would do any harm for her to go,' replied Samuel. 'What have you got against it?'

'Oh, I don't know. I've always heard that it's such a rough house. Kids from . . . from all over the place go, and heaven knows what they get up to when they all get together.' Iris had been going to say, *kids from the rough area of Haliford*, but had decided not to, remembering that she herself had hailed from those same mean streets. 'I like to know where she is and what she's doing . . . and who she's with an' all,' she added. 'I think it's time we met Pamela, don't you?'

'She sounds all right to me,' said Samuel. 'Evacuee, isn't she?'

'Not exactly. She's staying with an aunt and uncle in Coronation Crescent. It's not all that far from here. I tell you what, Samuel: I could call round and see them, and if they're agreeable, perhaps Pamela could come for tea one day after school.'

'Sounds all right to me,' said Samuel again. 'Haven't you enough to do, though, with our own two . . . visitors?' He motioned towards the ceiling. The two evacuees, Betty and Johnny, were asleep upstairs with his own three children. 'Without landing yourself with another of 'em.'

'One more won't make much difference,' said Iris crisply, 'especially at tea-time. They can have jam sandwiches and I'll make 'em a jelly. You've got to put yourself out a bit sometimes for your kids. Anyroad, it won't matter to you – you'll be at work.'

'Whatever you say, dear,' said Samuel, turning back to his *Haliford Chronicle*.

'Auntie Iris . . . Auntie Iris . . .' There was an impassioned cry from the room above. 'Come quick . . . I think I'm going to be sick.'

Iris sighed as she went up the stairs. If little Johnny wasn't 'going to be sick' – which he rarely was – he was wetting the bed, or crying for his mum, or forgetting to wipe his runny nose. He was enough to try the patience of a saint, and Iris knew that she was no saint. At times her tolerance was stretched to the limit, but she tried so hard not to let these two poor little mites know it. All the same, she would be relieved if their mother decided to take them home again.

'I think they're more likely to be her great-aunt and uncle,' Iris told her husband when she returned from her visit to Pamela's relations. 'Sixty-five if they're a day, both of them. A very nice couple though – Mr and Mrs Meredith – and it seems as though they're bending over backward to let that young Pamela have everything she wants. Mrs Meredith says she doesn't want the child to feel homesick, so she admits that she's spoiling her a bit. I only hope she doesn't live to regret it. It doesn't do any good. You always find that your chickens come home to roost when you spoil children.'

Iris tried to ignore Samuel's raised eyebrows. She was very well aware of what he was thinking . . . that she spoiled their Frances. Well, what if she did? She was an adorable little poppet, dainty and pretty and so affectionate, and she was showing no signs of being overindulged, no nasty temper or peevishness. Samuel wouldn't comment though. It was very rarely that he questioned her handling of the children; he wouldn't dare to do so when he knew full well that, more often than not, he left her alone to deal with them.

'We don't know what this Pamela's really like, do we?' he commented. 'Not until we've met her. What did they say about her coming for tea? Is it all right?'

'Yes, she's coming on Thursday after school. And I've agreed to let Josie go to the pictures with her on Saturday afternoon. It's only for a couple of hours. They finish long before it gets dark, because of this wretched blackout . . . But I'm not sure whether I've done the right thing . . .' Iris added doubtfully.

'She'll be all right,' said Samuel. 'She's a sensible girl, our Josie, and you can't have her tied to your apron-strings for ever. You've got to let her find her feet. Don't worry . . . she'll come to no harm.'

The idea of Josie ever being tied to anyone's apron-strings, especially Iris's, was laughable, but all the same, Iris knew what he meant. She and Josie may not have hit it off all the time, but Iris had always tried to keep a protective eye on the girl and to steer her in the right direction, even if it meant, at times, curtailing her freedom. Josie had been entrusted to her care and Iris intended to make a good job of bringing her up; and part of that care involved making sure she chose the right sort of friends.

And, after she had met Pamela Coates, Iris was far from sure. There was nothing that she could put her finger on. The girl was neat and clean, in a new green uniform that her aunt had bought for her so that she would be just like the others at school. She was well behaved and polite, saying 'please' and 'thank you' and passing the plates of jam sandwiches and buns to the younger children . . . rather too readily, perhaps? After all, it wasn't her family . . . And she had said, 'Thank you for having me,' so nicely when her uncle, beaming proudly, came to take her home.

'It's a pleasure, dear. Do come again,' Iris had said, somewhat bemusedly. There was something in those pale blue eyes that Iris couldn't quite fathom, a knowing look that made Iris feel as though the girl was laughing at her. One thing was certain; Pamela Coates had an old head on young shoulders. This was something that Iris, in the past, had sometimes said about Josie. But Josie, for all her bravado and bluster, was still a child at heart, although she had been forced to grow up pretty quickly, poor lass, when her mother died, Iris thought. She was surprised to find herself thinking of Josie as a 'poor lass', just as she had been surprised at the surge of affection she felt for her as she watched her at the tea table, so proud to be able to entertain her new friend.

Later that same evening as she pondered about Pamela Çoates, Iris felt that Josie was a babe in arms compared with that one. But it was too late, now, to retract about the Saturday afternoon pictures. She had already promised Josie that she could go.

Chapter 10

Josie's experience of the silver screen had been, up to the present time, somewhat limited. They went to the cinema occasionally as a family, as a very special treat. Recently they had seen *Snow White and the Seven Dwarfs* and *The Wizard of Oz*, but both times Frances had nearly spoiled it by screaming every time the wicked witch appeared. Bertie, too, had hid his head at the sight of the green-faced witch in *The Wizard of Oz*, but Josie had loved it all. She thought it was the best picture she had ever seen, far better than that soppy Shirley Temple and her *Good Ship Lollipop*, or Charlie Chaplin, whom Josie thought was too silly to laugh at. She had sat on the edge of her seat, entranced at the antics of the scarecrow, the tin man and the cowardly lion, to say nothing of Dorothy with her gleaming red shoes. Josie decided there and then that she wanted a pair just like them. Perhaps for Christmas. She would have to ask Auntie Iris . . . She had to admit, though, that she hadn't realized that the scarecrow, the tin man and the lion were really the three men from the farm, not until Auntie Iris explained it to her.

Auntie Iris had been quite like a child herself after that picture, talking about it for days afterwards, and Josie had found that, for once, she felt quite close to her stepmother. And she was feeling kindly disposed to her now for allowing her to go to the Saturday matinée with Pamela.

Dad had insisted on taking her, though, to her annoyance, because there were one or two roads to cross once you got through the park. She didn't want to look a baby in front of her friend, but she was surprised to see that Pamela's uncle had also escorted his niece to the cinema, in spite of Pamela's boasting that she went there and back on her own. The two men decided, however, that perhaps the girls could be trusted to come home by themselves, if they were very careful and promised to come straight back.

Josie had been to the Regal cinema before, but it was a vastly different place on a Saturday afternoon, filled to capacity with a hoard of stamping, yelling children. Never had she heard such a din, but it abated somewhat when the orange velvet curtains were drawn back and the adverts appeared on the screen. There was a concerted cheer, then the clattering of hundreds of tip-up seats as the youthful audience settled itself in readiness for the forthcoming entertainment. The adverts were not very interesting, being mainly for local shops, or for decorators, plumbers, hairdressers and the like. There was a lot of whispering and giggling and rustling of sweet papers, until the first certificate appeared on the screen when there was another deafening cheer.

The first film was a Mickey Mouse cartoon, followed by two 'interest' films. One was a nature film about woodland creatures – 'Boring, boring . . .' Josie heard two boys next to her telling one another in loud voices – and the second one about the manufacture of wool, all the processes from the sheep's back to the finished cloth. It should have been of particular interest to the Yorkshire lads and lasses, many of whom would, eventually, end up in a woollen mill, but

Josie's neighbours seemed to find it even more wearisome than the first one. 'It's like being at blinking school,' she heard one of them remark.

Then the orange curtains closed, the lights came on and it was the interval. Usherettes with trays of ice-creams, sweets and chocolates stood at the front of the auditorium and there was a stampede as the children who were fortunate enough to have a few pennies to spend hurled themselves down the aisles. There was nothing as dignified as a queue, just a mass of shoving bodies and thrusting arms, but the usherettes, who had seen it many times before, managed to serve everyone without losing their tempers, before the lights dimmed again. Josie and Pamela, who each had three pennies to spend, only just had time to scurry back to their seats and take the cardboard lids off their tubs before the certificate announcing the first of the 'big' pictures came on to the screen. Josie scooped up a morsel of ice-cream with her tiny wooden spoon, savoured its delicious creaminess on her tongue, then turned to grin at her friend.

'Isn't it good?' she whispered happily, then settled back to watch the antics of Laurel and Hardy. She thought they were rather silly really, though not quite as daft as Charlie Chaplin, but she laughed uproariously along with the other children at the buffoonery of the big fat one and the little thin one in their absurd bowler hats. The last film of the afternoon featured Tom Mix, the cowboy. Josie cheered herself hoarse, though she wasn't sure why, as he and his rivals chased along the roofs of trains, pursued one another on horseback and fired endless rounds of bullets from behind rocks. There was a concerted groan from the audience when, as the hero lay on the ground, presumably in the throes of death, the announcement flashed up on the screen that the epic was 'to be continued next week.'

It was all over for today, and Josie found the return to the real world a trifle disconcerting. She blinked as her eyes adjusted to the serene grey light of an October afternoon.

'Dead good, wasn't it?' said Pamela, tucking her arm through her friend's as they walked along the street. 'I'm ever so glad you could come. What shall we do now? Shall we go round Woolie's? It's only in the next street. I've been with me auntie Mary. Come on, I'll show you.'

'I know where it is. I don't need you to tell me!' retorted Josie. Honestly! She'd lived in Haliford for years and years – ever since she was born, in fact – and there was Pamela, who was only an evacuee, carrying on as though she owned the place. 'We can't go there anyway,' she continued. 'I've no money to spend. Besides, we promised we'd go straight home.'

'Pooh! Who's bothered about that? We'd only be a few minutes.' Pamela stopped in her tracks, looking defiantly at her friend.

'I don't care. I'm not going. If we don't do as we're told they might not let us go again.' Josie started to walk away. 'My auntie Iris can be awful if I don't do what she says, you've no idea.'

'Oh . . . all right then.' Pamela quickened her steps and caught up with Josie again. 'We'll go straight back. P'raps we could go next week . . . shall we?'

'We might . . . but we might not,' Josie answered edgily, and there was silence until they had crossed the road that led to the park.

'Why d'you call your mum Auntie Iris?' asked Pamela, breaking the silence. She was scuffling her feet through the piles of fallen leaves as they made their way across Victoria Park.

''Cause she's not my mum,' replied Josie irritably. She was still feeling cross with Pamela for trying to get her into bother. 'She's my auntie.'

'Not a real auntie though. She's married to your dad, isn't she? Why don't you call her Mum like your Bertie does, and your little sister? They call her Mum, I've heard them. Why don't you?'

'And why don't you mind your own business?' Josie snapped. 'I call her Auntie Iris 'cause it's what I've always called her. I remember my own mum, you see,' she added, less angrily.

'What happened to her?'

'She died when Frances was a baby. She had the baby, then Auntie Alice told me she'd died.'

'In childbirth?'

'What d'you mean?' Josie stared at her friend in puzzlement. This was a word she hadn't heard before, but then Pamela did seem to know an awful lot of things that Josie didn't know.

Pamela gave an exasperated sigh. 'She died having the baby, didn't she?'

'I suppose so . . . I don't know. Oh, shut up about it, can't you?' Josie kicked moodily at a pile of leaves, scattering them far and wide across the path. She didn't know why she was so cross, except that she hadn't thought much about her real mother for ages. She had been getting on quite well with Auntie Iris and now Pamela had stirred it all up again.

'Sorry, kid.' Pamela got hold of her arm again. 'I'm dead nosy, me. My auntie Mary says it's a wonder I don't trip over me nose, I'm such a busybody.'

Josie grinned back at her. ''S all right. Anyroad . . . me dad married me auntie Iris and that was that. I don't suppose our Bertie and Frances remember our mum. I know Frances doesn't.'

'Your auntie Iris is dead old, isn't she?'

'I don't know . . . is she?' Josie stared at her friend again, feeling bewildered. It was something she had never really considered. Auntie Iris was just . . . Auntie Iris.

'She's older than your dad, anyway.'

'Yes . . . I suppose so.'

'She's fat an' all.'

'She's not as fat as she used to be,' she retorted. 'She decided she'd got to lose some weight . . . a few years ago.' It was on the tip of Josie's tongue to tell Pamela about the drawings, but she thought better of it. Pamela Coates was too nosy by far. 'I don't think she's all that fat now,' she added loyally.

'She's a lot fatter than your dad though, and a lot older,' Pamela persisted. 'I wonder if they *do it* . . . you know.'

'Do what?' Josie frowned and shook her head uncertainly. Pamela had really lost her now.

'Do *that*, silly. What people do to make babies . . . but it doesn't always make 'em. You know, what people do in bed. I should think your auntie Iris is too old.'

'Why? What do they do?'

'D'you mean to say you don't know?'

Josie shook her head. 'No, I don't think so . . .' She stared, wide-eyed and open-mouthed as Pamela told her, but she didn't believe it. It was just ridiculous. Pamela told whopping lies sometimes. But Josie didn't want to start an argument, not about *that*. 'Oh . . . I see,' she said, trying to sound as if she wasn't all that bothered. 'How d'you know, anyway? Who told you?'

'Me mum,' Pamela answered brightly. 'She tells me lots of things. She's right young, is me mum, not an old codger like Auntie Mary – or your auntie Iris. She was only eighteen when she had me, and me dad was twenty. I think they had to get married 'cause I was coming, but they've never actually said so. I just guessed.'

Josie was lost again. Nobody *had* to get married, did they? You got married because you wanted to. There seemed to be a heck of a lot of things she knew nothing about. 'Have you got any brothers and sisters?' Josie asked now. She had never heard Pamela speak of any, nor of her mum and dad, since that first day when she arrived at school.

'Nope,' said Pamela. 'There's only me. Dad's joined the RAF now, like old Laycock, and Mum's working at a factory making aeroplanes. She gets a lot of money working nights, so that's why I'm staying with Auntie Mary.'

'D'you miss your mum?' asked Josie, remembering how she had missed her own mother at first, though not as much now. Pamela's mother hadn't died, of course, so it was different.

'Not much,' replied Pamela. 'She used to wallop me, me mum.' She rubbed her bottom ruefully. 'But Auntie Mary doesn't. She's dead soft, me auntie Mary. I can do what I like and she never says anything.'

They had reached the other side of the park now, and at the corner of the next street they went their separate ways.

'Ta-ra, Josie, see you Monday,' shouted Pamela as she skipped away.

'Yes . . . see you,' Josie replied. Her mind was in a turmoil as she walked along Jubilee Gardens, full of babies and people getting married and mysterious – happenings. She remembered her mother, all fat and bloated and poorly-looking – fatter even than Auntie Iris – and Josie had known, though nobody had told her, that it was because she was going to have a baby. But Josie had never had any idea how it had got there and she hadn't bothered to try and find out. Now, as she thought about her mum and dad, then her dad and Auntie Iris, together – in bed – she felt uneasy.

'Hello, dear. Have you enjoyed yourself?' called Auntie Iris cheerily, as Josie let herself in through the back door.

'Yes, it was smashing,' replied Josie, her disturbing thoughts already receding. For there on the table was a plate of Auntie Iris's lovely treacly parkin and, unless she was very much mistaken, she could smell a steak and kidney pie cooking in the oven.

Josie had never wanted to go to Woolworth's in the first place. She had known that it was being disobedient because she had promised to go straight home, but she hadn't liked to say no to Pamela again. For one thing, she didn't want to walk home on her own through the park – it was a lonely, scary sort of place on an autumn afternoon – and Pamela was determined to go to Woolworth's whether she, Josie, went with her or not. But when she realized what Pamela had in mind, Josie was horrified.

'I've only got threepence to spend,' said Josie as they entered the store which, to her eyes, was like an Aladdin's cave. It was full of all kinds of tempting goods; sweets and chocolates, of course, but also a myriad of other delights. Pencils, coloured crayons, rubbers, notebooks and drawing-books with crisp clean pages, just asking to be written on; ribbons in a multitude of dazzling hues, hairslides and combs; perfumed soap and bath salts in fancy jars; yo-yos, rubber balls, shuttlecocks, whips and tops, lead soldiers and celluloid dolls . . .

There were boring things as well, like nails and screws and electric light-bulbs, spades and plant pots and packets of seeds. Woolworth's was a store for everyone, as familiar to Josie with its distinctive red sign as the Co-op was, and no visit to town was complete without going there. Josie always saved some of her Saturday spending money for Woolie's. She hadn't been for a few weeks, though. Her Saturday afternoon jaunts to the Regal had curtailed her trips to town and also her visits to her aunt Alice; but, as Iris had told her, she couldn't have everything, and she had made her choice.

Now, as she and Pamela entered the store which, previously, she had loved so much, Josie was wondering if she had done the right thing. For one awful moment she wondered if she might encounter Auntie Iris in here. Oh crikey! She started to feel all trembly at the thought of it. No, she told herself, by this time Auntie Iris would be safely at home, getting the tea ready. Anyway, it wasn't as if she was doing anything wrong, going to Woolworth's. It wasn't a crime . . . except that she had promised to go straight home. But it was when Pamela replied to her remark about only having threepence to spend that Josie felt the first real stirrings of alarm.

'So've I,' said Pamela. 'Stingy old Auntie Mary wouldn't give me any more today.' Josie didn't answer, as she felt like doing, that she thought Pamela's auntie gave her everything she asked for. She just wanted to get her pennies spent as quickly as possible and get out of the place. 'Anyroad, I shan't let that worry me,' Pamela went on. 'If I want summat else, I shall just take it.'

'What?' Josie, in her horror, shouted much louder than she intended doing. 'What d'you mean? You can't—'

'Shurrup, you silly fool.' Pamela gave her a shove. 'We don't want everybody looking at us.' But the Saturday afternoon shoppers didn't appear to be taking any notice of the two girls. 'Come on, let's spend our money.' Pamela marched over to the sweet counter and Josie, feeling sick by this time, followed her.

'One of those, please,' said Pamela politely to the shop assistant, pointing to a wheel of liquorice with a purple aniseed ball in the centre, 'an' I'll have a sherbet dab . . . and two ounces of pear drops.' The assistant dropped the pink and yellow sweets, one by one, into the scales, then, when she turned her back to pop them into a cone-shaped bag, Pamela gave Josie a nudge. 'Watch,' she mouthed. And Josie watched, almost rooted to the spot with fright, as Pamela, as deft as a conjuror with a rabbit up his sleeve, reached out her hand, took a bar of Cadbury's chocolate and quickly secreted it in her coat pocket. Then, still smiling brightly, she handed her three pennies to the assistant in exchange for her purchases.

'It's your turn now,' Pamela said to Josie. 'Tell the lady what you want, and for goodness' sake, hurry up . . . We promised our mums we'd be home at four o'clock,' she added, as though butter wouldn't melt in her mouth.

The assistant smiled very kindly. 'What would you like, dear?' she asked Josie.

Josie didn't want any sweets. She felt that they would choke her, but she knew it might look funny if she didn't spend her money. Listlessly she pointed to a Fry's chocolate cream bar, some liquorice shoelaces and a penny bar of vivid pink spearmint toffee.

'Come on,' she said, tugging at Pamela's arm. 'Let's get

out of here. It'll be getting dark soon and Auntie Iris'll be really cross. We're ever so late.'

'We're not,' Pamela retorted, pointing to the big clock on the wall. 'Look, it's only quarter to four. We've only been in here a few minutes. It won't be dark for ages yet. Anyway, I've not finished me shopping.' She grinned wickedly. 'I want to look at them hairslides.'

'No . . . don't, Pamela. Let's go home.'

'Leave go!' Pamela shrugged herself away from Josie's restraining hand. 'You go home if you want to, you big soft baby, but I'm going over here.'

She strode away and Josie, sick at heart, knew that there was nothing else she could do but follow her. She didn't watch what Pamela did – she didn't dare – but she knew that when they walked out of the shop there was, as well as the stolen Cadbury's bar, a pair of pretty blue hairslides, which Pamela had previously admired, hidden deep in the girl's pocket.

'That's terribly wicked, what you did,' Josie admonished her friend as they walked across the park. Josie hadn't spoken for several minutes, anxious to put as much ground as possible between them and Woolworth's, a store which, now, she was sure she would never want to go inside again. 'It's stealing. You've broken one of the Ten Commandments. It says in the Bible "Thou shalt not steal", and God'll be ever so angry with you.'

Pamela burst out laughing. 'Where've you heard stuff like that?'

'At Sunday school, of course, where I go every Sunday,' Josie answered, a trifle piously. 'Don't you go?'

'Nope.' Pamela unconcernedly took a flying leap in the air, trying to touch one of the lower branches of a huge sycamore tree, now almost denuded of its leaves. 'I've never been to Sunday school, me. I'm not a goody-goody like you. Me mum never sent me, and Auntie Mary's a Catholic, so Mum told her she hadn't to take me to church with her. So I don't go anywhere.'

'Why did your mum say that?' asked Josie. She knew a bit about the Catholics – Roman Catholics was their real name – and she'd heard both her aunt Alice and her aunt Iris going on about them. She gathered that they didn't entirely approve of them, but it was Josie's view now that Pamela would be better going to some sort of a church, even a Catholic one, than none at all, if she was going to carry on stealing from Woolworth's.

''Cause me mum doesn't like 'em,' replied Pamela. 'They believe all sorts of potty things. Anyroad, they have to go to confession. Me auntie goes every Saturday, telling the priest what she's done wrong and asking him to forgive her. You wouldn't catch me doing that.'

'But I don't suppose your auntie does anything really bad,' said Josie, feeling perplexed, 'so why does she have to say she's sorry? That's what confession means, doesn't it? Saying you're sorry?'

Pamela shrugged. 'Don't ask me. But she goes. Not Uncle Bill, though. He's not one of them.'

Josie couldn't help thinking that Mrs Meredith, Pamela's auntie Mary, would be horrified if she knew the tricks that her beloved niece got up to. She was small and round and kindly, rather like Auntie Alice, but a lot older. It had come as a surprise to Josie, just now, to find out that the woman was a Catholic, though she wasn't sure why she should be so astonished. Except that she knew that members of her own church, including both her aunts, devoutly low church, all of them, considered the Catholics to be very peculiar. 'Too much like Rome,' she had heard Auntie

Alice say, after a visiting clergyman had lowered his head and crossed himself when reciting the creed.

And Catholics were disapproved of because they burned incense in their churches, said their prayers in Latin instead of the good old King's English, and had hoards of children. Josie didn't think it was just the Catholics, though, that had big families. Jimmy Clegg and Derek Watson both had loads of brothers and sisters and they weren't Catholics . . . at least, she didn't think they were. The Catholics in Haliford went to a different school, most of them, and wore brown blazers with yellow braid. It was all a great puzzlement, as were a lot of the things that grown-ups got into such a stew about. But Josie liked Pamela's auntie, Catholic or not, and she thought that Pamela was letting her down by behaving so badly.

'You can come with me, if you like,' she said now.

'Where to?'

'To Sunday school. I'll ask me dad if he'll take you with us in the car. There isn't much room, but we could all squash up. Me and Bertie go every Sunday morning and our Frances goes in the crèche while me dad and Auntie Iris are in church. It used to be Sunday afternoon, but they've changed it to morning now, 'cause they have the evening service in the afternoon 'cause of the blackout.'

'I don't know what you're chirruping on about,' said Pamela, laughing, 'and I don't want to go. No fear! Anyroad, I don't suppose Auntie Mary 'ud let me. She probably doesn't think much of your lot. What are they? Methodists?'

'No, of course not,' said Josie indignantly. 'It's a Church of England, St Luke's. You know, the one on the hill, the other side of town. We used to go there when we lived in Baldwin Lane, and the other houses . . . so we still go. It's a low church,' she added, somewhat uncertainly, repeating what she had heard her aunt Iris say.

'How can it be low? You said it was on a hill,' said Pamela, bursting out laughing. 'You're daft, you, Josie Goodwin. You don't know what you're talking about.'

'Oh yes I do,' said Josie crossly. 'That's what they said, my auntie Alice and auntie Iris, and they know a lot better than you, Pamela Coates.'

'Oh, you are in a way with yourself today, aren't you?' sneered Pamela. 'All because you're too scared to pinch a bar of chocolate.'

'I'm not scared! I think it's wrong, that's all,' said Josie, feeling tears of frustration springing to her eyes. She blinked them away rapidly. If Pamela saw them she would laugh more than ever.

''Tisn't wrong,' said Pamela blithely. 'Mr Woolworth's got pots of money. Me mum told me. He's a millionaire, so how can it be wrong to pinch a bar of chocolate from a bloke who's got millions of pounds? I bet he's got millions and millions of bars of chocolate in his house, so he's not going to miss one. Anyway, I'm only doing what Robin Hood did.'

'Robin Hood? What's he got to do with it?'

'He stole from the rich to give to the poor, didn't he? Well, that's what I'm doing.'

'But you haven't given it to anyone,' Josie retorted. 'You're going to eat it yourself.'

'How d'you know I am? I might be going to give it away for all you know. I might give it to Auntie Mary for looking after me.'

'But she's not poor . . .'

'She is compared with that Mr Woolworth,' Pamela grinned. 'On second thoughts I'll eat it myself.' She fished the bar of chocolate out of her coat pocket, tore off the purple wrapper and threw it on the ground, then broke off a piece. 'Here you are. You can have this.'

'No, thank you,' said Josie primly. 'I'm not going to eat that. It's stolen. I've got some sweets of my own.' She took out her bar of pink spearmint toffee, pushed back the wax paper and took a bite. The stiff confection stuck to her teeth and she chewed hard for a few moments, trying to ignore Pamela sniggering away at her side. 'What d'you think you're laughing at, anyway?' she asked indignantly, when she had swallowed the spearmint.

'That stuff, what you've just ate,' giggled Pamela. 'It makes you wee all pink.'

Josie, in spite of herself, burst out laughing. She, too, had noticed that phenomenon. 'Oh, Pamela, you are awful!' she said, staggering across the path in the throes of hilarity. 'It does though, doesn't it?'

The two girls gave another shriek of laughter, then they continued along the path arm in arm, the best of friends again.

Dusk fell early on those late October afternoons, and as Josie watched her aunt Iris draw the blackout blinds, then the curtains, before switching on the lights, she couldn't help thinking that the darkness might work in her favour. There was no way that they would allow her to be out in the dark, so her dad might suggest he should meet her from the cinema in future. That would put an end to the visits to Woolworth's. Or Josie might even decide not to go at all next week. She could go to her auntie Alice's instead. She didn't want Pamela thinking she was a softie, though. *You're a big soft baby* . . . That's what Pamela had said. *You're a goody-goody.* And that had hurt.

Chapter 11

Josie felt as though the lollipop was burning a hole in her coat pocket. Ever since she had taken it from the sweet counter and hidden it away it seemed to be making its presence felt, to be shouting out to everyone they passed in the street, 'Hey, look everybody. I've been stolen. Josie Goodwin's pinched me from Woolworth's.' It wasn't as if she even liked lollipops – they were pretty boring as sweets went; just like a big fruit drop on a stick, and Josie hated ordinary fruit drops – but she'd had to accept Pamela's dare. She'd had to . . . or else Pamela would have done something unbelievably awful. She'd said she would . . .

The afternoon had started off so well. Josie's original idea, that it might be too dark for them to come home on their own, had come to nothing as the cinema had changed the time of the matinée. It now started at one o'clock instead of one-thirty because of the early dusk and blackout, but there was still ample time for a trip to Woolworth's. So Josie had decided to come clean, not about Pamela's stealing, of course, but about the visit to the shop. She had asked Auntie Iris if she could go there with Pamela as they wanted to do their Christmas shopping, and Auntie Iris had said yes, provided she came straight home afterwards before the blackout.

Josie had half a crown to spend on presents for her

family – she had been saving up for ages out of her Saturday 'spends' – and throughout the picture show she kept feeling in her pocket to make sure that the large silver coin was still there. She knew that Pamela had some money as well, so maybe today her friend wouldn't be tempted to get up to her tricks.

Josie bought four presents – for her dad, Auntie Iris, Bertie and Frances – which didn't take very long because she already had a good idea of what she wanted. For Auntie Iris she bought a powder puff in the centre of a pretty gauzy handkerchief; Iris was forever powdering her shiny nose. A red leather diary for her dad; two lead farm animals for Bertie's toy farm, a cow and a sheep to add to his growing collection. (There was a splendid array of toy soldiers on the counter, but Bertie, unlike a lot of boys, was not very keen on soldiers.) And a tiny celluloid baby doll sitting in a pink bath for Frances.

That was all that Josie could afford today; presents for Auntie Alice and her family would have to wait a while until she had saved up again. But she was very pleased with her purchases and she packed them away in the space at the top of her shiny blue gas-mask case. The cardboard box that the gas mask came in had long since fallen to pieces and now the children in Josie's class vied with one another as to who had the poshest case.

'There, I've finished now,' she said with a satisfied smile as she fastened the two buckles. She nodded towards the clock on the wall. 'We'd better be going,' she said, beginning to walk hurriedly towards the shop entrance. 'It's half past three and it'll be dark soon. I promised Auntie Iris I wouldn't be late.' If she could just get Pamela out of the shop – quickly – then she would be able to breathe again. And Pamela appeared to have finished her shopping. She had bought a pencil sharpener and a red hair ribbon and three gob-stoppers – all for herself – and had seemed very amused at Josie's suggestion that she should buy a present for her auntie Mary.

But now Pamela refused to budge. She stood stock-still in the aisle between the toy counter and the sweet counter, her hands on her hips, grinning maliciously at Josie. 'What's the bloomin' hurry?' she asked. 'I've never known anybody like you, forever harping on about it getting dark and your silly old auntie Iris.' Her tone was mocking and Josie began to feel sick again, just like she had done last week. 'Anyway, just 'cause you've finished your rotten old shopping, Josie Goodwin, it doesn't mean that I have. And you know you've got to wait for me . . . 'cause "Auntie Iris says I haven't to go home on my own,"' she taunted.

'All right then . . . but for goodness' sake, hurry up,' said Josie miserably, not wanting to start an argument in the middle of the shop and have everybody looking at them. 'What d'you want, anyroad?'

'A bar of that nice smelly soap, for me auntie Mary,' said Pamela brightly. 'I've decided to get her a present, like you said.' But Josie soon discovered to her horror – although she had already guessed as much – that Pamela had no intention of paying for the soap. Quick as a flash the bar of soap in its gay rose-patterned packet was lifted from the counter and into Pamela's pocket. And the assistant, serving a customer at the other end, never even turned her head.

'Now it's your turn.' Pamela nodded at Josie, and she wasn't smiling now. 'Go on . . . you take something. It's dead easy – and I'm not going to go out of the shop until you've done it.'

'Don't be so daft,' said Josie in a whisper, but a very

emphatic one. 'I've told you, I won't do it. It's wrong. Oh, come on, Pam. Let's go.' To her dismay Josie could feel tears pricking at her eyelids. 'It's wrong, but I won't tell anybody what *you've* done, honest I won't.'

'You'd better not, kid, if you know what's good for you!' Josie had never heard such menace in her friend's voice before, and when she looked at Pamela, half fearfully, she could see that the pale blue eyes were gleaming with spite. But Josie couldn't for the life of her understand why. She had thought they were such good friends. 'An' I've told you, I'm not leaving here until you've done it.' Pamela leaned close to her and in that moment Josie was really terrified. 'Go on . . . I dare you!'

But still, in spite of her fear of Pamela, Josie resisted. 'No – I won't. I can't.'

'Oh yes you will,' sneered Pamela. 'You've got to accept a dare. Everybody knows that. You can't not accept a dare.' This was the unwritten code in the playground at Beechwood; but they were not at school now and so Josie stood her ground.

'I'm not doing it. I don't care how much you dare me—'

'If you don't do it I shall tell Jimmy Clegg that you love him, that you're potty about him . . .'

'I'm not! Don't talk so daft, Pamela Coates.' In her frustration and anger – and fright – Josie heard her voice getting louder. The other shoppers were looking at her. 'I'm not! I don't love him,' she repeated in a hoarse whisper. 'Don't you dare tell him.'

'Huh! If you don't love him, then why are you always drawing pictures of him?'

'Because he asked me to. He wanted one to give to his gran. Anyroad, what the heck's it got to do with you?'

'You love him, you love him,' taunted Pamela. 'I've seen you looking at him, all soppy, and if you don't do it I shall tell him. I shall tell Derek Watson an' all. An' I'll tell Hilda Ormerod and Vera Brown, and all the class'll laugh at you 'cause you love a snotty-nosed boy.'

'He's not got a snotty nose!' shouted Josie, feeling the dreaded tears begin to overflow. 'Oh, stop it, Pamela. I don't love him. I don't – and you're not to tell him. Please say you won't.' She knew that she was pleading now, but she had to make Pamela see reason. 'Don't . . . please.'

'All right then. But you've got to do what I say.'

Josie nodded numbly. She knew now that there was no other way. And they had to get out of there, fast, or she'd be in the most awful trouble with Auntie Iris. She glanced at the clock again and was amazed to see that it was still only twenty-five minutes to four. She seemed to have been arguing with Pamela for hours. Scarcely knowing what she was doing she walked towards the sweet counter, Pamela grinning wickedly at her side.

The lollipops were the first thing Josie saw, right at the front of the counter. The assistant was serving a lady at the other end and, at that moment, there was no one else around. Josie reached out and quickly snatched at a red lollipop, all the while expecting to feel a hand on her shoulder and to hear a huge policeman saying, 'Hello, hello; what have we got here?' That, or a thunderous voice from heaven – the voice of an angry God – publicly condemning her for her wickedness. But nothing like that happened and the lollipop was soon hidden away in the depths of the pocket of Josie's gaberdine mac.

'There! I told you it was dead easy, didn't I?' said Pamela in a gleeful voice, far too loudly for Josie's liking.

'Shhh! Shut up!' hissed Josie. 'Somebody'll hear you. We'll get caught.'

'Pooh! 'Course we won't.' Pamela looked at her scornfully. 'Nobody's listening. And nobody's watching. I'll bet they get tons of stuff pinched here, they're so stupid.'

'Anyway, I'm going now,' said Josie. 'I've done what you said and you can't stop me. I don't care if I have to walk home on my own. I'm going.' She started to scurry towards the shop door as though all the demons in hell were chasing her. And Pamela followed.

Josie hardly spoke to her friend on their way home through the town streets and across the park. 'Ta-ra, see you Monday,' she mumbled when they reached the end of Jubilee Gardens; then she walked away, turning every now and again and looking back over her shoulder until the figure of Pamela had disappeared round the corner. Then, after making sure that there was no one around, and hoping against hope that no nosy neighbours were peering out of their windows, Josie knelt down at the kerbside and shoved the offending lollipop between the bars of a drain cover. Only then could she breathe freely again.

She was quiet for the rest of the day, worrying about the next week and what would happen then, but Auntie Iris didn't seem to notice. She worried on and off for a few days, but she need not have done so because Auntie Alice called round and invited them all to tea the following Saturday to celebrate Uncle Jack's birthday. Then the Saturday after that there was a Christmas fair and sale of work at St Luke's, the church they all attended, and Josie just had to go to that.

Then, before they knew where they were, Christmas was upon them, with all the excitement – in spite of there being a war on – of shopping and gift-wrapping and baking. Iris had always made all her own mincemeat, puddings and cakes. She had put by a good store of dried fruit and sugar before the war started; this was condemned in some people's eyes as hoarding, but who cared? As far as Iris was concerned it was every man for himself, and the time to do without was when you couldn't get it. She had forgotten, for the moment, her former patriotic fervour; you had to make an exception for Christmas. And if she was surprised at Josie's willingness to help with the preparations this year she made no comment. Relations between the two of them were, for the moment, very cordial.

And after Christmas, as invariably happened in the hills and dales of Yorkshire, came the snow. The January of 1940, however, was more severe than normal and nobody with any sense ventured any further than they were forced to. For two days traffic was at a standstill and, to the children's delight, the schools were closed. The whole of the town of Haliford and the surrounding hills lay under a thick white blanket. Everyday sounds – the clang of the looms, sometimes heard through the open mill windows, the rumble of the big red buses in the town centre and the distant clatter of the trains – were strangely muffled, and in this silent white world you could almost imagine you were living at the North Pole.

The three Goodwin children built an enormous snowman in the back garden, near to the recently completed, but not yet used, Anderson shelter. Samuel rooted out an old sledge that he had had as a boy and the whole family trudged to the hills above Victoria Park, where Josie and Bertie – the latter somewhat tremulously – joined the other children of the neighbourhood whizzing down the snow-covered slopes. Frances, not quite four, was deemed by Iris to be too young to take part, but she stood there quite contentedly in her little red boots and pixie hood, holding on to her mother's hand. Occasionally she gave a shout of alarm as one or another of the sledges came to grief on the swift descent, tumbling the occupants out into a deep drift of snow, far too soft for them to be hurt very much.

When Samuel called out that it was time to go home Josie ran back happily to her family, dragging the sledge behind her, while Bertie, far less convinced of the bliss of the expedition, trudged along in her footprints. But for Josie this was joy such as she hadn't experienced for a long time.

First of all there was that exhilarating feeling of whooshing down the slope with Bertie's arms clinging tightly round her waist; then, the glorious sight of the setting sun, a glowing red ball low in the sky, painting the glistening silvery snow a pinky orange; her little sister's rosy cheeks and shining eyes and the red pixie hood that made her look like an adorable little elf – in that moment Josie felt nothing but affection for Frances. In fact, she felt that she loved everything and everybody, even Auntie Iris, not least because she knew that they were now going home to one of her special steak pies which had been left gently cooking in the oven. Her recent problems – Pamela and her recent peevishness, to say nothing of her stealing – seemed very far away.

She wondered idly, as they walked home, where Jimmy and Derek were this afternoon. She thought she might have seen them on the snowy slopes, but they were not in evidence. Neither was Pamela, and Josie was glad to have escaped her influence temporarily. It was as though the girl had tentacles, like some enormous spider, reaching out and ensnaring Josie against her will. But not today. It was Saturday, but Josie, more than happy in the bosom of her family, had never even thought of meeting her friend at the Regal, as she had half promised to do. But that was before the snow came. She knew, though, that it would be hard to make an excuse again for the next week; but she would think about that on Monday when they went back to school.

Chapter 12

As it happened, Josie had no need to worry, because when she arrived at school on Monday morning she found that Pamela was absent with a bad cold. Her aunt Mary had rung up to say so.

'Now then,' said the teacher, raising her voice and addressing the rest of the class. 'Pamela Coates is away today, so the desk next to Josie is empty. And I've had it in mind for some time to separate *you* two scallywags!' She pointed with outstretched arm to the desk where Jimmy Clegg and Derek Watson were sitting. 'You – Desperate Dan and Lord Snooty,' she added, to shrieks of laughter from the class. Mrs Faulkner always tried to be topical and to take an interest in what the children liked, but she didn't always get it quite right. Neither of the boys bore much of a resemblance to Lord Snooty of the *Beano*, although Desperate Dan might be nearer the mark. Still, it was good to have a laugh on a Monday morning; you couldn't do that with some of the teachers.

'Yes, it's about time you two parted company,' Mrs Faulkner continued when the laughter had abated. 'During lesson-time, anyway. The scholarship exams'll be upon us before we know where we are, and I want some good results from this class, if possible. Now, Jimmy Clegg, you can go and sit there, next to Josie Goodwin. She'll try to keep you on the straight and narrow.' There was another roar of laughter. 'And when Pamela comes back she can sit with you, Derek Watson . . . unless I have another change-round before the day's over. I may well do that! Now, Class 4A, get out your English grammar books, page forty-nine. We'll have a look at prepositions . . .'

Josie was covered with confusion at the turn of events – Jimmy Clegg, of all people! – and found herself blushing to the roots of her hair. She hid her embarrassment behind her desk lid, searching for her grammar book, her pencil and ruler, and when she emerged she hoped that her discomfiture no longer showed, or, at any rate, that nobody would notice. They didn't seem to. Jimmy just grinned at her, then appeared to be listening attentively to the teacher, and later to be getting on diligently with his work. He was much quieter recently, Josie had noticed. She knew that his father, who had joined up at the beginning of the war, had now been sent overseas.

'We want to talk to you,' said Hilda to Josie, as the class surged out of the classroom at playtime, towards the cloakroom. 'Me and Vera. Don't we, Vera?'

The girl who was Hilda's shadow nodded in agreement. 'Ye-eh, we want to talk to you, me and Hilda.'

Josie shrugged. 'All right then,' she said, as she buttoned up her gaberdine mac and tied her green pixie hood firmly under her chin. 'What d'you want to talk about?'

'Let's go over there by the lavs an' we'll tell you,' said Hilda mysteriously.

They found a patch of watery sunshine and stood leaning against the red brick wall. It was too cold to stand still for long. The recent thaw, which was causing the remaining snow to slither from the rooftops in intermittent avalanches and making sloshy puddles where there had been hard-packed ice, seemed colder than the frost and snow had been. Josie rubbed her gloved hands together and stamped her feet in their black wellington boots. 'What d'you want?' she said again. 'Hurry up – I'm freezing.'

Hilda and Vera looked at one another, then Hilda said, 'Seeing as Pamela's away, we want you to be our friend, me and Vera. Don't we, Vera?'

Vera nodded, then, to Josie's surprise, she smiled. Josie noticed how her pale pinched face, often petulant and complaining, suddenly looked pleasant and her green eyes, which had always reminded Josie of green boiled sweets, lit up with interest. 'Ye-eh, we want to be friends with you. Will you, please, Josie?'

Josie, to her own astonishment, didn't even hesitate. 'Yep, I can if you like. Don't see why not.' She knew that she would have to forfeit Pamela's friendship, but she had already come to the conclusion on her own that that wasn't worth having in the first place. Whereas these two . . . well, it was worth a try at least.

It was a rather subdued Pamela who returned to school a couple of weeks later. She looked pale, her nose was red, and she had brought some Victory Vs with her to suck at intervals. In the general shuffle-round of seats she had ended up sitting next to a girl called Shirley Plowright, not Derek Watson as had first been suggested. Shirley was a pleasant enough girl, but quiet and unobtrusive and she didn't easily make friends. It was soon obvious that Pamela had taken her under her wing and the two of them, plus three or four more girls, were soon a recognizable little gang in the playground. Pamela had shown with sidelong glances and narrowings of her eyes that she had noticed her former friend's new alliance with her one-time enemies, but she made no comment. Josie spoke to her when she had to – it was impossible not to do so – but, on the whole, she kept her distance and made sure she no longer walked home from school with her. Anyway, Pamela had taken to going the long way round with Shirley Plowright and company.

Very soon all petty squabbles took a back seat to the scholarship examinations. There were four of these, two intelligence tests, one Mathematics and one English, which took place on four mornings in late February and early March. Absolute silence was the rule and separate desks so that there could be no cheating. This meant that some classes had to vacate their rooms and double up elsewhere, while their teachers acted as invigilators for the scholarship candidates. All in all it was something of an ordeal, chiefly because of the strangeness of it all, and there was an overwhelming feeling of relief amongst the children of 4A when at last it was all over.

'It were dead easy though, weren't it?' declared Derek Watson to a large gathering of them during the afternoon playtime. 'I'd finished it in half the time,' he boasted. 'I was staring round, chewing me pencil, till Mrs F. told me to check through me answers.'

'Glad you thought it was easy,' said Shirley Plowright, quite talkative for once. 'I thought it was awful. Those meanings of words – honest, I hadn't a clue! I'd no idea what a blue-stocking was.'

'Blue-stocking? Huh, dead easy,' boasted Derek again. 'It's a sailor, i'n't it? They wear blue stockings, don't they?'

'Go on, yer daft beggar!' Jimmy Clegg gave him a flying push. 'Sailor, my aunt Fanny!' He threw himself about laughing. 'It's somebody what's dead clever – like

Josie here.' He playfully tweaked one of her plaits as he grinned at her.

'Shurrup you!' she countered, scowling at him, but she was unable to mask entirely the gleeful smile that was pulling at the corners of her mouth, and no one could know, thank goodness, about the warm happy feeling deep inside her.

'That's what it means though, doesn't it, Josie?' Jimmy persisted. 'Somebody what's always reading books an' all that.'

'I think so . . . I put "a studious person",' replied Josie. 'But I don't know whether it's right or not,' she added casually, shrugging her shoulders. She had realized, long since, that it didn't do to appear too brainy.

'Oh well, I gorrit wrong then,' said Derek, kicking his already scuffed toecap against the school wall. 'Ne'er mind . . . I knew what a cannibal was though. It's somebody what eats human flesh.' He licked his lips and several of the girls squealed. 'Oooh . . . Give over, Derek!'

'And what about them similes or whatever you call 'em?' asked one of the girls. 'What did you think about them?'

'Oh, they were dead easy,' said Vera. 'As blind as a bat, as bright as a button . . . Everybody knows those. Easy-peasy!'

'What about "as mad as"? What d'you put for that?'

'I put "as mad as a hatter" . . .'

'I put "as mad as a March hare" . . .'

'I put "as mad as Derek Watson",' exclaimed Jimmy, to widespread guffaws of laughter.

'What about "as drunk as" . . .? I didn't know that one, did you?'

'It's "as drunk as a lord", isn't it?'

'Oh, I put "as drunk as Hilda Ormerod's dad",' quipped

Jimmy again. This time the laughter was more restrained, several of the children casting covert glances at Hilda to see how she was taking it.

But Hilda didn't seem to be unduly put out. 'Ha-ha, very funny!' she replied scornfully. 'And d'you know what I put? "As ugly as Jimmy Clegg"!'

'Good for you, Hilda,' shouted someone, amidst the good-natured laughter.

Josie, listening to the banter, suddenly felt very happy. She liked Beechwood school now, and it was hard to recall the time, last September, when she had been so miserable there. She had her two new friends, Hilda and Vera, and since this little clique had been formed there had been a general falling-off of jealousies and rivalries in the class. Now, most of the children seemed to get on amicably together and even Pamela had caused no further trouble. And then there was Jimmy . . . Josie hugged the thought to herself. He had started walking home with her sometimes – not every day, just now and again – although it was out of his way. Yes, Josie was happy, more so than she had ever dreamed she would be at Beechwood school.

Pamela spoke then. 'Tell you what, everybody. Why don't we have a celebration on the way home tonight, now that the rotten old exams are over?'

There were cries of, 'Ye-eh, why not?' and 'Good idea,' and some of 'Where? What d'you mean?'

'There's a shop near us what sells ha'penny drinks of pop.' Pamela explained. 'Tizer and dandelion and burdock and sarsaparilla . . . An' they have lucky bags for a penny, an' sherbet dabs an' gob-stoppers an' all sorts of stuff. I think it's a sort of tuck shop for the kids what go to that Catholic school, but there's nothing to stop us lot going.

My auntie gets her papers there. Yours does an' all, doesn't she, Josie?'

Josie was surprised when Pamela addressed her directly. 'Mmm . . .' Josie nodded. 'Cardew's – we get our papers there. It's not all that near to our house though. It's a few streets away.'

'Pooh! It's not all that far,' scoffed Pamela. 'Don't come then, if you don't want to.'

''Course I'll come,' Josie replied quickly. She didn't want to invite Pamela's ridicule again, not when relations between the two of them seemed to be improving. She mustn't get too friendly, though.

Auntie Iris had warned her, several times recently, that on no account must she get too pally with Pamela Coates. Her aunt didn't seem to care for the girl at all; 'a bold, impudent madam,' she called her; and Josie, just lately, had been trying much harder to please Auntie Iris. 'She'll get you into trouble, you mark my words,' her aunt had said, and Josie knew that this was true.

But it sounded as though a lot of the kids intended going along. And, of course, Jimmy might go . . . ''S only about five minutes from our house,' she added. 'Ye-eh, it'll be great . . . That is, if we've all got some money. I've only got tuppence on me.'

''S all right – I've got a shilling,' declared Pamela. 'I can treat yer,' she added bountifully, grinning round at the group of children nearest to her.

'I've only got a ha'penny,' said one.

'I've got nothing,' said another, plaintively.

'Never mind,' said Pamela, who seemed to have taken upon herself the role of organizer. 'Them that wants to can come, and we'll see that everybody gets a drink and some sweets or summat. How's that?'

'Ye-eh, great,' shouted a chorus of voices as the whistle blew and they ran to form their lines. 'See you after school . . .'

In the end about ten of them trooped along the road arm in arm, in twos and threes, when school finished. Some of the others had changed their minds, some had no money and didn't want to be beholden to Pamela Coates, despite what she said, and for many the shop was in the wrong direction, away from their homes.

'Never mind,' said Pamela, suddenly linking arms with Josie, to Josie's surprise and not a little alarm. She would have preferred the girl to keep her distance. 'If everybody'd come it would have been too many. Old Cardew'd probably've turned us out . . . I'm real glad we're friends again, Josie,' she went on. Josie hadn't realized that they were. Josie herself was beginning to wonder what she was doing here. She decided that she would distance herself from Pamela as soon as they were in the shop.

Cardew's newsagent's shop was also a confectioner's and tobacconist's, a general store, in fact, which sold a bit of everything. Not groceries – that was the province of the Co-op further along the block where Iris did her weekly shopping – but most other things that the family required could be obtained at Cardew's. Stationery, hairnets, shoelaces, dishcloths, soap, toothpaste, toilet paper . . . Mr Cardew stocked a vast array of boring items which grown-ups always seemed to be needing, but he also catered for the requirements of his younger clientele and had, for the last year or so, been running a sort of tuck shop, patronized mainly by the Catholic school in the area.

Down one side of the shop ran a counter round which the children congregated, as their fathers did at the bars of their locals, sipping their gaseous, highly-coloured drinks of cherryade, limeade, cream soda, Tizer . . . There was a wide choice, kept in huge bottles on the shelf at the back and dispensed at a halfpenny a time in thick glass tumblers. There were halfpenny buns, baked by Mrs Cardew, each in its paper case with a tiny dab of icing sugar on the top, and a huge earthenware bowl of parched peas, moist and black, dispensed for a halfpenny in cone-shaped bags.

Then there were sweets and chocolates, all the usual favourites; liquorice wheels and shoelaces, sherbet dabs, coltsfoot rock, dolly mixtures (those were only for babies, though) floral gums, pear drops . . . and quarter-pound boxes of Dairy Box and Black Magic, which you could only afford if you were very, very rich. Surprisingly, sweets were still quite plentiful, despite the war. Some items of food had been on ration since earlier that year – Iris had registered for her weekly allowance at the Co-op – and it was rumoured that, eventually, sweets would be rationed.

Not today, though, and the children of 4A from Beechwood school stared at the profusion of goods in front of them as they entered the shop. Which items should they choose from such abundance? When you had only a penny to spend you had to make absolutely sure that you were getting the best possible value for your money. And that was what most of them had – a penny, no more – after pockets had been searched through, purses emptied and Pamela had magnanimously shared some of her bounty.

'Na' then, you lot, let's be having you,' said Mr Cardew, not unpleasantly, though. He knew that his younger customers provided no small portion of his income. He rubbed his hands together. 'Be sharp now and make up your minds. I haven't got all day. There'll be proper customers coming in soon wanting to be served. They won't want the place cluttering up with a lot of kids.'

Deftly he distributed pop and parched peas, sweets and halfpenny bars of chocolate, his wife hurrying in from the rear of the shop to assist him. Soon there was comparative quiet as the children sipped and munched.

'Don't often see you lot in here,' Mr Cardew observed, looking at their green caps and scarves. 'Not the Catholic lot, are you?'

'No, are we heck,' they told him. 'We're from Beechwood school.'

'Oh, are you now? Well, think on you behave yourselves. Them Catholics know how to behave, I've got to give 'em that. Come to think of it, there's not been any of 'em in here today. I reckon they must be having one of their saint's days or summat. P'raps just as well, or there wouldn't have been room for you lot . . . Now, put your glasses on the counter when you've finished and don't go littering my nice clean floor with your rubbish. Shove it in your pockets.' With a curt nod he disappeared round the back of the opposite counter.

'Surly old devil, isn't he?' remarked Jimmy to Josie. Holding his head back, he tipped up his paper bag and swallowed the last few of his parched peas. He licked his lips. 'Mmmm . . . them were good. I'll have to come here again. It's your paper shop, is it, Josie?'

'Yes. Old Cardew's not so bad,' Josie replied. 'I think he was injured in the war – that's why he's a bit crabby at times and it's why he walks with a limp. He was in the trenches. That's what my dad says. But his bark's worse than his bite – that's what my auntie Iris says.'

'You and your flippin' auntie Iris,' said Pamela, sidling up to them. 'Always on about her, aren't you? What are you two talking about, anyroad? Can't have you whispering in corners, you know.' She wagged a playful finger at them, but Josie could see that familiar malicious gleam in her eyes. 'The rest of the kids'll be saying that you—'

'We're not talking about anything,' Josie quickly interrupted, feeling a flush begin to stain her cheeks. 'It's none of your business, anyway.'

'Ye-eh, mind your own business, you!' added Jimmy.

'They'll be saying that you . . . that you love one another!' Pamela concluded gleefully. She turned round, raising her voice. 'Listen, everybody—'

'Shurrup, you . . . you rotten old evacuee!' Jimmy shot out his right foot, shod with a tough hobnailed boot, and Josie saw Pamela wince. But only for a split second. She soon bounced back again.

'Listen, everybody . . .' She dodged out of the way of Jimmy's raised fist. 'Who'd like . . . some more sweets?' she asked, grinning round at the group of children nearest to her, before sticking out her tongue in the direction of Josie and Jimmy.

'We can't, Pam. We've nowt left.'

'No . . . we're skint,' one or two voices replied.

'Well, I've still got tuppence,' Pamela declared, holding up the coins. 'Come on, who else has got some money left? Let's see if we've got enough for some of them Yorkshire mixtures. We can share 'em out between us.' But it seemed, after a perfunctory searching of pockets, that Pamela was the only one who hadn't spent up. 'Well, I'm not spending me money if you lot won't.' She glared at them. 'It's not fair. I've already spent loads and loads on some of you.'

'We can't . . . We ain't got none.'

'All right then. Suits me.' Shrugging her shoulders, Pamela quickly pocketed her two pennies. Then she glanced round. 'Old Cardew's disappeared anyroad . . .' She giggled. 'Not a very good shopkeeper, is he? Tell you what . . .' A wicked gleam lit up her pale blue eyes. 'There's no need to pay,' she whispered. 'Watch.'

The children nearest to her watched, silent and disbelieving, as she shot out a hand and closed it over a caramel chew, a box of which stood quite near to them, at the back of the pop counter. 'Go on, it's dead easy,' she incited them. 'He's not even here. You're daft if you don't.'

A few hands reached out, fearfully at first, then more confidently, a sense of togetherness making them foolhardy, snatching at halfpenny chews, barley sugar twists, lollipops, anything that was near to hand.

'You ought to see Josie do it, though. She's dead good at this, aren't you, Josie?' Pamela was leering spitefully at her. 'Go on . . . show 'em.'

Josie hung back, shaking her head. 'No . . . no, I can't!' she hissed. 'Don't be such an idiot, Pam, don't . . .'

'Aw, yer big soft baby! Cowardy cowardy custard,' taunted Pamela, but still in a low voice. 'Go on . . . I dare you! If you don't, I'll tell!' She glared at Josie with narrowed eyes, before glancing meaningfully at Jimmy. 'I'll tell . . .' she hissed, so quietly that only Josie – and possibly Jimmy – could hear her. 'I'll tell 'em all what you do, you and 'im.'

Josie could never explain afterwards what made her do it. She was only dimly aware of Pamela's grinning face, the wide-eyed stares of the other children, and Jimmy's warning cry, 'Josie – no!' as she stretched out a hand and grabbed at a banana chew.

At that moment there was an unmistakable voice behind them. 'What the hell are you lot up to?'

Chapter 13

Mr Cardew could not be dissuaded. He was determined to report them to their headmaster. It could have been worse, they tried to console one another afterwards. At first he had insisted that he would tell their parents. The worst Mr Edwards could do was give them the cane; he might not even do that as they were girls.

'I've seen you before, haven't I?' Mr Cardew thundered. Josie was caught red-handed with the banana chew still in her grasp. He grabbed her by the scruff of her neck and yanked her round to face him. 'Yes, you're Mrs Goodwin's daughter, aren't you? From Jubilee Gardens?'

Josie nodded silently, not arguing for once that the said lady was not her mother.

'And what's she going to say, eh, when she finds out her daughter is a thief?' Mr Cardew bellowed.

Josie wouldn't have believed that the pale thin man could have such a loud voice. 'Don't tell her. Please don't tell her,' she begged. 'I'm sorry, I'm real sorry, honest. I'll pay you back.'

'That's not the point,' Mr Cardew grunted. 'That's not the point at all. You're a thief. The whole lot of you are thieves.'

He turned on them all then and made them empty their pockets. It transpired that, out of the ten of them, six were guilty. Jimmy Clegg was not one of them, but Shirley Plowright – a very tearful Shirley – was. Pamela was soon identified as the ringleader; it was obvious from the accusing looks that the others were directing at her.

'An' I've seen you before an' all,' said Mr Cardew, grabbing hold of her shoulders and shaking her. 'You've been in with Mrs Meredith, haven't you? Aren't you her niece or summat?'

'I'm an evacuee,' said Pamela in a plaintive voice. 'Don't be mad at me, mister. Don't tell her . . .'

'Hmmm . . . Evacuee or not, you'd enough money to throw around before. I was watching you. And not content with that, you start thieving from me. I won't have this sort of carry-on in my shop. I've a business to run and it's hard enough as it is . . .'

The tirade went on for ages and it was a very subdued group who eventually found themselves outside on the pavement. Shirley Plowright was by now bawling her head off.

'Oh, for goodness' sake, shut up!' Pamela snapped at her. 'Nobody else is yelling, and we're all in it together.'

'Not all of us,' Jimmy pointed out. 'And it was your fault anyway, Pamela Coates.'

'Shut up, Jimmy Clegg! Nobody asked your opinion,' Pamela retorted. 'Anyroad, I bet he won't do anything, old Cardew. He was just threatening us.'

'Yes . . . his bark's worse than his bite, my auntie says,' Josie repeated, but not very convincingly.

It turned out to be a forlorn hope. Mr Edwards, the headmaster, was furious. The six culprits were hauled out in front of the whole school for a dressing-down. There was a good deal about the honour of the school and letting not only themselves but their parents down;

and some of them with fathers serving King and Country, as well.

'As you know, I don't believe in caning girls,' he said. Josie had thought that he might have done, just this once, and that wouldn't have been nearly as bad. But his concluding remarks filled Josie with such dread that she felt as though she was going to be sick, there and then, in front of all the school. 'I shall inform your parents,' he told them, 'and it will be up to them to decide how to punish you. Now go – and it will be a long time before I forget this disgrace.'

Mrs Faulkner, their teacher, seemed distressed rather than angry. 'I'm disappointed in you, Josie,' she said, shaking her head sadly. 'I would have thought that you of all people would have made an effort to keep the others out of trouble . . . I'm glad to see that you, Jimmy Clegg, were not involved in this. It seems as though you might be learning some sense at last. But nothing that you do really surprises me, Pamela Coates.' The long searching look that she levelled at the girl, as well as being sad, was reproachful, and even Pamela had the grace to hang her head.

'What the hell,' she muttered afterwards though. 'It were only a few rotten old ha'penny chews.' But nobody bothered to answer her and Josie was too terrified for words. What would happen when her dad – and worse, her auntie Iris – found out?

Iris's fury knew no bounds. The letter from school had arrived by second post the next day and Iris was holding it in her hand when Josie came through the door at dinner-time.

'What's the meaning of this?' She shook the missive in

Josie's face. 'You've some explaining to do, young lady, unless you can tell me that it's not true?' Josie hung her head. It would be useless to lie to Auntie Iris. 'Come on – I'm waiting. Is it true that you've been *stealing* – from Mr Cardew's, of all places?'

Josie nodded. 'But it was only a banana chew, Auntie Iris. That's all I took, an' I said I'd pay for it—'

'I don't care if it was a – a banana chew or – or a diamond ring,' spluttered Iris. 'You were stealing.'

'But it wasn't my fault. Honest, it wasn't.' Josie looked pleadingly at her stepmother. 'There were a lot of us, and we all went in . . . it was when we'd finished our exams. And we'd finished our pop, you see, and me and Jimmy were talking . . .' She was gabbling, falling over her words. 'And then Pamela came up to us, and she said—'

It was the mention of Pamela's name that did it. 'Pamela!' shrieked Iris. 'Come here . . .'

Josie tried to dodge back through the kitchen door, though how she thought she could possibly escape she didn't know, but Iris was too quick for her. She was a strong woman and now her rage was making her more powerful than ever. With one hand she dragged Josie to a dining-room chair and pushed her over the seat, then, with the other hand, she yanked up the girl's clothing and pulled down her bottle-green knickers. Josie hadn't realized before what strength there was in the woman's right arm, but she soon knew as Iris grabbed the nearest thing to hand – a hairbrush from the sideboard – and laid into her stepdaughter. Josie yelled and wriggled as the stiff bristles made contact with her bare flesh time and again, but Iris's grip was like iron.

'There now,' said Iris at last, flinging the brush away from her. 'Go and tidy yourself up, then I suppose you'll have to have some dinner – though you don't deserve any.'

'Don't want any dinner,' muttered Josie as she scrambled to her feet, 'and . . . I hate you,' she added under her breath, not caring whether Iris heard or not. Shamefacedly she fumbled with her underclothes; never in all her life had she felt so humiliated. To make matters worse, Bertie, just coming in from school, had witnessed the scene, and Frances, sitting up to the table on two cushions and with her bib on, awaiting her dinner, was staring at Josie, her eyes as big as saucers.

Josie did eat a small amount of shepherd's pie. It almost choked her, but Iris insisted. She didn't betray with even the tiniest wince that it was agony to sit on her chair, and she did get her own back on Iris, to a small degree, before she went back to school, although Iris wasn't to know about it.

'You got your bottom smacked,' declared Frances, in what seemed to Josie like self-righteous tones, when Iris was busy in the kitchen washing up. 'Our mummy smacked your bottom.'

'Shut up, you!' hissed Josie. 'Mind your own business.' She moved nearer to the child, keeping her voice low. 'Anyway, she's not my mummy . . . and she's not your mummy either. She's only your auntie Iris. Your mummy's dead. She died a long time ago, when you were a baby.' She stopped then, rather worried by the puzzled expression on the little girl's face as she frowned and looked in the direction of the kitchen. 'And you'd better not go telling her either,' Josie jerked her thumb at the kitchen door. 'Don't you dare tell her what I've said, or I'll . . . I'll take Mary Jane away from you. She belongs to me really, you know.'

Josie had the grace to feel a little ashamed as Frances hugged her doll, Mary Jane, closer to her. The doll, discarded ages ago by Josie, had become a great favourite with the little girl, continually nursed and cherished and taken to bed each night.

Frances answered meekly now. 'All right, Josie. I won't . . . I won't tell.'

Josie felt horrid. It had been Auntie Iris that she wanted to get at – mean, horrible old Auntie Iris – not Frances.

Josie crouched halfway down the stairs, her eyes on the chink of light visible through the slightly open door, listening to the muffled voices of her father and stepmother. She couldn't hear all that was being said, but she could follow the general gist of the conversation. And it seemed to her that her father was not entirely in agreement with his wife about her chastisement of Josie earlier that day.

Josie had gathered from the look on his face, when he had heard of her misdemeanour, that he did not consider it to be the heinous crime Iris thought it was. He had frowned, admittedly, and said that she should be ashamed of herself; but when mention was made of the article stolen – a halfpenny banana chew – Josie had detected a humorous glint in his deep brown eyes and he had seemed to be biting his lip, like she herself did sometimes, to stop a grin from breaking out. But he had controlled himself almost at once and said that she had to go to bed early without any of her favourite biscuits for supper.

Which was why she was now sitting shivering in the darkness, eavesdropping. She knew that that was the grown-up word for listening to other people's conversations, and that it was something you were not supposed to do. But how else were you to know what was going on? Grown-ups were always too ready to say that 'little pigs had big ears' and to stop talking when you came into the room.

It was Josie's villainous deed that they were discussing now.

'Don't you think you're making too much of it?' her father was saying. Good old Dad! 'A ha'penny toffee bar! For God's sake, woman, do keep a sense of proportion. It's not the crown jewels.'

'It's the principle of the thing, Samuel. Stealing is stealing, whether it's a penny or a thousand pounds.' And Josie, in her heart, knew that what Iris said was true. She had known it was wrong, like she had those times in Woolworth's, and she hadn't wanted to do it. But it had been Pamela with that horrible gloating look on her face, threatening to tell . . . She had tried to explain to Auntie Iris, but when she had mentioned Pamela her aunt had hit the roof. That was what she was saying now.

'It was her mentioning Pamela that made me see red. I'd told her quite clearly that she hadn't to have anything more to do with her, and what would happen if she did. And she deliberately defied me.'

'So you gave her a good hiding.'

'Yes, I did, and I'd do it again.'

'Against your principles, surely, Iris? Haven't I heard you say . . . ? And you know I don't believe in such harsh treatment.'

'Well, she asked for it.'

The conversation dropped to a murmur. Josie, cold and tired and miserable, was on the point of creeping back to bed when her father's voice suddenly became audible again. She heard a drawer opening and closing and she knew that he must have walked over to the sideboard which stood by the door. 'Well, I reckon you'd better see this, Iris. It came this morning. I wasn't going to tell you for a day or two, but you'll have to know.'

'What is it?'

Josie clutched at the banister rail, poking her ear towards the door. She'd be in trouble again if they caught her, but what the heck did it matter?

'Read it and you'll see.'

Iris's next words came in a shriek. 'Your call-up papers! Oh, Samuel . . . that's awful! I never thought . . . not yet!'

Josie stopped listening then for a moment or two, devastated by what she had just heard. Her dad had been called up to the Army, like Jimmy's and Derek's and some more of the dads, because there was a war on and he had to be a soldier and go and fight. And she would be left here on her own with horrible Auntie Iris. Josie had never felt all that close to her father, but in that moment it seemed to Josie that he was the most wonderful dad in the world . . . and he was going to leave her. He was saying so now.

'. . . So you'll have to manage them on your own. Sorry an' all that, but orders are orders. So I hope you'll try to get on a bit better with our Josie . . .'

Never, thought Josie. Never, never, never! I won't get on with her. I won't, I won't! I don't like her. In fact, I *HATE* her, and I'm not going to stay here. I'm going to run away, right now . . .

She decided she would go and live with her auntie Alice.

She made herself stay awake until she heard them come up to bed. The luminous hands on her little alarm clock told her that it was half past ten and she waited until the usual night-time sounds – the flushing of the toilet, the running of water and the closing of doors – had all finished. Then she let another ten minutes or so go by before she crept out of bed, dressed in the dark and stole out on to the landing. She stood motionless for a few seconds outside their bedroom door, but there was not a sound from Samuel and Iris, nor from Bertie and Frances in their separate rooms. She crept downstairs, fingers tightly crossed lest the step near the middle of the staircase should creak as it sometimes did, but she stepped on the very side, to make sure. She gave a sigh of relief when she reached the bottom, her breath sounding so loud to her own ears in the quiet stillness that she feared someone would hear her. Now there was only the front door to tackle, bolts at the top and bottom and a knob to turn, but her dad and aunt slept at the back, which was one small mercy. With her tongue held between her teeth with the effort of concentration she reached up on tiptoe and drew back one bolt. Not a sound; clever girl, she thought. Now the other one. This one was rather stiff and it made a clatter that almost frightened her out of her wits. But there was still no sound from upstairs. She breathed again, then, her face puckered with tension, she quickly turned the knob and pulled open the door. She stepped out, closing the door almost soundlessly behind her, and stood for a moment on the path, staring around.

It had been dark inside the house, almost completely so, for hardly any light could find its way round the edges of the blackout curtains, but out here, in the cold air of the March night, it seemed a little lighter. Josie could make out the shapes of bushes, trees, houses and lamp-posts in the faint gleam shed by the moon and stars. But the lamp-posts were, of course, no longer in use – except by dogs or for drunks to hold on to – because of the blackout. Josie had her torch, a shiny silver one that had been a Christmas present, and she drew it now from the pocket of her gaberdine mac and switched it on. No one ever ventured out at night without a torch, and Josie had felt very proud that she was considered grown-up enough to have one of her own. But this was the first time that she had used it by herself.

For a moment she didn't feel grown-up at all; just small and scared and miserable. But she wouldn't turn back; she couldn't, anyway, because she'd have to knock at the door and that would make it even worse. She had to get to her auntie Alice's and if she walked quickly it shouldn't take long. She hitched her gas-mask case more firmly on to her shoulder – something else you had never to forget to take with you – and set off walking.

She had forgotten momentarily that the park gates were closed at night and that she would have to go the long way round. But as she peered through the iron bars she knew she would not have dared to venture into that dark spooky place on her own. The trees looked menacing against the night sky, taking on fearful shapes like witches and demons and goblins. Josie knew that this was only her imagination – there weren't any such things – but she felt safer out here in the street. She stepped out quickly now, sure of the way that she had walked so many times before. Haliford was only a small town and you couldn't really get lost, but she had been unprepared for how different things looked in the darkness, especially when there was no grown-up to lead the way.

Once she had skirted the park she stood uncertainly at the main road that she had to cross. This in itself was no problem – there was no traffic – but which road was she to take from there? The road she usually took into town was opposite the park gates, much further along. There was nobody to ask, and that might not have been such a good idea anyway; they would be sure to ask her what she was doing on her own so late at night. The only people Josie had seen so far had been a couple kissing under the trees at the edge of the park and an elderly man wobbling about in the middle of the road on a sit-up-and-beg bicycle. None of them had taken any notice of her. But common sense told her that as all the roads sloped upwards, out of the valley in which the park lay, they all, surely, must lead to the town centre.

That was a bit tricky. However would she get through the main streets of Haliford without attracting the attention of a nosy policeman or an air-raid warden? And she wasn't even sure she was going the right way . . . In that moment Josie very nearly turned back. She would be in trouble anyway when they found out she'd gone. But she kept on going. Resolutely she lifted her head and marched across the road. She had heard her dad say that it was a couple of miles to Auntie Alice's house and she must have walked a mile already. So she was halfway there, she reasoned, forgetting that she had come the long way round.

She struck out up the first road she came to – one was as good as another because she had to admit to herself now that none of them looked familiar. A couple of cats jumped out of a privet hedge in front of her, startling her so much that she cried out in alarm. Then came the sound of a dustbin lid clanging – another cat, most likely. There seemed to be nothing abroad but herself and these creatures of the night . . . and they always knew where they were going. And then, just when she was beginning to think she was hopelessly lost, she recognized ahead of her in the murky greyness some familiar outlines. A builder's hut, scaffolding, a half-built brick wall; it was the building site near to the cinema.

She was approaching it from a different angle, but round the next corner there should be the Regal cinema, the furniture shop, the market hall . . . Yes, there they were, and Josie felt like shouting for joy. She ran now, forgetting how tired she was, round the next corner and up the street. Woolworth's, the Home and Colonial, Stead and Simpson's; all the scenes were familiar now, even in the blackout. Shining her torch in front of her she marched on resolutely. She just had to cross the big road by the roundabout, then she would be on the hill that led up to Baldwin Lane and Auntie Alice's.

'Little girl, where are you going?' She nearly jumped out of her skin at a voice behind her and her first instinct was to run. That was what she started to do, but she soon realized it was no use because a bicycle pulled up at her side and the man who was riding it took hold of her arm.

'Geroff!' She pulled her arm away, then she glanced up at him; at the heavy-jowled face staring at her in puzzlement, the dark uniform, the shiny buttons, the helmet . . . Oh heck! It was a policeman.

Josie wasn't normally scared of policemen as some children were. She knew there was no need to be if you were behaving youself, and this one couldn't possibly know about the stolen sweets . . . could he? Some mothers, she knew, threatened their children if they were naughty, 'You'd better watch out or the bobby'll come and get you!' But Auntie Iris, to give her her due, had never done that. She had always encouraged them to look upon policemen as friends, there to give a helping hand if you were in trouble or lost. But Josie wasn't lost. She knew her way to Auntie Alice's from here, if only she could get rid of him.

'Whatever are you doing out on your own?' he asked, peering closely at her. 'Does your mum know you're out? Where do you live?'

Josie wasn't quite sure which of the questions to answer. She couldn't possibly tell him that her mum – her auntie Iris – didn't know she was out, nor could she tell him where she lived. If she did he'd make sure she went back there – would take her, more than likely. Then the fat really would be in the fire! Oh heck, she thought again, deciding to tell a half-lie.

'I live with my auntie Alice,' she said. 'That's where I'm going now.' Well, it was nearly true; she would very soon be living there.

'Oh, and where might that be?' The policeman's eyes were penetrating, glimmering black pools in a big whitish-grey face. She wasn't sure yet that he believed her.

'Number fifty-eight Baldwin Lane,' she answered quickly. 'It's just over the road by the big roundabout, then up the hill. Please let me go, mister . . .'

She wasn't sure what to call him. To say 'Mister Policeman' would sound like the *Tales of Toytown*, still a favourite of hers on *Children's Hour*, though she knew it was really for little kids like her brother and sister. She had a sudden mental picture of Larry the Lamb bleating, 'Oh, Mister Maaaayor Sir . . .' and home – the fireside, toasted crumpets for tea, Bertie and Frances . . . even Auntie Iris – all at once seemed very appealing. She was lonely and frightened and cold, and she had just realized how tired she was. But she had to get to Auntie Alice's. 'I'll have to go now. I'll be all right, honest. Let me go, mister.'

'Indeed I won't, not on your own.' The policeman smiled at her for the first time. 'Baldwin Lane's a long way, more than a mile. Come on, hop up here and I'll take you home.

Then perhaps you can tell me what you're doing out by yourself, eh? Up to no good, I'll be bound.' But his voice was kindly and comforting now; he couldn't be thinking she was something dreadful, like a burglar.

He lifted her up over the high crossbar and sat her on the saddle. 'You'll have to hold tight, mind, or you'll fall off.' And Josie, clinging to the handlebars, the policeman's arm around her as he wheeled her through the silent dark streets, suddenly felt better. She didn't know what would happen when they got to Auntie Alice's, but she was too tired to worry about that now. She was finding it a struggle to keep her eyes open, but she knew that she must.

She wouldn't tell him, although he was probing and he was very near the truth. 'Had a bit of a row, have you, with your auntie? Decided to leave home, is that it? Then thought better of it?'

'Something like that,' said Josie evasively. If the policeman had only thought to look inside her gas-mask case he would have found her name, and her address – 6 Jubilee Gardens, not 58 Baldwin Lane. But he didn't look – obviously policemen were not infallible – although he did ask her name.

'Josie,' she answered sleepily. 'Josie Goodwin . . . but my auntie's called Mrs Rawlinson.'

It certainly was a long way up the hill. It seemed much further in the dark and Josie wondered however she would have got there on her own.

'Here we are,' said the policeman at last. 'Is this the one?' He was peering with difficulty at the numbers. 'Third one from the end?'

'Yes, that's it,' replied Josie, wide awake now and more than a little apprehensive. Whatever would Auntie Alice say? She would have to give her a sign – frown at her or something – to make sure she didn't spill the beans. But Josie need not have worried. It was Uncle Jack who came to the door, after what seemed an awful long time, with Auntie Alice close behind him. They were both in their dressing-gowns and Auntie Alice had a pink hairnet covering her head. After her first gasp of astonishment she seemed to take it all in her stride.

'Josie! Whatever . . . ?'

'You know this little girl then?'

'Yes . . . it's Josie. She's my niece.'

'And you're . . . What's your name, missus?'

'Mrs Rawlinson. Alice Rawlinson.'

The policeman nodded. 'That's all in order then. And she lives here, does she, this young lady?' He put a hand on Josie's head, smiling at her, though in a reproving manner.

'Ye-es . . .' Alice's voice was hesitant, but not for long. She soon seemed to put two and two together. 'Yes, I told you. She's my niece. But what . . . ? Where was she?'

'She was running for her life down by Woolworth's. Good job I found her. You hadn't missed her then?' The policeman was looking searchingly at Alice.

'No . . . no, we've been in bed for ages. She must have . . . Thank you very much, Officer, for bringing her . . . home.'

'All in a day's work, missus. I'll leave you to sort it out.' He turned to Josie again. 'Na' then, young madam, just see that you behave yourself in future. Think on, now!'

'Yes . . . thank you . . .' Josie faltered.

The policeman mounted his bike and rode away, and Alice closed the door. 'Now Josie love, you'd best tell me what this is all about.'

'Oh, Auntie Alice, Auntie Alice . . .' Josie buried her

head against the warm comforting softness of her aunt's bosom and the whole sorry tale poured out. '. . . And she hit me, she hit me right hard . . . and me dad's going in the Army . . . and I don't want to live there any more. Let me stay here, Auntie Alice, please let me stay . . .'

Uncle Jack, who had been just standing there taking it all in, spoke now. 'Er . . . don't you think we'd best let Samuel and Iris know she's here? They'll be worried sick. I'll just go and put my trousers on.'

'No, no!' Josie clung tightly to her aunt. 'Don't tell them. Don't tell *her*. She'll be mad at me again . . . She'll hit me.'

'Josie, stop it now.' Alice took hold of her shoulders and shook her gently. 'You're being silly. Nobody's going to hit you, and your uncle Jack and me'll sort it all out. But of course we have to let your dad and your auntie know where you are. Just imagine if they go into your room and find you're gone. They'll be out of their minds with worry.'

'They won't . . . *She* won't.'

'Yes, she will.' Alice paused. 'Your aunt Iris thinks a great deal of you, though you may not realize it . . . She may not even realize it herself,' she added quietly as an afterthought. 'That's right, Jack, you just nip along to the phone box and let 'em know she's safe.' This to her husband who was coming down the stairs pulling his braces over his pyjama jacket. 'And we'd best get you into bed, young lady.' She put an arm round Josie's shoulders and kissed her cheek.

'Now, don't you worry. We'll sort it all out in the morning. It was very naughty, you know. You shouldn't have run away, but we won't say too much about that, not at the moment. Now, just pop down the yard to the lavvy, and I'll go and put a bottle in the bed. The one in the little room's all made up, so you'll be snug as a bug in a rug in there. And I'll put a potty in, in case you need it. Run along now, and then I'll fetch you up a nice cup of cocoa to drink in bed.'

Josie had almost forgotten about the lav down the yard – freezing cold it was – and chamber-pots and jugs of water in the bedrooms; but as she sipped the delicious hot cocoa before slipping down between the cosy flannelette sheets, she felt that it might be worth any amount of inconvenience, if only she could stay here.

It was Iris, accompanied by little Frances, who came round the following morning. Leonard had gone to school and Jack Rawlinson to work, and Alice and a very subdued Josie were busy making the beds when Iris and Frances arrived.

Iris didn't rant and rave at her, as Josie had expected. She just nodded curtly as she said, 'Hello, Josie . . . Morning, Alice,' an unfathomable look in her grey eyes, but not one of anger or enmity. 'Well, this is a pretty kettle of fish, I must say.' She flopped down in one of Alice's fireside chairs as though she had run out of steam and of words.

Alice couldn't help but feel sorry for her. 'Josie,' she said. 'Just put your coat on, will you dear, and run to the Co-op for me? There's a few things I need.' Hastily she tore a page from a notepad and wrote *matches, fly-paper, bar of Sunlight soap, box of toilet paper*, all things which would come in useful, and handed Josie a florin. 'You can take Frances with you. That's all right, isn't it, Iris?' Iris nodded in a distracted manner. 'Look after her, mind, and keep hold of her hand,' added Alice. 'Off you pop, then . . .' And Josie seemed glad to escape.

'Ohhh . . .' Iris gave a long shuddering sigh as the door closed behind them, shaking her head sorrowfully. 'What on earth am I going to do, Alice? Tell me, what am I going to do? I've tried with her, God knows I've tried . . .'

It was the first time Alice had ever known Iris Goodwin to be at a loss for words or to ask for advice, and her heart went out to her. She hadn't cared much for her at first, when she married Samuel, so soon after poor Florence's death, she was the first to admit it; but the woman did seem to have mellowed, and she had done a jolly good job with Samuel's children, far better than he could have done by himself.

She could see, too, that the woman was having a tough job with Josie – six of one and half a dozen of the other, as she had thought before – but Josie was Alice's niece when all was said and done, a blood relation, which was more than Iris was, and she, Alice, had promised she would sort it out. Also, she thought that Iris's treatment of the little girl had been somewhat harsh. That was what she told her now, as tactfully as she could.

'Yes,' Iris answered regretfully. 'I know . . . and I'm sorry, believe it or not. But she made me so angry. To find out she'd actually been stealing! She's told you, has she, about that?'

'Yes, I think she's told me most things. Try not to condemn her too much for that, Iris. It seems that she was led on. It was that Pamela girl. And it wasn't the first time either. Apparently she made Josie pinch things from Woolworth's, a few months ago.'

'What? It's a wonder they didn't end up in the juvenile court! Just imagine, Alice, how dreadful that would have been. Whatever was she thinking about? I just can't understand it. I would have thought that our Josie had a mind of her own.'

The little word *our* didn't escape Alice's notice. As she had thought, Iris was fond of the child. 'I would say she definitely has,' Alice agreed, 'a mind of her own. But that Pamela sounds a tough little customer. I don't think we should underestimate the hold she's had on Josie. Threatening to tell tales about her to the other children, all about Josie and some boy or other, that they loved each other—'

'A boy?' Iris looked incredulous and she almost laughed. 'Our Josie and a boy? It's the first I've heard of it. Wait a minute – there's a lad called Jimmy she was on about. But they're only kids.'

'Yes, I know they are, and it all sounds very silly to us, but you can be sure it wouldn't be silly to them. Kids hate to be made to look ridiculous or to be shown up. And when they were caught pinching at the newsagent's, when there were a few of them involved, you can be sure they egged one another on. The herd instinct . . . You've seen 'em, haven't you, on the Golden Mile at Blackpool? All wearing daft Kiss-Me-Quick hats and shouting and careering about. I'm sure they wouldn't behave like that at home. And it's the same with kids. They're easily led. Try to understand, Iris.'

'I do . . . I do.' Iris seemed thoughtful. 'But I'd told her to keep away from Pamela.' She shrugged resignedly. 'I suppose she wants to come and live here now, does she? Is that what she's said?'

'Ye-es . . .' Alice replied slowly.

'And . . . how do you feel about it? Would you have her?'

'Ye-es,' said Alice again. 'You know I would. But I'm

not sure that she means it . . . or that you would want to part with her.' Alice raised her eyebrows, looking questioningly at Iris.

'You're right.' Iris shook her head. 'I don't want to part with her. I'm very fond of the child. Oh, I know I could strangle her at times, but I don't want to lose her, especially not now. Samuel's got his call-up papers, by the way.'

'Yes . . . Josie said so.'

'She what?' Iris frowned. 'But how does she know? We never said—'

Alice smiled. 'Eavesdropping, I daresay.'

'More than likely.' Iris's smile was one of understanding. 'She's very good at that. Happen that's why she left. Heard us talking, I shouldn't wonder. But I want her back, Alice, and that's a fact. I shall need some help with Bertie and Frances, and Josie's very good with them when she puts her mind to it. But it's not just because of that. She's one of the family.'

'Then why don't you tell her so? Tell her that you're sorry and—'

'I won't go crawling to her!' Iris's belligerence, the manner that was all too familiar to Alice, showed again for a moment. 'It's her that should say she's sorry. Running away like that just because I chastised her.'

'There'll have to be a bit of give and take between the pair of you,' said Alice patiently. 'Look, why don't you let the child decide for herself? Let her stay with me for a day or two. They've finished their exams at school, haven't they? So she won't be missing much. And I'll talk things over with her, put all the cards on the table and see how she feels. Unless you'd rather talk to her?'

Iris shook her head hurriedly. 'No, not me. I can't, not just yet. You do it – and thanks, Alice.'

'Don't condemn yourself too much,' said Alice gently. 'For what it's worth, I think you've done marvels with those children. They're a real credit to you, Iris, and I know I'm not the only one to think so.'

'I know you didn't like me stepping into your sister's shoes,' said Iris thoughtfully, 'and I can't say I blame you. But I've done my best, and that's all that any woman can do.'

'And Josie's not easy, I know that,' added Alice.

'No, she's not, but I daresay I'll have to go on trying. I tell you what, Alice, this 'ere war doesn't seem to have affected us all that much yet apart from the bloomin' blackout – and now Samuel being called up, of course – but I seem to have been waging a war of my own for the last four years, ever since I married him. It's been nowt but a series of battles with young Josie.' Iris sighed. 'And I was beginning to think we were getting on so much better, till this happened.'

'And I'm sure you will again, don't worry,' said Alice soothingly. 'Shhh – they're here now. Shall I tell her she can stay here for a bit, or will you?'

'I'll tell her.' Iris tried to smile at both the girls as they came into the room, but Alice noticed that her eyes were sad and her voice had lost its forceful timbre. 'Josie, love. Your auntie Alice and I have decided that you'd better stay here for a day or two.' Iris stood up, gathering together her bag and gloves and gas-mask case, fumbling around in an almost diffident way that was not like Iris at all. 'Be a good girl, now, and help your auntie.' She hesitated, making as if to go over to the girl, then changed her mind.

'All right. But I've no clothes, have I?' said Josie in a quiet little voice. 'No pyjamas or anything.'

'I'll ask your father to bring some round tonight.' Iris

sounded as near to tears as Alice had ever heard her. 'Come along now, Frances.' She took hold of the child's hand and hurried towards the door. 'Bye, Josie . . . bye, Alice.'

'Never mind about the clothes,' whispered Alice on the doorstep. 'She can borrow some of our Len's pyjamas and I can wash her undies through.' She took hold of Iris's arm. 'It'll only be for a day or two, you'll see.'

Iris nodded, sniffing hard. 'Just as you say. Thanks, Alice.'

And that was what Josie decided after some deliberation and a long discussion with her aunt Alice. She would go back home to Jubilee Gardens and help Auntie Iris with the younger children. She knew it was her duty to do so, now that her dad was going into the Army.

'It's my war work, isn't it?' she said to Alice in such an old-fashioned way that her aunt had to suppress a grin. 'We all have to make sacrifices in wartime. That's what our teacher, Mrs Faulkner, is always telling us.'

And that had been another very important consideration: school. Josie was very happy at Beechwood now, and couldn't contemplate going back to Queen Street. There were Hilda and Vera, her new friends . . . and Jimmy, of course. She tried not to think about Pamela. She didn't ever want to set eyes on Pamela again, but she would worry about that some other time.

'And this is your home as well,' Auntie Alice told her. 'You're a very lucky girl, having two homes, and perhaps Auntie Iris will let you come and stay for a week or two in the school holidays, if you're a good girl. You will try and behave yourself for Auntie Iris, won't you, dear?'

And Josie promised resolutely that she would. It was just another part of her wartime effort. When she got home she found that the whole episode – the stealing, Pamela, her good hiding and running away – was not mentioned at all, not by anyone. And when she returned to school she discovered to her relief that Pamela was no longer there. She had left, Mrs Faulkner told her briefly. She had gone back to Manchester.

'Really, Mrs Goodwin, I couldn't stand any more of it,' Mrs Meredith, Pamela's aunt Mary, told Iris. She had called round for a confidential chat the morning that Josie went back to school. 'The tricks that girl got up to, you just wouldn't believe. And the things she used to come out with! Well, really, for a child of eleven to know such things.' She bent nearer to Iris and lowered her voice to a whisper. '*Men and women*, Mrs Goodwin. I hardly like to mention it, but there didn't seem to be anything she didn't know about . . . what they do.' She gave an embarrassed laugh. 'More than me, I'll be bound. Of course I blame Priscilla – that's her mother – flighty little piece she always was. I thought so when Alec married her. Had to marry her, you see, Mrs Goodwin,' she mouthed, cupping one hand round her lips. 'He's my nephew. Well, no, I tell a lie. My husband's nephew—'

'So she's gone back to Manchester?' Iris broke into the flow. 'Well, I'm sure you're better off without her, though perhaps I says it that shouldn't. I know she caused a lot of trouble.'

'And that's one of the reasons I've come,' said Mrs Meredith. 'I know she led your Josie into trouble. Oh, I've heard all about it from the school. They didn't wrap anything up, I can tell you. Such a nice little girl, your Josie, and always so polite. She's a credit to you, Mrs Goodwin. I couldn't believe it at first, you know, about our Pamela. When she first came to us it was as though butter wouldn't melt. But all that stealing. I know she had things in her room that she couldn't possibly have bought. And her language! I've never heard the like.'

'Don't worry about Josie,' Iris told her. 'We've had a spot of bother, I must admit. But we'll get over it. Josie'll bounce back. She's gone off to school this morning as happy as Larry.'

'So I had to tell Priscilla that I couldn't be responsible for her any longer,' sighed Mrs Meredith. 'Dearie me, I do hope I've done the right thing. If they start dropping bombs on Manchester . . .'

'I shouldn't worry,' replied Iris. 'They're not dropping 'em at all, are they, at the moment. And most of the evacuees have gone back, anyroad. Our two went ages ago.'

So that's one problem out of the way, thought Iris as she said goodbye to her visitor. Pamela Coates. Thank goodness we've seen the last of her.

Chapter 14

As Iris had told Alice in the early spring of 1940, the war hadn't affected her all that much as yet, not in a personal way. The aggravations caused by restrictions and the enforcing of rules and regulations were the same for everybody. It seemed, indeed, that people grew more sociable as they shared the inconveniences of the blackout, evacuation and rationing. There was a sense of 'we're all in it together', words often uttered in the bus and food queues, which were gradually getting longer and longer; and when bacon, ham, sugar and butter went on ration in January, it was reassuring rather than alarming, as the Ministry of Food had promised fair shares for all.

It had been the coldest January for half a century. They were well used to such harsh climatic conditions in Yorkshire, but it had been bad in other parts of the country as well, so they read in the papers and watched on the newsreels at the cinema. The River Thames froze, and all over Britain it was a recurring story of frozen pipes, snow-blocked roads and paralysed railways.

A British Expeditionary Force had been sent to France, but seemed to be doing little except waiting for the enemy to attack. RAF bombers were flying over Germany . . . only to scatter propaganda leaflets. Neville Chamberlain, the Prime Minister, remained complacent, or that was the impression he tried to give. He announced at the beginning of April: 'After seven months of war I feel ten times as confident of victory as I did at the beginning . . . Hitler has missed the bus.'

But he spoke too soon, for on the tenth of May, the Germans burst into Holland, Belgium and France. The 'phoney war', or the 'bore war', as some had called it, was at an end. No one could deny now that Britain was at war with Germany: that evening Chamberlain was sent packing and Winston Churchill became leader of an all-party National Government.

'I have nothing to offer,' he told the British people, 'but blood, toil, tears and sweat. What is our aim?' he asked. 'Victory . . . victory at all costs, victory in spite of all terror; victory, however long and hard the road may be.'

At home in England it was a glorious spring. Every day brought sunshine and blue skies . . . but bad news. On the fourteenth of May Holland fell, followed on the twenty-eighth by Belgium. The British Expeditionary Force, facing the certainty of death or capture, was forced to retreat. The miracle of Dunkirk, when thousands of British and French troops were rescued from the beaches by an armada which included pleasure boats and amateur yachtsmen, touched the spirit of the British people more than any event in the war so far. It was, in reality, a defeat. The army had been largely disarmed; but, against all odds, it had survived and the reaction of the British was one of relief and satisfaction, pride almost, in their isolation.

Iris, sitting in the comforting darkness of the cinema with little Frances on her knee, breathed a sigh of relief as she watched the Pathé Pictorial News, that Samuel had not been involved in all this. He had not been in the Army long enough to have been sent over to France. He was still at Aldershot, doing his training in the Royal Army Service Corps. Iris was thankful that, for the moment, he was safe; as safe, that is, as any soldier could be with the threat of invasion looming large in everyone's mind. Not that these fears were ever voiced – that would have been condemned as defeatist talk – but it was obvious that the Government, the top dogs in charge of it all, were worried.

Squat, ugly-looking pillboxes were appearing all over the countryside; signposts, street names and placards on railway stations had been taken down, and the newsreaders on the wireless now announced themselves by name. 'Here is the nine o'clock news, and this is Alvar Lidell (or Bruce Belfrage or Stuart Hibberd) reading it,' was becoming the best-known sentence in Britain, a precaution in case some German should try to impersonate them, Iris supposed.

Yes, there was obviously cause for alarm, but this newsreel seemed to be making light of it, treating it as a victory, or, at the very worst, a temporary set-back instead of a defeat. 'Now, after a reissue of kit and a wash, they're anxious to get back and have another go,' a commentator with a cut-glass accent was proclaiming, as picture after picture of the 'gallant little ships' and hundreds of British Tommies scrambling aboard them, was flashed on the screen. But it was the nature of the British, thought Iris, to make light of adversity – real disasters, that was, because they were renowned for grumbling over petty things – and it seemed that it was only in times of war and danger that they all pulled together. It had been the same in the last war, she recalled.

J. B. Priestley had said something of the sort in his broadcast last night. Iris always listened to him on the wireless; first and foremost, of course, because he was one of them, a Yorkshireman, born and bred, but also because he was so homely and friendly and yet so inspiring. Iris even preferred him to old Winnie. What was it he had said? 'Our great-grandchildren, when they learn how we began this war by snatching glory out of defeat, and then swept on to victory, may also learn how the little holiday steamers made an excursion to hell and came back glorious.' Something like that, anyroad, although there isn't much sign of us sweeping on to victory as yet, Iris reflected.

Josie had asked her the other night, 'What if Hitler wins?' And she, Iris, had answered confidently, 'Don't be silly. He can't.' That was what anyone would answer; you could get into serious trouble for spreading rumours or despondency, but it didn't stop you from thinking or from worrying sometimes, in the secrecy of your own mind.

Josie was concerned, no doubt, about her father. Iris had never thought, in the beginning, that Samuel had been all that much of a father to his three children, but he had improved considerably of late, taking much more notice of them and showing more affection. And he was their real father when all was said and done, linked to them by the undeniable tie of blood . . . which was more than she, Iris, was.

She was pensive for a moment, her thoughts not on the silver screen, but with her own family. She was missing Samuel more than she could say, more than she had ever imagined she would. In the four years since they married she had grown to love him deeply. There had been many battles of will between the pair of them, but they had always been able to find consolation and forgiveness in each other's arms. Her arms felt so empty now. Even the love she felt for Frances couldn't assuage her longing.

But it was the same for thousands of women all over the country, she thought resolutely; the wives and sweethearts of those fellows she had been watching on the newsreel, no doubt they were feeling just the same as she did: lonely, sometimes depressed, but trying to put on a brave face. She returned her eyes to the screen where the credits for the big film were just appearing, *Sing as We Go* starring Gracie Fields. Iris had seen the film twice before, but she knew that the Lancashire mill girl with her melodious voice and impudent manner would be just the tonic she needed. Everybody needed to escape now and again from their worries; that was why the cinema, even on a sunny June afternoon, was more than half full. It would be time soon enough to go home and get the tea ready. She would have to be back before Josie and Bertie came home from school.

One of the men who didn't return from Dunkirk was Jimmy Clegg's father. Mrs Faulkner had told a subdued class what had happened and that they must be very kind to Jimmy when he returned to school the next day. He was red-eyed and unusually restrained, and Josie noticed that, at first, none of the children said anything to him at all. They just looked at him as though they were unsure how to behave with this quiet, uncommunicative Jimmy.

Josie plucked up courage and behind the cover of their desk lids she whispered to him, 'I'm sorry . . . about yer dad, I mean.'

Jimmy gave a tight-lipped smile and whispered back, ''S all right, thanks. I'll see you later, kid.'

And by playtime he seemed quite like himself again, shouting and laughing and kicking a football about with the lads. There were times, though, during the day, when he didn't do any work, just doodled in the margin of his book, and Josie was dismayed to see, just once, a large tear plop on to his page, making the ink all smudgy. She pretended she hadn't noticed.

He caught up with her soon after she turned out of the school gate at the end of the afternoon. 'I'll walk home with yer,' he said. They sauntered along in a silence which was growing embarrassing and Josie was relieved when Jimmy broke it.

'He were a good dad,' he mumbled, shuffling his feet and looking down at them. Josie could hardly hear him and she moved a little closer. 'He weren't like some of the other dads, you know, like Derek's and Hilda's, boozing and spending all their money on horses an' all that. He used to cough up all his pay packet to me mam. There's a lot of us, you see.'

'Yes . . . he worked at Hammond's, didn't he, like my dad?' Josie ventured.

'Not like *your* dad.' Jimmy sounded quite indignant. 'Your dad's one of the big bosses, isn't he? My dad was only a warehouseman. He had to work bloody hard, my dad.'

'And so does mine,' Josie retorted. 'He works very hard, too. Well, he did, but he's in the Army now, isn't he? How's your mum?' she asked, looking at him doubtfully. She wasn't at all sure what to say, but she had to say something. 'Will she be . . . all right?'

'She'll have to be, won't she?' Jimmy answered gruffly. 'Our Doreen's working at the mill now, and so's me brother, Frank. And our Joan leaves school soon so there'll be a bit more money coming into the house. Me mam's used to making ends meet.'

'How many of you are there?' asked Josie.

'Six of us. I've two brothers and three sisters. I'm just about in the middle,' replied Jimmy. 'You know the two little 'uns, don't you? Our Dottie and Georgie are in the Infants.'

Josie nodded. She had seen the two younger Clegg children, red-haired and tough-looking, smaller editions of Jimmy, but their elder brother took little notice of them at school and they found their own way home. The whole of the Clegg tribe seemed well able to look after themselves.

'I wanted to ask you something,' Jimmy said now, in a much more cheerful voice. He turned to look straight at Josie. 'Will you come to the pictures with me on Saturday? You know, the kids' show at the Regal. You used to go with Pamela, didn't you?'

'Yes . . . yes, I did,' Josie answered. She hadn't been since Pamela went back to Manchester. Somehow she had lost interest. 'Yes, why not?' she said brightly, feeling all happy and bubbly inside that Jimmy had asked her. 'I'd like to go. I haven't been for ages. But . . .' A couple of thoughts had just struck her.

'But what?' asked Jimmy.

'Well, d'you think it'll be all right for you to go so soon after . . . you know, your dad an' all that? What will your mum say?' Josie knew that there were certain conventions to be observed when someone died. Wearing black, for instance, and drawing the curtains, and not going to the pictures or to any place of entertainment was always high on the list.

'Me mam won't bother,' Jimmy replied. 'She says we've to carry on just as we always did. Me dad wouldn't want us being all sad and miserable. Me mam cries at night – I've heard her – but she's just the same during the day. It isn't as if we can have a funeral or anything. I 'spect they'll bury them in France, all those soldiers that've died there.'

Josie went all cold for a moment, thankful that her own father was still safe in England. How awful it must be for poor Jimmy. 'There's another thing an' all,' she told him.

'Go on. What's up now?'

'Well . . .' Josie felt a trifle embarrassed. 'What d'you think the rest of 'em'll say? The kids in our class, I mean. About us going to the pictures together. They might say all sorts of silly things . . . you know.'

'Then let 'em. Are you bothered what they say?'

Josie shrugged. 'S'pose not. But you know what they're like.' She was thinking about Pamela and her threats to *tell*, and all the trouble it had led to. But Pamela was no longer there.

'I know what Pamela Coates was on about,' Jimmy said now. 'That day in the shop when you got into all that bother. I'm not daft, y'know. But it's rude, that is. Proper dirty talk. She wasn't half a dirty-minded kid, that evacuee.' Josie could feel that she was beginning to blush, thinking about herself and Jimmy and . . . *that*. She looked away from him so that he wouldn't notice. 'I weren't thinking about anything like that, you know,' he went on. 'Nor about kissing neither. I think that's dead soppy. But I'd like you to be my friend, Josie . . . my girlfriend,' he added, almost shyly, with a sidelong look at her. 'You will, won't you?'

'Yes,' said Josie simply. She smiled at him. 'Yes, I will.'

'And you think your auntie'll let you come with me on Saturday?'

'Yes, I think so. I might have to bring our Bertie though.'

''S all right. I don't mind your kid brother. I wonder

what it'll be this week? I hope it's George Formby, don't you?'

Jimmy was a very different sort of friend from Pamela, Josie thought, as she parted from him at the end of the street. Not counting the fact that he was a boy, of course, he was also much more open and amiable and agreeable. It had been real nice of him to say that he didn't mind Bertie, although Josie couldn't help hoping that her little brother wouldn't want to go. She knew that in a few months' time she and Jimmy would not see much of one another because they would be at different schools.

When the scholarship results had been announced it transpired that about half the children in 4A had passed for the grammar school. Among that number were Josie Goodwin and Hilda Ormerod, who would be going to Haliford Girls' High School, and Jimmy Clegg, who would go to the Haliford Grammar School for Boys. Josie was glad that Jimmy had passed the exam, and Mrs Faulkner, too, had been fulsome in her praise of him. Josie hoped now that his mother would be able to afford the uniform and everything else he needed, but she hadn't liked to mention it. Derek Watson and Vera Brown had not been successful in the scholarship stakes and would therefore, in September, be attending one of the local senior schools.

Vera had looked upset, tearful almost, at the thought of their newly-formed threesome being split up so soon. 'Not that I ever really thought I'd pass,' she had said resignedly. 'I'm not dead brainy, like you two.'

But by the time September came the thoughts of everyone, children included, were on a much more serious matter. The bombing of London had started and it was feared that, before long, other cities would be under attack as well.

'It looks as though we'll be using that shelter after all,' Iris remarked to Josie at the beginning of October. Josie knew that her aunt was lonely, that she missed her husband very much and was concerned for his safety. Bertie and Frances were too young to be worried by the dismal war news, but she, Josie, was old enough to understand and her aunt often confided in her. 'I was beginning to think your father nearly broke his back for nothing, but I've a feeling we might be needing it soon. I'd best look out some old blankets and cushions and make it nice and cosy, just in case.'

'Why? Are the Germans going to bomb Haliford?' asked Josie in some alarm. 'There's nothing to bomb here, is there? Only the woollen mills, and there's not much point bombing those.'

'But we're quite near to Leeds and Bradford, aren't we, and all the munitions factories. Anyroad, it seems as if the Jerries are dropping their bombs here, there and everywhere now. Buckingham Palace has copped it and you never know who might be next.' Iris glanced apprehensively at her stepdaughter. 'Sorry, love; I didn't mean to scare you, but it's no use pretending everything's fine and dandy, is it? You're a big girl now and I know you understand.'

'It's all right, I'm not frightened,' said Josie with a show of bravado, such as all the girls in her class tried to present to one another. Gas-mask and air-raid shelter practices had been stepped up recently, and several times the air-raid siren had sounded. So far they had all been false alarms or practices, but Josie knew that one day – or night, more likely – it would be for real, and it would be up to her to help Auntie Iris look after Bertie and Frances as she had promised Auntie Alice she would do.

Sure enough, it wasn't long before the bombing of

the provincial cities began in earnest. The attack on Coventry on the fourteenth of November shocked the nation, and throughout the country many cities had their own tales to tell of death and devastation. Southampton, Bristol, Plymouth, and, nearer to home for the Goodwin family, Liverpool, Manchester and Hull. They feared that Leeds and Bradford might be next. At first, when the siren commenced its eerie wail, Iris gathered the children together, sometimes dragging them from their beds, and they ran for the safety of the Anderson shelter. But it soon became apparent that Haliford was to escape the worst of the bombing and that most of the warnings were false alarms. The neighbouring cities of Leeds and Bradford, however, 'copped it' on occasions. After a while they grew blasé and stayed in their beds and even, one night, watched a raid from a bedroom window.

'That's Bradford over there, isn't it?' said Josie to Iris in a hushed voice, as she listened to the far-off thud of bombs and saw flames shooting up here and there in the distant valley.

'I'm afraid so, lovey,' replied Iris. She sighed. 'It seems wrong, doesn't it, to thank God that we're safe when some other poor beggars are catching it.'

'Why, Auntie Iris? Why?' Josie implored. 'Why are they doing it?' It seemed senseless to her, all this destruction and people being killed, her dad having to go away and learn to fight and Jimmy's father never coming back. 'I don't understand it.'

'Neither do I, love.' Iris gave a mirthless laugh. 'If folks tried to understand one another a bit more, then none of this would happen. But they don't; they just go on being pigheaded, thinking they know best. Poor old Neville Chamberlain. He thought he knew best. He tried so hard to keep the peace, poor man, and now he's dead. I've heard it said he died of a broken heart . . . But we're all very good at thinking our way is right, aren't we? God forgive us,' she added quietly. She put an arm round Josie, gently stroking the long hair that flowed to her shoulders. It wasn't often that Iris showed much affection for Josie, not openly, although she was forever cuddling Frances and making a fuss of her; and Josie felt that this unusual gesture was Iris's way of saying she was sorry for the times, and there had been many of them, when the two of them had been at loggerheads.

'Auntie Iris,' Josie said now. 'I've been thinking. I know you don't like me talking about her, but I've been thinking about Pamela. D'you think they'll be bombing Manchester? D'you think she'll be safe? I know she was a nuisance, but I wouldn't like anything to happen to her.'

'And nor would I, lovey,' said Iris. She drew the little girl closer to her. 'But I shouldn't worry too much about Pamela if I were you. I have a feeling that that little madam's indestructible.'

It was in the summer of 1941 that Iris decided she and the children deserved a holiday. It was a pity that Samuel would be missing, but on the forty-eight-hour passes that he got he was content enough just to be at home.

And where else would they go but to Blackpool? They hadn't been back since the time, five years ago, when Samuel and Iris had spent their honeymoon there. They had had a couple of family holidays, but they had been at resorts nearer home, Bridlington and Filey. But now Blackpool beckoned with an urgency Iris couldn't resist; first and foremost because Eliza Pendleton, with whom Iris had kept up a spasmodic correspondence over the years, had at long last moved into her coveted North Shore private hotel and Iris couldn't wait to see it.

Civilians were constantly being urged to stay at home. One of the propaganda posters displayed on the station wall held a portentous warning. 'The time has come,' it read, 'for every person to search his conscience before making a railway journey. You need more than ever to ask yourself, "Is my journey really necessary?"'

But Iris considered that it was. Her earlier patriotism, when she had almost gloried in restrictions and deprivations, did not now burn so brightly. She was looking after three children single-handed, which was only what thousands of other women were doing, admittedly; but she could well afford a good holiday and that was what she was determined they would have.

In spite of the Government warnings to stay at home, dozens of train services were added that August Bank Holiday weekend to accommodate holiday-makers, and when Iris and the children arrived at Blackpool Central Station they found the whole area jam-packed with people. The queue at the left-luggage office – visitors, presumably, who were leaving their belongings before going in search of accommodation – reached as far as the road outside. But the Goodwin family's bed and board had been booked weeks beforehand, and they caught a tram along the promenade, northward to Cocker Square.

This was where Eliza and Norman's new hotel was situated, at the sea end of Cocker Street within a stone's throw of North Pier. 'It isn't quite on the promenade,' Eliza had explained in a letter, 'but it's as near as makes no difference and it is, of course, in North Shore, the more select part of Blackpool.' From the outside it looked, to Iris, pretty much the same as 'Elinorm' on Albert Road. The name was different, however. 'Sunset View', noted Iris with some amusement; then she remembered that Blackpool did have spectacular sunsets and that they would be visible from here, if you looked sideways.

Eliza and Norman were very little changed, Eliza a little more buxom, possibly, in spite of food rationing, and Norman a little leaner – like Jack Spratt and his wife. Their welcome was ecstatic and Iris felt in her bones that this was going to be a wonderful week; and so it turned out to be. She was dying to hear all Eliza's news, particularly about how she was faring in her new venture.

'It was very brave of you, wasn't it, to make a move in wartime,' Iris asked her friend later that evening. The children had all been ready to go to bed early, even Josie, who was tired after the long journey, and Eliza was entertaining Iris in her own little sitting room, the private sanctum where run-of-the-mill visitors never set foot. 'I should have thought it would be a tremendous risk with folks being told to stay at home instead of going on holiday. Not that we've taken any notice, have we?' she added with a laugh.

'Risk? Not a bit of it,' Eliza replied. 'There's the biggest property boom since the twenties here in Blackpool. Folks are beginning to think of a boarding-house as a way of getting rich quick, so Norm and I, we decided we'd best make a move before the prices went sky-high. Most of the south-coast resorts are closed to visitors, you know. Barbed wire all over the beaches and so on, in case the Jerries land. There's only Brighton still in business, I believe. So it stands to reason that Blackpool's reaping the benefit.

'Of course, we've had to take our quota of RAF lads – we inherited them from the previous owner – but we've still got room for visitors as well. I've every room booked this week,' she added proudly. Iris had noticed the 'No Vacancies' sign in the window.

'What about rationing, though?' asked Iris. 'Doesn't that make things very difficult for you?'

'Not really,' Eliza replied. 'The visitors have to bring their ration books, like you did, and I just collect 'em all up and take 'em along to the grocer where I'm registered. There are ways and means, you know,' she added slyly, tapping the side of her nose. 'Least said, of course, but my little grocer's very good to me.' Iris knew about under-the-counter goods and black market trading. It went on in Haliford, too, and although she hadn't been a part of it, she would never be so self-righteous as to report the miscreants to the authorities.

'You put on a good meal at any rate, Eliza,' she remarked now. They had all enjoyed their first meal of red salmon – a rare treat – with a generous salad, followed by home-made apple tart. The cream was only 'mock', to be sure, but Eliza was an excellent cook and Iris was looking forward to a week of meals that she hadn't had to prepare herself.

'I'm not saying there aren't any problems, though,' Eliza went on. 'Getting staff, for one thing. A lot of the girls here are working at the aircraft factory, getting better money, I daresay, than I can pay them. But I've managed to get two youngsters from Preston. They're staying with us for the season. But I'll have to ask you to make your own beds of a morning, Iris. There's a notice in the bedrooms. It'll leave the girls more time for other jobs.

'And then there's the pirate landladies. They're a big problem, taking the bread out of our mouths, you might say, and not even paying tax on the income neither.'

'What d'you mean?' Iris was lost here.

'What do I mean?' Eliza was red in the face and

very indignant. 'I mean private house-owners what are opening their doors to visitors. All on the q.t. an' all, most of 'em. A lot of the boarding-houses are full up, you see, with the RAF and civil servants from London, and the private householders are seeing it as a good way to make a quick bob or two. Some of 'em are building up quite a lucrative trade. But it's not fair, Iris. It's not fair at all on those of us who have a living to make from it.'

'But I don't suppose you're doing too badly, are you?' said Iris with a twinkle in her eye. It was the age-old cry of seaside landladies that they had a job to make ends meet, but most of them looked pretty prosperous, for all that. 'Be honest, now.'

'No, between you, me and the gatepost we're doing all right,' Eliza replied with a grin. 'I'm hoping this 'ere place'll be a little gold mine when this lot's over. Though God knows when that'll be,' she added, shaking her head sadly. 'There's not much sign of it yet, is there? It must be a worry for you with your Samuel being away. I daresay you miss him.'

'Yes, it's not easy,' said Iris, 'but we're all in the same boat and it's no use complaining. Your Norman didn't have to go, then? No – of course he wouldn't. He's older, isn't he? I keep forgetting with Samuel being younger . . . He's a few years younger than me, you know,' she added confidingly.

'Only a year or two, surely?' said Eliza. Iris knew that her friend was trying to be tactful. She had felt her age, and more, just recently. 'Yes, my Norman's turned fifty now,' Eliza went on, 'so with a bit of luck he won't have to go. He served in the last lot, of course, and I reckon one war's enough in any man's lifetime. Anyroad, that's enough of gloomy talk. What are you going to do this week? Have you any plans?'

'Well, there's the sands,' said Iris, smiling. 'That'll be a priority every day, I daresay, although our Josie's getting a bit big for sand-pies. She's twelve now, just finished her first year at the grammar school,' she added proudly. 'Then we'll have to pay a visit to Pablo's. I remember the last time we couldn't keep Josie away from the place. They're still making their ice-cream, are they, in spite of rationing?'

'Yes, they seem to keep going,' replied Eliza. 'I send Norman along for a few blocks of it a couple of times a week. It's lovely with tinned fruit, provided you can get the fruit, that is,' she laughed. 'And you'll have to take the kids to the circus, won't you? And *Happidrome*'s on at the Grand Theatre, the stage version, you know. Eeh, I do love *Happidrome* . . . "We three, in Happidrome",' she started to sing, '"Working for the BBC . . ."'

'"Ramsbottom, and Enoch, and me . . ."' Iris joined in, laughing. 'Yes, I like that an' all. I must certainly try and see that. You've seen it, have you?'

'Good gracious, no! What time do I have for going to t' theatre? You'd know if you were a seaside landlady. I hope you have a grand week anyway. You deserve it.'

And so they did. Wartime Blackpool didn't seem much different, in many respects, from what it had been in peacetime. The quality and variety of entertainment in the town's many theatres remained the same. As well as *Happidrome* at the Grand, there was a lavish season show at the Opera House, *Hullabaloo*, starring Nervo and Knox, Frank Randle and Anne Ziegler and Webster Booth. Iris decided, however, that this would not be to the children's taste, so they opted for the pictures. *The Ghost Train*, with Big-Hearted Arthur Askey and Richard (Stinker) Murdoch, both radio favourites of the children.

Then there was the Tower Circus, a continuous delight to the eye with its elephant sextet, pony revue, the Flying Devils on the trapeze, and the Cairoli brothers, Blackpool's own clowns. And, as a fitting finale, the Grand Patriotic Water Spectacle. Iris and Josie were both amazed, as they had been on their last visit, at the sight of thousands of gallons of water being pumped from below into the circus ring and at the aquatic display that followed; bathing beauties, sparkling fountains and flashing lights, all in shades of red, white and blue.

Frances was entranced by the Tower Ballet, *Babes on Parade* featuring a hundred local children. 'I wish I could dance like that,' she whispered to Josie. 'Aren't they lovely?' At the moment Frances was pestering her mother for dancing lessons, like some of the children in her class, and Josie thought that it wouldn't be long before Iris succumbed. Frances usually managed to get her own way. She, Josie, had never wanted dancing lessons, but as she watched the dainty little girls up there on the stage she could just imagine her pretty little sister as one of them.

'I bet you could do just as well,' she whispered back. 'I tell you what. I'll ask Mum if she'll let you go to dancing, when we get home.' She was feeling particularly friendly towards Frances at the moment. They were having a lovely holiday and she felt all happy and tingly inside.

She was rewarded by her sister's beaming smile. 'Gosh, will you really, Josie? I keep asking her, but—'

'Shhh,' Iris admonished them. 'For goodness' sake, stop whispering, you two, and watch the dancing. We've paid good money to come in here.' The sisters giggled and exchanged conspiratorial smiles.

One familiar attraction was missing from Blackpool, however, in the summer season of 1941. The Tower ascent had been closed after the 1940 season, and the structure converted into an emergency radar station. You could see the projections sticking out from the iron-work girders. They hadn't been up the Tower last time, Josie reflected, although Dad had half promised that they would, and they wouldn't be able to go this time either. Still, they were having a wonderful holiday. Every day there was the sea and the sands, weather permitting, because the week was a mixture of sunshine and showers. An added attraction was watching the RAF recruits exercising on the beach or marching in formation along the streets. The town was full of the lads in air-force blue. There were a dozen or so of them billeted at Sunset View, filling the place with their laughter and high spirits.

Also during that fun-packed week they visited the Boating Pool, the Pleasure Beach and Stanley Park, walked on the pier, sampled the delicious ice-cream at Pablo's, and stood in an enormous queue for sticks of Blackpool rock with the Union Jack running through them. Sweets were on ration now, but they were able to buy sticks to take back for Auntie Alice, Uncle Jack and Len, as well as a few for themselves. At the end of the week Josie was wishing she could stay here for ever. Just imagine living in Blackpool; how wonderful that would be.

A memory suddenly flashed into her mind, something she had completely forgotten. Auntie Iris and her father arguing on the other side of the bedroom wall. Iris saying that she would like a private hotel – and Dad shouting back at her, 'Have you taken leave of your senses, woman?' How funny . . . she hadn't thought about that for years.

Josie wondered if Auntie Iris still had ideas about becoming a hotel proprietress. And, if she had, how grand it would be . . .

Indeed Iris had. All her former aspirations, dormant for so long, sprang to the fore again during that week in Blackpool, especially as she watched Eliza, so contented and fulfilled in her work. She could just see herself in the same role, busy in the kitchen doing what she did best, baking and preparing meals; and then dressing up of an evening, as Eliza did, and socializing with the guests in the lounge.

She broached the subject to her friend one evening, tentatively though; she didn't want Eliza to think she intended to set up in opposition.

'Good heavens, no!' replied Eliza. 'Why on earth should I think that? There's room enough in Blackpool for any amount of us. I think it 'ud be a splendid idea, Iris, and if you take my advice you'll strike while the iron's hot. It would be just the job for you with Samuel away in the Army; it 'ud take your mind off things. What d'you think Samuel'll say?' She laughed. 'If he's owt like my Norm he'll say "Anything for a quiet life", and let you get on with it. And I should think you can wrap him round your little finger, can't you?'

'I don't know . . . I'm not sure.' Iris was doubtful. She had known at the time of their marriage that Samuel had a will of his own, but she hadn't realized just how strong that will was or how many ding-dong battles it would lead to. But they usually managed to patch up their disagreements amicably enough. 'I mentioned it once before,' Iris told her friend, 'and he didn't like the idea at all. But things are different now. I've a feeling he wasn't any too happy at the mill before he went away. He should be due for a spot of leave soon. I'll tell him about it then, rather than write to him . . .'

But it soon became clear that this was one difference of opinion which would easily not be resolved.

'No, never in a thousand years!' Samuel stormed when Iris brought up the subject. 'A Blackpool boarding-house? Are you crazy, woman? What the hell do I know about running a blooming boarding-house, eh? Or private hotel, as you keep calling it. My job's in the mill, always has been and always will be. I said so before, ages ago; I thought you'd forgotten all about this daft whim.'

'It isn't a whim, Samuel. It's something I feel I could do really well. I want to make something of my life . . . before it's too late,' Iris added quietly. She was becoming more and more conscious of the advancing years – every time she looked in the mirror, in fact. 'And it wouldn't be you running it, anyway, not at first. It 'ud be me. You're away in the Army, aren't you?'

'I shan't be in the Army for ever, woman.' Iris hated it when he called her woman, something he only did when he was really vexed. 'And what the hell am I supposed to do while you're being a seaside landlady, eh? Twiddle my thumbs? Or sell ice-cream on the sands, perhaps, or be a deck-chair attendant? Yes, I might be good at that.'

'Don't be ridiculous, Samuel. You'd be the proprietor, along with me, like Eliza and Norman are. They run it together. I thought you weren't too settled at Hammond's mill, anyway. You did nothing but grumble before you went away.'

'Only like every chap grumbles about his job. It's not all plain sailing you know, 'specially when you're an under-manager. I'm settled enough there. Wool's in my blood, I tell you, always will be.'

'And who can tell what the woollen industry'll be like after the war?' Iris persisted. 'There are all sorts of different ways of doing things now, more 'automation', don't they call it, needing fewer men? You've heard tell what happened in the old days when they brought in the power looms. The Luddites an' all that. How d'you know you'll have a job to go back to after the war?'

'Don't talk such nonsense, woman. My job's safe. And you think you can see into the future now, do you? The Yorkshire woollen industry'll never die, you take it from me. And I want to hear no more about blasted seaside boarding-houses. If ever you take a boarding-house then it'll be over my dead body!'

'Samuel!' Iris was shocked at his vehemence and suddenly fearful at his choice of words. 'What a thing to say, in wartime.'

'It's only a figure of speech,' Samuel replied hastily. 'What everybody says. I didn't mean it, not literally. But I don't want you to do it,' he added more gently. He moved across the room to sit beside her on the sofa. 'Come on, love. We mustn't quarrel, not when I've only a few days' leave.' He put an arm round her. 'You say you want to make something of your life. Well, this is your life, isn't it? Looking after our children while I'm away.'

Your children, Samuel, Iris thought, but didn't say, as she noted his puzzled expression. She tried to smile at him knowing that, for the moment, she would have to be content, or pretend to be. For the sake of her husband, who was a soldier serving his King and Country, and shouldn't have any distractions to worry him. 'All right, Samuel, you win,' she said, reaching out and stroking his dark, now slightly greying hair. Words which, at one time, she would never have uttered.

Chapter 15

Whoever christened it the 'bore war' was dead right, Samuel thought to himself after he had been in the Army a few months: For the lads in khaki, at any rate. Not so for the RAF; the boys in air-force blue were taking a hammering all right, in the skies above Kent and Sussex, but the main body of the Army, after the humiliation of Dunkirk, were in training camps up and down Britain. And they were becoming increasingly bored. There was square-bashing and manoeuvres, of course, to relieve the tedium; and it was then that Samuel, aged thirty-seven, began to realize that he was not as fighting fit as he had thought he was, not compared to his younger comrades, some of them mere youngsters of eighteen, scarcely out of the classroom.

There was the NAAFI of an evening, if he felt so inclined; the clubroom where you could partake of a snack to augment the Army ration, buy sweets and cigarettes, enjoy a drink, or congregate round the tinny piano for a singsong. Samuel joined in the camaraderie sometimes, but it was then that he felt his age the most, when he heard the raucous laughter and lewd jokes of the young servicemen. Samuel had never been much of a one for dirty jokes but he didn't want to be thought of as a killjoy with the lads who were young enough to be his sons. Instead he smiled and nodded agreeably as he quaffed his beer, and winked in a knowing way at their saucy pictures of Betty Grable or Veronica Lake pinned up above their beds. And thought about his home and family . . . and Iris.

He missed her more than he would ever have thought possible. In the five years they had been married, he had grown to love her deeply and to appreciate her more and more. It was a pity, he often thought to himself now, that he hadn't told her so very often. She couldn't compare with Betty Grable or Alice Faye or Dorothy Lamour, or even with some of the photos of young wives and sweethearts that Samuel was frequently asked to admire; not, that is, as far as looks were concerned. But there were other qualities that were more important than looks; love and loyalty, trust and family values, things to which, at one time, Samuel had paid scant regard.

He had a photograph of Iris in his wallet, a very flattering one of her on the promenade at Bridlington, and he showed this to his colleagues with as much pride as they took in their gorgeous womenfolk. She was smiling broadly at the camera, her dark eyes alight with the suggestive gleam that was so often in her glance when she looked at him, her dark hair, a little longer than she usually wore it, curling almost to her shoulders, a saucy hat tilted sideways over one eyebrow and her mid-calf-length, very fashionable dress covering her unattractive legs.

But it wasn't of her looks that Samuel was thinking as he gazed at this photograph, and at the others that he had of Josie, Bertie and Frances. He was thinking of the way Iris had borne with him the last few years, with his moodiness and his self-will; and with his children, too, because they hadn't always been easy, especially Josie. Now, thanks to Iris, Samuel had come to appreciate his children, and he loved them far more than he had at the time of his first marriage. They had shared some truly happy times together as a family, and Samuel had been relieved to see, when he left home, that his wife and elder daughter were now the best of pals.

There were still barneys, though, from time to time. With two people as strong-willed as he and Iris that was inevitable. There was the business of the Blackpool boarding-house, for instance. Samuel knew that he had been intolerant with her and dictatorial, too, but he honestly believed that now, while the war was on, was no time to be making such a momentous decision. Perhaps, when it was all over, he might even let her have her way.

Time frequently hung heavy; that was why he was lost, so often, in introspection. Samuel had found that the war was a great leveller. It didn't matter what your job had been in Civvy Street; in His Majesty's Forces you were all equal, whether you were a dustman or a milkman, a bank manager or . . . an under-manager at a Yorkshire woollen mill. In the barrack room you were all the same. There were the officers, of course, and Samuel had had to get used to taking orders from youngsters half his age, youngsters with a posh accent who had been to a swanky school. But he was learning to take it all in his stride. He was now a corporal himself, to his gratification and that of Iris, when he wrote to tell her.

To cope with the soldiers' boredom and their low morale after Dunkirk the ABCA – the Army Bureau of Current Affairs – had been formed. Army education was now compulsory for at least one hour a week. They learned, just as if they were at school, about the military course of the war, about social, economic and political affairs, and there were organized group discussions about such matters.

There were many unofficial discussions, too, in the NAAFI or the barrack room; and Samuel thought, privately, that old Winnie, despite his masterful handling of the war, would have a tough job getting re-elected to Number Ten once it was all over. Most of his comrades seemed to blame the Conservative Government for disrupting their lives, and vowed not to vote that lot in again. The Army was certainly a breeding ground for socialism and Samuel, a Tory all his adult life – because it had seemed a more respectable thing to be – was now beginning to have a change of heart.

Group discussions, however, not any amount of them, would win the war; neither would square-bashing or manoeuvres or singsongs round the piano. So it was with a sense of relief that Samuel found himself, in the summer of 1942, in the desert of North Africa as part of the British Eighth Army. Now, at last, he could feel that he was doing the job for which he had been called up, defending land which was part of the British Empire.

'Why the hell do we want to defend a God-forsaken place like this?' the soldiers frequently asked one another. But they did, of course, know the answer. Beyond the desert area lay the Suez Canal and the Middle East. The Germans were running short of oil, but if the Middle East and all its oil fields were conquered, then they could have all the oil they needed. By the time Samuel arrived on the scene the Eighth Army, after constant withdrawals and frequent changes of commander, had been forced back to a defensive position at El Alamein, only sixty-five miles from Alexandria, dangerously near to Cairo and the Suez Canal. At roughly the same time yet another new British commander arrived: General Montgomery, soon to be nicknamed 'Monty'.

Samuel had heard his father speak about the trenches in the last war – not often, because Harold Goodwin had not been one to dwell on his gruesome experiences – and he gathered that they had spent most of their time up to their knees in mud. At least they were spared that in the desert, but Samuel frequently wondered which was the worst evil, the mud or the dust. The dust was everywhere, in their food, their clothes, their hair and their tanks. The desert was an awful place, miles and miles of sand, as you might expect, and rocks as well, but mainly dust. From time to time the wind blew it into great billowing clouds – sandstorms – and tanks on the move made their own little sandstorms as well. By midday the heat was unbearable, but the nights could be bitterly cold.

Then there were the flies, crawling over your food, up your nose, into your mouth and round the corners of your eyes, anywhere where there was a drop of moisture. They would even drink the sweat off your back and Samuel had seen his comrades' backs black with them. And it would be heaven help you if you were wounded in the desert because they were seen to swarm in their thousands round even the slightest cut.

If the menu at the camp in Aldershot had been uninspiring, at least it had been varied; here it was monotonous, mainly bully beef and biscuits, tinned milk and tea. To brew up they made a desert fire from sand soaked in petrol. The biggest problem was water. Sometimes they found themselves down to half a gallon a day each, and that had to do for drinking and washing, as well as filling the radiator of the tank. The food had been better, some of Samuel's comrades told him, when they had been chasing the Italians. Then they had captured, along with the Eyeties, their tinned tomatoes and vegetables, and wine, too.

But that had been before General Rommel arrived with the German Afrika Korps. They had given the Tommies a run for their money, all right. They had brought with them some nasty weapons as well. Mines, known as 'Devil's Eggs', were planted all over the place. The only way to find them was to send the infantry ahead to prod the ground with bayonets, not an easy task to carry out with enemy shell fire all around you.

'But we'll soon send old Rommel packing, now that Monty has arrived,' they told one another. And on the twenty-third of October, 1942, the battle of El Alamein began.

Samuel had supposed that you might be safe enough in a tank. But he had supposed wrongly, he was to learn soon after his arrival in the desert, when he saw fire-blackened bodies hanging out of tanks. They were safe against a soldier with a rifle, but very little else. It was quite easy to get blown off course, and what they all dreaded most was the petrol tank or the ammunition locker being hit. If that happened, the tank would become a blazing inferno within seconds.

The Americans, however, had sent a supply of Sherman tanks, more than a match for anything the Germans had. Samuel, crouched in the turret of his Sherman Mark II tank, had convinced himself of this. He was invincible . . . wasn't he? When the explosion came, like the loudest clap of thunder he had ever heard, catapulting him into the air, knocking all the breath from his body, his last thought, before he was blasted into oblivion, was of the words he had spoken in anger to Iris, *Over my dead body . . .*

They were the words that flashed into Iris's mind, too, on that afternoon at the end of October, as she stood on the doorstep with the small yellow envelope in her hand. 'Over my dead body,' he had said. 'If you ever take a boarding-house it'll be over my dead body.' And now Samuel, her dear, dear Samuel was dead. She didn't need to open the envelope to know what the telegram said. The boy was staring at her, shuffling about uneasily, waiting for an answer.

'Thank you,' she mumbled, an automatic response. 'You don't need to wait. There'll be . . . no reply.'

Back in the living room she knelt on the hearthrug, a favourite place when she was in need of comfort, and drew out the thin sheet of paper. She read the words with a sense of fatalism. 'Regret to inform you . . . Corporal Samuel Goodwin . . . killed in action.' It was what she had dreaded, half anticipated, ever since she had known that he was to be sent to North Africa. It was what every woman feared, praying nightly that the loved one would be safe, but at the same time knowing that there was a certain futility in such prayers in wartime. Iris had prayed for him – and now he was dead. God doesn't answer prayers, she thought bitterly at that moment. He doesn't even listen.

She crouched closer to the fire, but the warmth could give no comfort this time to her frozen body and mind. She felt numb; it all seemed so unreal, and the tears, which might have brought some relief, would not come. She was still kneeling there some twenty minutes later when she heard the back door burst open and the children dash in from school. Quickly she rose from the hearthrug, pushing the telegram into her apron pocket, knowing that she must try to behave as though there was nothing amiss. The two younger ones, Bertie and Frances; she couldn't tell them, not just yet. She knew it was them: they always arrived home first. Josie would be a half-hour or so later, as the grammar school day finished later and it was further away. It was Josie that Iris was waiting for. Josie would have to be told first. Josie would know how she was feeling. Josie would help her to break the news to her younger brother and sister.

'Hello, you two. Had a good day?' Iris tried to act normally, but her voice sounded strange to her ears, far away and unnatural, and she still felt paralysed, in her mind and her limbs. Her legs would hardly carry her into the kitchen to put on the kettle, a routine task she always performed as soon as the children came in. They followed her, to her dismay. She usually loved to see them when they came home from school, bursting with the news of the day and chattering their heads off. But today was different. Iris wanted to be on her own at this moment; she didn't want to talk to them, not till Josie came home. To Bertie and Frances, however, this day was the same as any other; better, in fact, for they had a surprise for her.

'It was a smashing day, Mum,' Bertie was saying. 'We had to design a poster about the Squander Bug, and then write about what we're doing to help win the war. I wasn't right keen on that – the writing bit, I mean – but the teacher liked my painting. She gave me a gold star and put my picture on the wall.'

'Very good, dear,' replied Iris automatically, trying to smile at him. Damn the war, she was thinking; damn and blast it all, this bloody war that was even dragging children along in its wake, encouraging them to look on it as some sort of game.

'And Frances has got a surprise for you, Mum,' Bertie went on excitedly. 'Haven't you, Fran? Go on, show Mum what you've got.'

With a beaming smile Frances reached into the pockets

of her gaberdine mac and drew out an egg and a tomato, one in each hand. 'Here you are, Mum,' she said, hands outstretched, offering the gifts. They were rare treasures, both of them, since food had gone on ration.

Iris took them from her, blinking confusedly. 'What . . . what's this? Where did you . . . ?'

'It was a raffle, Mum,' said Frances, frowning slightly with impatience. 'Don't you remember? We told you we were going to have a raffle at school, and we took tuppence each for the tickets, Bertie and me. An' I won. Not the first prize – that was a bar of chocolate – but this was the second . . . What's the matter, Mum?' Frances was looking curiously at her. 'Don't you want them? I thought you'd be pleased.'

'Of course I'm pleased, darling. Thank you very much. You're a very . . . clever little girl.' Iris knew only too well that it was not cleverness that won a raffle, but luck, pure and simple. But how could she tell the child that she was a lucky little girl on such a day as this? She carefully placed the egg and tomato on the kitchen table and, bending down, drew Frances into her arms. 'Thank you, darling. Now we'll be able to have egg and tomato sandwiches for tea, won't we? I was going to open a tin of pilchards, but this will be a lovely treat. If I mash a drop of milk into the egg it'll happen be enough for all of us . . .' To her dismay her voice broke and the tears she had been trying to hold back started to flow down her cheeks. Abruptly she stood up straight, but Frances had noticed.

'What's the matter, Mum? You're crying.'

'Just a bit, dear.' Iris hastily dabbed at her eyes with a handkerchief. 'I'll be all right. It was such a nice surprise, you winning that raffle. And grown-ups sometimes cry when something nice happens . . . as well as something sad. Silly, aren't we? And I've had a bit of a headache today. I wasn't feeling too well when you and Bertie came in, but I'll be all right. Could you just go and play quietly upstairs, the pair of you? Do a jigsaw, or play with Bertie's farm, while I get the tea ready.'

Obediently the two children nodded, although they both gave her an odd look. Iris popped the egg in a saucepan of water and put it on the stove to boil. It was ages since they had had egg sandwiches. Dried egg was all right for some things, custard, for instance, and for putting into cakes, but you couldn't boil it or fry it. What a wonderful treat it would have been . . . on some other day. Perhaps she could keep the news from the children until they had enjoyed their tea.

Fighting back her tears, Iris cut the bread and spread it with margarine mixed with a little butter, then sliced the tomato thinly. There was home-made cake to follow, as always; Victoria sponge today and treacle parkin. She forced herself to spread the cloth on the table and set out the cups, saucers and plates. She wouldn't tell any of them, she decided, not even Josie, not until after tea. But when she heard the back door open for the second time, Iris knew that she couldn't keep the news to herself any longer. When Josie burst into the living room her stepmother was standing stock-still in the middle of the floor, staring into space.

The girl stopped in her tracks. 'What's wrong?' she said, the smile that had been on her face quickly replaced by a worried frown.

Iris just shook her head bemusedly.

'What's up? What is it?' Josie went over to Iris and took hold of her arm. 'Auntie Iris . . .?'

Iris put her hand into her apron pocket and drew out

the telegram. She handed it to Josie, her eyes downcast, not looking at the girl. 'This came . . .' she faltered, 'this afternoon.'

She heard Josie's indrawn breath, a gasp of horror, before the girl snatched the telegram and quickly read it to herself. The next minute the paper fluttered to the floor and her stepdaughter's arms were round her, her head buried against her shoulder. 'Oh, no . . . no,' Josie sobbed. 'Not Dad, not my dad. Oh . . . what are we going to do? Mum . . . what are we going to do without him?'

Iris held her close. 'Hush, hush my darling. It's terrible, I know . . . but we'll have to try to be brave. For the little ones, for our Bertie and Frances.' The tears were streaming down Iris's face now, her words interspersed with sobs that she was fighting to control. But amid the sadness was the realization that Josie had called her Mum, for the very first time.

'You haven't told them?' asked Josie, lifting a tear-stained face to Iris. 'Our Bertie and Frances, they don't know?'

Iris shook her head. 'No, dear, not yet. I want you to be a very brave girl, you see, and help me to tell them.'

'I'll help you, Mum,' said Josie sadly. The word seemed to be coming naturally to her now. 'I'll help you tell them. An' I'll help you look after them as well. I promised . . . my dad that I would, when he went away last time. He asked me to, you see.'

'And you have helped me, Josie,' said Iris, smiling warmly at her through her tears. 'You've been a real good girl, and I don't know what I'd have done without you.' She hesitated for a moment. Then, 'I'm sorry,' she went on, very quietly. 'Those times when I was cross with you, I'm sorry. I was only trying . . . to help you to be a good girl, you know. It's important to be good. It's wicked people that cause wars and trouble, and all this unhappiness. And I don't think we understood each other properly at first, did we, you and me?' Iris looked at her fondly. Her heart was almost breaking with her sorrow about Samuel, but she felt that there was now an accord between herself and Samuel's elder daughter that had not been there before.

'No,' said Josie simply. 'I didn't always . . . understand. And I know I was naughty. I was awful, sometimes. I'm sorry . . . I'm sorry, Mum. I'll try to be good now. I will, really.'

'I know you will, dear.' Iris shook her head sorrowfully. 'This war – this blasted war,' she whispered, almost under her breath. 'Why? *Why?* I'll never understand . . .' She was silent for a moment, then she turned to Josie, trying to speak in a normal voice. 'Listen, dear. Dry your eyes, and go and tell Bertie and Frances that their tea'll be ready in five minutes. It's all right, they won't notice you've been crying. They'll be too busy, I daresay. Then, after tea, you and I will have to try to be very brave . . .'

'I think you're doing the right thing, Iris,' Alice told her. 'It'll be a whole new experience for you, running a boarding-house in Blackpool.'

'It's a private hotel,' Iris interpolated.

'Same dog washed,' Alice went on. 'Just a more fancy name, that's all.' But Iris didn't take umbrage as she might once have done. Alice had been kindness itself to her since Samuel died, and a constant source of comfort to all three children as well. Iris was very grateful to her, and the two women were more friendly now than they had ever been, and so Iris had come to tell Alice Rawlinson her piece of news before she broke it to the children.

Iris had hardly given a thought to Blackpool during the grim, depressing weeks following Samuel's death. Like their elder sister, Bertie and Frances had wept bitterly on hearing the news, and all of them had needed a great deal of consolation and extra attention in the weeks leading up to Christmas. A somewhat bleak Christmas it had been, too, with memories of Samuel more vivid than ever at that poignant family time. But there again, Alice, along with Jack and young Leonard, had been a tower of strength.

When thoughts of Blackpool and her aspirations to be a hotel proprietress had resurfaced, as they did from time to time, Iris had been filled with an overwhelming sense of guilt. Samuel's words kept repeating themselves over and over in her brain. *Over my dead body, woman. Over my dead body* . . . She even felt, at times, though she knew such an idea was preposterous, that she had been partially responsible for his death; that she had, somehow, caused it to happen.

But with the dawning of 1943, and more especially as the days began to lengthen with the coming of spring, Iris knew she must endeavour to put her despair and her feelings of guilt behind her. She would continue to grieve for Samuel, of course, but she had to look to the future. She was certainly not an old woman – not yet quite fifty – and she had many years ahead of her, God willing. It was then that the thought of the private hotel entered her mind again, and it would not be suppressed.

She wrote to Eliza Pendleton, and that good lady perused the adverts in the *Blackpool Evening Gazette*, sending on to Iris any she deemed suitable. It was at the beginning of March that Iris made the journey to the west coast of Lancashire to view three possible properties, leaving the children in the capable hands of Alice for two days and nights. Alice had been in on the secret, but the children had simply been told that Iris had some business to attend to away from Haliford. They had assumed that it was to do with the coal haulage business that Iris's first husband had started. The business was now expanding into other west Yorkshire towns and Iris, a shareholder, still had some say in the running of it.

Six weeks later, all was signed and sealed. Iris had bought her longed-for private hotel. All that remained was for her to sell the house in Jubilee Gardens – she didn't anticipate much difficulty with that desirable residence – and to tell the children.

It was the children that Alice mentioned next. 'It'll be grand for the kiddies, won't it? I've often wished I could have brought up our Leonard in a nice seaside place, away from all the grime and smoke we get here. Although I must admit that it's not too bad up here on the hillside. But beggars can't be choosers, can they?' She laughed, without any sign of envy. 'Yes, it'll be just the job for those three bairns in Blackpool . . . I shall miss 'em though, Iris. God knows, I'll miss 'em.' Alice looked pensive. 'Especially Josie,' she added quietly. 'I shouldn't say it, I know, but I've always had a soft spot for that lass, even more than the others.'

'I know, Alice,' replied Iris. 'I know how fond you are of Josie . . . and how fond she is of you.' Iris remembered only too well how the girl, in the early days, had harped on and on about her auntie Alice, and how it had been Alice she had run to the time Iris always thought of as 'the big row'. But all bitterness had been laid aside long ago. 'It was Josie I wanted to talk about,' Iris said now, looking keenly at the other woman.

'Why, there's nothing wrong, is there?' asked Alice, with

a touch of alarm. 'I thought that you and Josie were getting on all right now.'

'So we are,' Iris smiled. 'Everything's fine between us, couldn't be better. She's no trouble at all. In fact she's been a real good help to me since her dad died, bless her. No, there's nothing wrong. But I can't help wondering if there may well be when I tell her we're moving to Blackpool.'

'She doesn't know then?'

'No, none of them do, not yet. There didn't seem to be any point in telling them until it was all sorted out. You know what kids are like for pestering the life out of you. When and why and what all the time; they never give you a minute's peace. I just wanted to get on with it on my own, nice and quiet, like. But now I'm wondering what Josie will say.' Iris hesitated. 'She may not like the idea at all. She's got all her friends here, you see. There's Hilda and Vera, those two girls she met at Beechwood. Well, it's more Hilda than Vera, now that the two of them are at the grammar school. Thick as thieves they are, our Josie and Hilda Ormerod. Then there's Jimmy Clegg. She still meets up with him from time to time.'

Alice grinned. 'Oh, so that's still going on, is it?'

'Yes, but there's nothing 'going on', not like that,' said Iris hastily. 'They're only kids, aren't they? And Jimmy Clegg seems a nice sort of lad, not so much of a scallywag as he used to be. I can't see our Josie coming to any harm with him.'

'They're growing up, though,' Alice pointed out. 'Your Josie's fourteen, isn't she? And I can hardly believe that our Leonard's nearly seventeen. If this blessed war goes on much longer he'll have to join up an' all.'

'Happen it'll all be over before then,' said Iris consolingly. 'Let's hope so, anyway. Our Josie's nearly finished her third year at that Haliford High School. Can you credit it? She's doing very well, too, from all accounts. There was an open day not so long ago; you know, where you can go and talk to the teachers, and they all spoke well of her. A real hard worker she is, so they say. And that's what's worrying me most, Alice. What's it going to be like for the lass when she has to change schools, apart from leaving all her friends? She's already lost her father, she won't take kindly to leaving you, either,' Iris added quietly, something which at one time she would never have dreamed of admitting to the other woman.

She stared into space. The truth was, she was more scared than she liked to admit of breaking the news about Blackpool to Josie. There had been a tacit understanding between the pair of them recently, a growing regard and a friendship that Iris felt amounted almost to love, and she was afraid of doing anything that might shatter their new relationship. She would miss the girl, she knew, if Josie were to stay behind in Yorkshire, but Josie's feelings had to be considered, and it might be what she would want. Her father was no longer here, and Iris was . . . well, she was only her stepmother, when all was said and done.

She wondered if she should suggest to Josie that she could, if she wished, remain with her aunt Alice. Iris knew she would be disappointed – devastated, in fact – should the girl choose to do so, but she felt that it was only right to give her the choice. But first of all she had to make sure that Alice was willing. She may well feel that she had already done enough.

Alice seemed to be aware of her dilemma. She nodded discerningly. 'So what you're saying, Iris, is can the lass stay here with me? Is that it?'

Iris looked at her gratefully. 'Only for the time being.

Just until she's finished her time at the grammar school, taken her school certificate or matric or whatever they call it. I think it might be better if she didn't have to change schools just now. That's if you would have her.'

'Of course I would. You know I would, and willingly,' replied Alice. 'You'd miss her though, wouldn't you? Just as much as I would miss her if she went to Blackpool with you.'

'I would that,' said Iris feelingly. 'I'd miss her all right. But I know I've got to consider the girl's wishes. There have been times when I . . . when I haven't done that.' Iris's voice petered out and she glanced down, fiddling with a button on her cardigan. 'It's up to Josie to decide what she wants to do. I've got to give her the choice.'

'Well, you put it to her then,' said Alice in a matter-of-fact way. 'Lay all the cards on the table. You can't do any fairer than that. But, d'you know, Iris, I've a feeling that you may well be surprised at her answer.'

Chapter 16

Josie was quite indignant that Iris should even imagine she would want to stay behind in Haliford. When the rest of the family were going to live in Blackpool? The very idea! At one time Josie would have thought her stepmother was trying to get rid of her by suggesting such a thing; but the girl had grown up tremendously in the few months since her father was killed, in mind as well as in body, and she knew this wasn't the case at all. She realized that Iris was trying to be fair to her, to consider her feelings in a way that she hadn't always done in the past; just as she, Josie, was now making the effort to help Iris as much as she could instead of being difficult.

Josie knew that in some ways it would be a big wrench, leaving Haliford and moving to Blackpool. Iris had been right about that. There were all her friends – not only Hilda, but the other girls as well that she had met at Haliford High School. Then there was her auntie Alice, and uncle Jack and Leonard. Their house had always been a second home to her and her auntie Alice a second mother – until recently, when Josie had noticed Alice taking, as it were, a step back. Josie, with her new maturity, saw that her aunt was trying to make sure Iris was given her rightful place as head of the Goodwin family. Yes, Josie would miss the Rawlinsons, although she hadn't seen very much of

Leonard lately since he had left school and started work as an apprentice electrician.

Then there was Jimmy . . . He had promised to write, but Josie had a sense that lads such as Jimmy were not great at letter-writing. With a feeling of resignation, she realized that the pair of them had come to a parting of ways. They were both growing up; there would be other friendships, other relationships; but she knew that leaving Jimmy behind would be hardest of all.

She had to go, though. Who in their right mind would give up the chance of living in Blackpool? Josie felt a little peeved that Iris, especially in view of their present harmony, hadn't confided in her sooner about her plans. But no matter; she had told her now. Bertie and Frances were so excited they could hardly keep still, whilst Josie, although she was looking forward to this new chapter in her life, was also experiencing more than a little trepidation. It would all be so very different; a new home, new school, new friends . . .

The private hotel into which the Goodwin family moved at the beginning of June 1943, was on Pleasant Street, a road adjacent to the promenade in the North Shore area of Blackpool. It was the area on which Iris, like Eliza Pendleton, had set her sights, the more desirable part of town; and, as her friend had pointed out, the hotel was near enough to the promenade to make very little difference. The difference being, of course, that Iris couldn't have afforded a sea-front hotel, and this was the next best thing. She was stretched to the limit as it was, but she felt sure that her outlay would pay dividends before long.

As stated in the advertisement, the property was an 'Old established private hotel in an excellent position near the promenade. Dining room, lounge, private living room, kitchen, pantry, fifteen bedrooms with wash-basins, WCs on each landing, one bathroom. Good bookings.' It was the last two words that had clinched the deal. Iris could see that Mr and Mrs Giles, who were retiring and moving to a small house at Marton, had worked long and hard to make the place a going concern. Iris acquired, along with the property, the bookings for the rest of the season, eight RAF recruits and the resident staff, which consisted of two young girls from Blackburn, and a woman who came in to 'do' on a twice-weekly basis.

Iris intended to do all the cooking herself. It was something at which she knew she excelled; she enjoyed it, too, and she had never been afraid of hard work. She thought that as time went on – and When the War was Over, a phrase on everyone's lips – she might enlist extra help. At all events, she had her two daughters who would, doubtless, follow her into the business. Josie very soon realized that this was to be her future occupation. Whether she would or no, it was what Iris wanted; and Frances, young as she was, often talked about the time when she would be old enough to help her mum.

Iris had seen this to be the case usually, in seaside towns; the children entering the family business as chef or bookkeeper or waitress, whatever was their bent. There was a very good catering college in Blackpool, and Iris had plans for both her daughters to go there on leaving school. She wasn't so sure about Bertie. He was now eleven, ready to begin his first year at the grammar school – a place had been found for him at the one in Blackpool – a studious boy, his head was forever in a book. Iris couldn't see him, somehow, as part of the milieu of the hotel trade, but time would tell.

One thing Iris changed quite quickly was the name of the hotel. She thought that the present name, 'Sunnydale', was trite and not very appropriate; Blackpool had its fair share of wind and rain as well as sun, although this never seemed to deter the visitors. Just as soon as Iris found a signwriter, it was altered. 'Irisdene', proclaimed the bold black lettering on a board swinging above the door. Iris folded her arms and gave a satisfied nod when she saw it up for the first time. Now all she had to do was welcome her visitors and carry on with the good work.

Josie had been apprehensive at the thought of changing schools, but a place was found for her, on transferring from Haliford High School, at the Blackpool Collegiate School for Girls, and she quickly settled in to her new routine. The building, situated on Beech Avenue, near to Stanley Park, was impressive. Elegant steps led up to the front door, flanked by four stone pillars on top of which was a triangular portico, reminiscent of a Greek temple. Topping the roof was a cupola from which, so it was said, could be viewed the distant hills and fells which gave their name to the school's four houses; Bowland, Longridge, Parlick and Pendle. But no one ever entered the cupola, just as no one except important visitors used the front door to the building.

Josie was to spend only two years at the Collegiate, as it was known, but they were two very happy years. She found just as much friendship and camaraderie here as she had enjoyed at her previous school. She tried to live up to the school motto, *Meliora Sequamur* – Let us aim for higher things – as she was determined to work hard and make her stepmother and her aunt Alice proud of her. She did wonder, at times, if working in a hotel could be called 'higher things', but maybe, if she did very well in her exams, Iris might change her mind about that. She seemed set on it at the moment, though, and Josie had decided not to argue.

Josie learned to wear her school blazer, with its distinctive blue-striped braiding, with pride. She learned, too, that the unique fringed hat, shaped like a pork pie, could be made much more wearable if the high crown was tucked in to half its size and the hat skewered to the back of the head with a couple of kirby-grips. To wear it in its original state would, indeed, brand one as an ignorant new girl. Clothes rationing had been in existence since 1941, which meant that the very strict rules about school uniform could no longer be enforced. However the girls were expected to wear navy-blue skirts and white blouses. This was fortunate for Josie, as the same colours had been worn at Haliford High School. She well remembered her early days at Beechwood, and how she had felt so conspicuous in that dreadful gymslip of the wrong colour.

Josie discovered that Blackpool, even in the middle of the war, was a comparatively peaceful place. You could hardly move for the RAF recruits, of course – the town was swarming with them – and there were huge water-tanks near North Pier, barricades across the promenade, and signs pointing the way to the nearest air-raid shelters. But very few bombs had fallen on the town, none, in fact, since 1941; and here, as at other north-west resorts, there was no barbed wire covering the beach. If the enemy were to invade, it was not expected that they would try to come ashore here. The sands were supposed to be out of bounds, though, after dusk, but it was evident that courting couples paid very little heed to that rule.

There were certain intimations, though, that there was

a war on, and that other towns, indeed, were suffering very badly. During 1943, when the bombing raids on Manchester were very severe, the Collegiate was host to many of the girls from Stretford High School. Josie had never known from which part of Manchester Pamela Coates hailed, or whether the girl had gone on to a grammar school when she left Haliford so suddenly. She curiously scanned the faces of the visitors, but to no avail. Pamela was not among them. In a sense, Josie couldn't help feeling relieved, although she often wondered what had become of her former friend and how she was faring.

Josie joined the 'Knit-Wits' Club, a group of girls who knitted socks for the forces whilst discussing current issues. Needlework was not really her forte, but she felt that she could at least do her bit for the war effort. More to her liking was potato-picking at a farm out at Great Eccleston. The need for labour in the Fylde was acute, and each autumn, girls from the fourth and fifth years went to help lift the potato crop on the local farms.

Then there were air-raid practices, still continuing though actual air raids were unlikely; queuing for sweets, always in short supply, at the tuck shop; munching sticky jam buns from the Beech Bakery (woe betide you, however, if you were caught doing so in your school uniform!). And, paramount among all these minor diversions, studying for that important milestone, the school certificate examination.

During the summer holidays Josie helped Iris at the hotel. It was one afternoon in August 1944, when she was setting the tables in the dining room in readiness for high tea, that she looked out of the window to see a familiar figure coming up the path. He wasn't familiar at first, however.

Josie didn't know any RAF lads, apart from the ones that were currently billeted at Irisdene – and those only by sight – and this young man was not one of that number. She looked again, then she gave a gasp of delight, for there was no mistaking that tousled fairish hair, on top of which the forage cap was perched incongruously, nor his good-natured grin and cheery wave as he spied her through the window. It was her cousin, Leonard.

She dashed from the dining room, along the dim hallway and flung open the front door. 'Len, Len! How lovely to see you! I'd no idea . . .'

'Hiya, young Josie.' His arms went round her in a bear-like hug. 'Surprised to see me, eh? I told Ma not to let on that I was doing my training in Blackpool. Thought I'd give you all a surprise.'

'You've done that all right.' Josie was pink-cheeked with excitement. 'We knew you were going into the RAF, when you got your call-up papers. But fancy you ending up in Blackpool. Mum, Mum! Come quick. Look who's here.'

Iris, hurrying from the kitchen, was also delighted at seeing her nephew. The young man didn't need much persuading to stay for tea, in fact Josie thought he was only waiting to be asked. The meal was taken in the private living room after the visitors had all been served, and Josie, Bertie, Frances and Iris hung on his every word as he told them about his training.

'Yes, there's never a dull moment. Drilling on the sands and square-bashing around the streets of Blackpool. We attract quite a crowd, I can tell you,' Leonard laughed. 'Anybody 'ud think we were a circus parade, the way folks goggle at us.'

'Some of us have better things to do, lad,' said Iris tartly, although with a grin on her face. 'When you've seen one bunch of RAF lads you've seen 'em all. We've had that many billeted here since we took the place over twelve months ago that they're all beginning to look alike.'

But Josie, stealing a sidelong glance at her cousin from behind her teacup, didn't think they were all alike. There couldn't be another one quite like her cousin Leonard. He wasn't what you would call handsome; he was very much like Uncle Jack, in fact, nice and homely-looking. The same unruly hair, mild bluish-grey eyes and amiable expression.

Rather more than amiable today, in fact. When she had dashed out to meet him he had looked at her as though he was really glad to see her, as though she was . . . special. She hadn't noticed that look until today. She had always thought that he regarded her as just a little kid; but not any more, perhaps? He was looking at her again now, his eyes narrowing and his lips curving in a slight smile as he became aware of her scrutiny. She returned his grin, a little unsurely, then quickly looked away. She felt a bit embarrassed, but happy all the same, happy and excited.

'Aye, we've had our fair share of you lads in blue,' Iris continued. 'One lot out and another lot in, but I'm not complaining. We've all got to do our bit, but it looks as though we might be on the last stretch now, doesn't it, after that – what do they call it? – that second front.'

'Let's hope so, Auntie Iris,' said Len with feeling. 'I'm glad I've had the chance to join up, though. I wouldn't have wanted to miss it all.'

'And where are you billeted?' asked Iris. 'Anywhere near here?'

'No, not really. Hornby Road, near the centre of town,' he told her. 'The grub's not bad, if you like spam and chips and corned beef hash. Not a patch on Ma's cooking though. Nor yours, Auntie Iris,' he added. 'I bet this is the best billet in Blackpool, isn't it?'

'Not so far off, lad,' said Iris with quiet pride as she smiled at him. 'That's what I'm aiming at, anyroad. And what are they training you for, Len? I don't suppose you'll be flying, will you, not just yet, anyway?'

'No, probably not at all,' replied Len ruefully. 'I wouldn't mind having a bash at old Jerry, but I daresay I'll end up as ground crew. Electrician, same as I was in Civvy Street, like as not. Anyway, it's my half-day today, Auntie Iris, and I promised Ma I'd come and have a look at you all. And I was wondering . . .' He looked at Josie, his eyebrows raised questioningly. 'I was wondering if Josie would like to come to the pictures with me? That is, if it's all right with you.'

'Of course it's all right with me,' said Iris warmly. 'But it's the young lady herself you should be asking. I reckon she's old enough to make up her own mind, isn't she?'

Josie didn't need asking twice. 'I'd love to go, Len,' she said delightedly. 'Thanks ever so much for asking me.'

'Who else would I ask?' replied Len, grinning at her again. 'You're my little cousin, aren't you?' But his expressive glance seemed to convey to her that that was no longer how he thought of her.

Josie was well aware that it was only because Leonard was her cousin that Iris was allowing her to go out with him. Despite her remark, just now, that Josie was old enough to make up her own mind, Iris was keeping a very strict eye on her stepdaughter, far more so than she had done back in Haliford. There, Iris had allowed her to knock about quite freely with her girlfriends, and even with Jimmy Clegg. But this was Blackpool; '. . . And you can't be too careful,' Josie had heard Iris say to her great friend Eliza Pendleton, 'not when you have daughters to bring up.'

Blackpool was not only swarming with RAF recruits, there were Polish, Australian and French servicemen there as well, and, last, but by no means least, the Yanks. 'Overpaid, oversexed, and over here,' was a phrase often uttered, especially by the RAF lads, who were no longer in such demand at the local dance halls now that Uncle Sam's GIs were in evidence. And so Iris was keeping an eagle eye on Josie, making sure she always knew just where the girl was going, and with whom.

Josie didn't mind. She was finding her life very full, what with school, homework, occasional visits to the cinema with friends, as well as helping Iris at the hotel at weekends and in the holidays. There had been little time or opportunity to take much notice of the opposite sex, and Josie, so far, had not been particularly interested. Until now, when Len had looked at her in that special way.

'Right, where would you like to go?' he asked her; although, on hearing her breathless reply that she didn't mind, he did seem to have already decided.

Cover Girl, starring Rita Hayworth, was showing at the Princess, and it was to that cinema, near the North Pier, that they walked, just as soon as Josie had helped Iris clear away the tea things.

It was a squally evening with spots of rain in the air, not much like August, but not untypical of Blackpool, a place well used to the vagaries of the weather. Josie was glad of her camel wraparound coat and she pulled the belt tighter and turned up the collar. The garment was rather short. Iris had bought it for her last year at the Co-op, but Josie had grown quite a lot since then. She was well aware that her red skirt showed a couple of inches at the hem, but no matter; the red did at least match her felt beret. She knew there was no point in moaning about her clothes. As Iris was forever telling them all, it was a question of needs must, and there were no clothing coupons to spare at the moment for new coats for any of them.

Josie clung on to her beret against the sudden gusts of wind as they walked south along the promenade, trying to match her steps with her cousin's long-legged stride. He slowed down, suddenly aware of her scurrying along beside him.

'Sorry – I'm going too fast, aren't I? It's all this marching, you see. And I'm not used to walking at the side of a girl neither,' he added slyly.

'Go on with you! Who are you trying to kid?' Josie teased him. 'I bet you've any amount of girlfriends,' she added, a little hesitantly. She wanted to find out, but she didn't want it to look as though she were being nosy. '. . . Haven't you?'

'Girlfriends? No, not me.' Leonard shook his head.

'Not back in Haliford?' Josie thought it was more than likely there would be someone back home. It was quite a while since she had had much contact with her cousin and she had lost touch with his doings.

'Nope. Not a one,' he insisted. 'Well . . . there was one, last year. But she went and found somebody else.' He gave an easy laugh. 'So there you are. I'm as free as a bird. What about you?' Len turned to look at her, his blue-grey eyes almost on a level with her brown ones. Josie had grown several inches since moving to Blackpool and now, in her wedge-heeled shoes, she was only a couple of inches shorter than Len.

'What about me?' Josie put her head on one side. 'Well, what about me, then?' she replied pertly.

'No boyfriends?'

'Nope. Not a one,' said Josie, just as her cousin had said. 'Not ever,' she added simply.

'Go on! With a house full of RAF lads? You're not going to tell me that some of them haven't been after you?'

'No . . . no, they haven't, honest, Len,' said Josie, stating the case. 'Not one of them.'

'There must be something wrong with 'em then.' Len gave her an appraising glance.

Josie could feel herself glowing with pleasure. He really must like her. She smiled at him, shaking her head. 'No, I don't think they've really noticed me. I'm usually in school uniform, you know, and Mum doesn't ever ask me to serve at their tables. I think she's trying to keep me out of harm's way. She usually tries to make sure I'm doing my homework when they're around.'

'And you don't mind?' Len looked at her curiously. 'I remember a time when you'd have done anything to defy your auntie Iris. Real little rebel you were, and no mistake. You've changed, Josie. D'you know that?'

Josie nodded. 'For the better I hope, Len. I think we both realized, Iris and I, that there was no point our both pulling different ways, especially after Dad was killed. We've got to live together, so we may as well try and get on. And we do get on very well now. Of course, I know that our Frances is the favourite. Always has been and always will be . . . Iris thinks the sun shines out of that child,' Josie added. But the words were said without any rancour.

'And that doesn't worry you?' asked Len.

'Funnily enough, no,' Josie told him. 'I was very jealous of Frances when she was born. I suppose it was more resentment, really, because she had come along and my mother had died. But I got over all that ages ago. Iris has done such a lot for all of us, you see. I realize that now.'

'Don't let her put out your spark though, Josie.' There was a warning note in Len's voice.

'What d'you mean?'

'Well, she's a very dominant sort of woman. Always was. Don't let her get all her own way, especially as you get older.'

'I'm fifteen already.'

'So you are. And very grown-up.' If Len's words were a tiny bit patronizing Josie tried to ignore it. 'Just stick up for yourself, Josie. Make sure you get what *you* want from life, not what *she* wants.'

'Don't you worry. I can look after myself,' Josie answered sharply. Who did Len Rawlinson think he was, bossing her around as if she were a little kid? And just when she thought things were going so well between them.

'Oh goodness, look at the queue,' she exclaimed as they drew near to Princess Parade. The queue of people, two and three deep, stretched right along the block and round the corner into Springfield Road. 'We'll never get in.'

'Yes we will,' Len assured her. 'There's loads of room in there. Come on, stand on this side of me and keep warm.'

Josie's momentary bout of crossness vanished as she stood huddled against the roughness of Len's greatcoat. He even put an arm round her to keep off the wind, just as though she were a real girlfriend. But once they got inside the cinema he didn't lead her to the back row, where she could see a few couples already ensconced, but to a seat in the centre stalls. Neither did he hold her hand during the film, but he did buy her an ice-cream at the interval. He didn't have one himself, but whilst she licked the somewhat watery confection from the little wooden spoon he lit a cigarette.

Josie looked at him in some surprise. 'I didn't know you smoked, Len.'

'Don't sound so shocked, little cousin.'

'I'm not!' Josie hated it when he called her that. 'I'm not shocked . . . and I'm not your little cousin, either. Not any more.'

'No, I know you're not. Only teasing.' Len held up his hand in an apologetic way. 'Don't get all huffy.' He took a long drag at his cigarette and puffed out the smoke. 'Ye-eh, I smoke now,' he said, tapping the ash into the ashtray in front of him. 'Never used to at home, but most of us do in the RAF. Good for the nerves, you see. Here – have a drag.' Josie sat back in her seat, startled. 'Go on,' he laughed. 'Have a puff. Have you never had a smoke before?'

Josie slowly shook her head. She took hold of the proferred cigarette, held it tentatively to her lips and sucked inwards. It tasted odd, a bit like the smell of her dad's pipe tobacco, which came back to her now. The smoke went up her nose and she suddenly coughed and spluttered. 'Here, take it back. I don't think I like it.'

'You're supposed to inhale, breathe it right in.' Len smiled good humouredly. 'Best not tell Auntie Iris, eh? She'd say I was leading you astray.'

'No . . . she wouldn't approve.'

'Don't suppose my ma would either. They never believe you're grown-up, do they?' Len looked at Josie keenly now. 'You are growing up, Josie. D'you know that? I got quite a shock when I saw you.'

'A pleasant one, I hope?' said Josie coyly.

'I'll say! An' I like your hair like that. It suits you. No more pigtails, eh?'

Josie had reservations about her hair. At times she hated it and wished she had been born what Iris called a 'dizzy blonde', like Betty Grable or Alice Faye. Or like her little sister, Frances, whose hair was pale gold and silky and curled in soft waves; just as their real mother's had done, although Josie's memories of her were now somewhat hazy. Josie's hair was dark brown, almost black, and although it was thick and glossy it refused to curl. She had thought of experimenting with a home perm, but Iris had advised against it. So she tried to coax it, with the aid of curling-pins on the ends, into a page-boy style, almost to her shoulders, with a heavy fringe that nearly touched her eyebrows.

'No, no more pigtails,' she said now, recalling how Len – and Jimmy – had used to tweak at her long plaits. 'Too grown-up for pigtails now, Len.'

He leaned towards her then, gently stroking her cheek with his forefinger. 'I'll say you're grown-up . . . little cousin,' he whispered softly. He took hold of her hand and squeezed her fingers, but let go of it almost at once as the curtains were drawing back in readiness for the big film.

Cover Girl was an extravaganza of escapism and Josie wallowed in it all, while acutely aware of the young man at her side. Her cousin Len so familiar, and yet, almost a stranger now, at times. He was bigger, bolder, much more mature. Josie was a little in awe of him, but she did hope that after this evening he would want to see her again. And when Rita Hayworth sang 'Long Ago and Far Away', Josie felt that it was just for her. She knew that it wasn't really the film star singing at all – she was just moving her lips and miming to the music whilst someone else sang – but it made no difference. The words were magic. As it said in the song, her dream really was beside her.

Josie breathed an inward sigh of contentment.

Len did ask her if she would go out with him again. 'Ivy Benson's band's on at the Winter Gardens next week,' he told her as they stood at the gate of Irisdene. 'How about it? Are you game?'

'You mean . . . go dancing?'

'Yes, of course. Why not? You've never been? You can dance, can't you?'

'Of course I can dance,' said Josie indignantly. 'I used to go to the dances at St Luke's in Haliford, you remember, but I was only a kid then. I've been to a couple of church dances here . . . but not to the Gardens or the Tower. Iris doesn't think I'm old enough, not till I'm sixteen, she says.'

'She'll let you come with me, though?' Len leaned forward, putting his hands on her shoulders.

'Yes . . . yes, I'm sure she will,' said Josie eagerly. 'Why don't you come in and ask her?'

'No, I'd best not,' replied Len. 'It's quite a walk back to Hornby Road and I don't want to get locked out. But if you say Iris'll let you go, then that's all right. Shall we say a week tonight? I'll give you a ring and let you know what time I'll pick you up. OK?'

'OK,' repeated Josie, a trifle breathless.

Len kissed her then, just a friendly kiss on the cheek. 'Goodnight . . . little cousin,' he said affectionately. 'See you next week then.' And with a genial grin and a wink he walked away. But it was enough for Josie. She glided up the path as though airborne.

'It was a smashing film, Mum,' she told Iris as she sipped her cocoa and munched a digestive biscuit. 'You should go and see it. It's just up your street . . . and don't say you haven't time, 'cause me and the girls from Blackburn'll look after things here for you. Why don't you ask Eliza to go with you? It's on for a few more days. I know you used to like going to the pictures in Haliford, didn't you?'

'Yes,' said Iris musingly, taking note of Josie's flushed cheeks and excited chatter. 'Yes, I did used to enjoy the pictures. I might ask Eliza. I think we're both due for a bit of a treat. Thank you, Josie. You're a real good lass. I'm glad you enjoyed it, love. It was nice to see Len again, wasn't it?'

Calf-love, thought Iris, as her stepdaugher nodded eagerly, her eyes shining. I hope she doesn't get hurt, because I don't suppose Leonard really wants to start anything . . . But he's a good lad. She won't go far wrong with Len Rawlinson, and that's for sure.

Chapter 17

Josie looked at herself critically in the full-length mirror in her attic bedroom. Mmm . . . Quite attractive, but not what you could call really stylish, she pondered. But who on earth could be stylish in these days of clothing coupons and make do and mend? That was what anyone who was good with a needle was doing these days, making do and mending. Josie wasn't at all gifted in that direction, but Iris was and she had made a very good job of the outfit that Josie was wearing now. Last year's dirndl skirt of cornflower-blue cotton, sprigged with white daisies, had been lengthened by inserting a band of bright yellow material six inches above the hemline. Iris had also made her a yellow blouse from the same material, and a wide white belt pulled tightly round her slim waist added a finishing touch and helped the garments look more like an ensemble.

Josie glanced down at her legs, long and slender and brown, and decided she would do very well without stockings. She possessed only one pair of silk ones, which she found itchy and uncomfortable; besides, that silly girdle and suspenders were too much of a palaver. Thank goodness the white sock mark that her school ankle socks had left behind had vanished during the long summer holiday. There hadn't been all that much sun, but Josie's skin tanned easily and she didn't need to resort to painting her legs with gravy browning as a lot of girls did. She slipped her feet into her wedge-heeled shoes. They might rub a bit, but it wouldn't have to matter. They were the only decent pair she'd got apart from her black school shoes and she couldn't wear those. At least these, though rather heavy for summer, were fawn suede and would go with anything.

She patted her hair, newly-washed and shining, deciding that it looked quite nice, then dabbed the tiniest touch of powder on to her shiny nose. Josie didn't wear make-up. Her skin was tanned and healthy-looking and her lips were a natural red. There was no need for artificial colouring; anyway, Iris wouldn't approve. Iris used a lot of make-up herself and she was forever popping into Boots the chemist's to see if they had an allocation of lipsticks, but as far as her stepdaughter was concerned, that lady had very definite views on what was permissible. Josie was only too pleased that she was allowing her to go dancing tonight. Iris had stressed, as Josie had known she would, that she was making a concession only because Len was her cousin, and that she had to make sure she was home by half past ten. Indeed, there wouldn't be any excuse for being late as the dance halls closed at around ten o'clock.

Josie smiled back at her reflection, noting that her eyes looked brighter, more sparkling, tonight. She didn't know, but Iris had already noticed the radiance in them. It had been there all week, ever since she returned from the cinema with Len. Her cousin would be here soon to call for her. Josie put her arms round her slender body, hugging herself at the thought, then, draping her camel-hair coat round her shoulders, she went downstairs to wait for him.

* * *

It wasn't the first time Josie had been in the Winter Gardens building. She had been to the pictures there, and to a pantomime at the Opera House. She had also taken a peek at the Empress ballroom with its balconies, plush seats and magnificent sprung floor, made from a quarter of a million separate blocks of wood; and she had watched the dancers swirling round, in an anti-clockwise direction, to the music of Horace Finch at the Wurlitzer organ. But it was the first time she had been dancing there herself – the first time, too, that she had been into the cloakroom to leave her coat in exchange for a little pink ticket.

'Wait here for me, won't you?' she said to Len, somewhat fearfully, as they entered the Floral Hall. The place was bustling already with crowds of young men, mostly in air-force blue, and young women, who all looked much more self-assured than Josie was feeling at that moment. Len promised he would wait just there, next to a huge potted palm.

Josie nipped down the stairs and joined the queue to dispose of her coat. Then, somewhat unsurely, she did what a lot of the other girls seemed to be doing; she followed a crowd of them into an alcove at the side to survey herself in a mirror. Her hair didn't really need any attention, but she took out a comb and tidied it up a bit, all the while glancing surreptitiously about her.

Many of the girls were very sophisticated, unlike Josie. She watched them opening enamelled powder compacts to dab at already over-made-up faces, and outlining Cupid's bows in brilliant red lipstick, even poking at eyelashes with a little stiff brush covered in gooey black stuff. The girl next but one to Josie at the long mirror leaned forward, pressing her lips together to distribute the colour evenly. Her mouth was painted cherry red, bright and glossy, which just matched her silky rayon dress. No make do and mend here, thought Josie, noting the padded shoulders and the sweetheart neckline, the bow trim at the waist and the way the material flowed round the girl's shapely hips.

As Josie watched the girl put her head on one side and gave a half-smile at her reflection as though satisfied at what she saw there. As well she might be, thought Josie. That young woman would never need to resort to a home perm, not with gorgeous curly hair like that springing all over her head, just like Shirley Temple's. Josie felt her heart skip a beat then. No . . . it couldn't be! Could it? How often Pamela had been told that her hair was just like that of the child star. Josie looked again, more closely. Yes, it was! Of all people, it was Pamela Coates.

The girl suddenly became aware of Josie's scrutiny and she turned from the mirror as if to say, 'Who d'you think you're staring at?' But she didn't say it, because at that moment recognition dawned in her eyes as well.

'Josie . . .'

'Pamela . . .'

They both spoke at once. 'Whatever are you doing here?' Then they laughed.

'I live here,' said Josie. 'I live in Blackpool now.'

'Go on, you don't!' Pamela pushed at her. 'Since when?'

'Since . . . just over a year ago, that's all. Iris – you remember Iris, my stepmother? – she decided to take a boarding-house here, well, a private hotel, to be exact.'

'Go on!' said Pamela again. 'Well, fancy that! Would you believe it? Yes, I remember Iris. The wicked stepmother. How is she, by the way? Still poisoning your apples, is she? "Mirror, mirror on the wall,"' Pamela chanted lugubriously, grinning at Josie's and her own reflection.

Josie giggled. She couldn't help it. 'No, she's all right now, honestly. We get on real well.'

'Well, that makes a change. And your dad? I suppose he's in the Army, is he?'

'He was in the Army . . . but he was killed. That's why we came to Blackpool.'

'Oh, kid, I'm ever so sorry. I'd no idea.' And Josie could tell from Pamela's expression that the girl really was sorry. 'Whatever must you think of me, blurting it out like that?'

'You weren't to know. How could you?' Josie smiled at her.

'When was it? D-Day, I suppose?'

'No, before that. El Alamein – he was with Monty. What about your dad? Is he all right? He was in the RAF, wasn't he?'

'Ye-eh, my old man's all right, as far as we know. I daresay he'll turn up like a bad penny when it's all over. And Mum's still on munitions. That's what I'm doing an' all. Have been ever since I left school.'

'You've left?'

'Yep. Don't sound so amazed.' Pamela gave a tinkling laugh. 'We're not all brain-boxes like you, you know.'

'But you were, Pam,' Josie insisted. 'You were real clever.'

'But I didn't *apply myself*, did I?' Pamela giggled. 'That's what they said, all them teachers. Anyway, I left last Christmas, soon after I was fifteen. I couldn't get away quick enough, I can tell you. You're still there, I suppose?'

'Yes, I moved to the grammar school here. The Collegiate, it's called.'

'Hmmm . . . very nice, I don't think!' Pamela grimaced. 'Still, you always were a bit of a swot, weren't you?'

Josie shot her a wary glance, but Pamela was smiling amicably enough. She decided to change the subject. 'So what are you doing here then, in Blackpool?'

'On holiday. What else?' Pamela shrugged.

'With your mum?'

'No! Perish the thought! No, I'm with a girlfriend.' Pamela glanced around. 'At least I was, but I think she must've gone on ahead. We're staying at the same boarding-house, Elsie and me, but apart from that we're free agents.' She gave a wink and a meaningful smile. 'She goes her way and I go mine. That's what we've done the other times we've been dancing, anyway.'

'You've been here already this week?'

'Not here. To the Tower.'

'With your friend . . . Elsie, did you say?'

'Ye-eh . . . Like I say, I start off with Elsie, but I don't always finish the evening with her. It just depends. I expect you've been here loads of times, haven't you, Josie? It must be terrific, living in Blackpool.'

'I've been . . . once or twice,' said Josie evasively. 'I've not been to the Tower though. It's Ena Baga playing the organ there now, isn't it, since Reginald Dixon joined up?' She must make it look as though she knew what was going on in her own town.

'Yes, she's dead good,' said Pamela, nodding enthusiastically. 'P'raps we could go one night, you and me, eh Josie?' Josie nodded, rather less eagerly. 'Who are you with tonight, anyroad? Some girls out of your class?'

'No, I'm not with them. As a matter of fact . . .' Josie hesitated. 'I'm with my cousin, Len. You remember Len Rawlinson, don't you? Auntie Alice's son. He's billeted here, in the RAF. And I'd better get a move on, too, or else he'll be wondering what's happened to me.'

'You mean to say you've actually got a cousin here, in the RAF?' Pamela's pale blue eyes gleamed with rather more than interest. 'Lead me to him! Of course I remember your Len; he was only about fourteen, though, when I knew him. Daresay he's grown up a bit by now, hasn't he?' Pamela nudged her slyly as they made their way out of the cloakroom and up the stairs. 'You've got something going, have you, you and Len?'

'No, of course not,' said Josie hurriedly. 'Nothing like that. He's my cousin, that's all.' She hadn't forgotten how spiteful Pamela had been on finding out that she, Josie, was keen on Jimmy Clegg. Pamela did seem nicer now, not so peevish and nasty, but there was still that wicked gleam in her eye at the mention of the opposite sex. In fact Josie had already gathered, in the few minutes she had spent with Pamela, that the girl was what Iris would call 'man-mad'. Josie didn't think Len would be Pamela's type – he was far too placid and easygoing – but she was taking no chances. Any suggestion of 'Hands off – he's mine', would, Josie knew, only serve to make Pamela more interested.

'Len and I used to be good friends when I lived in Haliford,' she said now, very casually, 'but I daresay he only called because Auntie Alice told him to. There he is,' she added as they reached the top of the stairs and Len turned to see them approaching. 'Would you have recognized him?'

'Wow . . . no!' said Pamela breathlessly, and Josie's heart sank.

Len was smiling questioningly, looking from her to Pamela, then back again. 'I was wondering where the dickens you were,' he said. 'Who's this? No – wait a minute – I know. It's Pamela, isn't it? Pamela . . . Coates?'

'That's right. I just bumped into Josie in the cloakroom.

Wasn't that a bit of luck?' Pamela grinned roguishly, holding out her hand. 'How d'you do? Don't think I'd have known you though. Shot up a fair bit, haven't you?' Pamela put her head on one side, smiling up at him, and Josie noticed that she only came to just above his shoulder. When they had been in the same class at Beechwood School Josie and Pamela had been much of a height. Now, Josie was a few inches taller. Pamela must have grown only a couple of inches since leaving Haliford; but she had grown in other directions, Josie thought now, noticing again the girl's rounded hips and the way her breasts pushed at the thin fabric of her dress. Josie was as flat as a pancake by comparison, the bra she had recently started wearing being more for convention than necessity.

'Yes, I remember you very well,' Len was saying thoughtfully.

'Once seen, never forgotten – that's me,' quipped Pamela.

'You were an evacuee, weren't you, in the same class as our Josie? Staying with your auntie.'

'Yep, until I was drummed out of the place.' Pamela threw back her head laughing. 'I didn't half cause a rumpus, eh, Josie? Did you hear about it, Len?'

'Yes, I think I did hear something about it.' Len's eyes were alight with amusement as he looked down at her.

Josie stood there feeling awkward and ill at ease. She didn't want to be reminded of Pamela's awful behaviour, which had resulted in that terrible row with Iris and Josie running away from home. She had put it all to the back of her mind . . . until now. 'Right then,' she said, rather more brusquely than she intended. 'Let's get moving, shall we?' The other two looked at her in surprise. 'I mean . . . if we're going dancing, then let's go, shall we?'

'Yes . . . of course.' Len tucked his hand companionably under her elbow, giving it just the tiniest sqeeze. Then he turned to Pamela. 'Are you joining us, Pamela? Or are you with someone?'

'Only my friend, Elsie, but it doesn't matter. I 'spect I'll bump into her before the evening's over. We're staying at the same boarding-house in Charnley Road.'

'Charnley Road?' Len's eyes widened with interest. 'Good gracious, that's practically the next road to where I am. I'm billeted in Hornby Road, would you believe it?'

Yes, I would, thought Josie, I'd believe it only too well. I'd believe anything of Pamela Coates. Although, in all fairness to the girl, she couldn't help it if her boarding-house was only a stone's throw from Len's digs. And what did it matter, anyway? Pamela would be going home with that Elsie, if they found her – Josie did so hope they would – whilst Len would be walking back with her, because Iris had said that he must.

'Right, girls, where shall we sit?' asked Len as he escorted them, one on each arm, up the steps that led to the ballroom.

'Sit? We're not going to sit down, are we?' said Pamela. 'We'll never get any partners, will we Josie, if we sit down all night. And you can't dance with us both at the same time, can you, Len?' she asked pertly.

Oh crickey! thought Josie. This was something she hadn't considered until now. What was she going to do while Len was dancing with Pamela? She knew he would, if only to be polite. She also knew that it would have very little to do with politeness; she had noticed the way Len had looked at Pamela. She would have to stand on her own, at the edge of the ballroom floor, as she could see groups of girls doing all around. Standing there looking all casual as though they were waiting for a bus, as though being asked to dance was the last thing on their minds. Most of them were in twos and threes though, not on their own as she would be if Len and Pamela took to the floor. Josie wasn't normally a shy or nervous girl – far from it – but here she felt more than a little out of her depth.

'Let's stand here,' said Pamela, stopping by a pillar at a corner of the ballroom. 'And you two go and dance. I don't mind, honest. Go on, don't just stand there gawping.' She gave them both a push with the flat of her hand. 'Somebody'll ask me in a minute, anyroad. They always do. An' I'll see you back here in this corner. Go and enjoy yourselves – it's a quickstep.' She grinned and fluttered her fingers at them.

'She's quite a case, isn't she?' laughed Len as they took to the floor to the strains of 'Mama, May I Go out Dancing?' 'Fancy you meeting up with her again.'

'Yes, just fancy,' said Josie flatly. 'She used to get me into no end of bother at school, you know. Iris couldn't stand her. She said she was leading me astray.'

'Yes . . . I remember that,' said Len slowly. 'Still, she seems OK now. A real live wire, but I don't suppose she's as bad as she used to be. I expect she's calmed down.'

'Mmm . . . maybe she has.' But Josie sounded doubtful. It wasn't likely that Pamela was still pinching sweets from Woolie's, or threatening to 'tell' if things didn't go her way. But calm down? Josie couldn't imagine that Pamela Coates would ever calm down. Still, she didn't want Len to think she was being uncharitable. We used to be right good friends,' she said, 'Pamela and me, until things started to go wrong. I expect she was unsettled, being an evacuee an' all that. She was the only one in our class; all the others had gone home. Like you say, Len, I daresay she's all right now.'

'You don't sound very sure.' Len was looking at her keenly.

'It was just a shock, seeing her again.'

'You didn't mind me asking her to join us?'

'No, of course I didn't.'

'You're sure?'

'Sure I'm sure.' Josie laughed. 'What else could you do? She'd tagged herself on to me, hadn't she? I don't suppose we'll see much of her, anyroad. She'll not be short of partners. Looks as though she's found one already.' For as they danced past their corner Josie could see that Pamela was no longer there.

Josie concentrated on her steps, noting that Len's dancing was about on a par with her own, adequate, but not what you could call polished. At the church hops back in Haliford she had more or less mastered a waltz and a quickstep, and a slow foxtrot after a fashion, but the tango was still beyond her. It was nice and comfortable dancing with Len and she leaned closer to him, feeling the rough serge of his uniform jacket rub against her chin and the firmness of his hand in the middle of her back. She decided she wouldn't worry any more about Pamela. She was going to enjoy herself.

When they got back to the pillar at the corner Pamela was just leaving the arm of an RAF lad and in a moment her friend, Elsie, joined them as well. Introductions were made and Josie began to feel much more at ease. At least she would have someone to stand with now that there were four of them. Elsie was just like Pamela, bright and bubbly and not very tall, but with dark curls in contrast to Pamela's fairish ones.

The evening was a mixture of modern dances and a few old time numbers, to suit all tastes. The latter were more to Josie's liking because the steps all followed a pattern and you didn't have to improvise, which usually involved falling over your partner's feet half a dozen times until you got the hang of it. Josie threw herself wholeheartedly into the veleta, the St Bernard's waltz and the military two-step, sometimes with Len and sometimes with other RAF lads who asked her to dance. She soon realized that she needn't have been afraid of standing on her own because that never happened, not once. The supply of young servicemen was more than enough to meet the demand of the local girls and the young women on holiday.

Veletas and barn dances and the like were not to everyone's taste, however. Josie wasn't altogether surprised that they were not Pamela's cup of tea. 'Dead tame, this, isn't it?' Pamela remarked with an exaggerated sigh as the organist at the Wurlitzer broke into a spirited rendering of 'Teddy Bear's Picnic'. He had taken over whilst Ivy Benson and her all-girl band had a break. 'It's just for kids . . . or old fogies.' But it didn't stop her jumping up and on to the floor a minute later when yet another of the RAF recruits came to ask her to dance.

The RAF were not the only servicemen to be seen at the Winter Gardens. Well in evidence that evening – as they had been, not only there but in other parts of Blackpool for the past couple of years – were the American GIs. Their well-cut olive-green uniforms, made from far superior material than those of the British troops, formed a vivid contrast to the all too familiar air-force blue. And it was not unknown for the more unscrupulous of these Yanks to adorn their uniforms with counterfeit medals and badges of rank to which they were not entitled.

It was little wonder that many female hearts were set fluttering, or that the lads in air-force blue, who had been around only too long, grew resentful. Tales were told of RAF lads misdirecting Yanks on to the wrong bus or tram when they were trying to find their way back to the camp at Warton. Many a man had found himself heading for Bispham or Cleveleys at the north end of the town, when he should have been travelling south. Or so it was said.

Josie had never been in such close proximity to these exuberant young men from across the Atlantic as she was that evening. She had seen them in town, of course, black Yanks as well as white – it was almost the first time she had seen a black face outside of the pages of a book. Now she stared, mesmerized, at the display of jiving, 'jitterbugging' as it was sometimes called, going on in the corner near them. Jiving, though not actually banned, was frowned upon by the authorities. But it didn't stop the GIs from indulging in this acrobatic cavorting at the very edges of the floor or in secluded alcoves away from the main ballroom.

Josie was even more amazed when Ivy Benson's band struck up with 'In the Mood' – one of Glenn Miller's numbers – to see Pamela begin jigging about on her own, moving not only her feet but her hips and shoulders in time to the music. She was la-laing the tune for all she was worth whilst her prominent blue eyes stared around as if to invite an audience. She didn't have long to wait. The next minute a dark-haired GI with a crew cut came along and, without a word, grabbed hold of her hand. Josie watched as the couple twisted and turned, pulled away then drew together again, every part of them, legs, arms, heads, shoulders and hips, gyrating wildly to the frenzied rhythm.

She could hardly believe it when the young man lifted Pamela off her feet, balancing her first on one hip, then on the other, at the same time giving the delighted audience a tantalizing glimpse of her brown legs – gravy-browned, Josie suspected – and frilly pink knickers.

He didn't stay with her afterwards, as one might have expected. 'Gee, thanks, that was swell,' was all he said as he grinned and bowed to her, then made his way back to his mates. But Pamela didn't seem at all put out, just flushed and excited and more full of beans than ever.

'Gosh, that was smashing!' she said, pulling her dress down and straightening the bow at the waist. 'Great dancers, these Yanks, aren't they? And aren't you Blackpool girls the lucky ones, having a camp right on your doorstep?'

'Don't you see any Yanks in Manchester then?' asked Josie, still feeling dazed by the display she had been watching.

''Course we do. They get everywhere, don't they?' Pamela giggled. 'Where d'you think I learned to jive like that? They come into our local Palais, not as many as you get here though. Phew! I'm sweating cobs after that lot.' She wiped at her red face with a lace hanky. 'And I could murder a drink. C'mon, Josie, Len, let's go and have one.' She stared around. 'Where's Elsie got to? Disappeared again, has she? The last time I saw her she was entwined round some RAF bloke, gazing up at him as though he were Clark Gable or somebody. I expect that's the last we'll see of her tonight.'

Pamela led the way to the bar. She certainly seemed to know her way around, thought Josie, as her friend dived for a table just ahead of another couple of girls and deftly procured three red plush-topped stools for them. 'There you are. Park yer bums and I'll go and get us a round,' she announced to Josie and Len. 'What you havin'? Shandy? Beer?'

'Indeed you won't,' said Len firmly. 'I'll go to the bar. And you're not having beer, neither, nor even a shandy. You're under age, the pair of you.'

'I'm sixteen, nearly,' Pamela protested, pouting at him. 'Will be in a week or two, anyroad.'

'Still not old enough,' said Len, frowning reprovingly, although Josie could tell that he was joking. 'And Auntie Iris'd never forgive me if I led my little cousin here into bad ways.' Josie glowered at him. 'Now, what'll it be? Lemonade? Ginger beer?'

The girls settled for the latter. 'Spoilsport!' Pamela taunted him. 'I'll pay, anyroad. I said I would.' She started to open her black patent-leather bag. It matched her peep-toe sandals, Josie noticed. Pamela seemed to be wearing the very height of fashion.

'Indeed you won't,' said Len again. 'Put that away. Never let it be said that I don't know how to treat a couple of young ladies.'

'Nice, i'n't he?' said Pamela as Len pushed his way through the throng near the bar. 'Even though he does act like a Dutch uncle. Nice and . . . safe. At least I should imagine so.'

Josie nodded. 'Yes; I don't think you could go far wrong with our Len,' she said casually, repeating something she had heard her stepmother say.

'Want to bet?' Pamela rolled her eyes meaningfully. 'He's worth a try, anyway,' she added, almost under her breath. Josie pretended she hadn't heard.

'He's got a girlfriend at home in Haliford,' Josie fibbed now, although she knew it wouldn't be likely to deter Pamela. 'He told me. He writes to her every week.'

'Oh . . . what's her name then?'

'Marjorie – I think that's what he said.'

'Oh well, that's that then,' Pamela shrugged. 'Pity. He's a nice lad.'

'Not your type, luv.' Josie tried to sound unconcerned.

'What d'you mean?' Pamela looked at her indignantly.

'Too quiet. You'd want somebody a bit . . . livelier, wouldn't you? Like that Yank.'

'Oh, I don't know. The quiet ones are best sometimes. Hidden depths, you know. And more of a challenge. Anyroad, he's spoken for, isn't he? Shhh . . . Here he is.'

Len plonked a brimming tankard on the table and two squat brown bottles with upturned glass tumblers over them. He poured out the frothy ginger beer and handed a glass to each of the girls. 'Cheers, both of you,' he said, raising his own glass. 'Nice meeting you again, Pamela.'

'My pleasure I'm sure, kind sir.' Pamela put on a mock-refined accent. 'It's so nice to meet a perfect gentleman.'

It wasn't that they excluded Josie from the conversation. As Pamela had remarked, albeit jokingly, Len was too much of a gentleman to do that. All the same, Josie did feel a little like a gooseberry as she listened to the chat going on between the pair of them. Mostly about Len's training – she had heard that before, of course – and Pamela's job in the munitions factory. Very hush-hush, and of the utmost importance to the war effort, she made it sound, but Josie guessed that all she was doing, in reality, like so many more women, was fastening rivets together or screwing nuts into bolts. But the girl was one of the world's workers and Josie, still at school, began to feel very immature and insignificant by comparison. Especially as Len was looking at Pamela far more than at her, Josie, as the conversation progressed.

He reached into his pocket for his packet of Craven A.

He did look at Josie then, to observe, 'I know you don't smoke,' and she had to admit that there was no scorn or attempt to belittle her in his remark. Indeed, he went on to say, smiling at her, 'You've more sense, haven't you?' Then he turned to Pamela. 'But I'm sure you do, don't you?' His eyes were appraising, calculating almost, as he held out the packet.

The girl met and held his glance for a few seconds. 'You're dead right I do,' she replied, taking a cigarette. 'Ta very much.'

Len lit it for her with his silver-plated lighter. Josie tried not to look too pointedly at Pamela as the girl inhaled deeply and expertly blew out a series of smoke rings. Instead she glanced about at her surroundings. The bar was just off the Floral Hall, the huge canopied entrance to the Winter Gardens, and Josie looked now at the high glass roof, the ornate pillars and the potted palms and ferns adorning each side and the centre of the walkway.

And at the hundreds of people coming and going, to the ballroom, the bar, the Indian Lounge. So many different faces, yet all strangers to Josie, except for the couple sitting opposite her. She thought she might have seen some of the girls from school here tonight – not all mothers were quite as strict as Iris about their daughters' whereabouts – but she hadn't done so. It was foolish of her to feel alone, she knew that. She had come with Len and she would go home with him; nevertheless that was how she did feel at that moment, alone and lonely.

Josie noticed that some men and girls already had their coats on. The dance halls did close ridiculously early, soon after ten o'clock. 'Come on,' said Len, rising to his feet. 'One more dance for each of you, then we'd best be off.

You don't want to stand in a mile-long queue for your coats, do you?'

Back in the ballroom a quickstep was playing. Pamela started to sing, tapping her feet and jiggling her shoulders. 'Don't sit under the apple tree, With anyone else but me . . .' She grabbed hold of Len's hand. 'C'mon, Len, let's dance. You don't mind, do you, Josie?'

Josie shook her head bemusedly while Len, raising his eyebrows and spreading his hands wide as if to say, 'What can I do about it?' followed Pamela meekly on to the floor. Josie leaned against the pillar trying to look blasé, but the dance was almost over anyway and in a couple of minutes the other two were back with her.

Then it was time for the last waltz. The band struck up with the tune, 'Who's Taking You Home Tonight?' and it was then that Josie began to wonder just that. What on earth was Len going to do about taking them both home? Pleasant Street and Charnley Road were in opposite directions.

Len seemed to notice her preoccupation. 'Don't look so worried,' he said, getting hold of her arm. 'It's your turn now. Come on, once round the floor, then we'll go and get our coats before the rush starts.'

At least I've had the last waltz with him, thought Josie, matching her steps to his. She was getting more used to his way of dancing now. Next time it would be better than ever – if there was a next time.

'What's up?' She felt Len turn his head to look at her. 'You're very quiet. There's nothing wrong, is there?'

'No, of course not. Why should there be?'

There was a few seconds' silence, then Len said, 'We'll see Pamela home. You don't mind, do you? It's only just down the road, then I'll walk to North Shore with you. Is that was what was worrying you?'

'No,' said Josie, too quickly. 'No, of course not.' But she felt as though a weight had been lifted from her mind. 'Who's taking you home tonight, After the dance is through . . .' she hummed softly to herself, feeling suddenly much happier.

Pamela, however, had other ideas. 'Pooh! The night's still young,' she declared. 'Who the heck wants to be going home at ten o'clock? Tell you what – we'll take Josie home first, then we'll walk back to my digs. That makes more sense, doesn't it? It's only a hop, skip and a jump from your place.'

Len glanced dubiously at Pamela's feet, at her red-painted toe-nails peeping out through the front of her sandals and at the height of her heels. 'Are you sure you can walk all that way in those things?'

''Course I can.' Pamela hooted with laughter. 'Don't be such an old fuddy-duddy, Uncle Len. I can walk for miles in 'em. Dead comfy they are.'

Josie doubted it, but she knew that Pamela would not be dissuaded. When had she ever been? And it seemed as though she hadn't changed. Dispiritedly she hung on to Len's arm, Pamela holding the other as they walked home through the unlit streets. Josie wasn't often out in the blackout and she found herself remembering now – her encounter with Pamela must have brought it to mind – the occasion when she had run away from home, when she had ventured out alone into the darkness to escape from Iris. Now all she could think about was getting home and pouring out all her troubles to that same woman.

Iris knew the minute she saw the girl's woebegone face that something was wrong, but she knew better than to start prying right away. It would be better to wait until

Josie chose to tell her about it. If she did . . . Iris knew that daughters didn't always confide in their mothers and Josie was, after all, only a stepdaughter. She was becoming more of a real daughter to Iris, however, with every year that passed.

'Had a good time, dear?' was all she asked. Josie nodded in an abstracted manner. 'I thought Len might have come in for some supper. You could have asked him, you know.' Iris looked at her questioningly.

'Wouldn't be any use. He's got better things to do.' Josie took off her coat and flung it carelessly over a chair before flopping down on to the couch. 'Oh, Mum . . . something awful happened. Well, it wasn't awful at first. I was quite pleased to see her really, but it was later . . .' Iris was startled to see that the girl's eyes were wet with tears which she quickly blinked away. Josie had never been one to cry easily. Whatever could have gone wrong? With Len Rawlinson, of all people.

'Who?' asked Iris. 'Who did you meet? And . . . what's happened?' she asked fearfully. If that lad had done anything to hurt Josie she'd kill him! But she couldn't imagine that he would.

Josie gave a deep sigh. 'Pamela Coates,' she said, a name that was once anathema to Iris. 'I met her in the cloakroom, and she tagged on to us – and Len's taken her home.' She hung her head despondently, biting at her lip.

'What! He let you walk home on your own, in the black-out? While he went home with that – that little minx?'

'No, of course he didn't.' Josie tried to smile, but it was a very weak, sad little effort. 'Len wouldn't do that. You know he wouldn't. No, they walked home with me, and now he's gone off with her. Arm in arm they were, chatting away as though they'd known each other all their lives.'

Iris had felt her hackles rise, as they had done before, at the mere mention of that girl's name, but she knew that all that trouble was now in the past and she must behave rationally. 'Well, she always was a chatty girl, that Pamela,' she said. 'She could talk the hind leg off a donkey, that one, and I don't suppose she's changed much. Len didn't . . . flirt with her or anything, did he? He didn't go off and leave you?'

'No,' said Josie flatly. 'He danced with both of us. He behaved like a perfect gentleman.' She told Iris about the events of the evening, even raising a faint smile as she recounted Pamela's dance with the GI. 'It was just seeing them go off together. He was supposed to be with me, Mum.'

Iris nodded understandingly. 'Yes, I know, love. But it seems to me that he had no choice, not really. And he didn't ignore you, did he, after he met . . . her?'

'No, I can't say he did.'

'And has he said he'll see you again? Is he going to come round?'

'Yes, he said he'd ring. He mentioned something about the pictures again, perhaps next week.'

'Well, there you are then,' said Iris consolingly. 'What are you worrying about? Len's a decent lad, I've always said so.'

'But she's here till Saturday, Mum. Pamela . . .' Josie looked at her imploringly.

'I know, I know.' Iris took hold of her hand. 'You were getting fond of him, I know that. But remember this, Josie, whatever happens – there are more fish in the sea than ever came out of it. And you're still only fifteen. Besides, Len's got his head screwed on the right way. I shouldn't think he would go for the likes of Pamela Coates.' But Iris knew, deep down, that men were suckers, the whole lot of them, when it came to a pretty face and provocative ways; but she had no intention of telling Josie that. The girl would no doubt find out for herself as time went on.

Iris was pleased, though, that the girl had confided in her. She knew that many mothers would give a lot to have had such a heart-to-heart chat with their daughters. And Iris also knew that Josie was far more open with her than she could ever imagine Frances being. The younger girl was only eight, admittedly, but she could be a deep one at times, full of her own little secrets, except when she wanted something, when she would chatter away twenty to the dozen.

Yet it was to Frances that Iris had always given the lion's share of her affection. She knew it, to her shame, but she was powerless to do anything about it. Her heart had gone out to the tiny golden-haired, blue-eyed, motherless infant all those years ago and she still felt the same. She loved the little girl with an intensity that hurt at times, though she tried hard not to let the others know. She loved the other two as well, Bertie and Josie, but it was Frances who had captured her heart and who, sometimes to Iris's dismay, still held it fast.

Chapter 18

Frances had been four years old when she first discovered that Iris was not her real mother. She had kept the knowledge to herself and had never told another soul; Josie had said she mustn't, anyway. She hadn't even said that she knew when Mummy, a couple of years afterwards, tried to explain the situation to her.

It had been much later, after Dad had been killed and they had moved to Blackpool, that Josie had told her more about it. About Samuel and Iris getting married when Frances was only a tiny baby and how they had all – even Frances, though she couldn't remember it – come to Blackpool for a holiday. And about how much Iris had done for them over the years, just as much, Josie had said, as any real mother would have done. Frances hadn't really needed Josie to tell her that, because she knew how hard Mummy worked to look after them all. She knew that her mother wasn't quite as young as some of her friends' mothers, or quite as pretty or slim, but it didn't matter to Frances. She was just Mummy, and Frances loved her.

Josie had shown her some photographs of their real mother, a very slender, fair-haired lady with big eyes and a rather sad expression on her face, even in the photo where she was with their dad, getting married. Frances had had a shock when she had seen how much like herself these pictures were; it was just like looking in a mirror.

'D'you remember her?' she had asked Josie, feeling very puzzled.

'Yes, of course I do,' Josie replied. 'I was nearly seven when she died; old enough to remember quite a lot.'

'And . . . d'you miss her? D'you think about her?'

'I did at first, a lot,' said Josie, 'but not so much now. Hardly at all, in fact. Iris is our mother now, and she's been so good to us, 'specially since Dad died. I thought you ought to know about it, you see, Frances, so you'll understand. When I first told you I was being nasty and spiteful, and I'm sorry. It was horrid of me to blurt it out like that.'

Again, Frances didn't say that Mum had already explained some of it to her. She was very good at keeping things to herself. She reflected that Josie was much nicer these days to all of them. She remembered a time when her sister and her mum had been forever shouting at each other, but that didn't happen any more. Frances had heard Mum remark to Auntie Eliza that Josie had grown up overnight. Josie was certainly very grown-up now, since she had left school, wearing make-up and high-heeled shoes and sometimes piling her long dark hair up on top of her head. But Frances didn't think that that was what Mum meant about Josie being grown-up. She meant that she had grown up inside, in her mind, and in the way she treated other people.

Whereas she, Frances, to her dismay, was still regarded as a child. She couldn't wait to be twelve because then she would be able to take part in the Children's Ballet at the Tower, if she was chosen, that is, but Frances had great confidence in her ability and knew that she would be. She had been bitterly disappointed to discover, when they had first moved to Blackpool, that she was too young – five years too young, in fact – and that seemed an awful long time to wait. But she worked hard at her dancing lessons – she was learning ballet and national and tap-dancing – and she knew that eventually her day would come.

In the meantime, Blackpool was such an exciting place to live. Frances had fallen in love with it on her first visit there – the first she remembered, anyway – in 1941, and now that she actually lived there it was even more wonderful. All that sea and sand; the delights of the Pleasure Beach, when Mum had time to take her there; an enormous Woolworth's, much bigger and better than the titchy little one in Haliford, where she could spend her Saturday pennies; and, above all, the Tower itself with all its amusements. For the admission fee of one shilling and sixpence (half-price for children) you could do all manner of things. Not only was there the Children's Ballet, on which Frances had set her sights, but the Aquarium, the Menagerie, the Roof Gardens where they had puppet shows and Punch and Judy, and the ballroom with the Wurlitzer organ. And at Christmas-time an enormous tree, brought from the Lake District, stood in the middle of the ballroom, from which, for the purchase of a shilling ticket, you could choose a present.

The Tower was the place to which Frances usually opted to go for a treat. She loved the mysterious greenish gloom of the Aquarium where a huge barrel-organ, called the Orchestrian, played to attract visitors into the building – you could hear its music out on the promenade – and where exotic fish swam around in tanks hewn from rock. And she never tired of the chimpanzee's tea party or the bear pit or the aviary. And always, of course, as a climax to the day, a visit to the Children's Ballet.

At long last Frances got her wish. In 1948, when she was twelve years old, she was chosen to be one of the hundred and fifty youngsters who were to take part in Annette Schultz's Tower Ballet. The director, known to all as simply 'Annette', ruled her charges with a rod of iron, but the youngsters seemed to worship her for all that. Very soon Frances's conversation at home was liberally peppered with references to her idol.

'Annette says that school's very important, Mum. And if we miss school, then we're not allowed to attend the rehearsal that day.'

'That sounds very sensible to me, dear,' Iris replied. 'You've got to work hard at school. Dancing isn't everything, though we're very proud of you.'

'And Annette says that we can only use a bit of stage make-up, so that it looks natural, like. And we can't use eye make-up at all. It looks cheap, she says. And we have to take every single bit off before we go home . . . And Annette says we haven't to talk to any members of the Tower staff, not even the people who play in the orchestra.'

'Hmmm . . . I don't know whether I like the sound of that, dear,' Iris commented. 'I don't want you to grow up snobbish and thinking you're better than everyone else, just because you do a bit of dancing . . . not that I think you ever would. So long as you're enjoying it, love, that's all that matters. It seems to me there's a lot of rules and regulations, but I daresay that's no bad thing.'

Frances didn't mind the rules; she was only too pleased to have realized her ambition. Now she had another goal. She wanted to be the one chosen to sit on the swing suspended high above the ballroom, waving, like a princess, to the audience down below. Maybe not this year – she was, after all, quite a new girl – but perhaps next year. And then . . . who could tell?

Frances kept to herself the secret that she wanted to be a dancer, a real dancer on the stage, when she grew up. She knew that Mum thought it was just a hobby, something she enjoyed doing but which she would, one day, grow out of. Mum had plans for her to go to catering college in a few years' time, to learn to cook all sorts of fancy things, and then to work in the hotel, like Josie was doing. But Frances had other ideas.

Josie's job at Irisdene was purely office work. She took charge of the bookings and accounts and everything to do with the financial side of the business, whilst the cooking and waiting at tables was left to Iris and to seasonal staff whom they appointed each year. Josie had insisted when she left school in the summer of 1945 that this was the way it must be. She was willing, though not ecstatic, to work at the hotel; Iris had taken it for granted for so long that she would do so and Josie hadn't wanted to let her down.

'I won't cook though, Mum. I most definitely won't do any cooking,' Josie had declared. 'I'm hopeless at it, and I'm not interested anyway.'

'You're only hopeless and not interested because you've never had a chance to learn,' Iris pointed out, though not very dogmatically. It was very rarely that she provoked an argument with Josie these days. 'You never had Domestic Science lessons, did you, with you being in the top class all the way through the grammar school.' The top stream, instead, had been taught Latin, because it was hoped that they would, as the school motto implied, go on to higher things. 'I thought it might be a good chance for you to learn to cook now, dear. If you went to the catering college—'

'No, Mum – no! I'll go to the technical college, and I'll learn shorthand and typing and bookkeeping. I've never had a chance to do that, either, at the Collegiate,' Josie told her. 'Then I'll be able to help you with the business side of the hotel. The teachers at school thought that might be the best idea. And they think I should keep up with my art as well, if I can.'

Josie's teachers had, in fact, been quite horrified at the thought of her academic abilities going to waste in a Blackpool hotel, and had advised her to continue with at least some form of higher education. They had recommended at first that she go to university or teacher training college, but Josie knew that that was out of the question. There had been a time when she had toyed with the idea of teaching, but not any more. Josie wasn't at all sure where her ambitions did lie. Somewhere in the world of art, she thought, which was why she had insisted that, as well as doing the bookkeeping course, she should also go to night school to continue with her drawing and painting.

'Whatever you wish, dear,' Iris had said, very agreeably. 'But that's just a hobby, isn't it, like Frances with her dancing. Your real job will be here, at the hotel. Yes – the more I think of it, the more I like the idea of having a trained accountant here – which is what you will be, won't it? I get in a muddle with all those columns of figures and trying to make things balance. I'm quite capable of doing all the cooking, though, at the moment. And by the time I'm ready to think of retiring, Frances'll be old enough to step into my shoes.'

'That's a long time off yet, Mum,' Josie had pointed out. 'Frances is only a little girl.'

'But it'll come, love. It's amazing how time flies. Frightening, in fact. D'you know, I'll be fifty-three next birthday.'

'No age at all, Mum,' Josie consoled her. 'And you certainly don't look it.'

But Josie was being tactful. Iris had, in reality, aged considerably since Samuel died, and moving to Blackpool, although it had given her a new lease of life, had also been a further strain on her constitution. She was a strong woman – boarding-house and hotel proprietors had to be or else they wouldn't survive – but she complained of feeling tired far more often than she used to.

To hear her stepmother even hint that one day she might think of retiring had given Josie quite a jolt. She had never imagined that Iris would retire at all. Her hair was now almost entirely grey and she had lost quite a lot of weight. Many people had, during the days of rationing, but the flesh had fallen from Iris's face as well so that she no longer looked quite as bonny. Her jawline, always round, had sagged, and the lines round her eyes and mouth were more prominent. Josie was telling a white lie when she said that she didn't look her age, and she guessed that Iris knew it too. Josie had grown very fond of the older woman over the years, much fonder than she would have thought possible, and wouldn't do anything to hurt her.

But Iris still loved to organize them all, to plan everyone's life out for them. It was second nature for her to do so, and it wasn't often that anyone really opposed her. Josie remembered how Len had told her to stick up for herself and not let Iris have all her own way. And so, over the question of the art classes, Josie was adamant.

The bookkeeping, shorthand and typing classes were examination courses which Josie passed with flying colours.

But the art classes were purely for enjoyment. She learned more about the use of colour, perspective and design, but her main interest, as always, was in lightning pencil sketches of landscapes, animals, interesting objects and, above all, people. She was streets ahead of the rest of her class, many of whom were housewives who wanted an outside interest, or businessmen relaxing after an intense day at the office. Josie knew this, but she didn't mind. She was drawing, often with an admiring group round her easel, and that was all she cared about.

Her tutor, though, was loath to see such talent not being used in a lucrative manner. And so it was that, in the summer of 1947, when Josie was eighteen, she found herself working three afternoons a week at R.H.O. Hill's department store in Bank Hey Street, doing lightning pencil sketches, for half a crown a time, of holiday-makers and – in the minority – Blackpool residents. The job had been acquired for her by a friend of a friend; someone her tutor knew who was friendly with a member of the store's board of directors. They were happy to let her have a spot on the ground floor so long as she paid a percentage of her earnings to the shop. Iris was satisfied with the arrangement as she was the first to admit that the office work at the hotel by no means occupied the whole of Josie's time or capabilities.

R. H. O. Hill's, in the late forties, was Blackpool's leading department store, a multi-storey building situated right behind the Tower. It was a bustling, exciting place, full of enticing merchandise, and Josie had been fascinated by it long before she went to work there. There had been nowhere in Haliford to compare with it, except maybe the Co-op Emporium, but this shop was superior by far. The layout was the same as most department stores of the time.

Handbags, make-up, perfume and jewellery on the ground floor, household goods in the basement, and, on the floors above, ladies' wear, gents' wear, furniture, and an elegant restaurant.

As well as these commodities, there were the 'here today, gone tomorrow' salesmen, who rented a stall for a few days, weeks or months. Down in the basement, at various times, there had been purveyors of polish guaranteed to bring a shine to your furniture such as no polish had ever done before; gadgets to take the tops off bottles and tins, slice onions, core apples, peel potatoes; bright pink liquid to clean your windows and tiles; and sticky adhesive tape to apply to hems and tears in garments, for those disinclined to sew. Schoolchildren in the crowd, whiling away a Saturday afternoon, had the salesmen's patter off by heart and waited for them to trot out the same old clichés. The words 'So shiny you can see your face in it, madam . . .' or some other such spiel was enough to reduce them to fits of hysterical giggles before they were sent packing by an irate vendor. Josie had been part of such an audience many a time when she first came to Blackpool.

On the ground floor there was a 'Polyfoto' booth where you could have your photograph taken in forty-eight different poses; a man who engraved names on identity discs, trophies and jewellery; a lady who cut out your likeness in silhouette from black paper; and, in the summer of 1947, Josie Goodwin, lightning portrait artist.

Her talent for highlighting the salient points of a person's face or figure had improved over the years, but she had also learned to be more sympathetic in her portrayals, emphasizing the good points rather than the bad. She recalled with shame her unkind sketches of Fat Iris – no wonder her stepmother had been angry and hurt – and of Vera Brown's drooping knickers and Hilda Ormerod's squint. Funny they may have been, but malicious too. Now Josie drew attention not to a long nose, a weak mouth or a double chin, but to attractive features such as a sweet smile, delicately arched eyebrows or a dainty turned-up nose. Her clients, gratified by her flattering portrayals of their ordinary selves, readily recommended her to their friends. It was seldom that Josie didn't have a queue of two or three customers waiting to have their portraits drawn.

But one Saturday afternoon in the August of 1948 – Josie's second season at Hill's – there was a lull, due no doubt to the warm sunshine which had lured many folks on to the sands. Local shopkeepers knew that inclement weather, of which Blackpool had its share, was good for business, but at the first ray of sunshine the shops would empty again, at least of holiday-makers. Josie was glad of the temporary respite. She had had a steady flow of customers since one o'clock, and now, by half past three, her head was aching a little. She, too, felt that she would like to be out there taking advantage of the good weather.

The shop was by no means empty, of course – it never was – but she guessed that the shoppers in there now were mainly residents, glad to be able to make their purchases or to browse without falling over visitors at every turn. Blackpool residents were often heard to moan about the 'flippin' visitors', milling round the shops or sauntering along the pavements, getting in the way of busy folk; their grumbles were without rancour, though, as they knew full well that the livelihood of the town depended upon these same holiday-makers.

Josie leaned back in her wooden chair, not a very comfortable one, and gazed round at the counters nearest to her. It wasn't often that she had the time to do so, but the fragrant aroma left her in no doubt as to where her booth was situated; opposite the make-up and perfume counters. There were attractive displays of lipstick, rouge, face powder, nail varnish, eyeshadow and mascara, items in which Josie was not particularly interested, although she had started using a pinky-orange Tangee lipstick which was nice and natural-looking.

She might treat herself to some perfume soon, she thought. Mischief by Saville, in that tiny little blue bottle, was an exciting sort of smell, or Coty *L'Aimant*, that Iris was so fond of, or Tweed . . . . Possibly they were for older women though. Josie didn't know a great deal about perfume. She only knew that she couldn't afford Chanel. There was a posh lady there now, sniffing at a dab of it that the assistant, Maureen, had put on her wrist. She would go over later, Josie decided, and ask the girl's advice. And perhaps she would ask Maureen to help her choose a present for Iris's birthday next week. Perfume, maybe, or, if she could afford it, one of those gorgeous Stratton powder compacts on the next counter. Josie had gazed at them longingly, not for herself, but she felt it was time she bought Iris something really nice; she worked so hard for them all.

Josie let her mind wander as she stared around, her eyes returning several times to a girl who was loitering near the display of lipsticks. She had moved away as though undecided a couple of times; now she was back again. The assistant in charge of the counter was occupied at the other end, filling in figures on a check sheet. Josie wondered idly why the girl didn't try to attract her attention if she wanted serving. Then, in a flash of horrified understanding, Josie knew why. She knew only too well. She found herself, in memory, back in Woolworth's with Pamela when she was ten years old, back in Mr Cardew's tuck shop . . . Oh no, she thought with growing dismay as she watched the girl glance furtively round – not at Josie, however; she didn't seem to have noticed her – then tentatively reach out a hand and grab at a shiny gold lipstick. Quick as a flash the article was secreted in the pocket of the girl's short jacket, and she started to walk away.

Josie didn't even stop to think about it. She jumped to her feet and hurried towards the girl, catching up with her just as she had her hand on the swing door. 'Excuse me,' said Josie, putting her hand on the girl's arm. 'I think you have something in your pocket, haven't you? Something you haven't . . . paid for?' She kept her voice low and didn't look round as she spoke, hoping, maybe, to gain the girl's confidence. Josie wasn't at all sure why she had acted as she did – it would have been much easier to let the girl get away with it – but she had just known that she must do something.

'What d'you mean? Let go of me!' The girl pulled her arm away, but Josie could see that her eyes – lovely luminous green eyes – held a trace of fear. 'I don't know what you're talking about. 'Course I haven't got anything! Are you calling me a thief or something?' But her words lacked conviction and her mouth was beginning to tremble.

Josie, remembering her own disastrous foray into shoplifting – the term now being used for this sort of offence – felt dreadful. She was beginning to wish she hadn't started this, but she had, so she was forced to continue. 'No, no, of course not,' she said gently. 'I know you've probably made a mistake – put it there without thinking, perhaps – but it's no use denying it, is it? I saw you put a lipstick in your pocket.'

The girl's eyes filled with tears. 'Who are you?' she asked, staring at Josie. 'Are you a policeman – a lady one, I mean? Or the manageress?' She glanced at Josie's black skirt and white blouse which she usually wore because it looked businesslike. 'I'm sorry. I'm ever so sorry . . . I didn't really mean—'

'No, I'm not the manageress,' said Josie kindly, smiling at the very idea. 'Nothing as important as that. I'm called Josie Goodwin and I work here. Over there.' She gestured towards her portrait booth. 'Come and sit down for a few minutes.' She put an arm round the girl's shoulders. 'No . . . come on, it's all right,' she said as the girl started to pull away. 'I'm not going to tell anybody. I shan't say anything at all, not to anyone. If you give the lipstick to me I'll sneak it back when nobody's looking.'

The girl flopped on to the chair opposite Josie as though her legs had turned to jelly. 'I don't know what came over me,' she said. 'I've never done anything like that before. I don't know why I did it . . . well, I suppose I do, really. Ohhh . . .' She gave a shuddering sigh. 'It's all so . . . so complicated. I'm so mixed-up.' She looked keenly at Josie. 'Why are you bothering, anyway? Why are you being so nice to me? You could get into trouble yourself, if they see you putting it back.'

'Don't worry, they won't,' said Josie. 'D'you see that woman over there? The one in the rose-patterned dress?' She nodded towards the accessories counter where a lady was nonchalantly fingering a chiffon scarf. She was dressed in a summery cotton frock and had a white handbag over one arm and a shopping bag in the other. 'Well, she's a store detective.'

'What!' The girl had blanched visibly. 'But . . . she's dressed so ordinary. You can't tell.'

'Precisely,' said Josie. 'That's the idea. What did you expect? A six-foot policeman stalking round? She's very vigilant, I can tell you, but she must have been far enough away. It would have been a very different story if *she* had seen you, and not me. And I'm bothering because . . . well, when I was a little girl – much younger that you are, I was only a child – I was involved in something like this. And I've never forgotten it.'

'You were?' The girl stared at her in astonishment. 'Shoplifting, you mean?'

'Yes, although I don't think the expression was used so much then. They just called it stealing. And I know that once you start it's so much easier to do it a second time. I never really wanted to do it at all in the first place, but I did. I was bullied into it by a friend. She said she'd tell tales about me if I didn't do it – you know the sort of thing. She was quite horrid.'

'Some friend!' said the girl forcefully.

'Yes, exactly,' replied Josie.

She was silent for a moment, deep in thought. It seemed as though she could never escape from Pamela Coates. If it wasn't the girl herself it was the memory of her, cropping up just when Josie least expected it. Iris had declared, when the girl returned to Manchester, 'Thank goodness we've seen the back of that one!' But they hadn't. She had turned up at the Winter Gardens.

Josie had known intuitively when she saw her cousin, Len, walking away arm in arm with the girl that they most certainly hadn't seen the last of Pamela Coates. As her aunt Alice was now finding out, to her cost . . . But there was no time to be thinking of that now. Josie shook her head rapidly, as if to rid it of distracting thoughts, then she smiled at the girl opposite her. 'Yes, as you say, some friend. But I couldn't blame her entirely, you know. I did do it. We're all capable of making our own decisions, and I don't want to see you starting on something you might regret – that you most certainly *would* regret. What's your name, by the way?'

'Karen,' replied the girl. 'Karen Hepworth. I'm seventeen.'

Josie was surprised. She had thought the girl would be much younger, whereas she, Josie, was only two years older. This was what she told Karen now, and couldn't help but be amused at the girl's reaction.

'Gosh, are you? Only nineteen? I thought you were years and years older than me. Not that you look it – I don't mean that – but you're so – what's the word? – sophisticated. Yes, that's it. You look so sophisticated, so mature, while I look . . . well, I look just like a kid, don't I?'

Josie laughed. 'I can assure you I don't feel mature at all, not inside myself, and certainly not when I compare myself with . . . with some of the girls I know.' She was thinking again of Pamela, a worldly-wise young madam if ever there was one. Not so worldly-wise, however, that she had been able to prevent herself from getting pregnant . . . Josie's mind was wandering again. 'It's these clothes I'm wearing, I daresay,' she said, smoothing down her black skirt. 'I like to look businesslike, as though I know what I'm doing. And my hair, perhaps.' She tucked a stray lock which had escaped from her French pleat back behind her ear. 'I look much younger when my hair's loose.'

'Oh dear, I am sorry,' said Karen. 'I seem to have put my foot in it. I'm always doing that. I've offended you, haven't I?'

'Of course you haven't,' Josie assured her. 'Tell you what – I'm going to shut up shop for half an hour and we'll go and have a cup of tea. I usually do about this time, and I seem to have run out of customers anyway.'

'Are you sure?' Karen sounded doubtful. 'I've already caused enough trouble. I don't want you losing trade because of me.'

'Of course I'm sure. I wouldn't suggest it if I didn't want to. Saturday's never the best day for business. It's change-over day at the hotels and the visitors are too busy getting settled in to spend much time in the shops. I sometimes get a few residents, but they'll have to wait.' Josie propped a card up on her counter, *Back in half an hour*. 'Come on, Karen. My tongue's hanging out for a cup of tea.'

In the basement snack bar Josie learned that Karen Hepworth was not a holiday-maker, as she had at first assumed. She lived with her father and younger brother and sister in Grosvenor Street, and her father had a photographic shop just round the corner in Caunce Street. Josie vaguely recalled having seen it, just once or twice; Caunce Street was on the fringe of the shopping area and she didn't often wander that far. Karen worked in the Borough Treasurer's department at the Town Hall. A good job, Josie thought to herself, and reasonably well paid. There was certainly no need for the girl to resort to shoplifting.

But as she knew from her own bitter experience, hardship was not always the main reason for stealing. When she learned that Karen's mother had died only a year ago, and that the girl was finding it hard to come to terms with her loss, she began to understand. Josie felt glad, now, that she had acted as she did in apprehending Karen, although she had wondered at first what she was letting herself in for. The girl seemed pleased to have the chance to open her heart to someone.

'It all seems so unfair,' she cried, her green eyes looking imploringly at Josie. 'D'you know what I mean? I still can't understand it. Mum was only thirty-six. Just imagine, God letting her die when she was so young, and she'd only had the flu. Why does He do it? Life's so unfair. Dad's only thirty-eight, and he's left with me and our Jacqueline and Brian to look after. Well, I look after myself and I help him as much as I can with the other two, but they'll be at school for ages yet.

'And then I saw this woman – done up to the nines, she was – at the perfume counter, trying a bit of this and a bit of that and wasting the assistant's time. I'm sure she didn't buy anything in the end. She was just about the same age as Mum; she looked a bit like her, too, same colour hair and same build, although Mum wasn't so peevish and spoiled-looking and she couldn't afford such posh clothes. And I thought, "You horrible, stuck-up cow!" I'm sorry, Josie, that's just what I thought, and I don't really know why. And I don't know why I took the lipstick either, except that I'd been thinking of treating myself to one, and I suddenly wanted to . . . to get my own back at somebody. Sounds stupid, doesn't it?' Karen hung her head, looking down at the green-checked oilcloth on the table, idly running her finger through a drop of tea that had spilt there.

'No, I don't think it sounds stupid at all,' said Josie. 'I know just what you mean about life seeming unfair, although I don't think we should start blaming God. It's so easy to do that when we don't understand. I know what you mean, though, because my mother died when I was only six, nearly seven, and then Dad was killed in the war.'

'Oh gosh!' Karen put a hand to her mouth. 'I'm sorry; I'd no idea. You're . . . you're an orphan, then?'

'Well, yes, I suppose I am,' said Josie. She smiled ruefully. 'Although I've never really thought of it like that. I have quite a good life now, you see, with my stepmother and my younger brother and sister. I didn't take to her at all at first – my stepmother, I mean – I was quite horrid to her. Like you, I suppose, I wanted to hit out at somebody, and poor Iris was the one who happened to be there. Things will get better for you, Karen, I'm sure they will. I'm not saying you'll forget your mum – you wouldn't want to, would you? – but it will get a little easier, I promise.' She smiled across the table at the girl with whom she was already beginning to feel such an affinity. It was amazing how quickly you could form an attachment to another person and sense the cementing of a new friendship.

'Haven't you got a boyfriend?' Josie asked. Karen was an attractive girl with lustrous green eyes and the auburn hair, gently curling, which so often went with them. Her mouth and chin were a little weak and her face lacked maturity, but she looked the sort who would appeal, in a 'little-girl-lost' sort of way, to the opposite sex. 'Someone to help you take your mind off things?'

'No, not at the moment,' said Karen. 'Dad's not keen on me going to the Winter Gardens or the Tower, not on my own, and most of my friends have got boyfriends now.'

'Dance halls are not the only place to meet lads,' said Josie. 'There are youth clubs and church socials and societies.' Thinking, as she said it, that she had very little room to talk. Since the bitter let-down over her cousin, Len, she hadn't bothered much with young men or with socializing a great deal. Boys of her own age were doing their national service anyway; and Josie had thrown herself wholeheartedly into her work, both at the hotel and here at R.H.O. Hill's. There had been one or two casual friendships with brothers of school friends or with young men who came to stay at Irisdene, but nothing of any great significance.

'I expect you have a boyfriend, haven't you?' Karen was looking at her admiringly. 'You must have.'

'No . . . I did have. I thought I had – but not any more.' And suddenly Josie found herself telling her new friend all about Len, probably because thoughts of him and of Pamela had resurfaced when she had seen Karen taking the lipstick this afternoon. Not that the thoughts had ever been buried very deep.

Len had continued to take Josie out during the time he was billeted in Blackpool in the autumn of 1944; to the pictures and dancing again, and they had exchanged more than a few kisses which could certainly not be termed cousinly. Then, after he had been posted to the south of England, he had continued to write to her and to spend an occasional forty-eight-hour pass at Irisdene instead of with his parents in Haliford. Josie was ecstatically happy at the way things were progressing, and Pamela Coates was never mentioned. Josie realized, in retrospect, that the silence regarding Pamela had been, in itself, significant. At the time, though, she was convinced that Len had completely forgotten the girl.

It had been when the war ended and Len, a few months later, had been demobbed, that Josie began to notice a change in him. His letters, although they had never been frequent, almost ceased and he no longer seemed very keen to visit her in Blackpool. And so, in the summer of 1946, Josie had gone to Haliford to stay with her aunt Alice and uncle Jack and her cousin, whom she had begun to think of as her boyfriend. And it was then, one balmy July night in Victoria Park, that he had told her . . .

All the time he had been seeing her, Josie, he had also been seeing Pamela. Only very occasionally at first, but then, after he was demobbed, much more frequently. It was only a short journey across the Pennines to Manchester – much nearer than Blackpool – and Pamela had been so very persuasive.

'Oh, come on, Len,' Josie had protested. 'Don't expect me to believe that. You must have wanted to go, or else you would have said no.'

'Yes, I wanted to go. Of course I did.' Len was looking a little sheepish. 'Pamela's good fun. I enjoyed being with her.'

I'll bet you did, thought Josie. 'But what about us?' she persisted. 'What about you and me, Len? I thought that we were – you know – we got on so well.'

'You thought we were courting, you mean?' said Len, using an old-fashioned expression of his mother's.

'Yes . . . well . . . we were, weren't we?' said Josie, a shade defiantly. 'We were getting on like a house on fire . . . and you made me think that—'

'Because I kissed you a few times?' said Len, but not in anger or impatience. His eyes were heavy with remorse and Josie knew that it was hard for him to tell her what he did. And so he was trying to diminish what had happened between them. 'It was only a few kisses, Josie,' he said again. 'You shouldn't have . . . have thought too much about it. You know I'm fond of you, very fond, but you surely couldn't have thought that we . . .'

Josie shook her head, blinking back the tears. She didn't believe him. She knew that he had been falling in love with her – as she had with him – until Pamela had got her claws into him. And yet, deep down, she knew that she was not altogether surprised at what she was hearing. There had been a flash of intuition, a portent of things to come, when she had seen them together.

She gazed steadily at the swans on the park lake – wasn't it said that swans mated for life? – trying to compose herself before turning back to Len. 'So what are you trying to tell me, Len? You and Pamela . . . you're getting married, are you?'

Len nodded numbly, staring down at his feet. 'Yes . . . soon. It'll have to be soon. She's . . . she's pregnant, you see.' Something which didn't surprise Josie one little bit. She had guessed what was coming. She also guessed that her aunt Alice didn't yet know about this turn of events. She couldn't, or she wouldn't have been able to behave so normally.

'Oh dear!' said Josie, a trifle sardonically, two insignificant little words which hid a wealth of emotion. She was, however, quickly coming to terms with it all; she had no intention of having a fit of the vapours, like a Jane Austen heroine. 'I take it Auntie Alice doesn't know yet?'

'No . . . I wanted to tell you first,' said Len. He looked steadily at Josie. 'Mam doesn't know about it at all, Josie. She doesn't even know that I've been seeing Pamela.'

'Good heavens, Len, she'll kill you!' exclaimed Josie, thinking more about Len in that moment than herself.

'Might be as well if she did,' mumbled Len. 'It 'ud be one way out. No, I don't mean that, but she'll be damned annoyed to say the least. She's every right to be, of course, 'specially as we'll probably have to live with her.'

'Oh crikey!' breathed Josie. 'Poor Auntie Alice.' She looked at Len searchingly then. 'Len . . . are you sure it's yours?' She wouldn't put anything past Pamela.

'Yes,' replied Len quickly, too quickly. 'I'm sure, of course I'm sure,' he added, as though it had only just occurred to him to doubt it. 'Pamela wouldn't do that.' But he obviously didn't know Pamela as well as she, Josie, did.

Alice Rawlinson had not been as angry as Josie had anticipated. Astounded, of course, but after the initial shock she had been very phlegmatic about it all, taking it in her stride as mothers so often did when put to the test. And when, some five months after the marriage, in the February of 1947, Pamela had given birth to a baby girl, there had been little doubt that the child was, indeed, Len's. Josie couldn't help but think that Pamela had been lucky. As little Linda grew older it became obvious that it was not only her colouring – fairish hair and grey-blue eyes – that was Len's, but also her features, mannerisms and disposition. She resembled her father in all ways far more than her mother, and again Josie thought what a stroke of luck that was.

'How awful for you,' said Karen, as she had been saying at intervals throughout the telling of the poignant tale. 'It must have damaged your friendship with this – Pamela, to say nothing of the way you felt about your cousin. How awful.'

'Oh, I'm over it now,' said Josie, trying to sound cheerful. 'Pamela and I weren't what you could call friends any more; I hadn't seen her since that night at the Winter Gardens. And as for Len, I suppose it wouldn't really have done, him being my cousin. It's Auntie Alice I feel sorry for. They're still living with her and Uncle Jack on Baldwin Lane, although they've got their names down for one of the prefabs on the outskirts of Haliford. But it means I can't stay with Auntie Alice now, when

I go over to Yorkshire. Not that I'd really want to, with them there.'

'No, I should think not.' Karen nodded sympathetically.

'The funny thing is that Pamela is all over me when I do go, just as though we were bosom pals again, as though nothing happened.'

'So where do you stay?' asked Karen.

'With Grandma Broadbent, Auntie Alice's mother – my real mum's mother too, of course. She's very quiet and deaf and I sometimes feel I don't know her very well, but she likes to see us. Our Bertie and Frances go with me sometimes during the school holidays. Anyway, that's enough about me. If you've finished your tea, I'd better be getting back to see if I've any more customers.'

'I've noticed you when I've been in here before,' Karen said as they walked back up the stairs from the basement, 'but I didn't recognize you at first when you came over to me, I was in such a state . . . You really are clever, aren't you?' she went on admiringly, gazing at the portraits which Josie had fastened to the wall, advertising her work. 'Are these your family? I can see the boy looks a bit like you.'

'Yes, that's our Bertie. He's sixteen – he's going into the sixth form at the grammar school in September. And that's my mum.'

'You mean . . . not your real mum?'

'No – Iris, my stepmother, but I think of her as my mum now.'

'She looks nice. Kind, and sort of . . . comfortable.'

'Yes, she is,' replied Josie. It was a kindly portrayal, unlike the ones she had drawn as a child, showing the warmth in the woman's eyes and the understanding in her faint smile.

'And that must be your sister.'

'Yes, that's our Frances.'

'She's very pretty, isn't she?' observed Karen. 'Like a doll, with that curly blonde hair and blue eyes. She looks as though she knows it though, if you don't mind me saying so.'

Josie smiled. 'Yes, you've just about hit the nail on the head. Frances is very well aware of her good points. She knows she's pretty, and she knows she's a good dancer, too. And she is – I was very impressed when I went to see her in the Tower Ballet. So was Mum, but she'd think it was wonderful, whatever our Frances did. She can do no wrong as far as Mum's concerned.'

'She's the favourite, is she?'

'Yes, I suppose she is. It's inevitable really, because Iris brought her up from a tiny baby and she was always an appealing little thing. But I don't mind any more. Iris and I are real good pals.'

'Yes . . . Mum and I were too,' said Karen sadly.

'Sorry . . .' Josie put a sympathetic hand on her new friend's arm. 'I wasn't thinking.'

''S all right, honest. I'm not going to cry or anything.'

'That's good,' Josie smiled at her. 'Listen – I've a feeling I'm not going to have any more customers today. Why don't you let me do your portrait? On the house, I mean – I don't want paying.'

'Gosh, would you? That 'ud be great.' Karen's green eyes were alight with enthusiasm. 'It's Dad's birthday next week, and I never know what to get him. I could put it in a frame.'

'OK, then. Sit yourself down.'

Karen was overjoyed with the finished portrait and insisted that Josie come for tea the following week so that her father could meet, in person, the talented artist. Josie protested – a birthday was a family celebration – but only a little. She could see that Karen was eager for her to accept the invitation, and she had a feeling that this new friendship, which had begun so incongruously, was going to last.

Chapter 19

Most of the friends that Josie had made at the grammar school were now away at training college or university. Her teachers had made it clear that that was where they thought she should be, too; and Josie sometimes wondered if she had, in fact, made the right decision in agreeing to work for Iris at the hotel. Her work was interesting and Josie enjoyed it, to a degree, but it was by no means totally absorbing or fulfilling. If it had not been for the extra little job at R. H. O. Hill's Josie often thought she would have grown somewhat dissatisfied. Even now, she couldn't envisage portrait-sketching as her ultimate aim in life. She had yet to find the right focus for her talents.

The birthday tea to which Josie was invited on the last Sunday in August was the second birthday that week. A few days earlier Iris had celebrated her fifty-fifth birthday and they had had a special meal, just the four of them, when the visitors' meals had all been cleared away and Frances had returned from her performance at the Tower Ballet.

'Well, it's as special as it can be, under the circumstances,' Iris had grumbled as they tucked into the boiled ham, cut rather thicker than usual, and the tinned peaches and cream which were still something of a treat. 'Would you believe it? The war's been over for three years now and we're still putting up with shortages and queues.

D'you remember? We used to say, "Won't it be lovely when the war's over?" Well, a fat lot of good it's done us, that's all I can say. All us women wanted to do was make a bonfire of the blackout curtains and our shabby old clothes, and chuck the dried egg out of the window, but we're still scrimping and saving.'

'Oh, come on, Mum; we do all right with the eggs,' said Josie with a twinkle in her eye. 'And that's thanks to me and our Bertie, isn't it?'

'Well – yes – I've got to admit that,' said Iris grudgingly, 'but it was against my better judgement, Josie. I don't like having to resort to shady goings-on like that. Tasty, though, aren't they?' she added, spearing a slice of egg with deep yellow yolk and popping it in her mouth.

Josie grinned at her. She had heard all Iris's grumbles before and knew that it was just a way of letting off steam. It hadn't been easy for her, keeping the hotel going in the last years of the war with all the rationing and restrictions, and, as she often said, it wasn't much better now. In some ways it was worse. At least bread had never been rationed during the war as it was in 1946. A world wheat shortage, they had been told, and were instructed to use more husk in the flour, resulting in an unappetizing-looking grey loaf of bread. There had always been the black market, something Iris had self-righteously shunned until Eliza had told her of a little farm out at Great Eccleston where you could get the most delicious new-laid brown eggs. And everybody was doing it, Eliza said. The temptation had been too strong, even for Iris, and now Josie and Bertie took periodic bike rides into the countryside to procure the illicit goods.

'I don't know how they expect you to bake, anyroad, without decent eggs,' Iris went on, as if to excuse herself. 'And it just adds the finishing touch to a salad, a nice bit of boiled egg. I must say, this ham's delicious.' She munched appreciatively. 'They can keep their horsemeat and their snoek and their bloomin' whalemeat. Would you believe it? That Ministry of Food tried to tell us that whalemeat was "Rich and tasty. Just like a beefsteak," they said. Beefsteak, my aunt Fanny!'

'Oh, be fair, Mum,' Bertie laughed. 'You've never tasted whalemeat, so how do you know?'

'Indeed I haven't tasted it and I never will, thank you very much! I can manage to run this place well enough without resorting to rubbish like that or my name's not Iris Goodwin . . . And you're off to another party on Sunday, aren't you, love?' She turned to Josie. 'What are you going to take? You can't go empty-handed.'

'Oh, I don't know, Mum. It isn't a real party – just a tea like this. I've never met Karen's dad, so I can't very well take a present.'

'I'll bake you a nice cake.' Iris nodded emphatically. 'Nobody could take offence at that, and from what you tell me I don't suppose that lass Karen has much time for baking. Poor girl, she must be run off her feet, working at the Town Hall and looking after a family as well. I reckon the best thing that chap could do would be to get married again.'

'It's only about a year since Karen's mother died,' said Josie. 'It's not very long. He's probably never even thought about it.'

'Your father did,' said Iris drily.

'Well . . . yes,' said Josie, feeling a little embarrassed. She hadn't even been comparing the situation with her own, and it was very rarely now that Iris referred to the matter. 'But everybody's different, aren't they? And we don't even know Mr Hepworth.'

Josie had told Iris a little about her new friend, but not the exact circumstances under which they had met; only that the girl had come to Hill's to have her portrait drawn and that they had struck up a friendship, and a little of Karen's background, as much as Josie knew herself.

She dressed with care on the Sunday afternoon, although there wasn't a great deal of choice in her wardrobe. It still consisted largely of 'make-overs' from last year's dresses and skirts and one or two blouses she had saved up and bought from R. H. O. Hill's; there was a percentage off for staff discount. The 'New Look' was the fashion now, and though Josie couldn't afford the real thing – who in their circle could afford Christian Dior? – she had an outfit which was quite a fair imitation.

Iris had made her a very full skirt from, of all things, a few yards of blackout material which had lain unused since the start of the war. It was gathered into a wide waistband which showed off Josie's slim waist to perfection, and the new mid-calf length accentuated her height. The mirror showed her now that she had developed into a tall slender young woman who was, she had to admit it herself, quite attractive. Her new red crêpe de Chine blouse with the collarless neckline fitted well beneath her jacket. This was also red, of a slightly deeper shade, made from a remnant of velvet which Iris had bought from Haliford market years before and never used. It had a narrow stand-up collar, hip-length peplum and rounded shoulders; and Josie felt sure that Christian Dior himself couldn't have made it any smarter, as she had told a highly gratified Iris. Her black ankle-strap, wedge-heeled shoes were taking some getting used to, but they did go well with the outfit, as did her neat black straw hat trimmed with a posy of red flowers that was perched on top of her upswept hair.

'Wow!' exclaimed Karen, when she answered Josie's knock at the door. 'Quite the fashion model! You do look nice, Josie,' she added admiringly. 'Did you make all those things yourself?'

Karen wasn't a girl to wrap anything up, as Josie was very quickly learning. Her outspoken remarks could be misconstrued as tactless, or simply rude, but Josie felt that it was simple naïvety.

'No, of course I didn't,' she assured her now. 'I'm no good at sewing. It's my mum – you know, Iris – who's the clever one.'

'But you're clever in other ways, aren't you?' said Karen. 'I've been telling my dad all about you, and he loved the portrait.'

Oh dear, thought Josie. What a build-up! I only hope I come up to expectations. She was shown into the living room at the back of the house where she could see the table was already laid for tea. A man rose from a fireside chair as she entered, and Josie's immediate thought was that he was rather like her father, what she could remember of him. Not exactly like him, of course, but he had the same dark hair, slightly greying, and deep brown eyes with a look of earnestness in them; he was also of roughly the same height, five-foot eight or so, and slim build, and he was, from what Karen had told her, about the same age – thirty-eight – as her dad had been when he was killed.

He stepped forward eagerly, his hand outstretched. 'How do you do? You must be Miss Goodwin . . . or may I call you Josie? Karen has told me such a lot about you.'

'Yes, of course you may,' said Josie as she shook his hand; he had a firm, decisive grip. 'How do you do, Mr Hepworth? It's kind of you to ask me to tea.' Although she knew that it was Karen who had asked her, not her father.

'Not at all,' he replied. 'We're only too pleased to have some fresh company. And it's Karen's prerogative to invite whoever she likes. She's made the tea after all, haven't you, my dear?' He turned to smile at his daughter who was looking, Josie noticed, flushed and pleased, much happier than when she had seen her in the store. 'And please don't call me Mr Hepworth.' He turned back to Josie. 'My name's Paul.'

'Oh, right.' Josie nodded, a trifle unsure. She didn't think she would have the audacity to call him by his first name; he was so much older than herself, old enough to be her father – just about – and Josie had been brought up to show respect to her elders. 'I believe it's your birthday,' she said now. 'Many happy returns . . .' She couldn't say Paul, so she decided not to call him anything. She held out the white cardboard box she had carried from home so carefully. 'I've brought you this. It's not really a present, but I hope you'll like it . . . I hope you won't mind.'

'Mind? Why should I?' He lifted the lid. 'Good gracious! I'll say I don't mind. Just look at this, Karen. Now, that's something like a cake.'

Iris had excelled herself. The Victoria sponge cake was topped with chocolate icing, glacé cherries and nuts, items which were kept in Iris's store cupboard and used sparingly, on special occasions.

'Gosh, that's terrific, isn't it, Dad?' said Karen. 'Much better than anything I can do. I can manage a few buns, but that's all. I told you Josie was clever, didn't I?'

'Oh, no . . . no, I haven't made it,' Josie hastened to tell them. 'It is home-made, but my mum made it, not me. I'm not much good at cooking and baking,' she added apologetically.

'It doesn't matter who made it, it's still very acceptable,'

Paul Hepworth assured her. 'And you're talented in other ways, aren't you? That portrait you did of Karen – it's excellent, it is, really. You've captured her exactly; that look of freshness and innocence. Though I suspect she's not always as innocent as she makes out, are you, love?' He smiled fondly at his daughter again and Josie got the impression that he was trying hard to be mother as well as father to the girl. Karen had already told her that she and her mother had been very close.

Josie couldn't help but be reminded of her own father and how he had made very little effort to befriend his children after their mother had died . . . and how quickly he had married Iris to do the job for him. But Samuel had changed. They had been much more of a family by the time he was killed, and Josie, comparing him now with Paul Hepworth, found herself suddenly missing him.

'I'm glad you liked the portrait, Mr . . . er . . . I'm glad you liked it,' said Josie. 'I see Karen has put it in a frame for you.'

The portrait, together with a few birthday cards, stood in pride of place on the sideboard. Further back there stood a wedding photograph, Paul and a young woman who was obviously his late wife. Josie was struck by the resemblance to Karen. The black and white picture did not reveal, of course, the colour of the woman's hair, but Josie guessed that it may have been the same rich auburn as her elder daughter's.

When the younger members of the family, Jacqueline and Brian, who had been playing a game upstairs, joined them, Josie could see that the girl resembled her father and the boy his mother and older sister. They were twins, Josie learned, ten years old, but not the least bit alike. They were polite, well-behaved children and as they all sat down to tea she reflected what a happy, united family they seemed to be. She was a little surprised at this; she had been wondering whether Karen's transgression had stemmed from some underlying unhappiness at home, as well as from the death of her mother. But she came to the conclusion now that it must have been an isolated lapse, one of those things which was difficult to explain. Maybe Karen's feelings of desolation had been exacerbated by the anniversary of her mother's death? At all events, the girl seemed to be perfectly at ease with herself today.

'You'll have to show Josie your works of art, Dad,' she told her father, her eagerness evident in her voice and the glow of her green eyes. 'She's a fellow artist, so she's sure to be interested.'

Josie looked inquiringly at Paul Hepworth. 'You're an artist, are you, Mr . . . er? What do you do? Draw, or paint?'

Paul Hepworth smiled. 'Well, I've done a bit of both in my time, drawing and painting. I've dabbled in both oils and water-colours, although I was never what you might call gifted. But what Karen is referring to is my photographic studies.'

Of course, how stupid of her. Mr Hepworth was a photographer; he had a shop round the corner, but Josie hadn't realized that he took photographs himself as well as selling cameras and film and all the paraphernalia. 'Oh yes . . . I'm sorry,' Josie said now. 'With Karen saying you were an artist I naturally assumed that—'

'You assumed that I was a painter.' Paul grinned at her, raising his eyebrows eloquently. 'A common enough mistake. We photographers get used to folk thinking that we're not real artists, because we don't work with a pencil or a brush. Do you know, Josie, there have been arguments going on ever since photography was invented about whether it's a science or an art.'

'And that was . . . when?' asked Josie. 'I don't really know much about it, but it sounds very interesting. When were the first photographs taken?'

'In the eighteen-thirties,' replied Paul promptly. 'Silver images on a copper plate, first produced by Louis Daguerre.'

Karen laughed. 'You've got him on his hobby-horse now, Josie. He doesn't need much encouraging, do you, Dad? He'll show you all his work later, especially now you've shown an interest. Just try stopping him!'

'Don't you make fun, young lady!' Paul spoke in mock-severe tones to his daughter. 'It's what helps keep the wolf from the door, I'll have you know.' He took a bite of the bun in his hand and munched thoughtfully. 'Mmm . . . not bad. Very good, in fact. So light it melts in the mouth, as they say. Don't underestimate your buns, Karen, my dear. You're improving by leaps and bounds.' He turned to the twins. 'Isn't she? Don't you think so?'

Jacqueline and Brian wrinkled their noses. 'She's not bad.' 'Can't wait for you to cut Josie's cake, Dad.'

'Later – supper-time, perhaps.' Paul stood up and pushed back his chair. 'Now, we'll all help Karen clear away the pots, then I'll take Josie on a conducted tour.'

Josie found that she didn't need to feign an interest in Paul Hepworth's work – which she soon discovered to be almost an obsession – as she knew it would have been only polite to do. As soon as she saw the masterpieces that he, with the aid of his camera, had produced, she was hooked and her curiosity grew very quickly into a desire to learn more about it all. The front room, or lounge, was sparsely furnished with only a three-piece suite and a bookcase, but the walls were covered with framed examples of Paul's art, which Josie soon recognized as that of a genius. There were lots of portraits, both of children and adults, some taken in what was obviously a studio setting and some in more natural surroundings; landscapes – Josie identified many as Blackpool; even still-life studies, with objects such as shells, books, candlesticks and bowls, had been grouped artistically and photographed with an eye for the minutest detail; Josie would never have considered this particular art form to be one that would interest a photographer.

She gazed in silence for several minutes, aware of Paul at her side, waiting, she felt, for her praise and an acknowledgement of his talent. He must be justifiably proud of his achievements and yet she judged him to be a modest man. Eventually she turned to him. 'They're wonderful. I'm almost speechless, Mr . . . er . . .'

He looked at her gravely, just the slightest twinkle lighting up his dark eyes. 'Do you know, that's the third time you've called me Mr . . . er? You'll have to do better than that, Miss . . . er . . . Goodwin, if you want me to explain a little about my work. And you must know that I'm simply dying to,' he added eagerly.

Josie laughed. 'Yes, I'm sorry . . . Paul. It's just with you being Karen's father, I wasn't sure. But you're right, I'm dying to hear more about all this. I know what you mean now about photography being an art, and how right Karen was when she said you were an artist. You are – and a brilliant one.'

'Thank you, Josie,' said Paul very quietly, but she could tell he was pleased.

'Tell me about your favourite ones,' she said now, knowing that many artists – but by no means all – loved to talk about the inspiration for their work. There were some who considered it too personal, but she guessed that Paul, though an unassuming man, would be glad of an opportunity to converse with someone in whom he recognized a kindred spirit. Josie was beginning to look upon her own talent as modest by comparison.

'I've always liked child studies,' replied Paul, 'and of course I've been lucky to have three of my own to experiment with.' He gestured towards a group of pictures. The twins, possibly a few years ago, splashing in the shallow waves at the edge of the sea, obviously unaware of the camera; another of the two children, again on the beach, heads bent over the contents of a child's bucket; a much younger Karen smiling up at the camera, momentarily distracted from the jigsaw puzzle in front of her.

Paul pointed to this one. 'The very instant a child looks up and notices you, that's the moment to capture on film. Karen had only just become aware of me. Or when they've forgotten the camera entirely, of course, like the twins had here . . . I feel that portraits, especially those of children, should be more than a mere physical likeness; you should aim to portray some essential facet of their character if you can.'

'And there was I thinking that you needed a pencil or a brush to make you into an artist,' said Josie. 'These are as good as any painting; better, in fact. I suppose I thought that all a photographer had to do was stand in front of his subject and – snap! Now I can see that there's so much more to it.'

Paul nodded. 'There is indeed. Tell me, Josie, what do you think is the most important factor in a photographer's work – or his art, if you will?'

Josie was thoughtful for a moment. Then, 'His camera . . .?' she said hesitantly, thinking as she said it that it was rather a silly answer. Too obvious; it must be something much more subtle, but she really had no idea. This was all foreign territory to her, but so fascinating.

'Apart from that,' said Paul, but he wasn't laughing at her. Josie shook her head. 'Then I can see I will have to tell you. It's light, Josie. That's what the word "Photography" means, in fact; drawing – or painting – with light.' He moved closer to her and she could feel that his enthusiasm was infectious. 'You know how a painter understands and manipulates colour to give him the desired effect? Well, a photographer – a skilled one, I mean – learns to use light in the same way to create the right mood and atmosphere.'

'Yes . . . yes, I can see that.' Josie was looking intently at two studies in front of her. One showed shafts of brilliant sunlight beaming through the bare branches of trees, whilst the one next to it, a summer-time scene, revealed dappled light and shade cast on the ground by the sun glinting through branches in full leaf. 'What a variation you have here; deep shadows and softer ones, and patches of sunlight, and yet it's all done in black and white. It has to be, of course, in photography.'

'For the moment, yes,' replied Paul, 'but I guess the time will come when coloured photographs will be the norm.'

'Really?' Josie looked at him attentively.

'Oh yes, it's only a matter of time. There's already Kodachrome film, which will produce colour transparencies, but they've yet to develop the technique for making coloured photographs. For my part, though, I can't see that anything will ever replace the dramatic contrasts you get in black and white, and all the shades of grey in between.'

'I have to agree with that,' said Josie. 'I work mainly in black and white myself, with the pencil sketches. I just add a touch of colour here and there if I feel the subject calls for it. But I do like to experiment and see just what the pencil can achieve on its own.'

'With you behind it,' Paul smiled.

Josie laughed. 'Of course.'

'And you can experiment with a camera in just the same way,' said Paul. 'Do you have a camera, Josie?'

'Only a box Brownie. I think it came out of the ark, but it takes good photos for all that, which is why we've never bothered to get a newer one.'

'I could help you choose one which would do rather more for you, without being too complicated,' Paul told her. 'There are all sorts coming on to the market now which use thirty-five millimetre film.'

'Oh . . . and what's that?' Josie was becoming aware of the extent of her ignorance, but Paul seemed only too willing to explain without showing the slightest impatience.

'Just the size of the film,' he said. 'It gives a much clearer image, you see. It was first used just for movie pictures, but now it's being more widely used in cameras. If you come to the shop sometime, Josie, I'll be able to explain to you better . . . I hope you will.'

'I'd love to, Paul,' replied Josie, really meaning it. 'It's as though you're opening a whole new world for me here. I'd no idea.'

'And that's what a camera is,' said Paul. 'It's a window on the world.' He was silent for a few moments. Then he went on, 'It was a world I didn't want much to be part of at first, when Kathleen died. I couldn't come to terms with it at all. But I had to pull myself together – I had the children to consider. I couldn't go under. And when I got myself moving again, as I had to, I found that it was a lifeline to me, all this.' He gestured towards the array of photographs. 'That's the secret, I've found, to fill your life completely, to work hard and leave little time for brooding.'

'Yes, I think that's what my mother felt, after my father was killed,' Josie told him. 'I think that's why we moved to Blackpool, to the hotel, so that she wouldn't have time to fret.' She looked at Paul sympathetically. 'But you enjoy your work as well, don't you? You must do, to achieve such excellence?'

'Yes, I enjoy it. I love it. There was a time, as I said, when my enthusiasm waned. It all seemed too much trouble; I didn't see the point any more. But my passion for it has come back, I'm glad to say. I'm starting to be full of new ideas again.'

'And Karen's a good help to you at home, isn't she?' observed Josie. 'I was pleased to see she's looking happier today. She was a bit . . . upset, the first time I met her.' Josie wasn't sure whether or not Paul knew the full story of how she had met Karen. Probably not, but it could do no harm to let him see that she, Josie, knew that Karen was still prone to bouts of grieving, that she hadn't the stamina or the strength of purpose her father had, and, if Josie was any judge, that she was still looking for someone on whom to lean.

Paul, from his reply, seemed to be fully cognizant of the situation. 'Yes, it's possible that Karen misses her mother more than any of us do. The two of them were very close, more like sisters really. She was inconsolable at first, and she still has her off-times. I do my best, but I know it's not like having another woman to talk to. I'm glad she's met you, Josie. She doesn't find it all that easy to make friends, and I suppose I've been guilty of over-protecting her since Kathleen died. It's a big responsibility bringing up a daughter.'

'That's what my mother says.' Josie smiled at him. 'Well, she's my stepmother, really. And she was left with two daughters and a son, the same as you. I'm the eldest, like Karen is.'

'Yes, so Karen has told me. But she hasn't got your resilience, Josie. I can tell that even though I haven't known you very long. You're a gutsy young lady, aren't you? Yes, I'm glad Karen met you. I'm sure you'll be good for her. That isn't the only reason though,' he added, looking at her intently. 'I'm glad to have met you as well . . . especially now you've shown such interest in my work.' He grinned. 'We fellows can lap up any amount of flattery.'

'It isn't flattery, it's the truth,' Josie replied simply. 'These are brilliant. I can't tell you how impressed I am. I'm so glad you showed them to me.'

'Yes, they're good, aren't they?' Karen added breezily, walking into the room at that moment. 'And while you two have been talking we've done all the washing-up, the twins and me. I expect you've told Josie all about your studio, haven't you, Dad? And the weddings you've got lined up.'

Paul hadn't, but he was to do so later in the evening. Josie was persuaded to stay for a game of Monopoly and a bite of supper and she learned, through odd snatches of conversation in between the wheeling and dealing over Mayfair and Park Lane, that wedding albums, a permanent reminder of the Great Day, were the up-and-coming thing with young couples. Paul had already done a wedding at a Methodist church, and his next booking, Karen informed her, as proudly as if it were her own achievement, was at none other than St John's, the parish church of Blackpool. He also had his studio at the rear of the shop in Caunce Street where he photographed clients, although he much preferred, he told Josie, the more relaxed atmosphere of their own homes or gardens.

Josie was to see for herself the following week both the shop and the studio. She was mesmerized at the array of cameras of all makes, shapes and sizes, as well as films, tripods, stands, flash units, light meters, filters . . . Some things of which she had never even heard and had no idea how they were used. And she was impressed at the studio with its elaborate lighting units and umbrella-like shades, curtains of various textures to be used as backcloths, and a box of assorted toys – dolls, teddy bears, building bricks, trains and cars – for the younger customers.

But it was the notice on the shop counter which grabbed her attention. *Assistant required for five afternoons a week, 2 p.m. till 6 p.m. Good pay and prospects. Experience not essential.*

'Your assistant's leaving then?' Josie asked, idly picking up a yellow film box and weighing it in her hand.

''Fraid so, miss,' replied Martin, the young man in the brown overall at the other end of the counter. 'Duty calls, you see. National service. I've just got my call-up papers.'

'Oh . . . oh yes, I see,' replied Josie. She put the film carefully back on the counter, standing there looking at it as though spellbound.

'Why? Are you interested?' Paul was at her elbow. His voice was low but he was looking at her earnestly.

Josie turned and smiled at him. She felt like flinging her arms round him, but she resisted the temptation. 'Yes, why not?' she said. 'Yes, I do believe I am.'

As she explained to Paul, she could do the work at the hotel with her eyes closed. 'Well, no, not exactly,' she amended.

'That sounds big-headed, but it certainly doesn't take as much time as I'm allowed for it. That's why I took the job at Hill's, because I had time on my hands, and that job comes to an end when the season finishes.'

The arrangements were perfectly acceptable to Iris, who knew that Josie would never let her down with regard to the bookkeeping; and so Josie started her new job as photographic assistant to Paul Hepworth at the end of September 1948.

At first she just served in the shop, assisting Paul in the darkroom and studio simply as a second pair of hands. That was all he had envisaged in the beginning, an assistant to take over the vacancy left by Martin, but only in a part-time capacity, whereas Martin had been in full-time employment. The taking of photographs and the developing and printing Paul saw as his province and his alone. They were skills requiring the hand of an expert, and Paul had decided, when he knew Martin was leaving, to cut his costs a little. He was well able to manage the real nitty-gritty of the business on his own, especially as trade had been falling off somewhat recently.

He soon realized how wrong he had been. Josie proved to be a very quick and willing pupil; and trade in the shop, instead of tailing off even more, as was so often the case at the end of the summer season, began to pick up. He was sure that his personable young assistant had a lot to do with it. Not only was she highly competent behind the counter and with the ordering of stock, but she had completely reorganized the displays both in the shop and in the window. She had persuaded Paul to bring some of his photographic studies from home to show in the shop window. It didn't matter, she said, that they were ones he had taken purely for his own enjoyment – a spider's web, moist with dew, or a silhouette of a lone figure on the beach, taken at dusk – they were examples of his art and could only help to attract new customers. She was right. New clients came, slowly at first, in ones and twos, but by Christmas he was inundated with orders and had several bookings for weddings in the New Year.

A great deal of the work was a puzzlement to Josie at first. She had had no idea how much was involved in the taking of a photograph, but she very quickly came to understand the intricacies of such things as light meters, telephoto lenses and filters, and to know what Paul meant when he talked about 'tonal range' or the 'angle of reflection' or 'backlighting'.

'And there was I thinking that you always had to keep the sun behind you,' she observed, with regard to the latter. 'That's advice for amateurs, of course, isn't it?'

Paul had shown her that, instead, it was often more effective to have the sun, or an alternative source of light, behind the subject. Backlighting, as it was called, was just one of many things he had taught her, and before many months had passed she was well on the way to becoming a professional, rather than an amateur, photographer. She was, Paul decided, indispensable, and when he offered her full-time employment instead of part-time, to help him in all aspects of his work, she jumped at the chance. The bookkeeping at Irisdene could easily be done in her spare time.

Chapter 20

'My sister's the girl in the swing this year,' Josie told Paul one day in the summer of 1949, about a year after she had first met the Hepworth family. 'You know, at the Tower Ballet. She's done ever so well and we're really proud of her. She's only thirteen, and it's only her second year in the ballet. We could hardly believe it when she told us that Annette had chosen her . . . She was convinced she was going to be chosen though,' she added. 'I've never seen her so determined about anything.'

'And what Frances wants, Frances gets, eh?' Paul looked at her meaningfully.

'Usually.' Josie gave a rueful smile. 'However, we're proud of her, and I thought it would be a nice idea if I had her photograph taken for Mum's birthday, in her ballet frock, perhaps, or the rainbow dress she wears in the finale. Would you do it for me, please, Paul?'

Paul nodded his agreement. 'Good idea. Your mother would like that. But I don't think I should do it. You'll take the photograph, won't you, seeing that it's your sister?'

'Oh, I'm not sure. I want it to be really good.'

'But you *are* really good, Josie, believe me. I wouldn't have let you take some of those wedding photos last week if you weren't really good. Do you want Frances to come here, to the studio?'

'Oh yes, I think so. It has to be a secret, you see. And I would like to have a go at it, if you think I can.'

'I know you can.' Paul's brown eyes held no shadow of a doubt as he looked intently at Josie.

It was only a year before that a portrait, to Josie, would have meant a lightning pencil sketch. She still drew and painted for pleasure, when she had time, but she hadn't taken the seasonal job at Hill's this year as she was far too involved with her photographic work. At last Josie had found her true vocation, work which she knew she could do well and which was absorbing her almost to the exclusion of everything else. She was only amazed that she hadn't stumbled upon it before. The scope was limitless, she had discovered. This could be, if she so wished, a lifetime career.

The portrait she took of Frances was proclaimed by Paul to be a remarkable achievement. Frances was standing with one foot raised on a stool, gazing straight into the camera, as though momentarily surprised in the act of tying up her ballet shoe, her head slightly to one side and a faint, enigmatic smile playing round her lips. Subtle lighting effects had enhanced the satin sheen of her short dress, and her golden hair, against the dark background, appeared like an aureole.

Iris was enchanted with her birthday gift, as were countless passers-by who stopped, during the last weeks of the season, to look at a duplicate of the picture in the window of Hepworth's photographic shop. And Josie knew that her mother was almost bursting with pride that evening as they sat on gilded chairs in the Tower Ballroom, waving to Frances, the golden-haired fairy in the floaty rainbow dress, blowing kisses to the audience below. From the back of the topmost balcony two large spotlights followed the rest of the rainbow dancers, now and again focusing on Frances, high on her flower-bedecked swing.

'Bless her,' said Iris fondly. 'Not a bit nervous, is she? At least she doesn't seem to be. It wouldn't do for me, I can tell you, our Josie. I've never had much of a head for heights. It takes me all me time to climb up a stepladder.'

Josie laughed and squeezed her mother's arm. 'No, I can't say I'd like to be up there either. Like you say, Mum, she doesn't seem nervous. In fact I would say she's lapping it all up; she's loving every minute.'

'She'd best make the most of it then; it won't last for ever. Nothing does,' Iris went on, as the swing was lowered to the floor and Frances stepped out, curtsying, blowing kisses, spreading her arms wide as if to embrace the audience. 'I daresay she'll find she hasn't time for this dancing lark before long, when her school work gets harder. But you've got to give credit where it's due and she's a lovely little dancer. I'm that proud of her!' Iris's cheeks glowed like two red apples and her eyes shone with delight.

'We're all proud, Mum,' said Bertie, on the other side of Iris. 'I didn't think this would be my cup of tea, but I'm glad I came. It's nice to have a family celebration and a meal out for a change,' he added as they waited on the edge of the ballroom floor for Frances to join them. 'And this time next year, Mum, I most likely won't be here for your birthday. I'll be in the Army.'

'Oh, forget about that now,' said Iris. 'That's ages off. Let's enjoy ourselves.'

They were to round off the festivites for Iris's birthday with a fish and chip supper – like real Blackpool trippers – at Hesketh's near Central Station. Frances had wrinkled her nose at first and said, 'How common!' but she was quickly outvoted. And, in spite of her hints that fish and chip shops were only for the *hoi polloi*, she appeared to be enjoying herself, Josie thought later that evening, watching her sister sprinkle her crispy golden haddock and chips with liberal doses of salt and vinegar.

Josie smiled at her across the red checked tablecloth. 'You were very good, Frances, especially in the ballet scenes. We all thought so. Quite the professional.'

'Mmm . . . I know.' Frances daintily swallowed her mouthful of fish and chips then dabbed at her lips with a paper serviette. She graciously inclined her head – she might almost be Princess Margaret, thought her sister in amusement – acknowledging what she knew to be her due. 'Thank you. Annette says that ballet is my strong point. And she says that I'm one of the best girls in the swing they've ever had, even counting Little Emmie.'

Josie doubted that Annette had been quite so fulsome in her praise – Little Emmie had been before Annette's time, anyway – but she knew it would be best to let her young sister have her moment of glory. Little Emmie's fame was legendary. She had been renowned, not only in Blackpool, but throughout the rest of Great Britain and even on the Continent. Her picture had appeared on sheet music and she was often known as 'La Petite Pavlova'.

Josie wondered if this was what Frances had in mind for herself. It wasn't the first time she had mentioned the famous Emmie Tweesdale, and whenever she did there was that rapt look in her eyes. If that was the case, then Josie feared her sister might be in for a shock, and possibly the first major disagreement with Iris of her life. It was clear that Iris, even though she was proud of Frances, regarded it all, deep down, as a lot of tomfoolery, all very well as a passing interest, but certainly not the sort of thing that right-minded folk would want to do for a living.

Not that Frances had expressed such an idea as yet, not openly – she was a tight-lipped little madam when she wanted to be – but Josie felt sure she hadn't mistaken that starry-eyed expression. Still, time would tell.

At first Josie didn't recognize the voice on the other end of the phone, especially as the caller didn't say who she was. 'Hi there, Josie. When are you going to come over and see us? It's been ages, and now we've moved into our prefab.'

Prefab . . . Of course, it was Pamela, but how different she sounded over the telephone wire. Josie hadn't realized how much this contraption distorted the voice, emphasizing the broad vowel sounds and the somewhat piercing timbre. She held the receiver a little away from her ear. There was a lot of crackling and whistling as well as Pamela almost deafening her. 'Oh, hello there. It's Pamela, isn't it?'

''Course it is! Who d'yer think it was?' There was a high-pitched laugh. 'Always getting phone calls, are yer? Well, I suppose you might be, seein' as 'ow you're a career girl now.'

Josie wasn't sure whether or not she imagined the irony – or a touch of envy? – in the last few words, but she chose to ignore it, just as she chose to hold back the remark that came into her mind, that it was Pamela's own fault entirely that she was stuck at home with a two-year-old child to look after. Although, if Auntie Alice was to be believed, she didn't do all that much staying at home.

'Anyroad, when are you going to come and see us? I asked you to come over for me twenty-first, but you never came, did yer?'

'I couldn't, Pam. I did explain. September's a very

busy time at the shop – and at the hotel as well – and I couldn't ask Paul for any more time off. I'd already had my fortnight's holiday.'

'All right, all right, don't bother with the chorus. It's October now, so you've no excuse. The season's over.'

'Not this year it isn't. The lights are on again.'

'What lights?'

'Blackpool illuminations, of course. They didn't have them during the war because of the blackout, but they've switched them on again this year for the first time. The boarding-house keepers are tickled pink about it, I can tell you. It adds another few weeks to the season, you see.'

'Yes, I'm sure it does . . .' Pamela didn't sound as though she was all that interested. 'Your wicked stepmother'll be rubbing her hands in glee then?'

Josie smiled a little, in spite of herself. 'Half and half. Iris is a bit tired. I think she could have done without the extra weeks, to tell the truth. But she never likes to admit defeat.'

'And are they good then, these famous lights?'

'Yes, spectacular. The prom was jam-packed with folks the night we went to see them. I went with Paul and—'

'Aye, aye!'

'What d'you mean?'

'You went with Paul, did you? He's not just your boss then? Shady goings-on in the darkroom eh, Josie?'

'Don't be ridiculous, Pamela!' Again, Josie bit off the retort that sprung to her lips, *We're not all like you . . .* 'I was just going to say, when you interrupted me, that I went with Paul and Karen and the twins. His children, Pamela.'

'All right, all right. Keep your hair on. They're worth seeing then, are they, these lights?

'Yes, great. Your Linda would love them.'

'Huh! Chance 'ud be a fine thing. We're lucky if we get a day in Bridlington, I can tell you. It's cost us a fortune moving into this place, what with carpet squares and curtains and God knows what else . . .'

Josie grinned to herself. It sounded strange to hear details of domesticity falling from Pamela's lips. 'Oh yes, your prefab. I am looking forward to seeing it, Pam, honest I am, but it just hasn't been possible.'

'So when are you coming?'

'November.' Josie suddenly made up her mind. It wasn't as if she'd actually be staying there with Pamela and Len; there wouldn't be room anyway. 'I'll come, let's say, the first week in November. I'll stay with Auntie Alice, if that's all right with her.'

'Oh, it'll be more than all right with her, you can be sure. Whatever her precious Josie does is all right with Alice. Will your Bertie and Frances come as well?'

'No, they'll be back at school. Half-term's only a few days. But I might ask my friend Karen if she'd like to come with me.' Josie had only just thought of this, but it might help to ease the tension that she always felt whenever she spent any time in the company of her cousin Len and his wife. Not that it ever seemed to worry Pamela.

'Okey-dokey. 'Spect your friend'll find Haliford a bit tame though, after Blackpool.'

'Oh, Karen won't mind. We can go on some bus rides into the country. We might even get to York – it's ages since I've been there. Karen likes seeing new places.'

'Very thrilling, I'm sure.' Pamela sounded as though it would be anything but. 'So long as you leave some time for us and our humble abode.'

'Have you got a phone as well?' Josie suddenly realized

that she didn't know where Pamela was ringing from. She hadn't heard her press button A, so she couldn't be in a phone box.

'Have we heck as like! D'you think we're millionaires? No, I'm ringing from Alice's. We've brought Linda round. We do sometimes on a Sunday afternoon, and her doting grandma has taken her for a walk. Len's talking to Jack in the garden. Garden! Honestly, anybody 'ud think it was Victoria Park – it's only a few rows of veg and a privvy at the end. So I'm all on my owny-own, an' I just thought, I'll give me old friend Josie a ring.'

At my auntie Alice's expense, thought Josie indignantly, annoyed, too, at the way Pamela always referred to her in-laws as Alice and Jack. Iris always said it was most disrespectful and Josie didn't like it either. She brought the conversation to a close.

'Cheerio then, Pamela. I'll see you in a few weeks' time. I don't want to use Auntie Alice's phone any longer. It's cost quite enough already.' She put down the receiver with more force than was necessary.

Poor Auntie Alice, thought Josie. She had had the phone installed only a few months ago after she had been rather poorly and unable to get about. She still regarded it as a supreme luxury, only to be used on rare occasions. She must have been relieved when Len and his family finally moved to their prefab, after three years of living under the same roof. And she seemed, like so many middle-aged women did, to be finding solace in her grandchild. Josie was looking forward to seeing her aunt again.

Josie thought that Yorkshire was at its best at this time of the year, and when she saw the trees in their glowing autumn foliage and the purple sweep of the heather on the moors as the train cut through the Calder Valley, she wondered how she could ever have exchanged this wild, rugged beauty for the flat and featureless landscape of Blackpool and its environs. She was thoughtful as she gazed through the train window. There was very little scenic charm in Blackpool, apart from the sea, sand and sky.

And that, in essence, was Blackpool. As a photographer she had come to notice for the first time, and to capture on film, the ever-changing patterns of light and shade – and colour, although this, of course, didn't show – upon the seascape, brought about by the variations of wind and weather.

And the clouds. Never before had she been aware of the powerful influence of clouds on a landscape. Paul had taught her that pictures could be lifeless without the relief of even a few white wisps in an otherwise clear sky. And the heavier banks of cumulus, such as were hanging over the Pennines now, had a beauty all their own.

And where but in Blackpool, Josie reflected, did you ever get such an expanse of sky or such clarity of light? She found herself thinking about her job, which brought her such satisfaction and joy; about her family, all of whom had found new interests and friends in the seaside town – she knew that Iris, in spite of finding the hotel work increasingly hard, would never want to live anywhere else now. And she thought about Paul . . . Yes, it had been a wrench at first to leave the hills and valleys of Yorkshire, but she knew that she had made the right decision. It would be lovely to see Auntie Alice again though.

'A penny for them.' Karen broke into her reverie, nudging gently at her foot.

'What?' Josie came to with a start.

'You were miles away. Your eyes had gone all glassy. What are you thinking about?'

'Oh, this and that. About Yorkshire . . . I was comparing it with the Fylde. Not much comparison, is there?'

'No, not really,' replied Karen, staring out of the window. 'I was thinking myself how beautiful it is round here. Wild though, and very lonely, I shouldn't wonder. Just imagine living there, 'specially in winter when the snowdrifts are piled high against your door.' She pointed to a row of grey stone cottages teetering on the edge of a rocky cliff. 'There's a great deal to be said for town life as far as I'm concerned. Anyway, your home's in Blackpool now, isn't it? And your job and your friends?'

'It's true,' agreed Josie. 'And I wouldn't want to come back here, not for good, believe me.'

'Dad'll miss you this week, won't he?' Karen was looking at her quizzically.

'Oh, he'll be all right,' Josie replied casually. 'We're not very busy at the moment, now the season's over. And the Christmas rush hasn't started yet. I should imagine he's more likely to miss you, Karen. He's not much of a hand at cooking, is he? I know he leaves a lot of it to you.'

'He can do it when he has to, and the twins'll help. And I expect they'll have a few of their meals round at Brenda's.' Brenda Sharples had a café a few doors away in Caunce Street. It was only a small place, specializing in snacks – various items on toast, egg and chips, bacon barmcakes and the like – and ready-packed sandwiches for holiday-makers and local office-workers to take away. 'She'll make sure they won't starve.'

'Oh yes, Brenda. I like Brenda. She's a good sort, isn't she? Real friendly, without being too pushy, if you know what I mean.' Josie had warmed at once to the pretty, plumpish brunette in the bright pink overall when she had popped into the café for sandwiches that Paul had ordered for his midday snack. 'She's got a soft spot for your dad, hasn't she? I can tell.'

'Yes, I think so,' replied Karen. 'About a year after Mum died – round about the time I met you – I thought they were getting rather friendly. He went round once or twice in the evening – she has a flat over the shop, you know – but nothing came of it.'

'You wouldn't have minded?'

'No, I don't think so. I like Brenda. She's about the same age as Dad.'

'And single?'

'Yes, she's never married. Anyway, it all seemed to fizzle out. Dad threw himself into his work again; he didn't leave time for anything else. And then we met you, and now . . . well, I just don't know.' Karen was looking at her questioningly again.

'No, I don't know either,' Josie answered. But the smile they exchanged across the compartment was perfectly amicable.

The two girls were made more than welcome at Alice Rawlinson's, and Josie enjoyed showing her friend, who was visiting Yorkshire for the first time, the glories of the place of her birth. They marvelled particularly at Knaresborough with its splendid view from the castle ruins of the viaduct spanning the River Nidd, and Josie thought that the tiny railway station, nestling in the valley, was like something out of a bygone age. Harrogate, too, was charming, with its elegant shops and the Valley Gardens at the climax of their autumn grandeur; even Haliford, now that Josie was seeing it with the eyes of a visitor, seemed to have acquired an attraction that she hadn't noticed before.

She found herself scouring the shops and market for familiar faces and was surprised to see none at all. She remarked on it to Karen. 'I had quite a lot of friends here. School friends, you know. I can't help wondering what has happened to them all.'

'You didn't keep in touch?'

'No, I'm afraid not. You know how it is. You intend to, and then you never do . . . And boys aren't much good at letter-writing, are they?' she added pensively.

'Boys?' She felt Karen's ears prick up with interest. 'Or do you mean one boy in particular?'

Josie turned to grin at her, tucking her hand companionably beneath Karen's elbow as they walked up the steep hill of Baldwin Lane back to Aunt Alice's. 'Yes, I suppose I do. I was thinking about Jimmy. Jimmy Clegg. I used to sit next to him at Junior school. And after we left we were still good friends.'

'He was your boyfriend?'

'Not really. I was only fourteen when we left Haliford. There was nothing . . . like that, you know. But if I'd stayed, there might have been.'

'But you didn't stay.'

'No, I didn't.'

'I've never heard you mention him before. It was only Len that you told me about.'

'Yes, Len; that was after we moved to Blackpool. And now that's all ancient history. You'll be meeting him later – and Pamela. There were two girls I was friendly with as well at Beechwood School, besides Pamela. Vera Brown, and Hilda. D'you know, I haven't thought about Hilda Ormerod for ages. Isn't that dreadful? And we were such good friends. The last I heard she was at training college. And I'm twenty now, so she must be – gosh! She must be teaching already. Just imagine that.'

'Perhaps Pamela will know something about them. She knew them, didn't she?'

'I doubt if she'll know anything,' said Josie briefly. 'She didn't like them very much and the feeling was mutual. Of course we'll all have grown up a good deal since those days.'

Josie was remembering now, with more than a little guilt, her own spiteful behaviour towards the two girls who were later to be her friends, to say nothing of her frequent squabbles with Pamela. Children could be so terribly cruel to one another, whereas adults, on the whole, did learn to conceal their feelings of animosity. 'I should imagine Pamela will have some new friends now,' she remarked. 'Other young mums, perhaps.' Although the idea of Pamela discussing the weight of babies or some such topic over the dried milk and orange juice at the clinic did seem somewhat incongruous.

They didn't see Len and his family until halfway through the week. The two girls had been invited for tea at the prefab, and Len had promised to finish work a little earlier so that he could pick them up in the small van he had now acquired.

'Our little Linda's a lovely child, and as bright as a button, too,' Alice told Josie and Karen over the breakfast table, and Josie noticed that her aunt's eyes lit up with affection and delight whenever she spoke of her granddaughter, a response any mention of her daughter-in-law certainly didn't evoke. Josie had to admit, though, that Alice was very fair, and apart from the odd remark to the effect that Pamela still liked to gad about whenever she got half a chance, she didn't indulge in overt criticism of the girl.

'They're happy, are they?' Josie asked tentatively. She found she was unable to resist rubbing salt in the wound, although by now the wound was largely healed.

Alice gave a slight shrug. 'Suppose so. They've got to be, haven't they? They've made their bed and they'll have to lie on it. At least they're in their own home now, which is a blessing. I must admit I've been very impressed with them prefabs, Josie. I thought it was a rum idea at first, living in an aluminium shed – that's all they are when all's said and done – but it's ever so cosy. Inside bathroom and lav an' all, that's not to be sneezed at. It's more than we've got here.'

'Isn't it time you got the landlord to do something about that?' asked Josie. She knew that her aunt and uncle, unlike her own father, had never owned the property on Baldwin Lane. Samuel Goodwin, ages ago, had had the boxroom in his house converted into a bathroom. Looking back, it seemed many moons to Josie since she had lived there. 'We're nearly in the nineteen-fifties now, Auntie. If you lived in a council house you'd have one.'

'Yes, happen you're right, love,' replied Alice. 'In fact I know you're right. If only your uncle and I could scrape together enough money we'd buy this place, and a bathroom 'ud be the first priority.'

'You'd most likely get a grant from the Government if you owned the property,' Josie told her.

'Aye, maybe we would . . . Pigs might fly, I sometimes think,' Alice said ruefully. 'We should have thought about buying this place years ago, but somehow we never did. Your uncle Jack never had as much go about him as your father, Josie. Not that I'm criticizing him, mind – he's been a wonderful husband – but he's always been inclined to take life as it comes, nice and easy like, instead of getting the bull by the horns. Still, we're all as the good Lord made us.'

'Mmm . . . I suppose so.' Josie was thoughtful as she spread marmalade on her toast. Her aunt belonged to that generation of women who had never gone out to work, and though she was now commenting, half ruefully, that Jack Rawlinson was easygoing, Josie knew that Alice was pretty much the same. There was no reason why she couldn't have worked, especially after Len had left school – the war had been on then and she could easily have got a job in a munitions factory – but she had chosen not to do so. Most likely she had never even thought of it. If Auntie Alice had worked, Josie found herself thinking, they could have bought this house years ago.

Probably a day would come when women would automatically go out to work, just as the men did. Josie enjoyed her own job so much that she couldn't imagine herself not working. Times were certainly changing. She could see that her aunt's horizons had always been restricted to the needs of her family; she hadn't even considered trying to broaden them. Whereas Iris had forged ahead and carved out a whole new life for herself. If Dad had lived, goodness knows what he and Iris, together, might have achieved. Been joint owners of a string of hotels, maybe. They had been so much alike, her father and stepmother.

'Wakey, wakey.' Karen waved a hand in front of her friend's face. 'You've gone all dreamy again. What are you thinking about?'

'What? Oh . . . nothing really.' Josie smiled. 'Just about . . . houses. I used to live at the end of the row, you know.'

'And you've lived in goodness knows how many places

since then,' her aunt added. 'Iris always had itchy feet. Have you shown Karen all the houses you've lived in?'

'No, of course I haven't,' Josie laughed. 'Why should she be interested in that? It's what's happening now that's important, Auntie, not what happened years ago. It's a sign of old age, raking up the past.' She gave a roguish smile. 'Eeh, I don't know what things are coming to. It were never like this when I were a lass . . .' Although Josie had found herself continually reminiscing since her return to Haliford.

'Give over, you cheeky monkey!' Alice grinned at her good-humouredly. 'Now, if you've both done, you'd better get yourselves out. Don't waste this nice sunshine. It'll be winter before we know where we are and another year gone. And don't forget you're at our Len's for tea.'

Josie knew that she wouldn't be likely to forget. She was only glad that Karen and Linda would be there to defuse the situation a little.

The prefab was one of a whole colony of cream-coloured, single-storeyed, aluminium structures that had been erected on the outskirts of Haliford, an area Josie didn't know very well as it was at the opposite end from Victoria Park. The rooms were small – a living room, kitchen, two bedrooms and a minute bathroom and toilet – but everything was clean and bright and sparkling with newness. Josie noticed as Pamela proudly showed them round that the gas cooker was spotless and she hazarded a guess that it wasn't required to work very hard. Not that she, Josie, had any room to talk. She knew that she was no great shakes as a cook and sometimes wondered how on earth she would manage when – and if – she ever got married.

She was forced, however, to change her opinion as they

tucked into the meal that Pamela had prepared. It was not the inevitable limp-lettuce salad, the stand-by of inexperienced young housewives, which she had expected, but ham and eggs and golden-brown chips, followed by apple tart and cream. The latter, Pamela admitted, she had bought from the local bakery, but she had made an excellent job of the first course.

'My wife's a good cook,' Len said proudly. 'Don't you think so?' And Josie was forced to agree.

She found herself wondering if, after all, her one-time friend was settling down to married life. She felt almost peeved at the thought, realizing, to her chagrin, that the cooker was clean because Pamela kept it that way, as she did the rest of the house. The linoleum round the edge of the carpet squares gleamed with recent polishing; so did the taps and the mirrors, the oak furniture and brass ornaments – Josie recognized one or two pieces from her aunt Alice's home. It was all very neat and tidy, and Pamela, in her flowered pinny, was playing the part of competent housewife to perfection. It was almost, Josie thought, as though she were a little girl looking after a doll's house.

But no, she admonished herself, she mustn't be uncharitable. The young woman was making a good job of it, much better, Josie feared, than she herself would be able to do. There was something lacking, though. It wasn't what you could call a home. It was just . . . a house.

Josie realized as the meal progressed that if it was Pamela who cooked the meals and kept the house clean then it was most certainly Len who looked after little Linda. As Josie had hoped, the child, with her constant chatter and appealing ways, helped to ease the tension she always felt in the presence of her cousin and his wife.

'I'm two and three-quarters,' Linda told them proudly, not at all shy of the unaccustomed company. She smiled engagingly at the two young women, entertaining them with rhymes and little songs she had learned at the nursery, where she went three mornings a week, and the retelling of the story of the three bears which she had heard for the first time that day.

It was Len who persuaded her to stop chattering for a while and eat her tea, who wiped the egg from her chin and helped her to hold her cup of milk; and, after Josie and Karen together had read her a story from her favourite book, it was Len who took her to her bedroom to put on her pyjamas. That was reasonable enough, Josie thought, considering that Pamela, with the assistance of herself and Karen, was doing the washing-up. She couldn't help noticing that Pamela was ill at ease. She seemed nervy and preoccupied. In the short time they had been in the kitchen she had dropped a cup and saucer and had spilt the contents of the milk jug on the floor.

'Damn!' she exclaimed, hurriedly mopping it up. 'It's a good job there wasn't much left in there. That child'll drink milk till it comes out of her ears. I sometimes think we should have our own cow. And Len 'ud buy her one an' all if she said she wanted one. Spoils her rotten, he does.'

Josie hadn't got the impression that he did spoil the child. He was obviously very fond of his little daughter, but she felt he could be firm with her when necessary. She didn't say so however, merely commenting, 'I'm not surprised. She's a delightful little girl. You must be very proud of her.'

'Of course I am,' replied Pamela sharply, and Josie wasn't sure whether or not she imagined the hostile glance which vanished as quickly as it appeared. Pamela took off her apron and hung it on the back of the door. 'Come on, let's have a sit-down for five minutes. Because soon I'll have to . . .' She didn't finish the sentence, and again Josie was aware of the girl's unease.

The three young women sat on the easy chairs in the living room, Josie feeling that she hardly dared rest her head against the pristine cleanness of the chair-back cover. Pamela was certainly house-proud, but where on earth did the child play, she wondered? There was no sign of any toys, the teddy bears, building bricks and half-finished jigsaws she remembered from her own childhood. In her bedroom, perhaps?

The silence was beginning to be uncomfortable, even Pamela, for once, seeming to have run out of words, when Len reappeared with Linda to say her final goodnight. Josie was glad to see that Pamela kissed the little girl quite affectionately, then there was a kiss each for Auntie Josie and Auntie Karen before Len carried her away again. It was when he came back, flopping thankfully into a fireside chair and picking up his newspaper – just like his father, Josie thought – that Pamela dropped her bombshell.

She rose to her feet, smiling brightly – too brightly – at them all. 'Well, I'm afraid I'm going to have to love you and leave you. I hope you won't mind, folks, but I've arranged to go out.'

Len put down his paper with a sharp crackle, glaring at his wife over the top of it. 'What! What d'you mean, you're going out? Where?'

'Oh, stop it, Lennie, being so boring and bad-tempered,' Pamela chided, but Josie could tell that the girl was jumpy and on edge. 'You know I sometimes go out with Peggy on a Wednesday, to the pictures. It's one that Peggy badly wants to see, so I said I'd go with her. I did tell you.'

'I don't remember.' Len was scowling at her. 'I'm sure you didn't. Anyway, we've got company.'

'Oh, don't be so difficult, Lennie. Josie's not company, she's family – and Karen won't mind. That's one of the reasons I said I'd go, because I knew you'd have two nice young ladies to look after you. You'll look after your cousin, won't you, Josie?' Pamela was smiling fatuously, but there was a trace of fear lurking in those big blue eyes, as though she were wondering if she had gone too far.

Josie didn't answer – how could she? – but just nodded non-committally. Len wasn't returning his wife's smile. He looked blazing mad, but was obviously trying to keep his true feelings under control.

'Seems you've got it all worked out,' he said, 'you and Peggy. Yes, I know you sometimes go out with her on a Wednesday, but I did think that tonight . . . What are you going to see, anyway?'

'Oh, some Deanna Durbin musical,' replied Pamela airily. 'I'm not sure which one. They're all pretty much the same, but Peggy's nuts about them.'

'Where's it on?' asked Len, looking at her with narrowed eyes.

'The Regal . . . What's this? Twenty questions or summat?' Pamela gave a shriek of laughter which, to Josie's ears, sounded false. 'Anybody 'ud think you didn't trust me, Lennie. You know that Peggy and me—'

'All right, all right.' Len was getting very impatient. 'Don't be late, that's all. I've said I'll run the girls home and I can't till you get back. Eleven o'clock, OK?'

'Yessir!' Pamela gave a mock salute. 'Right, sir. Will do, sir. Shouldn't think Alice'll lock them out though, will she? They're big girls now.'

'That's beside the point. Just make sure you're back.

D'you want me to run you to Haliford?' Len added, though his tone was icy.

'No.' Pamela's reply seemed to come too quickly. 'No, thanks. I'm meeting Peggy at the corner of her street. We'll get a bus.'

Josie felt slightly embarrassed when Pamela had finally departed, with fulsome promises that she and Linda would meet the two young women in Haliford the next day. Len's angry face seemed to relax, however, when his wife had gone.

'Whew!' He gave a deep sigh. 'So that's that. No use arguing with Pamela when she's set her mind to something. It's best to try and keep the peace, if you can.'

By letting her have her own way, thought Josie. And this was the same Len who had once advised her, Josie, not to let Iris rule her. She was remembering, though, how persistent Pamela had always been, to the point of being vindictive, so that it was easier in the end to let her win. It seemed as though she hadn't changed much. It was to the same Regal cinema that they had gone, as children, to the Saturday matinée. She wondered if Pamela ever gave a thought to those far-away days.

'Who's Peggy?' she asked now, just for something to say.

'A girl Pamela met at the clinic, about the same age as her. She's got a baby boy. They go out to the pictures quite a lot. I don't usually mind.'

'A bit of peace and quiet, eh, Len?' said Karen with a grin. Josie smiled to herself. Her friend certainly wasn't one to hide her feelings.

'You could say that.' Len also grinned wryly. 'She looks after the house a treat, though,' he added, almost as if to defend his young wife. 'I've got to give her credit for that.'

But are you happy, Len? Josie wanted to ask, as she had already asked her aunt Alice, but she didn't. She could see that Len was determined to be loyal to the girl he had been obliged to marry. But that was Len: ever ready to make the best of things. Josie thought, with a sudden spurt of anger, that Pamela didn't deserve him. But that was something she had always known.

'So – what are we going to do?' Len looked inquiringly at Josie and Karen. 'Radio? A game of cards? If we just talk we'll only end up going down Memory Lane, and it wouldn't be fair on you, Karen.' He smiled at her.

Karen giggled. 'Yes, I've heard a lot about Haliford this week, but mainly from your mum. I don't mind though. Have you got a Monopoly set? That's something I really love.'

'Of course! A brilliant idea.' Len went to fetch the game from the bedroom and the two girls exchanged meaningful glances.

'Heck! I thought there was going to be a row, didn't you?' Karen whispered.

'He doesn't like rows,' Josie whispered back.

'No . . . he's nice, isn't he? I can see why you – you know. I didn't like *her* much, though. I'm glad she's gone out.'

'Yes, a little of Pamela goes a long way, I'm afraid. It always did. Shhhh . . . he's here.'

About three and a half hours later, after Karen had become a millionaire for the evening and they had all partaken of two cups of tea, Len was getting restless. He picked up his *Haliford Chronicle*. 'Let's see what time this picture finishes. I did warn her not to be late.'

'Don't worry, Len,' said Josie. 'She'll be back before eleven. It's only ten-to. I expect they've had to wait for a bus.'

There was silence except for the crackling of the newspaper, then a more ominous silence as Len stared at the page in front of him. 'That's funny,' he said, frowning.

'What is?' asked Josie.

'The Regal . . . There's nothing here about Deanna Durbin. It's *Gone with the Wind*. Retained for a further week, it says.'

'Right up to the minute with your pictures in Haliford, aren't you, Len?' said Josie, trying to make light of the situation. 'That's ages old.'

'Yes, I know. But it's still popular. It must be, or they wouldn't have retained it.'

'They'll have gone to see that picture then,' said Karen. 'Pamela and that Peggy. They mustn't have realized it's still on.'

'They've seen it,' replied Len flatly. 'They went last week. Pamela's seen it umpteen times.'

'Don't worry,' said Josie again, although the atmosphere was becoming very tense. She could feel a prickle of fear down her spine, though she wasn't sure why. After all, it was not yet quite eleven o'clock. 'She'll be here.'

'If Peggy was so nuts about Deanna Durbin she'd have known,' said Len, a frown creasing his brow. 'What the hell is she up to?' He gazed unseeingly into the embers of the fire while Josie and Karen looked at one another uneasily.

A knock at the door disturbed the silence and Len sprang to his feet. 'At last! About time too, but I might have known she'd forget her key.' The relief was evident in his voice.

When he returned to the living room, however, his frown was even deeper. It wasn't his wife he was ushering in, but a burly policeman.

Chapter 21

'You'd better sit down, sir,' said the policeman. 'I'm afraid I've got some bad news.' He looked inquiringly at Josie and Karen. 'These young ladies . . . ?'

'My cousin and her friend,' said Len, in a voice that was almost inaudible. He sat down on one of the easy chairs, his knuckles gleaming white as he grasped the arms. 'It's all right. You can say . . . What is it you have to tell me, Constable?'

'It's your wife, Mr Rawlinson. Pamela Rawlinson . . . she is your wife?' Len nodded silently. 'I'm afraid there's been an accident. She was rushed to hospital – they both were – but . . . I'm sorry to say that they were dead on arrival. I really am sorry, Mr Rawlinson.'

The gasp of horror came from Josie, not from Len. This was devastating news, horrendous; she couldn't believe this was happening. All evening she had felt the resentment building up inside her against Pamela and her casual attitude towards her husband and that dear little girl, a resentment that was very close to hatred; but never, never in a thousand years would she have wanted this to happen. Poor Len. She felt that he really did care for Pamela in spite of her careless treatment of him. Tears sprang to her eyes and she didn't bother to check them as they rolled down her cheeks.

Len was staring at the policeman, struck dumb. It was several seconds before he spoke. 'But where . . . ? How? Did I hear you say they were both . . . dead? Peggy as well? What were they doing?'

The policeman, who was still standing, his bulky presence filling the small room, now lowered himself on to one of the dining chairs. He didn't look at Len but at the top of the table as he answered. 'They were in a car, on the moorland road, the Bradford road. It seems like they took a corner too fast and crashed into the drystone wall. There was no other vehicle involved.'

'But . . . but they were supposed to be at the pictures, my wife and Peggy. What the hell were they doing up there?'

'I'm sorry, Mr Rawlinson. There was no one by the name of Peggy. The young lady – your wife – she was with . . . a young man. A Mr Malcolm Forrest. Does the name mean anything to you?'

Again Len shook his head. He had blanched visibly now, his grey-blue eyes dark with anguish in the stark-white face. It was a few moments before he replied. 'No . . . not a thing. No, but whoever he is . . . Did you say he was dead, too? It's perhaps just as well . . .' A shade of feeling, sadness tinged with anger, had crept back into his voice now.

'Yes, sir. We assume that they were both killed immediately. There was nothing that could be done. I'm sorry, sir. But she wouldn't have suffered.'

'Hang on a minute . . .' Len was muttering as if to himself. 'Forrest . . . Forrest . . . I think that was the name of another of my wife's friends. Yes . . . Evelyn Forrest. She lives at the other end of the estate, I believe. Prefab, like this.'

'Quite so, sir. Another of our chaps has gone to see

her. I shouldn't jump to conclusions if I were you, Mr Rawlinson. There's most likely an explanation.'

'There's an explanation all right,' replied Len grimly. 'Don't know why I didn't realize before. I might have known . . .' He paused, then, 'I suppose you'll want me to . . . Where is she?' he said, his voice no longer angry now, but tormented.

'To identify the body, sir? Yes, if you would. But it's just a formality. Tomorrow morning will do, Haliford General Hospital.' The policeman rose. 'I'm very sorry to be the bearer of such sad news.' He turned to the two young women. 'I should make a pot of tea if I were you. Nice and strong, lots of sugar – good for a shock.'

A sudden thought seemed to have struck Len. 'You said it was just a formality. You already knew it was Pamela and . . . and that other one. How? There couldn't be . . . a mistake?'

'Identity discs, sir. We got used to wearing 'em during the war, didn't we? Old habits die hard. And her name and address were in a diary in her handbag. I'm afraid there's no doubt that it's your wife. I'm so sorry, sir. Goodnight . . . I'll let myself out.'

Len and the two girls stared at one another after the policeman had gone. 'I'm sorry,' said Josie, words that the constable had already uttered several times. But what else was there to say? 'This is terrible, Len. I can't believe it.'

'Nor can I. I just can't take it in.' Len's tone was expressionless. 'Pamela, and that – that fellow. Her friend's husband, for God's sake.'

'You had no idea?'

'No, none at all. I thought she was happy. Well, happy enough. She seemed to be. She kept this place lovely. And we were . . . all right, you know.' His eyes grew misty, and

Josie guessed he was referring to the more intimate side of his marriage. 'But she was always a restless sort of girl, my Pamela. You know that, don't you, Josie?' The little word *my* didn't escape Josie, and she was sure Len must have loved his wife.

'I'll go and make that tea.' Karen rose suddenly and went into the kitchen.

Len stared at her departing back. 'I said I'd run you home, you and Karen. I can't now. There's Linda . . . I can't leave her. What'll you do? The last bus'll have gone.'

'We're staying here, Len,' said Josie decisively, although the idea had only just come to her. 'We wouldn't leave you on your own, we wouldn't dream of it. We'll sleep on the settee, or the floor – anywhere. But I'll just have to let Auntie Alice know. She'll be getting worried. Is there a phone box?'

'On the next corner. What will you tell her? It'll be a shock.'

'Oh . . . nothing much. I can't tell her over the phone; it'll have to wait till morning. I'll say we got talking and didn't realize the time.' She looked at her cousin concernedly. 'I'll break it to your mother, Len, tomorrow. Don't you worry about that. Just concentrate on . . . what you have to do.'

Len's eyes were wet, for the first time since the appalling news had come, as he tried to smile at Josie. 'Thanks, Josie. You're a great girl. I don't know what I'd do without you.'

'You'll stay for the funeral, won't you, Josie love?' asked Alice. 'I don't think I can face it without a bit of moral support from you. And she was a friend of yours, wasn't she? You and Pamela were good pals once, when you were kiddies, weren't you? In spite of . . . what she did. To you, and now to our Len. Eeh, Josie, I don't know.' Alice shook her head sorrowfully. 'She's been a naughty lass, a real wicked lass, though I know you shouldn't speak ill of the dead. And yet she could be so nice, so charming, when she wanted to be . . . You will stay, won't you, love?'

'I can't stay, Auntie,' Josie told her. 'These things take time. It'll be next week, more than likely, before Len can arrange a funeral. But I'll come back, I promise. I'll have to go home with Karen. She's due back at work on Monday and I'll have to put in a day or two with Paul before I can take some more time off.'

'Poor Karen,' said Alice. 'It's turned out to be a rum sort of holiday for her, and for you as well. She's a nice lass, isn't she? It was grand of her to take Linda off our hands, wasn't it? Not that the bairn's any trouble, but I don't want her to hear anything she shouldn't.'

Karen had taken the little girl down to Victoria Park to feed the ducks, leaving Len and his mother and Josie to cope with the distressing details surrounding the sudden death. So far Linda didn't appear to be unduly worried about her mother's absence, accepting without comment the story that Mummy had had to go away for a while. Josie guessed that she would miss her daddy far more, were he suddenly to disappear from the scene.

'Don't worry about Karen,' Josie told her aunt. 'She's only too glad to help. She's grown up tremendously in the time I've known her. She was very mixed-up and insecure when I first met her. You would hardly know it was the same girl.'

'Your influence, Josie, I'll be bound.' Her aunt looked at her fondly. 'I can see she looks up to you more than a bit.'

'Oh, I don't know about that, Auntie,' said Josie dismissively. 'We just get on very well, that's all. And I'll be back next week to give you a hand with everything, never fear.'

'Thanks, love. I don't know what I'd do without you,' said Alice, just as her son had said the night before.

'We sang this hymn at your father's wedding, when he married Iris,' Alice whispered to Josie. 'Our Len asked me to choose the hymns. He's been in such a state, poor lad, and I thought it was appropriate.'

Josie nodded, although she was frowning to herself. How could a wedding hymn be appropriate for a funeral?

> Dear Lord and Father of Mankind,
> Forgive our foolish ways . . .

they had just sung. Yes, Pamela had, indeed, been a foolish girl, but was it quite the thing, Josie wondered, to remind her assembled friends and relations of her waywardness at such a time? Or maybe they wouldn't be attaching as much significance to the words as Josie found herself doing. It was a beautiful hymn, very moving, she thought, as they sang the next to last verse.

> Drop thy still dews of quietness
> Till all our strivings cease;
> Take from our souls the strain and stress,
> And let our ordered lives confess
> The beauty of thy peace.

Perhaps it was for these words that her aunt had chosen it. Josie said a little prayer now for Len and her aunt Alice – for Pamela's mother and father, too – that they would be able to cope with the strain and stress of this awful, awful event, now and in the days ahead.

She felt her eyes drawn time and again, as they always were at a funeral, to the oak coffin reposing near the chancel steps of St Luke's church. It was covered with a huge wreath of chrysanthemums and dahlias, almost the only flowers in bloom in mid-autumn, in vivid shades of orange, vermilion, deep russet-red and gold. Rich, vibrant colours, seeming to glow with life and energy, just as Pamela had done. Josie found it almost impossible to believe that in that box there lay the now useless body of the young woman who had created so much havoc in all their lives; yet who had been able, in her better moments, to make them laugh and to stop taking themselves too seriously.

And later, when the mourners assembled round the graveside and the clods of earth fell on the coffin, it all still seemed like a terrible dream. Not very many people gathered at Alice and Jack's home for the simple buffet lunch – prepared earlier by her aunt, with Josie's assistance – but Josie found it rather an ordeal. She didn't know these friends of Pamela and Len, nor was she acquainted with Pamela's mother and father; she had stayed away from her cousin's hasty marriage in Manchester.

They were sad, naturally, still dazed and shaken by their daughter's death, but Josie suspected that they were very wrapped up in each other, and always had been if what Pamela had told her was true. It was maybe just as well, as she had been their only child. Josie was glad to see two familiar faces; Pamela's auntie Mary and uncle Bill, with whom the girl had stayed as an evacuee, looking sad and much older, but delighted to see Josie again.

Apart from a few moments' chat with them and with Pamela's parents, Josie spent most of her time in the kitchen, washing up. She was relieved when, the following morning, she was able to board the homeward-bound train at Haliford station. A very subdued Len, accompanied by his lively little daughter, came to see her off. Linda would be a great comfort to him, Josie was sure. How he would manage on his own, though, had been discussed hardly at all. Josie suspected that much of the burden – although she knew her aunt wouldn't regard it as such – would fall on Alice, as it had done when her own mother had died, leaving Frances as a tiny baby.

'Thanks for coming, and for all you've done. You've been grand,' Len told her as they waited on the draughty platform. 'Come and see us again, won't you? And let's hope it'll be a happier time, eh?' He hesitated, then, 'Perhaps you could bring Karen with you again?' he said. 'Poor girl, it wasn't much of a holiday for her, was it? I thought she was . . . nice. And Linda liked her, didn't you, darling?' he added hurriedly. 'You'd like to see Auntie Karen again, wouldn't you?' He stooped down to the child in the pushchair as if slightly embarrassed.

'Yes,' the little girl agreed. 'Auntie Karen . . . and Auntie Josie.'

Josie smiled to herself. She had thought, even at their first meeting, that Len might, in different circumstances, have been attracted to her pretty, auburn-haired friend. And now, of course, circumstances had changed, drastically, although Karen was still only eighteen. 'I'll give her your best wishes, shall I?' she asked. 'Tell her you'd like to see her again, sometime?'

'Yes . . . please,' said Len quietly. 'This last week has been terrible. I know it'll take me a while to pick up the pieces, but . . .' He didn't finish the sentence. The train was just approaching round the bend.

He kissed Josie warmly as she entered the carriage, almost, but not quite, on the lips; and the looks they exchanged were ones of compassion, friendship, true affection . . . but nothing more.

Josie was thoughtful as she leaned back in her corner seat, her eyes fixed on the sepia prints of Yorkshire market towns – Skipton, Thirsk and Richmond – on the wall opposite. Her aunt Alice had said to her confidentially that morning, her bright brown eyes filling up with tears, 'D'you know what would make me really happy? If you and our Len . . . There, I know I shouldn't have said it, but it's what I've thought many times, and it's what should have happened right at the start. Then there'd have been none of this mess, all this upset.'

'You wouldn't have had Linda either,' Josie reminded her gently, 'and you wouldn't want to be without her, now would you? Don't worry,' she said as she kissed her aunt's shiny, apple-smooth cheek. 'Things'll work out, you'll see.'

But Josie knew, as Len did, that what had once happened between them could never be revived, no matter how convenient it might be. Too much had come along since. Karen had asked her on their journey home, in her usual forthright way, 'D'you think you're still in love with Len?' And Josie had replied, in perfect honesty, 'No, not at all.' The relief on Karen's face, though she might not have realized it, had been transparent. And Josie knew that she hadn't misinterpreted the tenderness in the girl's eyes as she had told Josie to give her very best wishes to Len. Now it seemed that the affection might be reciprocated, sometime in the future.

And earlier that week, just before she departed for her second visit to Yorkshire, Paul had asked Josie if she would go out with him, to a play at the Grand Theatre, followed by supper at the Temple Grill. Josie, feeling flattered and delighted, had said yes. It would be the first time that the two of them had been out on what might be called a date. Before they had always been accompanied by the rest of Paul's family. Josie knew that Paul Hepworth was a cautious man, one who wouldn't make a move unless he was very sure. She had worked closely with him for over a year now, and the rapport between them had developed into a deep friendship. Now she felt that they might be on the brink of something more than that. She was already very fond of him.

The confusion had arisen in Frances's mind when she had discovered that, as well as being able to dance, she also had a good singing voice. She knew, of course, that she could sing in tune. Members of the Tower Ballet sometimes had to join in the vocal numbers, and she had always enjoyed singing along to the wireless at home, to *Family Favourites* and *Music While You Work*, which her mother always had on. But dancing was her first love, and she hadn't really thought that her voice might be anything out of the ordinary until she was invited to join the church choir.

St Matthew's, adjacent to the sea front, was the nearest church to the hotel, but Iris didn't attend every week as she had done back in Haliford. She had found that her duties as a hotel proprietress didn't permit this. She had to be on the job, cooking the Sunday dinner for hungry visitors, rather than attending morning service. Or Matins, as it was called at St Matthew's, which was a rather high church compared with St Luke's in Haliford. Too high for Iris, if she were honest, although she did try to attend evensong – as opposed to the 'evening service' of the lower churches – at least once a month. And, when she did, Josie or Frances, one or both of them, usually went with her. Bertie, too, when he was at home, but by the summer of 1950 he was far away at Catterick camp, doing his national service.

It was during that summer that Mrs Gilchrist, an important personage on the Parochial Church Council of St Matthew's, first heard Frances singing. She had turned her head surreptitiously once or twice during the service to see who was making such a 'joyful noise unto the Lord' in the pew behind her.

'Your daughter has a beautiful voice, Mrs Goodwin,' she remarked to Iris as the congregation filed out of church. 'Do you think she could possibly be persuaded to join our choir? I know that Mr Beaumont, our organist and choirmaster, is crying out for good sopranos. A lot of young girls today don't want to be bothered, and it's nice to have a mixture of different age groups. At the moment it seems to be mostly the boy choristers and middle-aged men and women.'

Iris was gratified that such an important lady not only knew her name, but was complimenting her on her daughter's voice. Iris herself had been a person of some importance at her church in Haliford and she didn't find it easy now to be something of an outsider, even though she had little time for further involvement with church affairs. But if Frances were to join the choir that would be a feather in her, Iris's, cap, and it might help to take the girl's mind away from all that silly dancing. It was still, in Iris's view, playing too large a part in Frances's life, although she never voiced her feelings about it. It was very rarely that she criticized Frances.

'Thank you, Mrs Gilchrist, how kind of you,' Iris said

now in her Sunday-best voice. 'Yes, she does sing lovely, doesn't she? I think it would be a very nice idea for her to join the choir, but it would be up to Frances herself, of course. Perhaps you might like to ask her . . . then I'll work on her,' she added in a confidential manner. 'She's over there, talking to one of her school friends.'

Frances had hemmed and hawed at first. She was too busy; not only was there her dancing, but her school work as well, although, if the truth were told, she didn't attach too much importance to that. But, as Iris pointed out, the Tower Ballet came to an end after the season and the choir would then be a nice interest for her. And so, in the autumn of 1950, when she was nearly fifteen, Frances joined the church choir of St Matthew's, North Shore. She soon found that she loved every minute of it.

First, there was the attractive uniform which the lady members wore, maroon gowns and a floppy hat like a soft mortarboard, which Frances knew suited her admirably. And the music, which until then was of a kind almost unknown to her, she found too beautiful for words. Previously the only sorts of music she had experienced were the popular melodies to which Annette's youngsters danced, interspersed with light classical pieces from well-known ballets. Now she found herself, as it were, transported to another sphere – a phrase she had heard before, but never truly believed in – by the strains of '*Panis Angelicus*', 'How Lovely are Thy Dwellings', or Mozart's 'Ave Verum'. She had never had any formal teaching in music, but she soon learned to read the notation and as a soprano it was comparatively easy because they always sang the melody.

When rehearsals began for the Tower Ballet of 1951 Frances was amazed to find that she was having doubts as to whether or not she should be part of it. But she had promised Annette that she would. She was one of the principal dancers now and she couldn't let her down. And when Annette discovered that Frances's voice had developed both in clarity and in strength, she was given a solo number in the performance. Dressed in a South American costume, reminiscent of Carmen Miranda, she was to sing the catchy number, 'I-Yi-Yi-Yi-Yi, I like you vai – ry much.' It was what she had wanted ever since she had been the girl in the swing two years ago, another chance to shine in a solo spot, so how could she even consider that she should turn it down?

Once the performances started she was unable to attend all the choir practices at church, but Mr Beaumont was very understanding. If she just popped in for the last half-hour on a Friday evening, after she had finished at the Tower, then that would be fine, he told her. She knew most of the music and didn't find it difficult to learn new pieces. Frances was enjoying being lauded as a leading light both at church and at the Tower, but at the same time she was confused. Wasn't it somewhat incongruous, she wondered, dancing with such abandon – showing her shapely legs and rolling her eyes – on the stage every night, and then singing demurely in the church choir on a Sunday?

She didn't, however, let it worry her unduly until Janet and Megan, girls in her form at school, started to pester her. She had always tried to give these two a wide berth, as most of the girls did. Bible in hand, they were forever trying to get you into a corner of the cloakroom where they would exhort you to 'turn away from your sins and come to Jesus'. The 'God Squad', they were nicknamed, and Frances knew that Janet and Megan and a few others belonged to a religious sect known as 'Friends of the Carpenter'. They were not Church of England or Methodists or even Baptists, she had heard them proclaiming devoutly, but a group of friends who had broken away from the established churches – which, according to them, were full of imperfections and errors – and met in one another's houses, seeking to serve the Lord in their everyday lives.

Frances was impatient with them. She knew all about Jesus – who didn't? – and she had gone to Sunday school and church all her life. Her mother had made sure of that. She didn't understand all this business of getting to know Jesus in a more personal way. What was wrong with *her* way, she thought indignantly. She went to church, didn't she? And she sang in the choir as well. What more could you do?

Janet and Megan cornered her at mid-morning break one day in July when she hadn't been able to escape in time.

'Frances, there's something we feel we must say to you,' said Janet, a bonny girl with shiny red cheeks and straight black hair like a Dutch doll. Frances had often thought she could make much more of her appearance if only she would. 'Isn't there, Megan?' Janet turned to her friend.

Megan, her counterpart, a frail-looking girl with a pale complexion and wispy blonde hair, nodded earnestly. 'Yes . . . we think that what you are doing every night, up on the stage, must be very displeasing to God.' She turned soulful blue eyes upon Frances.

Frances felt her mouth opening wide in astonishment. How dare they? Of all the barefaced cheek! But the comments forming in her mind – What the hell has it got to do with you? Why can't you mind your own flipping business? – didn't come. She just gaped at them. 'Why? What d'you mean?' she faltered. 'How d'you know what I do, anyway?'

'We've been to see the show, haven't we, Megan?'

'Yes, we felt it was our duty. That's a very provocative number you sing, Frances.' Megan shook her head sorrowfully. 'Very . . . sexy.' She breathed the word in hushed tones. 'All about . . . lips and . . . hips.'

'Yes, we feel that you are making yourself look cheap. It's unworthy of you, Frances,' Janet told her, nodding fervently. 'We felt we had to say something before it was too late.'

Frances was speechless for a moment. She knew the number to which they were referring – and they'd been lapping it up, too, hadn't they, she thought indignantly, every word of it. The Carmen Miranda song, where she waggled her hips in a seductive manner and rolled her eyes naughtily at the audience.

She had felt rather self-conscious at first and had wondered if what she was doing might be a little too suggestive, but Annette had told her to give it all she'd got and so she had complied. Yes, she knew what they meant, these earnest young Friends of the Carpenter, but she wasn't going to admit it. Was she like heck!

'I can't see that it's anything to do with you,' she said eventually, far more evenly than she intended. 'Anyway, I'm only acting.' She shrugged, giving a careless laugh. 'You know me. I'm not really like that at all.'

'No, we know you're not, Frances. That's why we want to help you.'

There was more in this vein until the bell sounded for the end of break. Frances was churned up with righteous indignation, but only partially so. Hadn't she already been turning over in her mind the inconsistencies of her life? Besides, she had always had a sneaking admiration for these two girls, pious prigs though they might be at times. They would never take part in the telling of rude jokes or the passing round of 'sexy' books that went on in the form room from time to time, and in which Frances, to her shame, had sometimes indulged.

Nor were they part of a clandestine group who took a drag at a cigarette behind the bike sheds. This was something, however, that Frances had not been persuaded to do. Always, in Frances's mind, there was the thought of how upset her mother would be if she knew. Iris had brought her up to be a good girl, and Frances usually tried not to stray too far from her precepts.

The conflict waged in Frances's mind over the next few weeks. She found herself, to her surprise, chatting with Janet and Megan from time to time. She couldn't help but like them, although she wished they weren't always so blooming goody-goody. They made you feel positively wicked at times. Sinful, that was the word they were always using. They made you feel that you were full of sin.

They asked her several times to come to their meetings, but she always refused. She was performing nightly at the Tower, in spite of what they thought of it, and on Sunday she attended her own church. When, however, they told her that the Friends of the Carpenter were holding a beach mission on the second Sunday in August she finally agreed to go along.

It was on the second Saturday in August, 1951, that Josie and Karen boarded a train bound for the north Wales coast, where they were to spend a week at a Butlin's holiday camp. The romance that had entered both their lives had flourished over the previous couple of years, and both young women now wore an engagement ring. Josie wasn't wearing hers at the moment, though. At the last minute, just as she was getting ready to come away, one of the tiny diamonds had fallen out, so she had tucked the ring away in her dressing-table drawer for safe keeping during her holiday.

As Josie had guessed he would, her cousin Len had contacted Karen, after what was considered a decent interval of several months, and it was obvious that the couple were now very much in love; quietly, but unmistakably so. They spent whatever time they could together, although it was difficult with Karen in Blackpool and Len and his little daughter in Haliford.

Linda, of course, had been one of the deciding factors in the relationship. She adored her auntie Karen; there had been an immediate bond between them even at their first meeting, which had quickly developed into affection and trust. The couple planned to marry the following summer when Karen would be twenty-one. Now they were both saving hard, as Len was determined that they would start married life in their own little house, and not in the prefab where he still lived. They were to live in Yorkshire, as by now Len had a responsible job at the firm of electricians for which he had worked since he was a lad.

Josie would be sorry to lose her friend when she married, but she knew it was inevitable. She saw, now, from Karen's shining eyes and air of excitement, how much the girl was looking forward to seeing Len again. For he and Linda were meeting them at the camp in Pwllheli for a week's holiday. Josie, for several reasons, had felt reluctant at first to be one of the family party.

'I shall only be playing gooseberry,' she had said laughingly to Karen. 'You and Len want some time on your own. You don't want me with you.'

And, 'You can't possibly spare me from the business,' she had told Paul. 'You know it's our busiest time. Besides,

I don't really want to go away on holiday without you,' she had added. 'How do you feel about it? Don't you mind?'

'Of course I don't mind,' Paul had said, drawing her into his arms and kissing her tenderly. 'It was my idea, remember? It's only for a week, and then you'll be back with me. I shall miss you, you know I will. I love you, but I trust you as well, my darling Josie. Anyway, I'd like you to be there to look after Karen.'

'She's a big girl now, Paul,' Josie reminded him. 'And Len'll be there to take care of her. She doesn't really need me.'

'You'll be company for her on the journey,' said Paul. 'And in the chalet at the holiday camp. It's better that there should be two of you. And you need a holiday, darling. You haven't had a proper one for ages, only a week now and again at your aunt Alice's. You go and enjoy yourself, and don't forget to bring me back a stick of Welsh rock.'

So Josie had given in to the persuasion of the others. She suspected that Paul wanted her there as a chaperone to his daughter and Len, although he had never admitted it. She might also have added that a holiday camp was not her scene, the ceaseless round of fun and games organized by the jolly Redcoats, which she had heard was the fare at these places. She wasn't sure she could stomach that. But, as Paul had said, it was only a week, and she was certainly ready for a holiday.

She had been engaged to Paul for over a year now, and she knew that many of her friends and relations wondered why they were not already married. There was nothing to stop them. Josie was twenty-two, plenty old enough to be sure of what she was doing, and it was now four years since Paul's wife had died. Like Len and Karen, they too were saving hard, putting as much as they were able into a building society account so that they could start married life in a different, newer house – one which didn't hold memories of the first Mrs Hepworth.

Josie was now a partner in the photographic business and all their efforts were channelled into the enterprise. To the exclusion of everything else, Josie sometimes thought, for it was only rarely that the two of them went out, except on business engagements. An occasional visit to the cinema or theatre was all they indulged in; for the rest of the time they were content to stay in and play records or listen to the radio, when they were not busy working in the darkroom or completing orders for their customers.

'You're like an old married couple already,' Iris had told Josie recently. 'I can't help thinking that you should be out and about enjoying yourself while you're still young. Middle age creeps up on you soon enough, Josie, believe me.' Iris didn't add, as she might have done, that for Paul, now turned forty, it could be said to be already here, although he was quite a youthful-looking man.

Iris had said very little about the relationship since the couple got engaged, when she had remarked, though by no means critically, that the age difference was quite a large one; almost twenty years. Iris, indeed, had no room to be critical: her own first husband had been twenty-five years her senior, and her second, ten years her junior. 'Yes, I must admit that the age factor isn't important,' she had added thoughtfully, although Josie wasn't altogether sure of the truth of her remark. 'If you're happy with each other, then that's the main thing. Paul's a fine man. I like him very much, Josie, and I can see he makes you happy.'

Josie had assured her stepmother then, as she did now, that she was very happy with Paul. She was content and relaxed in his company, they were business partners and very good friends. As for being like a married couple, Josie didn't tell Iris – she would have found it impossible to do so – that they weren't, exactly, not in every respect. Paul had never made love to Josie, not in the real sense of the expression, although he frequently kissed her and, at times, left her longing for more . . . much more. But Paul, as well as being cautious, was an honourable man, and Josie knew that their union would not be consummated until their wedding night. She hadn't considered that there might, possibly, be something lacking in their relationship. Excitement, perhaps, passion, high emotion . . .

By the summer of 1951, Butlin's holiday camps had become very popular. Billy Butlin's idea was to take all the organizational worries out of a holiday and fill the holiday-maker's week with a ceaseless round of fun and frolic. For those that wanted it, that is. You could, if you so wished, decline to take part, but you would hardly choose to go to a holiday camp unless you liked a bit of fun. Josie hoped that there would be a happy medium.

In return for a single payment the camper received accommodation, three meals a day and all the entertainment without any additional charges. There was nothing left for the campers to spend their money on but drinks, snacks and cigarettes. Even, so, the prices were not cheap, and were often well out of the range of the lower wage-earners. But they attracted a broad cross-section of the public. The habit of mixing with all types, not just your own social class, had come about during the war years, and still hadn't worn off.

Josie's first impression as she walked through the grounds soon after their arrival, was that it was like a Blackpool in miniature – the funfair, the swimming pools, the numerous cinemas, theatres and bars – and that couldn't be bad. The chalet she was to share with Karen, a creosoted wooden hut, was functional though somewhat spartan, with an inadequate little rug on the wooden floor and cold water in the taps. But the sun, shining from a cloudless blue sky, made all the difference, though it couldn't be guaranteed to shine all week, and the thousands of rose-bushes, now in full bloom, which had been planted in profusion throughout the camp made the otherwise bleak surroundings look truly beautiful.

'Hi there, young lady. Enjoying yourself?' called out a cheerful young Redcoat passing near to Josie. She smiled and assured him that she was. She hoped that she was . . . She had left Karen to spend a little time on her own with Len and Linda and she would meet them later for their first evening meal.

They had handed in their ration books on arrival and they found that the first meal was surprisingly good. Tomato soup, followed by braised steak and onions – Josie had feared, for one awful moment, that it might be the dreaded whalemeat, but it turned out to be beef, not the best quality, but undeniably beef – with tinned peaches and ice-cream as a sweet. A real boon to the campers was the babysitting patrol provided by the staff, and when Linda had been settled down for the night in her daddy's chalet, the three of them met in one of the many bars for a celebratory drink.

'Cheers, and here's to a wonderful holiday,' said Len, raising his glass to the two girls. 'I must say we've got off to a good start. A smashing meal, and brilliant sunshine, and Linda's gone to sleep without any trouble.' He glanced about at his surroundings. 'And this seems a jolly sort of place. I must say they try to get you into the party spirit.' The walls were festooned with garlands of flowers, coconuts and imitation pineapples and bananas to give a South Sea Island atmosphere. 'Good heavens!' he exclaimed suddenly, staring towards the bar. 'I don't believe it. I just don't believe it . . .'

'What's up, Len?' asked Karen.

'You go on holiday to get away from folks, and then you find they've come to the same flippin' place.' But Len was laughing, Josie noticed, so whoever he had seen, it couldn't have been such an unpleasant shock. 'See that lad over there – the dark-haired lad? It's Derek. He works at the same place as me. Talk about a small world.'

Josie looked, then she gave a start of surprise and looked again. It couldn't be . . . 'Derek – what's his other name?' she asked.

'Derek Watson. And that must be his wife. Vera, she's called, but I've never met her. Yes, he's sitting down with her, that red-haired lass.'

'That's Vera Brown,' said Josie in disbelief. 'Well, of all the things! Derek Watson and Vera Brown. I can't believe it.'

'Why? D'you know them?' Len was staring at her in surprise.

'I'll say I do. I was at school with them. Beechwood Juniors. Come on, Len . . .' Josie rose to her feet, picking up her glass of shandy. 'We'll have to go over and say hello.'

Chapter 22

Her two old school friends, Derek and Vera, were just as amazed as Josie at the coincidence of their meeting. It transpired that Derek worked with Len, but he hadn't been with the firm very long and the two young men didn't know each other well. Derek had known Len was a widower and that he had a little daughter, but he had had no idea that the girl to whom Len had been married was none other than Pamela Coates, the evacuee from Manchester. He and Vera had both known, however, though not in great detail, about Pamela's return to Haliford and her subsequent tragic death. And when they found out that Len and Josie were cousins, their incredulity knew no bounds.

'Well, I'll go to the foot of our stairs!' exclaimed Derek, adding, as Len had done, 'It's a small world, it is that!'

'And what about you two?' asked Josie, when all the introductions had been made, the exclamations of surprise had died down and they were all sitting round the table with their drinks. 'I'd no idea. How long have you been married? I didn't even know you were . . . well . . . all that friendly.'

'Oh, we were friendly all right,' Derek grinned, and Josie caught a glimpse of the cheeky, good-natured lad that he had been when he was ten years old. It seemed he hadn't changed very much. 'You could say that we were more than friendly, weren't we, Vee?' He turned to his wife, giving her a saucy wink, then back to Josie.

'Yes, we got friendly when we both went to the secondary modern. You went to the grammar school, if I remember rightly, you and Hilda Ormerod.' Josie nodded. 'Anyroad, you remember Vera, don't you?' He leaned closer to Josie, whispering behind his hand, but making sure the others could hear him as well. 'You remember the trouble she had with her knickers, how they were always falling down?'

'Derek, honestly!' Vera gave him a hefty push.

He pushed her back, still grinning. 'Well, you might say that they fell down once too often!'

Josie burst out laughing. She couldn't help it. Derek Watson was as outrageous and irrepressible as ever. She glanced at Vera to see what her reaction was to this revelation. The young woman had turned a bright pink, but she was smiling and shaking her head, obviously well used to Derek and his banter.

'Aye, her father came after me with a shotgun, I can tell you,' Derek continued. 'I thought of fleeing the country, but I was doing me national service, y'see, up at Catterick, and I thought they might shoot me for deserting if they caught me.'

'Derek, honestly!' said his wife again. 'You don't half tell some whoppers. He hasn't changed much, has he, Josie? Take no notice of him. It wasn't like that at all. Me mam and dad think the world of him, though God knows why! But we did have to get married in a bit of a hurry, you might say.'

'You've a child then?' Josie smiled at Vera, sensing the girl was not a mite embarrassed by all these intimate disclosures and that she, Josie, didn't need to be either.

Vera had always been outspoken, just as Karen was. Karen's candid manner of speaking, however, stemmed more from naïvety, whereas Vera was a true Yorkshire lass who wasn't afraid to call a spade a spade.

'Two kids, not just one,' Vera replied proudly, 'and another 'un on the way, though nobody can tell yet.' She patted almost reverently at her stomach where there was not the slightest bulge to be seen. Vera was as thin as a yard of pump water, to use one of Iris's expressions, but she was quite attractive in an angular sort of way. She was sharp-featured, her nose a shade too long and her mouth too wide, and her hair was still the brightest shade of ginger that one could imagine, though it had now been brought under control by a permanent wave and no longer stuck out so alarmingly. She had an engaging smile and her pale green eyes, which Josie had once likened to boiled sweets, lit up with humour and affection as she countered her husband's sallies. Josie felt herself warming again to the girl, who had once been a bitter enemy and then, later, a friend.

'Aye, our Julie's four now and our Jackie'll be two next month,' Vera told her. 'They're both fast asleep in t'chalet, thank goodness. They were that excited about coming here, we thought we'd never get 'em off, didn't we, Derek? But they were out like lights, the pair of 'em.'

'Good gracious,' remarked Josie. 'Two children already. I can't get over it. You're leaving me far behind, aren't you?'

'Don't you believe it,' said Vera. 'I'll bet you've done well for yourself, haven't you, Josie? Even though you're not wed yet. I'll bet you've got a right good job, haven't you? What are you? A teacher or summat? You were always a real brain-box, you and Hilda Ormerod.'

'No, I'm not a teacher,' said Josie. 'I'm a photographer.' She felt, suddenly, though she wasn't sure why, that she didn't want to talk about herself. 'Tell me about Hilda,' she said. The girl's name had been mentioned twice already. 'We were such good friends, Hilda and I, but I'm afraid we've lost touch, you know how it is. It's the same with you and me, Vera, but we must try to keep in touch now, mustn't we? Anyway, what's Hilda doing? She'll be teaching, I daresay?'

'Yes, she's been teaching for two years,' Vera nodded, 'although I must admit I don't see all that much of her now. She's at Millbank, that new school on the outskirts of Haliford, teaching Infants, I believe.'

'Len, d'you hear that?' Josie turned eagerly to her cousin. 'Millbank – that's the school Linda's going to in September. Just fancy that! Wouldn't it be strange if Hilda turned out to be our Linda's first teacher?'

And while they all exclaimed over yet another coincidence, Josie reflected that there was one person who hadn't so far been mentioned. She wondered how she could casually drop his name into the conversation. When, a few moments later, there was a slight pause in the flow of chatter, she decided that there need be no prevaricating. There was no harm in asking after an old school chum; she wondered why she was being so guarded about it.

'How's Jimmy going on?' she asked, as nonchalantly as she was able. 'Jimmy Clegg. I haven't heard anything of him for ages. I don't suppose you still see him, do you?'

'Old Jim? 'Course I see him,' said Derek, grinning widely. 'And I'll tell you summat else.' He took a swig of his beer, wiped his hand across his mouth, then leaned forward across the table. 'You'll be seeing him an' all in a few minutes.'

'What? Jimmy Clegg – he's here?' Josie felt as though she could have been knocked down with the proverbial feather. She was trying to speak normally, but she feared her voice sounded odd and there was a fluttery, fidgety feeling – half excitement, half panic – taking hold of her. Don't be such a silly fool, she admonished herself, clenching her hands tightly together beneath the table. 'What on earth is he doing here?' she asked, giving an airy laugh.

'What d'you think he's doing? He's on holiday, same as the rest of us,' replied Vera.

'With . . . his wife? And family?' asked Josie, hardly daring to utter the questions.

'Good grief, no!' exclaimed Derek. 'He's not married, not our Jim. He's got more sense.' He gave his wife a friendly nudge. 'Hasn't he, Vee? No, he's as free as a bird – at the moment, that is, though I daresay there'll be a few broken hearts before the week's out. He's like a bloody butterfly, is Jim, flitting from flower to flower. Anyroad, when he knew we were coming to Butlin's he asked if he could come along with us. I don't imagine we'll see much of him, though.'

'Why didn't you say earlier?' asked Josie, feeling all faint and funny.

'You never asked, did you?' retorted Derek. 'Anyroad, I couldn't get a word in with you women nattering. Hey up, he's here now. It always takes Jim ten times as long as everybody else to get ready for an evening out.'

'And he said he had to ring his mam,' Vera observed.

'Oh aye, he's a good lad to his mam, he is that,' agreed Derek. 'You remember Mrs Clegg, don't you, Josie? Jim's dad was killed in the war and she'd six kids to bring up.'

Josie nodded, her thoughts not on Mrs Clegg and her brood of children, but on just one of that number, the tall auburn-haired young man who was now making his way alongside the bar, his eyes scanning the various groups of people to locate the whereabouts of his friends. He was wearing a pair of well-fitting, neatly pressed khaki trousers and a blue checked, cowboy-style shirt. He was casually dressed, but, at the same time, immaculately groomed. Josie could see that his hair, once a bright ginger such as Vera's, had darkened considerably, or maybe it was the effect of the Brylcreem with which he had slicked it down, suppressing the unruly waves.

There was no sign now of the unkempt, sometimes scruffy schoolboy of Josie's remembrance. This young man was neat and tidy, strikingly attractive – almost handsome – and Josie felt her stomach beginning to turn somersaults in a most alarming way. Calm down, don't be such a fool, she told herself again. It's only Jimmy, your old school chum. Besides, time has moved on, you are different people now . . . and you are engaged to be married, she almost reminded herself, but hastily stifled the thought.

Derek had hardly changed at all, nor had Vera, but it was obvious that Jimmy Clegg was not as she remembered him. Would she have recognized him, Josie wondered? Possibly . . . the firm, squarish jawline and the resolute set of his mouth were still the same, and he had been unable to do anything about the liberal scattering of freckles across his nose and cheeks, unlike Vera, who had hidden hers with pancake make-up. His clear grey eyes were unchanged, too, eyes that had so often glinted with mischief and cheer.

Now Josie saw them light up with awareness as he spied his two friends and lifted his hand in acknowledgement, then his look changed to one of puzzlement, disbelief, then gradually dawning recognition as he stared at Josie.

His mouth opened wide in an amazed O, becoming a delighted smile as he hurried across the room.

'It can't be!' he said, his voice hushed and incredulous as he stood there, just looking at Josie. 'I don't believe it. What on earth . . . ?'

'Yes, it's me, Jimmy, it's Josie Goodwin,' smiled Josie. 'And it was just as much a surprise for me, I can tell you, when I found out you were here. And Derek and Vera . . .'

'This is amazing . . . it's wonderful!' Jimmy hooked his foot round a stool, pulling it towards the table, then sat down, plonking his pint of beer in front of him. The frothy ale spilled over the top and down the sides. 'Now look what you've made me do,' he laughed. 'I've spilt me flippin' beer . . . I can't get over seeing you again, Josie, after all this time. How long is it? Must be . . . let me see . . . seven or eight years?'

Josie nodded, feeling very, very happy. 'We moved to Blackpool in forty-three, so it's eight years, isn't it?'

'Far too long, I know that,' replied Jimmy quietly. They looked at each other in silence for several seconds, and as the years rolled back Josie recalled the affection she had held, even as a child, for this lad who was once such a scallywag. Affection that she knew could so easily be rekindled. It was useless to tell herself that this was a different time, that they were different people. She knew in that moment that her feelings for Jimmy were unchanged.

'Come on then, let's hear all your news,' he said, after what seemed like an eternity, but was really only a few moments. 'Who are these?' He cocked his head, smiling in a friendly manner at Len and Karen. 'Aren't you going to introduce me?'

So introductions were made once again and, inevitably, much of the same ground was covered.

'And what do you do, Josie, for a living, I mean?' asked Jimmy, leaning forward intently. 'No, let me guess – I bet you're a teacher, an art teacher.'

'Just what I said,' Vera interrupted. 'A teacher, anyroad. But she's not. Come on, Josie. We've not heard much about your job yet.'

'I'm a photographer,' said Josie simply. 'I work with Karen's father, Paul . . . Paul Hepworth. He has a shop in Blackpool. I'm his . . . assistant.' She was aware of Karen looking at her keenly, and Josie felt herself involuntarily glancing down at the bare fingers of her left hand. But she didn't say anything more about Paul. Neither, to her relief, did Karen.

'So you are making use of your art, aren't you?' Jimmy remarked. 'In a different way, though, taking photographs instead of drawing.' He turned to the rest of the group. 'She was brilliant. You should have seen the lightning sketches she did . . . Of course, you lot'll all know that,' he added. 'How daft of me. D'you know, Josie, my old gran still has the one you did of me, with my bright red hair and freckles. She wouldn't part with it for anything.'

'Good,' said Josie, feeling rather awkward. 'You don't look much like that now, do you, Jimmy?' She was recalling, to her embarrassment, the less than flattering sketch she had done of Vera and she wondered if she, too, remembered. She glanced across at her and Vera gave a knowing wink. Obviously it was remembered, but forgiven. 'Never mind about me,' said Josie dismissively. 'I'll tell you more about it some other time. What about you, Jimmy? What job do you do?'

'Well, that's something you'll never guess, not in a

thousand years,' said Derek, opening his eyes wide. 'Will she, Jim?'

'No, I suppose not,' Jimmy grinned. 'Go on – have a guess, Josie.'

She suspected that he didn't do manual work, like Derek and Len. He was so smart and well turned-out. Not that the other two young men weren't, but Jimmy had a certain bearing about him, not exactly of importance, but of . . . authority. Yes, that was it; an air of being in charge that she would never have dreamed he could have had when he was a scruffy lad, plaguing the life out of the other children, and the teachers, too, when he could get away with it.

'You're not a teacher, are you?'

'No, not on your life!'

'A . . . doctor? No, you couldn't be. It takes years to qualify. A chartered accountant? A solicitor – or training to be one?'

'A librarian?' suggested Karen. 'No – I know – a manager of a big store. No, you're not old enough . . . A trainee manager?'

'You'll have to tell 'em, Jim,' laughed Derek. 'You're miles off the mark. I knew you would be. Go on, tell 'em.'

'I'm a policeman,' said Jimmy, grinning.

'Go on with you, you're not!' said Karen. Already the girl seemed to be at ease with these new-found friends. 'You don't look a bit like a policeman.'

'And what are we supposed to look like, eh?' laughed Jimmy. 'I'd look well coming to a holiday camp in me helmet and shiny black boots, marching in and saying "'Ello, 'ello, 'ello!"'

Josie had felt momentary surprise on hearing Jimmy's

news, but it soon subsided. Why shouldn't he be a policeman, she thought? He had the height and the demeanour and even though he had been a rogue, he had always been honest. Jimmy hadn't been one of the guilty ones in Mr Cardew's shop, she found herself remembering.

'So I hope you've stopped pinching sweets from the corner shop, young Josie Goodwin!' said Jimmy severely, as if reading her mind. 'Or I'll be after you with my truncheon!'

Yes please! thought Josie, feeling a rush of excitement and delighted abandon flowing through her, such as she hadn't experienced for a long while – never, she found herself realizing, with Paul. She looked steadily back at him. 'Fancy that,' she said, grinning mischievously. 'I shall have to watch my ps and qs, won't I?'

'So will I,' chimed in Karen. 'Won't I, Josie? We've got a dark, dread secret, haven't we? I've got a wicked past as well!'

'What's all this?' Len was frowning.

'Oh, something I haven't even told you, darling.' Karen put an arm round him. 'When Josie first met me, d'you know what I was doing? I was – shoplifting!'

'Oh, come on, Karen, it wasn't as bad as that,' said Josie, realizing that too much cider, drunk too quickly, had gone to the girl's head. She would have to try and make sure that Karen stuck to lemonade from now on.

'Oh yes it was. I was awful. I pinched a lipstick!' Karen's cheeks were flushed, her eyes over-bright and her voice over-loud. Len was looking distinctly worried, and the others somewhat embarrassed. 'But Josie – good old Auntie Josie here – she made me give it back.'

Josie held her breath. Soon there would come the revelation, she was quite sure, that Josie would one day be Karen's stepmother. If the girl blurted it out then she would have to admit it, and that would be that. End of story. Josie knew that it was wrong to withhold this vital information. It would serve her right if Karen, already more than a little merry, told everybody. But, again, the girl didn't, and for the second time Josie breathed a sigh of relief. Len, she knew instinctively, wouldn't say anything. Even though he got on well with his future father-in-law, Josie had the impression that he wasn't too keen on the idea of her marrying Paul.

Len was frowning perplexedly, as well he might. 'First I've heard of it,' he mumbled.

'Oh, it was nothing, Len, honestly,' said Josie. 'Karen was in rather a state . . . about her mother, you know,' she added in a whisper, and Len nodded understandingly.

'Well, it's hardly a hanging matter,' said Jimmy, laughing and rising to his feet. 'I'll get another round in. Come on now, what are you having, folks? This one's on me, PC Clegg of the Haliford constabulary. I think you girls had better switch to the soft stuff, hadn't you? Before you start confessing to murders and God knows what!'

Normality was at once restored and Josie felt a surge of gratitude towards Jimmy. How he had matured. Jim, the others called him now, a more grown-up name, but Josie knew that to her he would always be Jimmy.

It was inevitable that they should stay together. There were three couples; Derek and Vera, Len and Karen . . . and Jimmy and Josie. And, during the day, the three children as well, Julie and Jackie Watson and little Linda Rawlinson. These three soon made friends, especially as Linda and Julie were almost the same age. Many happy hours were spent on the beach, paddling in the sea, watching Punch and Judy, eating ice-cream, and sampling the various rides – all free – in the children's amusement park.

Vera was persuaded to enter Jackie in the Bonny Baby competition, the one to two years' section, but, unfortunately, he didn't win. He was, indeed, a bonny little boy, with his mother's ginger hair and his father's round face, merry blue eyes and cheerful grin. He came third, beaten by two little girls, a blonde-haired beauty and a dark-haired, dark-eyed little charmer. Josie thought it was a shame, and wondered about the wisdom of such contests. All babies were beautiful, and understandably the best in their parents' eyes, but Vera seemed well pleased. She had developed into a very easygoing, adaptable young woman.

And any disappointment was forgotten when it was announced, to much cheering and whistling and rounds of applause, that Derek had won the Knobbly Knees competition. He had quickly become a favourite among the campers with his jesting and ready quips, his willingness to join in all the fun and games and his easy repartee with the jovial Redcoats. Derek was always one of the first on the ballroom floor of an evening, leading the prancing and the raucous singing of the campers' song:

> When you're at Butlin's,
> Jolly old Butlin's,
> It's the place to make you gay,
> Chase your worries all away . . .

Len and Jimmy were not nearly so exuberant although they, too, were enjoying themselves. You could hardly fail to do so in such congenial company. Neither of them could be persuaded, like Derek, to bare their knees for a crowd of screaming girls to gawp at. Jimmy would have done so willingly at one time, Josie mused, although Len had always been somewhat diffident. But Len and Jimmy redeemed themselves by coming second in the darts contest, so, all in all, the little group hadn't done too badly.

None of the three young women, however, could be talked into taking part in the Bathing Beauty competition at which a winner was chosen each week to go forward to the final of Miss Pwllheli, 1951.

'Not on your Nellie!' scoffed Vera. 'I'm not having all them fellows leering at me in me bathing cossie! Besides, I'm too thin. Like a beanpole, I am. They'll want somebody with a bigger bust and bum than what I've got, won't they, Josie? You're as thin as a rake an' all.'

Josie laughingly agreed. She hadn't been on the front row either when the vital parts had been given out, though she wouldn't have voiced it in quite the same way. Karen, though, might be said to have had what it took, with her neat rounded figure, baby-face smile and glossy, shoulder-length auburn hair. But she, too, had demurred. Karen had calmed down considerably after that first evening when she had been more than a little tipsy. It had been due, Josie saw, to the excitement of arriving at the camp, seeing her beloved Len again and meeting a host of new friends. She suspected, also, that Len had given his fiancée a good talking-to. Karen adored him and was, more often than not, a very compliant partner. This marriage would be a very different set-up from his first one, Josie often reflected.

'Go on, why don't you?' whispered Jimmy, putting an arm round Josie's shoulders as they strolled through the camp, a few steps behind the rest of the group. 'As far as I'm concerned you'd knock spots off all the girls here, you and those two smashing redheads.' He nodded towards Vera and Karen. 'But especially you,' he added, wrinkling his eyes in that funny bewitching smile she was getting to know again. It was odd that out of their little group of six, three of them had auburn hair, thought Josie; Karen and Vera . . . and Jimmy.

'No, not me,' she said, shaking her head. 'Beauty contests aren't my scene. You know that, don't you, Jimmy, if you're honest? Anyway, as Vera put it – in her well-chosen words! – I'm too thin.'

'You look all right to me,' said Jimmy, giving her a squeeze. 'More than all right. No, come to think of it, I wouldn't want all those other fellows ogling you . . . I can't get over finding you again, Josie. It's amazing, isn't it? You think so too, don't you?'

'Yes, Jimmy . . . You know I do,' replied Josie quietly.

Then the familiar panic seized her again. Here they were, more than halfway through the week already, and she still hadn't told him. She had tried to, but the words wouldn't come. She knew, though, deep down, that she hadn't tried all that hard; that she had no intention of telling him until the very last minute. Maybe, subconsciously, she was waiting for Karen, in her usual gregarious way, to spill the beans. She had waited that first evening, but the girl had kept mum and there was little likelihood that she would say anything now. Karen, for some reason, was being very close-mouthed. Why shouldn't I have this week of happiness? Josie tried to convince herself. It isn't as if I'm doing anything wrong. I've come here to enjoy myself after all. Paul would want me to enjoy myself . . . But he had also, she recalled, said that he trusted her. And all the while she was falling more and more in love with Jimmy Clegg, as she suspected he was with her, and she was unable to do a thing about it.

They had danced together that first evening, and Josie had discovered that this was something at which Jimmy was very proficient. Josie hadn't been dancing for ages – it wasn't much in Paul's line – and her terpsichorean abilities had never progressed much beyond a waltz and a quickstep. Now, as Jimmy led her expertly round the ballroom floor, she found herself, to her amazement, mastering the intricacies of a slow foxtrot.

'You're some dancer, I must say, Jimmy,' she remarked, smiling up at him. 'Where did you learn?'

'Oh . . . I've been around, you know,' he replied breezily. 'I'm a man of many talents. You don't know the half, Josie.' But he wasn't showing off, she could tell, only teasing.

'Yes, Derek says you've – er – spread your wings a bit,' Josie ventured, half fearfully. Soon would come the disclosure that he had a girl at home, and that would be that.

'Oh, take no notice of him,' replied Jimmy. 'Old Derek exaggerates wildly, always did, and he hasn't changed. Actually, I was engaged to be married last year, but it fizzled out. "A policeman's lot is not a happy one," as dear old G and S said. It's a damned hard one at times – night duties and awkward shifts an' all that, and she got fed up. So I'm fancy free, you might say, Josie.' He smiled down at her, his grey eyes glowing with warmth. 'And I'm so glad I've met you again.'

She waited then for the inevitable question, but it didn't come. Maybe he assumed that if she had a steady boyfriend she would have said so. But she didn't say so, and the moment passed.

'Beware, my foolish heart,' crooned the girl vocalist that first evening.

Yes, take care, you silly fool, Josie told herself. You're falling for him, and you can't have him. You belong to someone else. You've promised Paul Hepworth that you will marry him and he's waiting for you back home in Blackpool. But her foolish heart wouldn't listen to what her head was trying to tell her.

It was a week, come what may, that Josie knew she would remember for ever. Besides dancing, which they managed to fit in during some part of every evening, they watched the amateur talent contests, joined in singsongs in the bars and visited the cinema and the variety theatre. During the day they swam, played putting, crazy golf or tennis, or, when the weather was kind, just sat and sunbathed. On some afternoons Josie and Jimmy, Karen and Len, leaving Linda in the care of her new 'auntie and uncle', went on coach trips to the various beauty spots of the Lleyn peninsula; Abersoch, Criccieth, Portmadoc and the Italianate village of Portmeirion.

The landscape had a breathtaking beauty, the like of which Josie had not seen before, even in Yorkshire. There were rocky coves, wide bays and sandy beaches; dramatic cliffs falling sheer to the sea; whitewashed cottages sitting atop rounded hills and quaint fishing villages. Trees were scarce on the windswept peninsula, but the hillsides blazed with the gold of gorse and the purple of heather. Josie was entranced by it all and found that she was falling in love with the Principality of Wales, which she had never visited before. Or maybe, she admitted to herself, it was a person with whom she was falling in love, and not just the scenery.

Josie knew that, in the company of Jimmy, pleasures were heightened and she was more appreciative of the beauty around her. She had thought it was just in romantic ballads that the grass was greener, the sky bluer, the song of the birds sweeter, but she found now that it really was so.

She became aware, too, that qualities she hadn't realized were lacking in her relationship with Paul, such as excitement, laughter . . . and passion, were there in abundance in this new-found friendship. The passion, as yet, was dormant, but it was there all too clearly in Jimmy's loving glances, in the way he took her hand or held on to her arm, in the way he kissed her at the end of each joyful evening. His kiss, the first time, had been just a friendly one, chaste almost, but as the week progressed and their feelings for one another increased, so did the fervency of Jimmy's embraces. He hadn't yet said that he loved her, but she knew he did and that, before the week came to an end, he would tell her so.

And what would she say to him in return? She knew that she loved him – she felt, indeed, that this was the love she had been waiting for all her life – but she wasn't free to admit it. She had given her promise to marry someone else.

She dressed carefully on the last evening, deciding to wear the pink taffeta, ballerina-length dress which had been hanging in her wardrobe all week. She had wondered if it was rather dressy for Butlin's, but now she was glad she had brought it. She was sure everyone would make a special effort tonight, and she wanted to look her best. In the past Josie had rebelled against wearing pink, condemning it as an 'Iris' colour. Now she knew that the deep rosy hue enhanced her long dark hair, worn loose tonight, and the halter neckline showed off her recently acquired suntan.

Karen, in her apple-green dress with the big white collar, was too absorbed with her own grooming – brushing her glossy auburn hair and applying her orange-pink lipstick –

to pay much attention to her friend. Josie did so wonder what the girl was thinking. It was unlike Karen to be so silent, but Josie had to admit that she was glad of her reticence.

The band was playing once again the tune that had become 'their' song:

'Beware my foolish heart,' sang the vocalist, as she had sung so many times that week.

And Jimmy, at last, whispered the words that Josie had been longing, yet dreading, to hear. 'I love you, Josie. You know that, don't you?'

'Yes, I know, Jimmy,' she answered quietly.

He held her close, his cheek nestling against her temple, his hand stroking her hair and her bare shoulder before settling firmly again in the small of her back. The revolving crystal ball, suspended from the ceiling, shot out tiny shafts of light, like silver butterflies, alighting on the dancing figures. It was a moment that was made for love and romance and Josie, in all her life, had never felt so happy . . . or so sad and bewildered. She knew, as the song said, that it was love, but she also knew that this dream was one which must, inevitably, fade and fall apart. How could it be otherwise?

They spoke very little as they returned to their seats with the rest of the group. Then, when the band struck up with the camp song, and Derek and Vera, Len and Karen eagerly dashed on to the floor, they were left on their own.

'You don't want to join in, do you, love?' asked Jimmy quietly, and Josie shook her head.

'Let's go outside,' he said, picking up Josie's white woollen stole and placing it gently round her shoulders. 'I don't think you'll be cold, but you'd better have this.'

As they made their way round the edge of the dance floor and out through the door, the sounds of revelry followed them.

The holiday that's well worth waiting for, ta-ra-ra!
B-U-T-L-I-N-S,
And we hope that you'll be back again for more, ta-ra-ra!
Butlin's for evermore!

The noise of singing and the stamping of feet died away as they strolled through the grounds, their arms round one another and their heads close together. In a secluded thicket behind the farthest group of chalets Jimmy drew Josie into his arms. Then his mouth was upon hers, his hands were caressing her hair, her shoulders, her breasts and slender hips. Josie was conscious of an overwhelming desire to belong to Jimmy, now . . . and for always.

It was Jimmy, though, who called a halt to their love-making. 'No . . .' he said, suddenly drawing away from her. 'I won't . . . I can't. I love you far too much, Josie, to spoil everything. You know I love you, don't you?' he asked, for the second time. And again Josie nodded.

'And you . . . ?' He looked at her perplexedly. 'You love me too, don't you? I know you do. Then why . . . why can't you tell me?'

'Yes, I love you, Jimmy,' Josie replied simply, knowing that these were words she shouldn't be saying.

'Then why are you looking so sad? You'll marry me, won't you, Josie? I think I've always known it – you and me – ever since I was a little lad. And then I went and lost you. But now I've found you again. Josie, what's the matter?' Jimmy took hold of her shoulders as she hung her head, gazing unseeingly at the ground. He put a finger beneath her chin, lifting her face up, forcing her to look at him. 'Josie, darling, what is it? You must tell me.'

'We can't, Jimmy. I can't marry you.' Josie gave a long shuddering sigh, then she took hold of his hands, looking down at the firm, square-tipped fingers and the sunburnt wrists below the sparkling whiteness of his shirt. 'I should have told you, I know. But . . . I couldn't. I'm – I'm engaged, Jimmy. I'm engaged to be married . . . to Paul. To Karen's father.'

She had had no idea what his reaction would be. Now his response startled her. 'Don't be silly, Josie,' he said softly. 'You love me. I know you do. Don't try to pretend—'

'I'm not pretending anything, Jimmy,' Josie cried. 'Yes, of course I love you. But I shouldn't – I mustn't. I'm engaged to Paul, I tell you. You must believe me. I've promised.'

'Yes, I believe you, Josie,' said Jimmy, so very calmly. 'But don't imagine for one moment that I'll let you go. We'll have to do something about it, won't we? Well? Won't we?' He cupped his hands round her face, his grey eyes gazing intently into hers. 'It's not the end of the world, darling. It won't be the first broken engagement. And this man, Paul – he'll understand. He'll have to understand.' He took hold of her hand. 'You're not wearing an engagement ring.'

'I lost a stone . . . It's at home,' Josie muttered, not knowing what to say or think.

'That's fortuitous,' Jimmy grinned. 'Not that I'd have been warned off, I can tell you.'

'But – aren't you angry with me? I thought you'd be furious. I hardly dared tell you.'

'No, Josie, not angry. A bit puzzled, perhaps. But I thought there was something. You mentioned him – Paul

– that first night, and there was something in the way you said his name that made me wonder. Aye, aye, I thought, she's hiding something. I knew you'd tell me in your own good time. That was why I told you I'd been engaged; I thought you might say something then. But I'd made up my mind right at the start that I was going to marry you. And marry you I will.' He pulled her into his arms again, kissing her fiercely, and Josie was powerless to resist, she loved him so much.

It would be easier when she had returned home, when Jimmy was no longer with her. So she tried to convince herself in the quiet darkness of the chalet, as she lay awake listening to Karen's rhythmic breathing.from the opposite bed. Lucky Karen; her love-life was so uncomplicated. Josie decided that she would say as little as possible to Jimmy. He was so insistent, anyway, that she must break off her engagement, that he wouldn't listen. She would write to him once she had returned to Blackpool; for how could she possibly let down such a good and honourable man as Paul, who had already known a great deal of unhappiness? She couldn't. It would be too, too heartless.

'Josie – Josie, listen to me. You mustn't do it.' Karen leaned across the tea-stained table in the refreshment room of Crewe station and took hold of her friend's hand. The train from Pwllheli had been crowded, and so had the one to which they had changed at Shrewsbury, and only now, as they waited for the third and final train of their journey, had there been a chance to talk. Josie had been relieved; it had given her time to work out what she was going to say in reply to Karen's unavoidable comments.

The girl's green eyes were anxious now, her forehead creased in a frown. Josie looked back at her seriously, unable to force her lips into even the smallest semblance of a smile. 'Don't worry, Karen, I won't,' she replied steadily. 'I've already decided – I won't let your father down.'

'No, no, no! That's not what I meant.' Karen dropped Josie's hand in an impatient gesture. 'I mean you mustn't marry Dad. It wouldn't be fair. It wouldn't be right, feeling the way you do about Jimmy. You love him – I know you do – and he loves you.'

Josie was silent for several seconds. Then, 'Yes . . . we do,' she replied quietly. 'I admit that we love each other. But I promised Paul, ages ago. He'd be so hurt, Karen. He's a fine man. I couldn't do that to him . . . and he mustn't know, either. You mustn't tell him,' she added, knowing what a little busybody Karen was at times.

'I won't say anything,' Karen sighed. 'It's not my place, is it? But I think *you* should. Besides, you and my dad, I don't think you're right together.'

Josie stared at her in surprise. 'But – I thought you were pleased about it. You seemed to be.'

'Oh, I was at first. I thought it was great. But you should have been married by now. Why aren't you? I think it's because neither of you is really sure. You work together, and Dad depends on you – in the business, I mean – and I know you're fond of one another. But is it enough, Josie? Besides . . .' An impish grin spread over Karen's face. 'You can't cook!'

'Oh, Karen, honestly!' Josie laughed, in spite of her misery. 'As if that mattered. I can when I have to, and I'm improving. Even your dad says I am. Anyway, even if I were to marry . . . Jimmy, I still wouldn't be the world's greatest cook, would I?' But Josie knew that it wouldn't matter in the slightest, if she were married to Jimmy.

Karen's next words echoed Josie's thoughts. 'I don't

think Jimmy would think it was all that important, would he? But Dad would. He likes his creature comforts. He likes being pampered, and Mum was a marvellous cook,' she added wistfully.

'He's never complained,' replied Josie a trifle irritably. Really, Karen was a menace at times.

'No, of course he hasn't, because I do most of it,' Karen reminded her. 'Or he goes round to Brenda's café. He hasn't complained yet . . . but he might do. If you got married and he was having to eat egg and chips every day.'

'Oh, mind your own business, Karen,' Josie retorted. Then, seeing her friend's look of hurt and bewilderment, she added, 'Sorry, I didn't mean to snap. Everything's got so complicated . . . but I'll have to deal with it in my own way.'

Mum looks tired, thought Josie, the minute she set eyes on Iris. She looked as though she'd been crying, too, which was very unusual. There wasn't time to pursue the matter, however, as Iris and her helpers were busy making the salad for the visitors' tea when Josie arrived home; and very soon Josie, too, had her apron on, lending a hand. Frances was nowhere to be seen.

It wasn't until they had washed up and retired to their private living room that Josie was able to ask what was on her mother's mind. Her engrossment in her own affairs had diminished slightly in her concern over her mother. She had noticed how Iris collapsed wearily into the easy chair as though she couldn't stand up another minute. Her dark eyes were ringed with shadows and she looked not just tired now, but really ill.

'Mum . . . whatever's the matter?' asked Josie. 'Come on, you must tell me. I know there's something wrong.'

'It's our Frances,' Iris replied, looking imploringly at Josie. 'I don't know what to do, Josie love. I'm at my wits' end. She's changed so much. She's gone all religious. She says she's become a Christian.'

Chapter 23

'But our Frances has always been a Christian, Mum,' replied Josie, feeling very puzzled. 'What are you talking about? Ever since she was a little girl she's gone to church and Sunday school – we all have – and just lately she's been in the church choir. So what's different? What do you mean?'

'Don't ask me to explain, Josie.' Iris was shaking her head in dismay. 'It's beyond me. It's this religious lot she's got in with at school, those Friends of Jesus, or whatever they call themselves. You knew about that, didn't you?'

'Friends of the Carpenter,' said Josie. 'Yes, but I only knew a bit about it. You know how secretive Frances can be. But she did mention that they'd been pestering her.' Josie smiled. 'They seemed to think her act at the Tower was a trifle suggestive.'

'Yes, so they did,' replied Iris grimly. 'Well, they've brainwashed her all right. She's given it up.'

'What! Her part in the ballet?' cried Josie. 'She's not in it any more?'

'No, not the Carmen Miranda part, anyroad,' said Iris. 'She told Annette she couldn't do it any longer. I gather Annette was rather annoyed to say the least, but the understudy'll be pleased, I daresay. So Frances is just in the chorus now, and I think she'd like to pull out of that as well, if she could.'

'But – what's happened, Mum, to make her behave like this? She loves the ballet. I used to think she'd like to go on the stage. Properly, I mean, to make a career of it, when she was old enough. Except that you wouldn't have approved—'

'And d'you think that would've stopped her?' said Iris. 'D'you really think she'd have taken any notice of me? But believe me, Josie, I wish that *was* what she wanted to do, to go on the stage. That, at least, I would be able to understand. But this . . .'

'So what's happened?' asked Josie again.

'She went to a beach mission,' said Iris in a toneless voice, staring vacantly into space. 'With these Carpenter people. It was the Sunday after you went away. And when she came home – nearly midnight it was, later than she's ever been; I was worried sick about her – she said she'd been "saved". She'd "seen the light"; she'd "become a Christian". You never heard such stuff as she was talking.'

'But she was a Christian before,' Josie persisted. 'She's been christened and confirmed, like I have and our Bertie. You always insisted we went to Sunday school, Mum, and I've been glad of it, too. It gives you something to hang on to, especially when things start going wrong. I remember when Pamela made me pinch those sweets. I knew it was wrong, and I remember telling her that Jesus would think so too.' Josie smiled reminiscently. 'I must have sounded a real little prig. But what I mean is, going to church and Sunday school gave us a sense of moral values, what was right and wrong.'

'Huh!' Iris gave a bitter laugh. 'That's not enough now,

according to our Frances. It's not enough to go to church every Sunday, it's not enough, even, to try and lead a good life – and God knows, Josie, I've always tried to do that.' Iris's voice was breaking with emotion. 'I know I've sometimes failed. We all do, God forgive us, but I've always thought He understood. That's what being a Christian is all about, surely, trying to do your best. I've brought her up to be a good girl, to do what was right and proper, and then for her to turn on me like this; to tell me that I need to – to confess my sins and come to Jesus. I just can't bear it.'

'Surely not, Mum.' Josie was horrified. 'She didn't say that?'

'As good as. I was cross with her, as I might well be, coming in late like that and getting me all worried, and I reminded her that I'm her mother and that she's only fifteen and she has to do as I tell her. And do you know what she said?'

'No, Mum, I can't imagine.'

'She said, "Who is my mother?"'

'What!'

'Yes, she just stood there, smiling serenely and . . . and that's what she said.' Tears welled up in Iris's grey eyes and she hastily brushed them away. 'After all I've done for that little girl. Brought her up as if she were my own, right from a tiny baby. I've spoiled her, Josie, I know it now. I've made more of her than I did of you and our Bertie, and I'm – I'm so sorry, love.'

'Never mind that now, Mum,' said Josie. 'It doesn't matter. The youngest one always gets spoiled. What did she mean, saying that dreadful thing to you?' Josie felt that if she could get her hands on her little sister right now she'd throttle her, and that wouldn't be a very Christian thing to do! A thought suddenly struck her. 'Mum – you don't think it's because you're not – I mean, perhaps it's my fault. You see, I told her once, when I was mad with you about something, I told Frances that you weren't her real mother. And I felt terrible about it afterwards—'

'No, no, it's nothing to do with that,' said Iris gently, trying to smile at Josie. 'I knew all about that anyway. I knew a lot more than you gave me credit for. No, it's something that Jesus is supposed to have said. I turned on her, you see. I felt like giving her a damned good hiding, which I didn't do, of course – but I did ask her what the heck she was talking about. And she said it was something Jesus said to his disciples. I looked it up in the Bible later. She's always quoting the bloomin' Bible at me now, I can tell you.'

'And did he say it?' asked Josie, more bemused than ever.

'Oh aye, he said it all right. They said to Jesus that his mother and his brothers were looking for him – I never knew he had any brothers, did you? – and Jesus said, "Who is my mother? Who are my brothers?" Then he went on to say that whoever did the will of God was his mother or his brother. And, according to our Saint Frances, I'm not, I suppose. I'm not doing God's will.'

'I'll give her God's will when I get hold of her,' Josie seethed. 'The little madam, upsetting you like this.' She got up and went to sit on the arm of her mother's chair, putting her hand fleetingly on the wiry iron-grey hair before getting hold of her mother's hand. 'I should try not to worry too much about it, though, Mum. You know what she's like. It might just be a phase. At one time it was all dancing – though I must admit that's gone on for ages – then it was the church choir. She might calm down. I remember when I was at school there were some girls who went all religious. Perhaps she'll get over it.'

'I wouldn't be too sure,' said Iris darkly. 'You should hear the things she's told me this week. You've only been away a week, Josie love, but it seems more like a year, believe me. She's not going to catering college, she says. She wants to go to Bible college, like this Janet and Megan she's got friendly with. She's at their houses till all hours, after she's done her dancing at the Tower; that's where she'll be now. Or she might train to be a nurse and go on the mission field. So I'd best forget my ideas about her taking over when I retire.'

'Well, I certainly wouldn't worry about that, Mum,' said Josie, patting her mother's hand, then going to sit in the opposite chair again. 'Her heart's never been in the hotel, has it? I doubt if she'd have wanted to do it anyway.'

'No, I suppose not,' said Iris pensively. 'Ironic, isn't it? I came to Blackpool to take a boarding-house – well, hotel – thinking I'd three children who'd be able to come into it, and none of 'em are interested. Bertie's going to train to be a teacher when he's finished his stint in the Army, Frances has got religious mania . . . and you've never been keen on the idea, have you, love? You're a photographer, anyroad – a real good one an' all – and you'll be getting married before long, I daresay.'

'Mmm . . .' replied Josie, who had temporarily shelved her own problems. There would be time enough for those later. 'But you don't need to carry on with the hotel if you don't want to. You're tired, Mum, aren't you? It isn't just this business with Frances that's getting you down, is it? You're really weary, I can tell you are.'

'Yes,' Iris sighed. 'I must confess I am. It gets harder every season, and since they lengthened it with those bloomin' illuminations it's been worse than ever. I know you have to make your money while you can – Eliza told me that when I first came into the business – but I'll be damned glad when the season finishes, Josie love, and I never thought I'd say that. I don't know how I'm going to summon up the strength to carry on till the end of the Lights, and that's a fact.'

Josie looked at her in concern. She had never heard Iris talk like this before. 'What about extra help, Mum? You can afford it. Somebody to help you with the cooking, perhaps?'

'I've already seen to that,' replied Iris, 'while you were away. I've a woman starting on Monday. She's a friend of Eliza's and she's recently lost her husband. Eliza reckons it'll be a godsend to her to have something to occupy her mind, and it will be for me, if she's any good. I've got to have some time to relax a bit more, Josie. At the moment it seems to be nowt but bed and work, and when I do get some time to myself I'm usually sitting here on my own.'

Josie felt remorseful. She was often round at Paul's of an evening, and she had just been away on a week's holiday, whereas Iris hadn't had a real break for ages. 'I'm sorry,' she started to say, but Iris interrupted her.

'Now don't you start feeling guilty. I didn't want that, and I shouldn't have said it either. It's just that I'm feeling a bit low. I know you've got to spend time with your fiancé. That's only right.' Josie looked down at the floor, not wanting to meet Iris's glance. 'I've had my chances as far as fellows are concerned, and I don't begrudge you any time you spend with your Paul.'

'Mmm . . . You're lonely a lot of the time, aren't you, Mum?' said Josie. She felt a surge of compassion for the woman whom she had once vowed she would never accept

– it was incredible to think of that now – who had been such a true friend and mother to her. 'After all you've done for the lot of us . . . and now, when you need us, none of us are here for you.'

'It's life, Josie,' said Iris resignedly. 'Your children grow up, they grow away from you, leave home sometimes. It's part of the whole scheme of things. How could it be any different? Our Bertie'll probably never live at home again, and you, you'll be getting married soon.' Again, Josie didn't meet Iris's questioning glance. 'But if there's something else there, something . . . deep in the relationship, then you never lose your children. And somehow I know that I'll never lose you, will I, Josie?'

'No, Mum, you never will,' replied Josie, feeling the truth of this with all her heart.

'But as for Frances, I've lost her, Josie. I know that she'll never be part of me again. I know she never was, not really. I didn't give birth to her, but I loved her so much, as if she were my very own child. But she's gone away. Even though she's still at home, she's moved away.'

'She's always been rather . . . selfish, Mum,' Josie pointed out quietly.

'Oh, I wouldn't go so far as to say that.'

'Thoughtless, then. Wanting her own way.' And you let her have it, Josie added to herself, but didn't say.

'Yes, but you can't say that giving your life to Jesus is thoughtless, surely?' said Iris pensively. 'And that's what she says she wants to do.'

'Time will tell,' replied Josie crisply. She was feeling heartily sick of these tales of her sister's conversion, or whatever it was. 'It's early days. Let's see how she goes on. Just start thinking about yourself a bit more, Mum. I think it's a great idea that you've gone and got some extra help.'

But Iris's thoughts were still with Frances. 'She's not the only one who thinks about God, you know. I've always tried to do my best for Him. It's only because I've been so busy here at the hotel that I haven't been going to church every week. Anyway, I've got myself on to the flower rota now at St Matthew's, doing the arrangements for the communion table. The vicar there calls it the altar, but I can't bring myself to do that – too high in my opinion. And Mrs Gilchrist has asked me if I'd like to be on the Parochial Church Council. They've got a vacancy.'

'Don't do too much, Mum.'

'No, I won't. But I've missed being involved in things, Josie, and now that Mrs Evans – that's Eliza's friend – is starting on Monday, I'll have more time. Now, that's quite enough about me and my problems.' Josie was pleased to see that her mother was perking up a bit. 'What about you, love? Did you enjoy your holiday? You'll have to tell me all about it. I expect Paul'll be glad to see you back again, won't he? When are you going to see him? If you want to go round there tonight don't let me stop you. I know I've been going on and on. I sound like that Mona Lot on ITMA, don't I? "It's being so cheerful as keeps me going."'

Josie was relieved to hear Iris laugh, but she couldn't join in. She just smiled abstractedly.

'Josie, what's up?' Iris looked at her keenly. 'Oh dear, I've been so wrapped up in my own affairs, I haven't taken any notice of you. I thought you were quiet – a bit strained, like – when you came in. What is it, love? There's nothing wrong, is there?'

'I don't know, Mum.' Josie leaned back against the cushions, closing her eyes. 'I honestly don't know what to think or to do. Or how to begin to tell you.'

'Begin at the beginning, then. That's always best.'

Iris said very little as Josie told her tale, just nodding now and again, sympathetically, and saying how she remembered Jimmy as a very nice lad whom she had always liked. Josie, indeed, hadn't intended to tell her so much, but she found that once she started she couldn't stop. She had wanted to confide in someone all week, and Karen certainly wouldn't have been the right person.

'You mustn't marry Paul out of a sense of duty,' Iris told her. 'That would be even worse than breaking off the engagement. I know he's a good man, a really worthy man in every way and I can't speak too highly of him, but—'

'But he doesn't deserve this,' Josie interrupted. 'How can I let him down? I can't, Mum. The last thing he said to me was that he trusted me.'

'I realize you're in a dilemma, love. It isn't easy, but when is life ever easy? You must think carefully, but I know you already have done—' Iris suddenly stopped speaking, her head to one side, listening intently. 'Here's our Frances. We won't say anything, of course, about what you've just told me.' She sounded wary, frightened, almost. 'Although I doubt if she'd be interested.'

Josie frowned, shaking her head. 'No, that's my problem, Mum.'

'And you won't start going on at her, will you, Josie? About what I told you. Please, for my sake, love. I don't want any more trouble.'

'No, Mum. Don't worry – I won't.'

Frances stood on the threshold of the living room smiling radiantly. 'Hello, Mum. Hello, Josie. It's good to see you back again. Had a good holiday?'

'Yes . . . very nice, thank you,' replied Josie guardedly. She was finding it difficult to come to terms with what her mother had told her, to know how to speak to her sister. 'Good weather, good food . . . it was great.'

'Mum's told you, hasn't she?' Frances was still smiling and Josie had to admit that the girl looked happy; sort of glowing. 'I can see she's told you about me becoming a Christian. It's so wonderful, Josie. I just want to tell everyone about what's happened to me.'

'Well, that makes a change, I must say,' replied Josie, although she knew she must try not to be too sarcastic. 'You were always such a terror for keeping secrets, weren't you? Sometimes we never knew what was going on in that head of yours.'

'Not any more, Josie. I feel so . . . so . . . liberated, so free,' Frances spread her arms wide. 'I just want to share the Good News with everyone. Let me tell you—'

'Some other time, if you don't mind, Frances,' said Josie mildly. 'It's been a long day and I'm tired. And I know Mum is. I tell you what, if you feel like showing us what a good Christian you are, you can go and make a cup of tea.'

The flicker of annoyance on Frances's face was only fleeting, then she beamed again. 'OK, will do.' She turned towards the kitchen door, then, looking back over her shoulder she added, 'I'll say a special prayer for you tonight, Josie. Like I've been doing for Mum.'

'Thank you, Frances,' replied Josie. 'Do you know, that's just what I need.' She wasn't being sarcastic.

Mum didn't understand. Neither did Josie. Frances could tell by the faintly amused expression on her sister's face, but her friends had warned her that this was the usual reaction of one's family. It was only to be expected. Hadn't Jesus said that he had come not to bring peace, but a sword?

To set a daughter against her mother; yes, he had actually said that. He had said that if you didn't love God more than your own mother and father then you weren't worthy of Him.

Frances had hated upsetting Mum. It had been dreadful to see the look of hurt on her mother's face and to know that she was responsible for it, but it had been unavoidable. It was all part of being a Christian. Her new friends had told her that she had to witness for Him and that, after all, was only what she had been doing.

Frances had felt, even before the beach mission, that something of importance was taking place in her life, that God was calling her to serve Him in a more meaningful way. In the solitude of her room at night she had prayed, asking God to help her understand what it was that Janet and Megan kept telling her, because sometimes, for the life of her, she couldn't make head nor tail of what they were on about. And then, that Sunday evening at the mission on the sands, it had all become crystal clear.

It had been a cool, blustery evening, threatening rain, not at all like August, when the Friends of the Carpenter had gathered on the beach just to the south of Central Pier. They were hoping that a good crowd would gather to listen to their guest speaker, a young man from Wigan, who, it was said, was skilled in the art of winning souls for Jesus.

In spite of the inclement weather they were not disappointed. Quite a few holiday-makers, out for an evening stroll to walk off the effects of a substantial high tea, stopped when they heard the music of the piano accordion and vigorous voices raised in the singing of choruses. For this group of Friends certainly sang lustily: what they lacked in musicality was made up for by enthusiasm. Some of the choruses were familiar from Sunday school days or from listening to the Sally Army in the town centre, and many of the onlookers found themselves joining in, restrainedly at first, then more animatedly as numbers grew.

A few, admittedly, had come to scoff, but they didn't do so noisily. There were no jeers or catcalls, just the shaking of heads and the tapping of fingers on temples – 'They've got a screw loose!' – as the 'unbelievers' walked away, muttering that that sort of carry-on was nowt in their line. Crowds at such gatherings, in the early fifties, were generally well behaved.

Frances, standing at the back away from the rest of the crowd, was still unsure. Janet and Megan, their heads raised – their hands raised, too, she noticed from time to time – were singing joyously. They had asked her to join them, but she had hung back. She was beginning to wonder, in fact, why she had come at all. She had missed the service at her own church, St Matthew's, to come here, and that had made her feel guilty. Although, according to her new friends, the worship at St Matthew's was too idolatrous, too *popish*, to be pleasing to the Lord. At times Frances felt utterly confused by it all.

Her bewilderment continued throughout the community singing, the fervent prayers – no set petitions and responses here, such as you got in the Church of England, but impassioned pleas from the heart – and the solo spot.

> 'All that thrills my soul is Jesus,
> He is more than life to me . . .'

sang a young girl with a sweet voice and an even sweeter smile.

But it wasn't until the preacher, the young man from

Wigan, began to speak that Frances felt her heart stirred to any degree. She couldn't have repeated afterwards exactly what he had said or even described what he looked like. She was vaguely aware of the fact that he was a thickset, dark-haired lad with a pronounced Lancashire accent, but such extraneous details were of no consequence. She only knew that he seemed to be speaking to her and to her alone . . . But she also knew that it wasn't him speaking at all; it was the voice of God speaking through him. When they sang the closing hymn,

> Out of my bondage, sorrow and night,
> Jesus I come, Jesus I come . . .

and the invitation was given to come forward, Frances was the first to respond.

> Out of my sin and into Thyself,
> Jesus, I come to Thee.

She walked to the front of the crowd, and at once Janet and Megan pounced on her.

Paul pushed aside his empty plate which had held beans on toast, all that he felt like preparing when he was on his own. Karen was working late, the twins were at a party, and Josie had dashed off home as soon as the shop closed as she had often done just lately. She had promised, however, that she would be back later that evening.

Paul wished he knew what was troubling Josie. She had been behaving strangely ever since she returned from the holiday camp. Karen, also, had been giving him the oddest looks, then turning away again quickly when he caught her eye. But all Josie would say was that she was concerned about her mother and her sister.

Quite rightly, too, from what she had told him. This religious thing certainly seemed to have got a hold of young Frances, but Paul had tried to assure Josie that it would pass. The girl was only fifteen – still a child – and not old enough yet to know her own mind.

And he could understand why she was worried about her mother. The last time Paul had seen Iris he had been alarmed at how tired the woman looked, so strained and tense and lacking much of her usual gusto. And, according to Josie, this business with Frances had knocked her back even further.

Paul knew that now was not the time to discuss with Josie the matter that was uppermost in his own mind. The girl was troubled enough already, preoccupied and nervy; how could he possibly tell her that he was having doubts about their relationship, that he was wondering, in fact, whether he ought to marry her at all? He loved her very much, although he did ponder, at times, as to whether his love for her was more that of a father for a daughter than that of a husband.

And he admired her greatly, both as a person and as a working partner. The work that she produced now, both in the studio and on outdoor assignments, was exceptional, and Paul had no doubt that very soon she would overtake even himself in her talent and expertise. And that had come about mainly through his guidance and tuition, although she had attended night school as well to improve her technique.

Wasn't that the main reason that he had asked her to marry him, he questioned himself? Because he had been her mentor, because they worked so well together . . . and because he had been flattered by the attention paid to him by so much younger a woman? Josie was such a vital person, and this was the quality that enabled her to breathe life into her work. But was such vitality as she possessed – he had to admit it left him speechless at times – necessary, or even desirable, in a marriage . . . in a marriage such as Paul wanted?

His first wife had been so very different. Kathleen had been placid and easygoing, a restful sort of person, whose chief aim in life, it seemed to Paul, had been to create a happy and comfortable home for her husband and children. Josie was definitely not of that ilk. She made him happy, though, of course she did, and he didn't want someone who was a carbon copy of Kathleen, when all was said and done. But he could never envisage Josie as a placid wife, one who would calm him down in moments of crisis or when life, as it did occasionally, seemed to be too much to cope with . . . in the way Kathleen had done.

Paul was trying hard to consider Josie's feelings as well as his own. He had asked her to marry him, he had bought her a ring and they were looking for a house. It would be churlish to tell her now that he had changed his mind. But would it not be even more dreadful to go ahead and marry her, and then find that Josie herself was having regrets, as she very well might, married to someone who was so much older?

Paul had spent quite a lot of time at Brenda's during the week that Josie was away. Only for meals in the café, however, sometimes with the twins as well, and she had popped in several times with sandwiches she had prepared for him. It wouldn't have been right for him to go up to her flat, not when he was engaged to someone else, and Brenda, understanding this, hadn't invited him.

Brenda: now she was a restful woman, just such a one as Kathleen had been. Paul wasn't in love with her though, as he was with Josie. But she was comfortable to be with; he felt relaxed and easy in her company and he knew that, if Josie hadn't come along when she did, then he and Brenda might easily have become more friendly.

This was all supposition, though, dwelling on what might have been instead of what was, and Paul certainly wouldn't want Josie to think that he was breaking off his engagement to her because he preferred Brenda. That was if he ever managed to pluck up the courage to talk things over with her. He didn't know what the dickens to do, and that was a fact . . .

'Dad, is there something the matter? Why are you scowling like that?' Paul looked up to see his elder daughter standing in the doorway looking at him curiously. He had been in a brown study, still sitting there with the remnants of his makeshift tea before him. He would have to get a move on or Josie would be back before he had even washed up.

'No, why should there be anything the matter?' he answered. 'And I didn't realize I was scowling. I had to get my own tea ready tonight,' he smiled ruefully, 'with everyone being out, so I suppose you could say that didn't go down too well. I was just sitting here enjoying a second cuppa.'

'But your tea's stone cold.' Karen gestured towards the obnoxious-looking brown liquid on top of which a scummy film had formed. 'You haven't even started to drink it.' She pulled up a chair and sat down. 'Come on, Dad. You can tell me. There is something wrong, isn't there? I've felt that you were being . . . odd, ever since I got back from Pwllheli.'

'No odder than you, young lady,' Paul retorted. 'You've been giving me very funny looks all week.'

'I don't think I have. I didn't mean to, anyway.'

'Well, you have, whether you meant to or not. And as for Josie . . .'

'What about Josie?' Karen was looking at him strangely again. 'Has she said something? Is that what the matter is?'

'No, what should she say? Only about her mother and her sister; family problems. What should she say?' he asked again, disturbed by Karen's eloquent silence.

'Nothing, Dad. Nothing I can tell you, anyway.'

'I wish I knew what the heck was up with the pair of you,' Paul exploded. 'There's something, I know that. And then you have the gall to ask what's the matter with me!' A sudden thought occurred to him. Maybe his uncertainty about their future had been apparent to Josie; perhaps she had already guessed what was in his mind. And if she had, then she may well have confided in Karen who was, he supposed, her best friend.

He sighed. 'No, you're quite right, Karen love. I'm sorry I shouted at you. There is something wrong, something troubling me, that is. You see, I'm not absolutely sure that I'll be doing the right thing if I marry Josie. I love the girl, but damn it all, Karen, she's not much older than you. And there are other reasons as well,' he added quietly. 'Has she guessed? Is that what's up with her?'

'No, Dad. I don't think she's guessed at all.' Karen was smiling at him now, almost grinning, as though it were a huge joke. 'But you'll have to tell her, won't you? It wouldn't be right for you to go on with it, feeling like that.'

'I'm damned if I know how I feel, except, like you say,

that it wouldn't be right. But how the heck am I going to tell her?'

'Just go ahead and tell her, Dad.' Karen was grinning broadly now. 'Josie'll understand. I know she will. Is she coming round tonight?'

'Yes, quite soon in fact.' Paul stood up hurriedly. 'I'd better get a move on and wash these pots, or else she'll be here before—'

'I'll do them, then I'll make myself scarce.' Karen pushed him out of the way. 'Go and read the paper. And – promise me you'll tell her?'

'All right. I suppose I've no choice.' Paul gave his daughter a shrewd glance, his eyes narrowing. 'You know something, don't you?'

'I'm saying no more, Dad. You'd better ask Josie, hadn't you, if you think there's something wrong.'

Paul nodded perceptively. Light was suddenly begining to dawn. The holiday camp, Josie's absent-mindedness, Karen's peculiar looks . . . why on earth hadn't he twigged before? Josie had gone and met somebody else.

Chapter 24

Iris stood back, looking pensively at the floral displays on the Communion table. The pink carnations and the long-stemmed white roses, surrounded by a cloud of gypsophila, looked well, she thought, in those lovely silver vases. There was a vase at each end of the table, complementing the silver cross in the centre and the brightly burnished silver salvers. Iris had no garden at the hotel, as some of the other parishioners had; only a paved area with a tiny flower-bed at the front – this was where the visitors sat, on a green-painted form – and a yard at the back. She could afford, however, to buy flowers for the adornment of the church instead of plucking them from a garden, and this she did willingly.

She could, in fact, afford most things she wanted now. The hotel business had proved to be a lucrative one and in the eight years she had been in Blackpool, Iris had managed to save up a good sum in the bank. If she wanted to she could even retire, and it was surprising how often that thought flashed into her mind these days, she who had once thought that she would carry on working till they carried her out feet first.

A team of women worked hard to keep the parish church of St Matthew looking beautiful, and Iris was pleased to have been asked, recently, to be one of their number. She hadn't even stopped to consider that she was too busy, which, if she were perfectly honest, was the truth. But a change was as good as a rest, as the saying went, and she hoped that her church involvement – working for the Lord as well as for herself – would help to make her feel less wearisome and ease, maybe, the worries that were on her mind.

This business with Frances had hurt her dreadfully, and she was still feeling the pain of rejection by a beloved daughter to whom she had given so much. No – maybe rejection was too strong a word. Excluded – that was how she felt, as though Frances no longer wanted or needed her in this new life, a way of life which was fast becoming an obsession. Frances was still working with her mother at the hotel, when she was not dancing or out with her new friends; it was the school holidays, and she had always done so, but her heart and her mind were elsewhere. Iris was finding that the two of them seldom conversed. It was as though the girl had thoughts and ideas which she knew her mother would not understand, and so she didn't even try to explain them.

Then there was Josie. Iris was concerned about Josie, knowing that she still hadn't told Paul she couldn't marry him. Iris was convinced that she shouldn't do so when she was obviously head over heels in love with that Jimmy Clegg. She hadn't said so, but Iris knew that she was. It was Josie's affair, though, when all was said and done, and she, Iris, wouldn't interfere.

Bertie, at least, should be happier soon, when he came out of the Army. Iris knew that he had never taken to the rough-and-tumble of national service life, and she hoped that the teacher training college where he would be going in the autumn would be more to his liking. Bertie was the one whom she had always felt she knew the least well of Samuel's three children. He was also the one who had given her the least trouble.

Iris sat down in the front pew, where the vicar's family usually sat on a Sunday, although there was, she had been glad to see, no pronounced hierarchy at St Matthew's. The vicar often told them that they were all God's children and all equal in His sight. Something Frances would do well to remember, Iris mused. Frances seemed to have the strange idea, since this conversion of hers, that some were more equal than others; that she and her cronies were special, somehow, in the eyes of God.

Iris closed her eyes for a moment. When she was tired these depressing thoughts weighed more heavily. She was not feeling too well either, although she had mentioned this to no one, not even Josie. She had been having a few odd pains in various parts of her body, vague aches which were difficult to explain away. There was one now, stabbing in her chest, although like as not it was just indigestion. Iris loved her food and even her worries never seemed to put her off eating. Idly she opened her handbag and popped a Milk of Magnesia tablet into her mouth as she looked up at the stained-glass windows behind the Communion table.

Her favourite was the one of Jesus at the well, talking with the woman of Samaria. It was not one of the best-known stories of Jesus, but as Iris gazed now at the stylized figure in the white robe and the conventional blue gown of the woman holding the pitcher, she felt that it had a special significance for her. For Jesus had known all about the woman, even though he had never met her before. Just as he knew all about her, Iris Goodwin, her thoughts and her fears and all the wrong things she had done. This knowledge had not come to her in a blinding flash, as it seemed to have done with Frances, but all the same, Iris knew that it was true.

She turned at the sound of footsteps coming down the aisle. It was the vicar himself, the Reverend Stephen Hunt, and Iris didn't know whether to be glad or sorry. It was time she was getting back home. Tomorrow, Saturday, would be a busy day, change-over day, and on a Friday evening she always checked all the bedding to make sure there were no sheets or pillowcases that needed mending. It would be impolite, though, to dash off without having a few words with him, and she had had the feeling of late that she would like to have a chat with him about the things that were troubling her.

'Hello, Mrs Goodwin,' he greeted her. 'I've just popped in to prepare the register for tomorrow. It's a busy day – we've two weddings. And those beautiful arrangements will be much admired, I'm sure.' He nodded towards the flowers on the altar. 'Your handiwork, I presume?'

'Yes, that's right, Mr Hunt,' Iris replied. 'I've arranged them. It's a job I haven't done for ages, not since I was at St Luke's in Haliford, but I'm enjoying it. I'm so glad Mrs Gilchrist asked me to join her team of helpers.'

'Good, good. We're very glad to have you. It's great that you can spare the time. I know how busy seaside landladies are, so it never ceases to amaze me how so many of them will give the time to do some work for the church as well.'

He sat down in the pew beside her. He was an unassuming man, fiftyish, Iris guessed, with unexceptional features and thinning hair, but in the pulpit, in his Sunday attire, he seemed to possess an authority of which you would not be aware if you were to meet him in the street in his ordinary weekday garments. There were many in the congregation, acknowledging this supremacy, who called him 'Father', but Iris could never bring herself to do that. It was too reminiscent of Rome for her liking. Neither could she call him Stephen in the familiar way that many of the younger folk did. She considered that that was lacking in respect for a man of the cloth. To Iris he was always the vicar, or Mr Hunt.

She looked at him now somewhat hesitantly. She had wanted to talk to him, but now that he was here it was so difficult to know how to begin. It was he who spoke first, and when he did it was incredible, because he mentioned the subject that was uppermost in her mind. It was just as though he had read her thoughts.

'You're worrying about your daughter, aren't you, Mrs Goodwin?' he said soothingly. 'About Frances.'

'Yes . . . yes, I am. But . . . how did you know?'

'Oh, let's just say it's . . . intuition. I know she hasn't been with us for the last couple of Sundays, and that she's come out of the choir.'

'Yes, she has, but it's not because she's not going to church, you know, Vicar. Just the opposite. She's got in with some . . . peculiar religious lot. They meet in one another's homes, and I think they've just got a wooden hut or something down South Shore way.'

'Yes, I've heard all about that, too.' He nodded understandingly. 'Someone told me that Frances had joined their ranks. I'm afraid that we at St Matthew's, and a lot of other churches like us, are considered to be far too high, far too – what shall I say? – ritualistic in our approach to the Almighty, according to our evangelical friends, that is. I daresay that's why Frances has left the church, isn't it? Because of all the ceremonial in our worship? I know the group she's with don't approve of it. Neither do a lot of our low-church brethren, I might add.'

'Yes . . .' breathed Iris, looking at him in amazement. It was astounding how much he knew without being told. 'That's it exactly. Not that she tells me all that much, and when she does I can't understand the half of it.' Frances had even gone so far as to say that the manner in which Reverend Hunt conducted his services was not pleasing to the Lord, that he was not really walking 'in the way', whatever that was supposed to mean. But Iris had no intention, of course, of telling him that. To her, this pleasant middle-aged vicar was serving God in the way he knew best, and if he liked dressing up on a Sunday and doing a bit of bowing and crossing himself, well, what did that matter?

Again the vicar seemed to take the words out of her mouth. 'You see, Mrs Goodwin, I've always believed in giving to God the very best that I can. I love beauty in worship. Lovely music, stained glass, beautiful things on the altar . . .' He gestured towards the silver objects and Iris's flowers. 'And the ornate vestments that I sometimes wear – but only on special occasions, mind you – and even the burning of incense, though I know some disapprove of that very strongly; to me they are all part of showing God that you love Him and want to serve Him. But one has to try to serve Him in practical ways as well, of course, and I hope I can be said to do that,' he added humbly.

As indeed he did, Iris thought. The Reverend Stephen Hunt was well known and admired in the parish for his care of the sick and the bereaved and his compassionate treatment of the tramps and ne'er-do-wells who, from time to time, turned up on his doorstep.

'What has happened to Frances has been so very sudden,'

Iris tried to explain now. 'Like – I don't know – a bolt from heaven, you might say.'

'Yes, a typical Road to Damascus experience,' Mr Hunt commented.

'You mean, like St Paul?' asked Iris. She wasn't all that conversant with the more obscure parts of the Bible, but she did know that story.

'Yes, that's right. Some people do say that they come to know God like that, in one sudden moment of revelation.'

'Yes, I can see that, I suppose,' said Iris thoughtfully. 'But now Frances seems to be saying that . . . that because I haven't had something like that happen to me, I don't know God properly. And I do, Mr Hunt, I do. But she's convinced that she's right, and I'm wrong.' She shook her head sadly.

'Then thousands more of us are wrong as well,' said the vicar, half-chuckling. 'I, for one, certainly cannot remember the time when I came to know God. He's always been there, ever since I was a child. Then, as I grew older, it was a gradual realization that I wanted to do more for Him. And so I think it is with most people; an awareness of God that develops slowly.'

Iris was already feeling heartened. 'So you think they're wrong, do you, these 'Friends' or whatever, that Frances has got in with?'

'No, certainly not wrong. They are sincere in their beliefs, just as I am and as I know you are, Mrs Goodwin. We're all God's children, as I often say in my sermons, and there's room for all of us in the Kingdom of Heaven.' He smiled. 'I think our "born-again" friends – that's what they like to call themselves sometimes – may get quite a shock when they get to heaven and find out that they are not the only ones there.'

'I've always tried to believe that I'll go there – eventually, I mean,' said Iris smiling. 'Not yet, I hope. It was Frances that got me all upset and started me thinking that I might not.'

'Yes, their chief fault is their intolerance,' said the vicar. 'I've known them to cause trouble in families, even to break up marriages, by their uncompromising attitude – the most extreme of them, that is. I sometimes think that their God is too small. They try to confine Him to a small space to fit in with their own rigid beliefs, but you can't do that with God. Personally, I believe in a more ecumenical view of religion.'

'Ecu . . . what? That's a big word,' laughed Iris. 'I don't think I've heard that before.'

'It means worldwide Christian unity, that's all,' The vicar smiled at her. 'All the denominations – Church of England, Roman Catholics, Methodists, Baptists – all realizing that they're heading for the same place and working together.'

Iris was getting rather lost now. 'I've always hoped that God loves us and that he forgives us, whatever we do,' she said. 'We sang a lovely hymn when I married Samuel – the children's father, you know, Vicar. I'm not really their mother, you see – "Dear Lord and Father of Mankind" . . .'

'. . . "Forgive our foolish ways,"' the vicar continued. 'Yes, a beautiful hymn, as you say.'

'I've done a lot of foolish things.' Iris was pensive. 'I've made too much of Frances; I've spoiled her . . . I know that was foolish. And, because of that, I've not taken as much notice of the other two as I should have done, sometimes.'

'We all make mistakes, Mrs Goodwin,' said Mr Hunt

gently. 'I didn't know you were their stepmother. They're a credit to you, all of them. And Frances will come back to you. I'm sure she will. She'll realize that she's hurt you and she'll learn to be more tolerant as time goes on. I know that children can bring you sadness, but they bring joy as well, don't they?'

'Yes, they do indeed,' Iris replied slowly. 'I've had so much heartache and trouble, with one of them in particular. But, do you know, she's brought me more joy that I could ever have imagined.'

'Yes, Frances is a lovely girl,' said the vicar.

Iris looked at him sharply. 'I didn't mean Frances. I was thinking about my elder daughter, my Josie.'

She went on to tell the vicar, briefly, about her fears that Josie might marry the wrong man, and again he listened sympathetically. It was amazing the things she had told him, thought Iris, as she made her way home. But she felt better for having relieved herself of the problems that were troubling her – better in her mind, at any rate but not in her body. The pain in her chest was quite severe now, and she couldn't wait to get home.

She subsided thankfully into the armchair and looked at the clock. Quarter past eight. Josie was round at Paul's and she wouldn't be back for a while, but Frances should be home soon, from the Tower. Iris was suddenly frightened at the thought of being here on her own for much longer. All at once a violent pain seized her and she fell forward, clasping at her chest. 'Help! Oh . . . somebody, please help!'

It was Frances who found her, some twenty minutes later, slumped on the hearthrug.

'Don't you think it's time you came clean with me, Josie?'

said Paul. 'I know there's been something on your mind all week.'

'It's only my mother and Frances,' Josie replied wearily. 'I've told you I don't know how many times. And of course I'm worried. You worry about your family, don't you?'

She still didn't know what on earth to do about Paul, or about Jimmy. It wasn't as clear-cut or as simple as Jimmy tried to make out. He had written to her, such a lovely letter, saying how much he loved her and wanted to marry her, but also stating emphatically that she had to tell Paul how she felt – and at once. Josie hadn't yet replied. She had intended, on returning to Blackpool, to write to Jimmy and tell him that she was going to marry Paul after all, and that he, Jimmy, had better try to put their brief romance behind him, just as she would try to do.

But she hadn't done so. When she saw Paul again she knew she didn't love him, not in the way she loved Jimmy. But how on earth was she to tell him? On the other hand, marrying Jimmy would mean going to live in Yorkshire, and how could she even think of doing that when Iris needed her here? She could never leave Iris.

'There's something else though, isn't there?' said Paul, leaning forward and looking at her intently. 'No, don't look away, and don't try to fob me off again with tales about your family. Something happened, didn't it, when you were at the holiday camp? I know it did, Josie, so you'd better tell me about it – now.' Paul looked stern, more so than he had ever done in the time she had known him. He leaned back, drumming his fingers on the chair arm. 'Come on, I'm waiting.'

Josie looked at him confusedly for a moment or two, then she gave a tut of exasperation. 'It's Karen, isn't it? What's she been saying? I might have known she wouldn't be able to keep anything to herself. Wait till I get my hands on her! I told her—'

'Now don't go blaming Karen,' said Paul, quite evenly. 'She hasn't told me anything. She refused to. But I must admit I asked her if she knew what was troubling you, and she said I had to ask you. So that's what I'm doing. You've met someone else, haven't you?' he added quietly. 'Tell me about it, Josie . . . please.'

'Oh, Paul.' Josie hung her head. 'I didn't want to hurt you. That's why I haven't said anything. Yes, I met a young man. He's called Jimmy. He's an old schoolfriend . . .' She told him how they had met the crowd from Haliford and that they had all, inevitably, spent a lot of time together. '. . . But we didn't do anything wrong, Jimmy and I. I swear we didn't. And I don't want to hurt you, Paul,' she said again.

'But you care for him, don't you?'

'Yes, of course I do. I've always cared about Jimmy. And it was lovely to see him again after all that time.'

'You love him, don't you?' Paul persisted. 'More than you love me. That's why you've been in such a state all week.'

'But I'm not free to love him, am I?' cried Josie. 'I'm engaged to you, and I promised to marry you . . . and I'm very fond of you, Paul.'

'Yes, I believe you are . . . fond of me.' Paul smiled rather sadly. 'But to be fond isn't enough, is it? I'm not being entirely fair with you, Josie, my dear. But I wanted you to tell me yourself about this . . . Jimmy. I felt that you ought to do that. But there was something I wanted to tell you as well, something I've been plucking up courage to say all week, just like you have. Josie, I'm afraid I can't marry you.'

'But . . . why, Paul?' She stared at him, perplexed. 'Not because of Jimmy?'

'No; because I know that it wouldn't be right, and we might come to regret it, both of us. I'm very fond of you too, Josie – I believe I love you – but I'm so much older than you. And I feel that our friendship developed mainly because we work together so well. We're a good team aren't we, you and I? And I see no reason why we can't continue to be, if you are willing?' Josie nodded slowly. 'But I can't marry you. I didn't know how to tell you. But now – well – it's just what you wanted to hear, isn't it?' The glint of humour had returned to Paul's brown eyes now.

Josie smiled back at him, but somewhat sadly. 'Yes, I suppose so. There's no one else then for you, Paul? That's not why . . . ?'

'No, there's no one else.' But there was a tiny flicker of uncertainty in his eyes and Josie knew that quite soon there might very well be someone to take her place. She knew, too, who that someone might be, and she didn't mind in the slightest.

The shrill ring of the telephone sounded in the hall and Paul went to answer it. He was back in a few moments. 'Josie, it's Frances. She wants you. She sounds as though she's in quite a state.'

'Josie . . . Josie, come home quick!' Her sister's voice was distraught. 'It's Mum. She's collapsed. I think it's her heart. I don't know what to do—'

'Mum? You don't mean she's . . . ?' Josie couldn't utter the word. 'She's not . . . ?'

'No, she's alive. She's asking for you, Josie. Come quick, please . . . I don't know what to do,' Frances said again, her voice petering out pathetically.

'You don't know what to do?' Josie almost screeched

down the phone. 'Ring the doctor, for God's sake, you silly little fool. Or ring an ambulance. Use your common sense, girl. No, on second thoughts, don't bother. I'll ring the doctor. Honestly, Frances, you're so bloody heavenly-minded that you're no earthly good! I'll be with you as soon as I can,' she added, more calmly. 'Just look after Mum.'

When she turned round Paul was right behind her. 'I'll ring the doctor,' he said, 'and then I'll take you home.' Then his arms were round her and she was crying against his shoulder.

The doctor arrived at almost the same time as Josie and Paul, who had driven there in Paul's Morris Minor. Iris was lying on the settee, fully conscious, but her eyes were dark with pain, luminous grey pools in a chalk-white face. She looked frightened. Josie couldn't remember ever seeing Iris look frightened before. She reached out a hand. 'Josie . . . Josie love, I'm so glad you've come. Frances, well, she panicked a bit, but I told her, Get Josie – Josie'll know what to do.'

'Right, Mrs Goodwin, let's take a look at you. You can talk to your daughter later. Just take it easy, there's a good lass.' The doctor stepped forward, brisk and efficient, and the rest of them stood to one side while he made his examination.

He took hold of Iris's hand. 'Mmm . . . you've had a nasty turn. But you'll be all right. That is to say, when we get you into hospital, you'll be all right. That's where I want you to go. Up to Victoria—'

Iris gave a start. 'Hospital? Not on your life! I can't go there. Folks die in hospital. Anyroad, I've got a hotel . . .' She tried to sit up, but the doctor put a restraining hand on her arm.

'Now steady on, Mrs Goodwin. That's where you're going, whether you like it or not.' Gently but firmly he took hold of her shoulders and pushed her back against the cushions. 'Die in hospital, indeed! There are skilled doctors and nurses there to take care of you.'

'But I can't!' Iris protested. 'Don't you understand?'

'I understand that you're a very argumentative lady! But you'll have to do as you're told, or I won't be held responsible for what might happen. You've had a heart attack, Mrs Goodwin. Not as severe as it might have been, thank goodness, but bad enough. So we've got to take every precaution. It's Victoria Hospital for you.' The doctor turned to Josie. 'The phone? I'll ring for an ambulance. We can't waste any time,' he added quietly, in an aside.

'It's in the hall, Doctor,' said Josie. She followed him across the room. 'She will be all right, won't she?'

'As far as I know.' The doctor pursed his lips guardedly. 'I would say the worst is over . . . this time. And we want to make as sure as we can that there won't be a next time. I can see she's a headstrong woman. She'll have to take advice, and she'll have to ease off a lot. I would say she's been doing too much. Now – this phone.'

'So there you are, Mum.' Josie sat on the edge of the settee and took hold of her mother's hand. 'Are you listening? You're to do as you're told, for once in your life!' she smiled.

'But hospital, Josie!' Iris looked at her fearfully. 'I've never been in hospital in all me life. Hardly ever had a day in bed, for that matter. Anyroad, the pain's eased off a bit now, quite a lot in fact. So what's the point?'

'Every point, Iris,' Paul joined in. 'We all want you to get well again, and you won't if you stay at home. You'll be dashing about like a flea on a flitting, like you always do, then you'll be ill again.'

'But there's so much to do,' Iris insisted, although she was looking much more resigned now. 'I've a house full of visitors and more coming tomorrow. I can't be ill, right in the middle of the season.'

'You can't choose your time, Mum. None of us can,' said Josie. 'And you've not to worry about a thing. That new woman you've got is quite a marvel, isn't she? I'll go round and see if she can live in for a while. She's no ties, has she? And I'll help. I'm not much of a cook, but I can do the other things. Paul will let me take a few days off, won't you, Paul?

'And we mustn't forget Frances. You'll put in a few more hours, won't you, Frances?' Josie turned to her sister who, so far, had said hardly anything. The girl was looking very subdued and afraid. There was little evidence now of the radiant young woman who had declared that she wanted to serve the Lord.

'Won't you, Frances?' said Josie again, pointedly, but trying to smile encouragingly at her sister. It was on the tip of her tongue to remind her that it would be an excellent way of putting into practice what she had been so earnestly preaching, but she resisted the temptation. Now was not the time for backbiting.

'Yes, of course I'll help,' said Frances, somewhat peevishly. 'You know I will. I help already while you're at the shop, don't I? You don't know what I do because you're never here.'

'A few *more* hours, Frances,' Josie told her patiently. 'You'll have to do a bit extra.'

'Yes, try to pull your weight, there's a good girl.' Iris sighed. 'Help Josie and Mrs Evans as much as you can.

I'll be back home as soon as I'm able, you can be sure of that.'

'You'll do as you're told, Mum,' said Josie, grinning at her. 'And don't worry, we'll manage.'

'Yes . . . I'll ask Annette if I can have some time off from the Ballet,' said Frances in a quiet little voice. She cast an apprehensive look in her mother's direction. 'I think she'll let me. I'm only in the chorus now.'

'Aye, all right then. Good lass.' Iris nodded, but there was none of her previous indulgence of the girl evident in her tone now. Ever since Josie entered the room she had been aware of an undercurrent between the pair of them; she knew that this atmosphere had been building up gradually over the last two weeks. It was little wonder that Frances was feeling peeved. She had been the centre of attraction for so long, the apple of her mother's eye, ever since she was a tiny baby. Now it seemed as though Iris's attention was being given entirely to Josie. It was to Josie that Iris was looking for help and moral support and the words of reassurance that would calm her fears.

The panic surfaced again when the ambulancemen arrived and Iris was lifted on to a stretcher and covered with a red blanket. 'Come with me, Josie,' she begged, holding out both her arms. 'Don't leave me . . .'

'Of course we'll come with you, Mum,' Josie assured her. 'But we'll have to leave you later, when you're settled in.' This was an Iris that Josie had never come across before. She was obviously afraid of illness – for herself, that is – although she had been well able to cope with it in others. Josie turned to her sister who was standing back, almost cowering behind the settee. 'Are you coming, Frances? We'll both go along with Mum, shall we?'

The girl shook her head. 'No . . . I don't want to. I

– I don't like hospitals. They give me a funny feeling.' Josie raised her eyebrows. This was a strange reaction, she thought, for someone who had ambitions to be a nurse, to go and serve overseas, hadn't she said, a veritable Florence Nightingale? But again Josie reminded herself that there must be no recrimination. Frances was no doubt as upset about their mother as Josie was, but hadn't the maturity to know how to deal with the situation. It must have been a shock for her to find Iris, who had always been so fit and well, collapsed in a pitiful heap.

'No, I'll stay here if you don't mind,' Frances faltered. 'I'll go round and tell Mrs Evans, shall I? Ask her if she can come and stay?' Her blue eyes were filling up with tears and her lip was trembling.

'Yes, that would be a great idea,' said Josie brightly. 'Thank you, Frances.'

The girl dashed forward then, flinging her arms round her mother. 'Oh, Mum . . . Mum, I'm sorry. All those awful things I said. I'm sorry, I didn't meant to upset you.'

'All right, darling. It's all forgotten.' Iris's eyes softened as she reached out a hand and stroked her younger daughter's cheek. 'Don't think about it any more.'

'Get better, Mum, won't you? Please get better.'

'Of course I will. Nothing more sure than that.' Iris kissed her on the cheek, then she turned to Josie. 'Come on, lass. Our carriage awaits.' She was trying hard to be brave, but fear was still lurking in her eyes.

'I'll follow you up in the car,' said Paul as the men carried Iris out to the ambulance. 'Then I can bring you home later.'

'Thanks, Paul. You're sure?'

'Of course I'm sure. I haven't stopped caring, you know. I'll always care . . . about all of you.'

And Josie knew that he would. Paul was a good man, none better. But now she was free to love Jimmy. That was too complicated, however, to think about at this moment in time. For now, all her thoughts must be for Iris.

Josie sat down thankfully after all the Sunday tea things had been washed up and cleared away. She hadn't realized how hard it was working full-time at the hotel. Apart from short visits to Iris in hospital, she had been on the go all weekend, from six o'clock in the morning until late in the evening. She hadn't done the work single-handed, though. There were the two girls from Preston – waitresses-cum-chambermaids; Mrs Evans, the new cook, who was turning out to be a veritable treasure; and Frances, who, to give her her due, had worked like a Trojan. Josie had been able to report to Iris that it had all gone very smoothly. The seeing-off of one lot of visitors and the welcoming of another, the changing of beds, weekend shopping, cooking and baking, laying tables, washing-up, clearing away . . . There had hardly been a hitch, apart from Frances dropping a loaded tray and breaking most of the pots. She had burst into tears – she was very much on edge at the moment – but Josie had assured her that it didn't matter at all.

The house seemed so quiet without Iris. It couldn't really be quiet, of course, not with twenty guests milling about. But it seemed as though the place had lost its driving force; Iris had been the kingpin around whom everything else revolved. Josie had been glad to see, though, when she and Frances had visited her that afternoon, that her mother was not bursting to be 'up and at it'. She seemed to be resigned to her stay in hospital – it would be the best part of a week, the doctor said, although she was out of danger now – and Josie felt that the time might be ripe, soon, for them to talk about the subject of Iris's retirement. Josie had no doubt in her mind that that was what her mother must do. She had had a severe warning and to ignore it would be foolhardy.

She looked up as Frances entered the room. The girl had changed out of her old blouse and skirt into a floral cotton dress and matching cardigan, ready to go out. 'You don't mind, do you, Josie?' She looked apologetically at her sister. 'I did say I'd go to the service . . . if it's all right with you?'

'Yes, of course it is.' Josie smiled at her. 'You've worked hard this weekend. We couldn't have managed without you.'

'Really?' Frances looked pleased, but surprised as well.

'Yes, really. You're not going to St Matthew's, I suppose?'

'No, I can't very well. I came out of the choir, you know. I haven't been for two Sundays, and I've not been to the practices. No, I'm going to the Friends' service.' Frances sounded hesitant, though. 'They've got a new place, down South Shore.'

'I see. You enjoyed the choir, though, didn't you?' Frances was lingering, and Josie guessed that there might be something she wouldn't mind talking about. 'I was surprised – amazed, in fact – when you came out of it.'

'Yes . . . I loved the music,' replied Frances wistfully. 'But Janet and Megan, and some of the others, they told me it was wrong to attach so much importance to it. They said that God prefers worship to be simple. And I got confused. I do miss it, though.'

'Then why don't you go back? You can do both, can't you, if you want to? Go to St Matthew's and meet these . . . 'Friends' as well.'

'Mmm . . . I might. They'll argue with me though.'

'Then let them! Argue back. Stick up for yourself. Look here, Frances,' Josie looked at her earnestly. 'It's all very well being swept along on a tide of emotion, like you were—'

'It wasn't just that. Nobody made me. I felt I wanted to.'

'All the same, it hasn't helped much, has it? You went to pieces when Mum collapsed, didn't you?' Josie pointed out gently. She knew she had been less than sympathetic at the time and wanted to make amends now. 'You couldn't cope.'

'I was frightened. I don't want her to be ill. She will get better, won't she, Josie?'

'She'll get better a lot quicker if she doesn't have to worry about you,' said Josie kindly. 'Or about me. I'm not going to marry Paul, you know.'

'Oh . . . why ever not?' Frances looked stunned. 'Won't that worry Mum even more? She likes him.'

'Yes, but she also knows that he's not right for me,' said Josie. 'Our mum's a very wise woman, don't you ever forget that. I'll tell you about it some other time. It's a long story. Off you go, or you'll be late for your service. And, Frances – stick up for yourself!'

Frances smiled and nodded, looking more cheerful than she had all weekend.

Josie leaned back and closed her eyes. For the moment she was quite alone. It was strange not to have Iris there, or Paul. She had been in the habit of going round to Paul's on a Sunday evening, but she wouldn't be doing so tonight.

She didn't know, in fact, when she would be seeing him, as she would be working in the hotel this week. Yes, it felt strange, as though she were in limbo. Next week she would have to write to Jimmy and tell him . . . What was she to tell him? That it was all over with Paul; but how could she embark on another relationship when she was needed so badly at home?

When the doorbell rang several minutes later, she rose to answer it. Mrs Evans would be taking a well-earned rest in the attic bedroom they had quickly made ready for her, and the two girls were out. When she opened the door she almost fainted with shock.

'Jimmy! Whatever are you doing here? I was just thinking about you—'

He didn't wait for an invitation. He strode into the hallway, closing the door behind him, before taking Josie in his arms. 'Thinking about me? I should jolly well hope you were! It's been a whole week, Josie.' She couldn't answer because his kisses were smothering her words and there was silence for the next few minutes. Then, 'Why didn't you write?' he asked. 'I've been frantic.'

'It's only been a week, Jimmy—'

'Only a week! A week's a hell of a long time when you love somebody as much as I love you.' Jimmy tightened his hold of her. 'I have to know, Josie. Have you told him?'

'Yes, Paul knows about us—'

'Thank God for that. But I couldn't wait any longer for you to write. So I changed shifts and wangled a whole day off. I don't have to be back till Tuesday. You can put me up, can't you?'

'Of course . . . Oh, Jimmy, it's wonderful to see you.' As Josie relaxed against the comfort of his shoulder she knew, suddenly, that everything would be all right. Jimmy was here. They would sort it out together. 'So much has happened. Come in and I'll tell you. Iris is ill . . .'

'Don't they have policemen then, in Blackpool?' asked Jimmy with a twinkle in his grey eyes, some time later. Josie had made him a pot of tea and a sandwich, and they had talked and kissed, and talked again. She had told him all about Iris and Frances and Paul. But chiefly about how poorly Iris had been and how she would need Josie here with her, how she couldn't possibly think of going to live in Yorkshire . . .

'What d'you mean?' She frowned at him. 'You don't mean . . . You can't mean that you would come . . . But your job's in Haliford, and your family.'

'Josie, darling, I'm not tied to my family. I love my mam, of course I do, and I help her all I can, but there are five more of us, you know, and they're all in Yorkshire. Besides, Mam doesn't expect me to be dancing attendance on her all the time. She knows I have my own life to lead. And from what I know of Iris, that's what she'll feel as well.'

'But she seems so helpless at the moment, Jimmy. So . . . dependent. On me, particularly. I've never seen her like this before.'

'She's been ill, Josie. Very ill, from what you tell me. It's sure to have made her more vulnerable. And it sounds to me as though she's discovering what a treasure you are – especially after Frances hurt her so much – and she's making the most of it.'

'Yes, we're certainly closer than we've ever been. That's what illness does, I suppose. But she's making it up with Frances as well, I'm glad to say. She'll need me though, Jimmy, when she comes home.'

'Darling, you must get things into proportion.' Jimmy put an arm round her shoulders. 'Iris will want you to live your own life, just as she's always lived hers. I know she's looked after you three, but she's done what she wanted to as well, hasn't she? You and Iris are an awful lot alike, you know, though you may not realize it. The last thing she would want would be an over-protective daughter fussing round her all the time. Anyway, Frances will be with her for quite a while yet, won't she?'

'You make it sound so easy, Jimmy.'

'So it is. Why complicate matters, eh? You're going to marry me. I decided that the minute I saw you at that holiday camp, and if I'd decided to stay in Haliford you'd have had to come and live there. Oh yes you would . . .' he said, tapping her gently on the nose as she opened her mouth to protest. 'I don't take no for an answer. You should know that by now. And Iris wouldn't have objected at all. But, as it is, I've decided to move to Blackpool. I'll ask for a transfer. Then we'll get married.'

'When . . . ?'

'I'd like to say next week. I can't wait, darling.' Jimmy kissed her fiercely. 'But I suppose we'll have to say . . . next spring?'

'That sounds wonderful,' said Josie happily. 'It's just like a story-book, isn't it?' She really did feel that she had been swept off her feet, like some fairy-tale princess, by a prince on a white charger, a role in which she had never seen herself. But that was before she had met Jimmy again. 'And they got married . . .'

'. . . And lived happily ever after,' Jimmy finished for her, before he kissed her again.

Yes, they would be happy. Josie was certain of that. But she was by no means a stereotypical story-book heroine. Josie Goodwin was no fawning female. She knew that with two characters as volatile as herself and Jimmy, the sparks would be sure to fly. Just as they had between herself and Iris. But it would be great fun watching the fireworks.

Also available from Headline

There's a Silver Lining

An evocative Blackpool saga full of warmth and colour

Margaret Thornton

It's 1918, the war is finally over, and Sarah Donnelly and her cousin Nancy are filled with hope for the future. In particular, Sarah eagerly awaits the safe return of her cousin Zachary, whom she has adored since childhood. But when Zachary returns to Blackpool, shattered by the horrors of war, he can barely face his family, let alone reciprocate Sarah's affections.

Refusing to be thwarted by rejection, Sarah throws herself into her job at Donnelly's tea rooms, where her father, the owner of Blackpool's most popular department store, has allowed her to work. Then Sarah spys a run-down building to let near North Shore, and decides to set up in business, running her *own* tea rooms.

Meanwhile, Nancy, forever a dreamer, has chosen to follow in her mother's footsteps on to the stage. But it is not long before her youthful naivety lands her in trouble.

There's a Silver Lining is an evocative saga, steeped in warmth and nostalgia, in which heartache, happiness, tragedy and triumph lie in store for a close-knit Blackpool community.

FICTION / SAGA 0 7472 4875 3

Also available from Headline

STAY IN YOUR OWN BACK YARD

The enthralling Liverpool saga from the author of HOME IS WHERE THE HEART IS

Joan Jonker

In her terraced house in Liverpool, Molly Bennett struggles to bring up four children on her husband's meagre wage. Skint by Tuesday, they live on tick for the rest of the week. But Molly doesn't complain; she has an abundance of things money can't buy – and a home filled with love and laughter.

When her eldest daughter, Jill, is offered a place at high school, Molly is racked with guilt. She needs Jill working to relieve their poverty. But Jill eases Molly's conscience by getting herself a job in a baker's shop while signing up for night school.

Molly's best mate is Nellie McDonough; they spend hours laughing, gossiping and lending a helping hand to others. And when they discover one of their neighbours, Ellen Clarke, is being beaten by her violent husband, the friends roll up their sleeves and move into action. Meanwhile, Jill starts dating Nellie's son Steve, and both families are delighted. But Jill lands herself an office job that takes her into a world beyond the confines of their close-knit community and she and Steve seem to be drifting apart . . .